Tales of Mundus

Puppets

CHRIS SIFNIOTIS

Tales of Mundus
Copyright © 2021 by Chris Sifniotis

All rights reserved. No part of this publication
may be reproduced, distributed, or transmitted
in any form or by any means, including
photocopying, recording, or other electronic
or mechanical methods, without the prior
written permission of the author, except
in the case of brief quotations embodied
in critical reviews and certain other non-
commercial uses permitted by copyright law.

Tellwell Talent
www.tellwell.ca

ISBN
978-0-2288-2198-4 (Hardcover)
978-0-2288-2197-7 (Paperback)
978-0-2288-2199-1 (eBook)

Introduction

The land of Mundus has a rich history that many humans and elves are currently piecing together. Historical study is a relatively new scientific discipline championed by Midgardian man William Stevington PhD. During his higher learning, Stevington studied Alchemistry in the Sage's Guild of Midgard. However, he decided to abandon his studies and turn his attention to what he found as 'an intellectual disinterest in a critical aspect of global culture'. Stevington left Midgard and, with minimal funding, support from students and professors, and the recent wave of peace across the land, travelled the Nine Realms of the continent for the sole purpose of learning and understanding the known history of each nation.

During the start of the Fifth Age, Stevington travelled to all the accessible nations over a period of four years, culminating into his two theses: *Immortality: The History of the Elf Clans*, and *Ingenuity: Humanity's Effect on the Nine Realms*. These works established him as an authority on global history. Doctor William Stevington is currently an honorary doctor and fellow of the Sage's Guild of Midgard.

Mundus today lives in the one hundredth year of the Fifth Age, notated as 100FIA – FIA is the shorthand for the Fifth Age. A secondary name for the Fifth Age is 'the Age of Peace'. All the ages have been given similar names based on the events that defined their change.

The First Age is known as 'the Age of Life'. No one knows how old the First Age is because writing in the Ancient World did not develop until the Second Age. Due to this uncertainty, events in the First Age are generally notated unusually; the birth of Lian Jie for instance is written as taking place in -17SA, seventeen years before the Second Age. The Age of Life is perceived as an interim period that describes the origins of the High Elf clan and possibly the Goblins who live underground.

The Second Age is defined as 'the Age of Schism' and is written as SA after the year of a date. It is defined by the young rebellious elf Lian Jie who defied the traditions of the ancient High Elves and rallied a group of fellow elves to find a new home elsewhere. After a year Lian Jie established a city within the Udoerufu Forest and a home for his followers. The Age of Schism was the period where the elves successfully separated from their strict traditions.

The Third Age is known as 'the Age of Discovery' and is written as TA after the year of a date. The Midgardian men made landfall on the mainland for the first time and discovered the other races. The relations between the humans and other races enriched the minds of everyone, the men included. The Midgardians provided the mainland the Scientific Method, a pursuit that is uniquely human without the introduction of magic. The other races provided Mana crystals to the men, giving them a new object to study and understand. This meeting of science and magic changed the nature of the races of the earth, and all nations entered a scientific revolution that is collectively known as the Age of Discovery.

The Fourth Age is known as 'the Age of Destruction' and is written as FOA after the date of the year. It is defined by a series of terrible events; an experiment was grossly underestimated, and a large explosion which caused the creation of the ninth and forbidden race, the orcs. As a result, the experiment caused a frightening new enemy that over time, threatened every race with war and suffering.

The current age is defined by the boldness of human diplomacy and the unity of the races to achieve peace, the then King Dalton III of Midgard bought land from the halflings to establish a city and bring the leaders of the other nations together. The grand strategy was to organise a plan to contain the orcs and establish peace amongst the races. Over a period of years, the city of Beacon was founded, the Council of the Earth was built, and the leaders congregated. The union of races repelled the orcs and created the infrastructure to bring the Dark Elf Khan to Beacon.

The council succeeded in all these tasks as the orcs discovered their plan and sent waves of soldiers to destroy the city. The assault failed and the leaders united. The orcs surrendered, and the other leaders agreed to many new laws to maintain their existence, placing strict embargoes against them and patrols around the borders. For the past century, Mundus has been in a state of peace. No major conflict is playing out against races, and while aggression itself has not been resolved, hatred against races has largely subsided.

Chapter 1

The sun was high over Mundus. A temperate warmth, excellent for a leisure walk. A clear day shone over the Nine Realms and blessed the land with spring warmth. The great river glistened, the Foirceannadh River – that sparkling blue divider of land. Far along the river, at the edge of the sea where the water exited, the Halflings dwell at the hilly banks. They live in a quaint nation, a small group of cities at the mouth and along the great river. Life was idyllic here. The perfect hills and clear water inspire a beauty few others can imagine. The rural folk have a more simplistic view of the world, preferring to enjoy themselves in the natural beauty. The breeze gently brushed the grasses of the hills, the current trickled quietly along the bank. It was a heaven, a sight, sound and feel of divine things.

The town of Béal na Habhann bustled, a small hamlet out west. Much energy was felt by the men and women. They all hurried about their day, they gossiped and chatted, argued and discussed, haggled and bought.

Amongst the hubbub and noise two gents slowly made their way, one in a simple green jacket and little else of note, the other in a fashionable navy suit. They let the crowd sail past them as they discussed the affairs of the day. "Gees, there's a lot of people out here today," the green fellow said as he looked about, "is it really such a big deal?"

"I reckon it is," the other replied, "the Dogess doesn't come by this part of the river very often."

"Or ever. I've never once seen her visit this ol' town. I bet she doesn't get out of her house much at all." He chuckled at his own quip.

"House? You call that big thing a house? That's a whole bloody city she has there. Imagine this town, all of this here, for a residence."

"Bugger off Óir."

"I mean it mate. I've seen the thing." Óir made great gestures in the air. "A huge golden dome, far up high as the clouds met the sky. A big structure, from here to the docklands."

The green jacketed man peered over the shoulders of a stocky gent in front. Past him he saw the length of the town, the dirt road through the markets and taverns, across the recreation parks, and down to the wharfs and piers of the docks. "Down there? Really? All the way there?! Isn't that a clear 250 yards?"

"Aye! 250. I swear by it."

"You swear on your father's life?"

He fell silent for a moment, he looked back at the man with a sigh and a slight shake of his head. "I don't reckon that was called for."

"Well, I don't mean to be rude, but you can't just expect me to believe that. You know me better than that mate. How big was it really?"

"I don't know Cean. It was big alright?" The men carried on down the street for a few seconds. "It was big enough to impress me."

"Hang on!" Cean stuck out his hand and they haunted. "I've just realised, you've dodged my question earlier. Did you get your contract? What happened with the Dogess?"

Óir sighed briefly. "You sure you don't want to complain some more?"

"I don't like complainin', what happened?"

He sighed again. "Fine. I got knocked back." Immediately he continued to walk, he was visibly sullen. Cean promptly followed.

"Hang on! What do you mean 'knocked back'?"

"I mean knocked back. I didn't get the contract." He shook his head and waved his hand to explain himself. "Apparently I don't have the 'prestige' to work a national trade house. Says I'm too small to invest in."

"That's a damn shame. You worked hard for that."

"Too right. I reckon university training ought to be enough, or at least that's what I was told," he sighed, "but I guess that wasn't enough."

"What will you do? Will you stay here?"

"Oh, I have no plans to leave Cean, that was never the deal. I like this place too much, its got a quiet peace."

"That's good!" The gentlemen continued to walk for a moment of two. "Prestige though."

"Cean, don't start this now. She's here and she has her bus-"

"But there's something about this that seems off." He interrupted. "What does she mean by prestige?"

"Acclaim. Note. Fame. I'm not well known."

"No, I get that. But see, don't businessmen get more fame with a Royal Seal? Like, how did Uisce herself become a name in trade? She didn't happen to be known about the land, right?"

"Eh, I don't know. I guess it wasn't enough."

"Hey, hold on a minute." Again, he stopped his friend, this time just outside a store with a homely charm and a fresh smell of food. "I need to pop into the bakery for some lunch. You want anything?"

"Aye. I'll join you." The window enticed the men to divert themselves into the building. Rows of breads and pastries of all kinds and sizes lined the shop front.

Inside the bakery was a medley for the senses. The interior matched the exterior, a rustic store surrounded by wooden shelves of all manner of loaves and breads. Long breads, shortbread, fat rolls, flatbreads, loaves sprinkled with grains and herbs. A wooden counter separated the customers from the bakers who worked at the ovens. Only they were made of stone, a lower chamber to stoke fires and an upper cavity to cook the breads. All else about the store was wooden, even the decorations were carvings into wood and wooden planks. The smell beckoned Cean to the counter, the sharp smell of freshly made bread. The yeast, the dough, the piping hot crust of fresh bread. It was the most delightful aroma that excited his tastebuds. The counter was clear save for an elderly man off to the side. He made his way to the attendant, a lovely young woman with short, wavy hair about her face. She wore a white, thick apron and a bonnet rimmed with lace atop her head. She tended to a fresh loaf upon a shelf. "Excuse me, miss?"

She turned about and her locks flitted across her eyes. "Good day mister Ceannte. How are you today?"

"Please, call me Cean." He blushed at the formality. "The day's been fine so far, plenty of trout for the morning catch. I'm angling for some lunch, what's the specialty right now?"

"I figure a bloke like you could enjoy some chicken on pumpkin seed. What do you say to that?"

"Bleh! I'm all for chicken, but pumpkin seed bread is horrible. Could I have that on green bread?"

"That's fine." She turned around again to search for the loaf. "Mister Ceannte, may I ask you a question?"

"Cean dear, and of course."

"Well first of all, if you insist on it, may I ask you call me by my name?"

He blushed once again. "Alright, Álainn. Didn't mean to upset."

"Oh, I'm not upset, it's just rather strange. You're a regular customer and we chat every so often," upon sighting the cut bread, a lime green colour with an odd brightness, she took it down and placed it upon her counter. A metal box filled with poultry was set beside the bread. She began to create the meal. "You've known me long enough to address me, surely."

"My apologies miss, uh, Álainn. I can be a bit giddy sometimes."

"Nothing wrong with giddy Cean, I reckon you fancy me though."

"Uh," Ceannte faltered slightly, he cleared his throat and his voice squeaked briefly, "didn't you have a question you wanted to ask?" Both Óir and the old man chuckled quietly to themselves.

"Aye, I do." She completed the meal and handed it to him. "It'll cost you though."

"I'm good for cash. 10 pounds, right?"

"Ah ah ah," Álainn retreated her offer. "I don't mean that. I want to know; do you like me?"

"Well of course I like you. You're a charming young lass."

"Alright, but do you like to take me for a dinner?"

"He better bloody not Ály!"

Her father came out from the kitchen, he carried a large tray with a round pie. "I reckon he ain't worth your time."

"Don't be mean daddy."

"Mean? I'm mean, am I? I hear he gets into bar fights with cross words about all kinds of nonsense."

"Oi! It ain't nonsense!" He protested. "I don't take shit like that! When some bloke insults me for no good reason I'll have at 'im, but I'm not wrong to defend myself."

"No, you're not, but you start up fights with your drunkenness and bloody temper. I'm not letting my dear Ály near you until you calm the hell down."

"I'll calm down when you calm down. I don't blow up unprovoked."

"Hey guys," Álainn bellowed over them, they stopped suddenly, "can you two stop? This is a bake house, not a pavilion." With her hands raised the men retracted, and after a moment both Ceannte and her father settled. "Now, Cean, just calm down. Daddy just wants to protect me okay?"

He nodded slightly. "I can understand that. That's fine, but it's no excuse to just freely lambast me like that."

"Aye, I reck-"

"No, it is not, Daddy!" She interrupted over him, turned over to see him, and rose her voice to drown his out. "There's no reason for that kind of villainy. I don't want that."

"Aye!" Still by himself, pie in hand, the old man finally made an utterance. His voice cracked mildly yet was clear as day. "Don't be such an arse Athair. It's an ugly quality."

"Oh, and he isn't Eagna?" He pointed at Ceannte.

"I don't reckon. All I saw was this bloke come in with his friend, ask for a sandwich, and hide his taking a fancy at your daughter, only for you to bloody well badger and bark at his flaws. Them I only saw after you go harassing him." He blushed again at the man's observation. "So nah, I don't know him well enough, but I don't think he's the problem here. It's you that's offside, so how about instead of acting all inhospitable-like you just nick his gold and let him go on his way aye?"

He sighed with an air of frustration. "Alright. Alright." But as soon as he did, he turned back and returned to the kitchen behind. As he did, he muttered words to himself, nothing audible or clear.

Everyone all looked at each other for a moment, Eagna decided to break the tension. "Ah, don't mind 'im. He doesn't like being wrong is all. It's part of his upbringing."

"How do you know that?" Ceannte asked.

"He's a friend of Daddy's," she explained, "old man Eggy we call him. He's known him for ages, we're almost family."

"Aye. I've known Athair since he was a wee boy. He was always a mule really, much too stubborn to let live is his problem. He thinks everything can be solved in a jiff you see, it's all so simple and straight ahead." Eagna turned about and faced him. "Young man, the name is Ceannte right?"

"Yes sir."

"I'm sorry you had to deal with that nonsense today. 'Ere." He reached into the pocket by his side and revealed a stack of gold coins. "Let me trouble your meal."

"Oh no, that's not at all necessary." He waved his hands about. "I cop that a bit here and there, but I wouldn't dare take the money of elderly folk. Besides, you hardly did anything to make it worse."

He remained with his hand outstretched, the shining gold glinted from the few spots of sunlight that struck the metal. "I made it worse by letting it happen mate. Plus, I insist. There's plenty more of that where that came from." He still hesitated for a moment, Óir and Álainn watched on from about the store, each contemplated the same scenario. Ceannte decided to reach out and take the offer. "Attaboy. There's no shame in that."

"Thank you, sir." He looked up to Eagna with great fondness and admiration. "I don't often get such generosity. Would you care to join me and my company for some tucker in the city?"

"Ah, it's a lovely idea, but I best be off to my own companion. She's waiting on the pie and it might already be a bit cold for her liking." He then began to make his way out of the bakery.

"Cheerio!" said Ceannte.

"Hooroo!" she added afterwards.

"Bye to you all. Oh, and Ály."

"Eggy?"

"Take this chap out for a dinner, will you? The poor sod's hurt his pride." And with that he exited.

Álainn laughed roundly. "He seems like a top bloke." Ceannte tried to talk over her mirth.

After a second, she calmed down. "Aye, he's got a sharp wit but a gentle soul. He makes for a good friend." She sighed. "That was a lovely offer you made for him. For all the talk floating around, you certainly have a more reserved side no one really sees. Why is it you get into so much trouble Cean?"

"I haven't a clue if I'm honest. All I know is I speak my mind and I often get into a scuffle. Sometimes I drink, sometimes I get vulgar, sometimes I'm just down right mean. But I never get into other people's face about it, not unless I get offended anyway." His stomach interrupted. "Oh right, could I have my meal now? I'm getting famished."

"Of course!" She handed over the sandwich to him. It was wrapped in brown paper and the crust of the green bread outlined the edges. He gave her the very coin he was compelled to take from Eagna, she took it and for a few seconds she stared at the coin. Álainn was deep in thought for a length of time. Ceannte and Óir both noticed and looked to each other briefly, they ensured each saw what the other noticed. "He's right." She said finally. "I really should get to know you better mister Cean. Are you free this evening?"

"Uh," he stammered for a moment, "um, I am yes. But does that mean you like me?"

"I fear I might need to get used to you a bit, but on the whole yes. You're not as unpleasant as people make you out to be, I reckon I can tame you a bit."

"He needs more than that." Óir jeered from behind. His friend turned about, looked right at him, and cleared his throat in a loud and deliberate fashion. "I mean, may I have a Barley Square please?"

Again, she laughed. "Of course!" As before she turned and moved about the space with precision and professionalism, that of a mindful worker who knows where all her things are. He headed to the counter, and a moment later the pastry was packed into another bit of paper and handed over. "7 pounds please." He was prepared himself. He presented a small brown purse made of silk where he paid his lunch. As she opened the till, she checked the room behind her for a second, then turned back to address them again. "So, Cean. The Sheriff's Serpent, around sunset, sounds good?"

"Sounds like a date, but what about your pa?"

"He doesn't have to know." She winked at Ceannte and smiled. He responded similarly and the men were about to head out. "Cean, wait!" They turned about at the door when she asked him. "I didn't get to ask my question earlier, do you mind?"

"Not at all, but I have to eat at the minute." No sooner did he announce this when he began taking bites from the sandwich.

"That's fine, I just really want to know. You come by at least three times a week and ask me what's on special, yet you always get the same green bread every time. The meat changes, but never the bread. Why? Do you not want to have something different?"

"Nuthin rong with green bred." He was muffled by a mouth full of chicken and bread. "Fool of vitamins and meel. That's nuff for me."

"Well of course, but why not just ask for it from the beginning?"

"I ca-" he finished chewing and swallowed. "I can eat the other stuff, it's no big thing. Green bread is my favourite though. I love the taste and the colour. It's a beautiful mix of herbs, plants and dough."

"I agree, but that still doesn't explain very much. You love the bread, alright then." She shrugged at the response. "Whatever. If that's all then I'll see you tonight. Bye now." She waved them off as the men stepped out and left the bakery.

Outside Ceannte and Óir ate their meals and continued their discussion. "Why do you do that?" Óir asked.

"Do what?"

"What she was going on about. That bread thing."

"Ah." He began to walk and Óir followed behind. "Well, you see, I try to start a conversation with her. It's stupid really but I want to chat with her."

He took several moments to process that response. The idea of small talk about fishing and bread as some sort of playful dialogue confounded him. "Aye," he replied eventually, "you're right. That is stupid. That's not how people talk at all you know."

"Yeah, I know. I know. I just get all embarrassed and flushed about her. She gives me the jiggly knees." Ceannte ate another bite of his lunch. "I don't know much about her. I try to chat, but I get all smitten and my head goes blank."

"Gees. You've got it bad." He shook his head. "How long has this been going on?"

"A month and a bit. I just stumbled into that place. I swear I took one look at her and went all giddy, just like that. After a bit of time I decided to visit her daily and try to spark a conversation, but I always say stupid things."

"Gee I can imagine, if it's anything like just now."

"Don't be like that." He moaned.

"I've never heard of this Cean. We've been good mates for seven years, you never bothered to tell me. I'd be insulted if it wasn't hilarious."

"Oh please. I don't like sharin' this right now. It's not the most flattering thing about me."

Óir shook his head. "I think the word you're after is 'elegant', that I'll agree with, but I beg to differ. It's nice that you fancy a lady like Álainn, charming actually. I reckon you need a bit of charm at the minute."

"You reckon?"

"Aye. That bloke isn't the only one who's got a stick up their arse about you. This ain't a big city you know, I think you just about upset every family and some of the lords here at some point."

"Oh, now you're just talking nonsense!"

"I'm not mate. I mean sure, you have a few friends who don't mind you and know you better, but you're not the most amenable person. Most of us lot like to be jolly. You're not a grump really, but you can aggravate people at times. Have you tried to just calm down when it happens?"

"It's not as easy as that." Ceannte held out his arm and they stopped once again, just as before. "I'm smart enough to know I shouldn't. I mean I really don't want to blow my top, but I can't let things lie, especially if someone decides to insult me. Most people seem to think it's fine to call me no good or too angry, -"

"That's because you are quite angry." Óir interrupted. As he ate, he waved about his hands. "You don't take a moment to just listen to someone explain their grievance. That, or you take it so personally, you feel affronted by it. Haven't you noticed people act very differently when they're pissed off than normally?"

"Ah! They act different because they are different!" He pointed out. "Uncouth and short sighted. They bring out the worst in everyone around them, so I get riled up and assert the truth."

"Your truth you mean. I mean gees. I've not met a lot of people so stubborn, but you're something else mate."

"Well I'm not wrong…" he paused to think for a moment, "…most of the time. I don't reckon I'm so bad as all that."

"No Cean, you're not bad. You just have an ill temper you don't seem to want to fix presently. Honestly, you're alright mostly, but you have no tact, no comfort in your voice or manner, and you don't mean to get some. I reckon some tuition in speech and diplomacy will do the trick."

"Ha! So, I can get myself a silver tongue like you?"

"It'll do you good mate. Talk better, argue clearer, don't talk down, keep it clean. It's not tricky at all."

"Aye sure. Those fancy words don't confuse issues or insult anyone who don't know their meaning do they?!" His response dripped in sarcasm. The very sound of his voice stabbed into Óir and cut him down to size.

"Of course, bloody not." He sighed. He took several breaths to calm himself down and compose his thoughts. "For God's sake Cean. You don't move."

"Huh?" He raised his eyebrow at his friend.

"You're unmoving. You don't yield. You have this strange desire to hold your opinion and fight for it, even if it means challenging your mates. I figure getting you to brush up your speech will help you with this problem. It'll definitely make you less abrasive and hostile while still getting your point across. But hell, you'd rather rubbish it and risk losing a friend than even consider the idea." He paused. He watched Ceannte slowly sink his head. "Is that what you think of me Cean? Some charlatan that tricks people for greed?"

"No, I don't." He looked back up at him. "It's just, I don't really trust people who don't talk plainly. Big words feel wrong to me. I think they hide true intentions." He stuck out his finger and pointed directly at Óir. "But not you. I've known you well enough to know you don't do that."

"That's my point mate. I speak well and I don't cheat you or anyone else. That's not what speech does, it's what people do with it."

"Aye, I know." He nodded along with him.

"And I bet that's the problem," he produced a pocket watch and slightly gasped at the time, "but we can't hang about. I've got a meeting to get to." He ate the last of his pastry, scrunched the paper bag, gave Ceannte a pat on the back and continued walking again. "Oi Cean," he turned about to him one last time, "tell me how the date goes, and try to relax. A lady'll be present."

"Aye. Cheerio." He waved back to his friend and they both went their separate ways.

* * *

As the sun sunk into darkness, the town became loud and bright. It was festive. The streets were all lined in candlelight and buntings, and the halflings dined and convened outside. Children played with each other in small groups and chased about down open alleys.

Merriment was all about the town. Taverns and inns were all popular with patrons. Beer and meat and music filled every open area that was not drowned out by the gossip of the day. Down one of the many streets of noise and cheer a pub stood out from the rest. The building was tall and impressive, it looked over its neighbours. Darkened wood with many windows and shutters. The lower most floor supported a shade cloth over the entrance. The crowd outside was smaller than the rest. The noise was not so offensive to prohibit conversation. The sounds inside the inn were of music and dance, and the rhythmic clapping of the audience. Above the doorway a wooden sign hung, the image of a blue snake. The Sheriff's Serpent.

Outside and aside from the crowd Ceannte leaned upon the tavern's wall. He checked his watch. 6:25, a good nine minutes after sundown. He sighed and replaced his watch into his thick jacket. He sat back and continued to watch the people about him. By his right were the Serpent's customers, many jolly men and women sat at a long table to dine and laugh and revel in each other. Across the road not much else was about, he observed the stones set into the street, the footpath beyond, and the foundations of the buildings. His thoughts moved towards Álainn. He looked down along his attire; a green jacket kept him warm and covered a simple tunic. White made beige by the dirt and dust of wear. The buttons of the jacket gleamed gold in the candlelight. Ceannte looked up and brushed his hands into his auburn curls. He kept his eye on one particular street in the middle distance when suddenly;

"I apologise for my tardiness mister Cean."

He turned about his left to find her not more than a few feet away. She was a vision. A blue dress with lace, ruffled and subtitle, a white bonnet to keep safe her golden hair, and something new to Ceannte, a gold necklace with a jewel of some sort, a deeply blue gem. A lustrous sapphire perhaps. "I let Daddy know I went out to the Serpent for the night. I come here often."

"I see. Does that mean your father'll let you out with me?"

She chuckled. "I told him where I was, I didn't tell him why."

"Gees." He outstretched his hand. She took hold. "You're a cheeky deviless, aren't you?" They laughed as he escorted her into the tavern.

"Cheeky yes, but a deviless?" She asked upon the threshold. The noise of the inn grew much louder. Inside they found the room alive with energy. Folks of all kinds sat and ate and cheered and sang and drank and banged upon the tables. At the centre of the space performers carried the melody upon a large circular stage. Musicians fiddled the tune and banged the beat, while dancers moved with the elegance and motions of the wind. They tapped their feet and skipped about in synchronous rhythm to the music. The wooden stage clacked a complex beat in response to the drum and the tables. Porters and waiters hurried about the gaps between the rowdy diners and performers, they noted dinner orders and handed them all over the inn. "It's a good night tonight. The place is packed."

"Aye, tis." Álainn walked and shepherded Ceannte across the table, they passed drunk men and loud women, the occasional crowd of young people celebrating anything at all, elderly halflings enjoying a steak and a beer, humans cheering at the music and dance. They reached the bar at the back of the inn, two men in fancy garments tended the thirsty patrons.

One of them noticed her and, after serving another ale, made has way to them. "G'day Missy. Back so soon are you?"

"Aye. I'm here with a friend, Óstach. Can you get a quiet spot for us?"

"Course I can. Follow me." He came out from the bar and beckoned them. Óstach directed them through the noise like a ranger tracking his prey through jungle. After a moment of movement and sensation he led the couple to a quaint nook by the side of the inn. "This'll do, I think. Have a seat you two and I shall get your drinks if you want 'em."

"A beer for each I think." She declared. "Is that fine with you Cean?"

"Aye, please."

"Right then, won't be a jiff." He headed away, and the two were left by themselves in the loudness behind them. Ceannte tried to talk but the crowd was much too powerful.

"What?" She called out.

"I said I wish this place wasn't so damn loud," he repeated. His voice projected just enough for Álainn, "it's not exactly a good place for a candlelit dinner."

"True, but I'm not looking for romance." She responded. "I like this sort of thing more, you know. This place is as good as any eatery I reckon."

"Can't argue with that."

Before he had an opportunity, she began to ask. "So, mister Cean. How is the fishing business?"

"Huh? You want to know that?"

"Well, I see you at the shop and you chat about it. And I know no others who fish. I am quite curious about it."

He chuckled for a moment and shook his head. "You must be the only person I know that wants to know about it. At all!" She smiled back at him. "Well, if you really do want to know, business is fine, although I wouldn't mind some more. I can get by well enough with the catch I get. It's just enough for a living though, food and taxes. I can't afford none of that high class, nobleman stuff. So, I have a modest little home for now. That's all I need really, a roof over me head, a loaf of bread, and a flagon of beer."

"Do you get on with the other fishermen about?"

"Eh, kind of. Most of us blokes just settle down and fish. We don't do much chatting, unless it's complainin' about the taxman or getting done over by merchants. I'm alright with them, but occasionally I shoot my mouth off." In between conversation a barmaid appeared and placed two wooden mugs in front of them. "Thank you dear." He grabbed one and set it down by him. "I know I kinda make people angry sometimes, but my friends know me well enough. I don't often go to places like this,

I'm not a real sociable type. I enjoy long and meaningful talks with people, not this racket really."

"Oh, I'm sorry. I had no idea."

"Ah, don't worry about it," he took a brief sip of his beer, "it's easier if I'm with people I really like and it's not noisy." He looked about at the space, the moving and the shouting. "Actually, this is quite a quiet spot."

"This place doesn't get so loud as tonight, I guess with Her Highness up and about town is a good reason to celebrate."

"You mean the Dogess?" Álainn nodded. "Maybe, but I reckon we'll take any old excuse to get drunk at a pub."

She laughed heartily. "You're not wrong, I reckon. I bet if I asked Óstach he'd tell me this place is packed every single night."

"Even Ananday?"

"Why not?"

"It's the middle of the bloody week!" He chuckled.

"So what?" She shrugged. "I bet there's always someone here just wanting to have a drink." He laughed and his cheer encouraged her to laugh with him.

Óstach returned to their table, he caught them in their joke. "Does anyone want anything to eat? It's quite a bit past dinner time."

Ceannte had just calmed down and let his hand drop onto the table. He let out one last sigh and ordered. "Aye, I'm quite famished. I'll have a quail if you've got it."

"I'll get a Mutton Salad please and a pitcher of water too."

"Quail, aye? We don't get that very often, but we've got some for you sir. And water, righto then." The man carried on and left.

"You don't seem like a man with such particular taste Cean. I didn't know you liked quail."

"Nothing wrong with quail, a nice small bird like that. What do you think I eat?"

"Oh no I don't mean that. Quail is quite expensive. For a man of simple tastes and pleasures, such a thing is very odd."

"Ah, yeah I see. Anytime I go out to somewhere like this I like to have something nice now and again, if I can afford it of course."

"I see, I get that." She nodded along to his answer. There was a brief pause between them, the conversation stopped unexpectedly. They both drank, and Álainn carried a new topic. "I'm curious Cean, what compelled you to fish for a living?"

"Why do you work in the bakery?" He handed his open palm onto the table and asked back.

She tilted her head slightly. "Mum and Dad own the shop. They want me to become a baker like them. So, I work there."

"It's the same deal for me. My Pa taught me to fish when I was young, gave me math and business skills so I could continue the family business. I'm a third-generation fisherman in the town. My grandad taught my pa, and my pa taught me. We Macántacht's have been catching trout by the river since just about the turn of the age."

"Oh wow, I had no idea about that."

"Yeah well, we've not had a lot of luck really. We're not one of them big names around here. How about you? I've been prattling on about myself this whole time, how are things at home?"

"Oh, you're not prattling. I'm enjoying listening." She smiled again. Her gladness blushed his cheeks as he chuckled quietly. "Home is fine. I spend my free time their either knitting with Mum in winter or traveling about with Dad in the summer. I will be visiting the capital soon. Daddy wants to start a new shop and sell there."

"He's building a franchise, is he?"

"Yes. We need to do business with the Dogess to secure the land and the loan, but if all goes well, we will earn quite a bit of gold." She paused to drink some more and sighed. "Can you imagine it? The first business ever in Béal na Habhann to become a franchise. I reckon that's why she's here really, just to take a look at this place."

"Aye. I have a friend who works in the money changing business, that bloke who was with me at lunchtime." He pointed his thumb behind him, an imaginary direction towards nothing. "He went for a similar thing this week, just a little pawn shop to exchange things. It didn't work out for 'im."

"Aw, that's a shame."

"Ah, he'll be fine. If all else fails, I'll sell my books to him." He drunk more of his beer when Óstach returned with a tray of food and a wooden pitcher.

He set the tray down and uttered quietly the items he presented. "Mutton." He handed Álainn a plate of salads and cooked potato with slices of a roasted lamb. "Quail." He put Ceannte's dish in front of him, a whole bird that glistened in a glossy marinade, steam rose gently from the meat. "And water." The pitcher sat in the centre of the table, as the patrons sat about their cutlery. "Enjoy your dinners." He departed again, taking the tray with him. In the distance a cheer erupted, they turned over to see the performers had finished another dance. The audience gave their applause, and the dancers took this moment to take a break.

The violinist bellowed an announcement to the crowd. "The Taibhiú Sisters are taking a breather at the moment. They'll return after a brief intermission."

He then returned to his seat on the stage and played a slow tune. They turned back to their meals and began to eat. "So, Cean, you read do you?"

"Oh yes. I quite like reading. Historical books really, learning about the past. It's good to learn about that stuff."

"I see. Anything interesting?"

"A great deal actually. This place is full of history. Just up the road, past the northern towns, that's where the High Men live. The oldest continuous culture of men you know."

"I see. Did they interact with us much back then?"

He was slightly taken aback by the question. "Uh. On the whole, not really. The men were much more interested in the elves and magic. Don't you know that?"

"No. Am I meant to?" She looked puzzled.

"Aye. It's one of the most important points in history. Man's discovery of magic. The Elvish Peace. Didn't you learn that in school?"

"I didn't go to school." Ceannte nodded and mouthed a blunt 'oh' under his breath as she finished her beer. "Dad did not teach me much learning. Just simple maths; counting, multiplying, all that. Enough really to keep the books and get by. Mum taught me to cook meat and bake bread, and really that's it. Did your mother and father send you to the schoolhouse?"

"Yep. Pa gave me a whole song and dance about it. He saved up the gold to send me off. I reckon it's worth it. You get to learn more stuff you'd never know anywhere else."

"Aren't I too old for that?" She chuckled.

"Probably yeah, but there's plenty of books out there. You can pick up whatever you fancy. Plus it wouldn't hurt to try."

"Indeed. Perhaps you can tell of anything you think I can enjoy." She poured herself a drink of water. She offered the jug, but he refused. He gestured to the remaining alcohol in his pint. "Very well."

"In terms of your question, really it depends on the person. But if you really do want a suggestion, then it's hard to go past anything by Mr Stevington. He writes the most vivid accounts of the world. The problem with him though is that there's not a lot of good stuff out there."

"Really? How do you mean?"

Ceannte paused for a moment, he simply stared back at Álainn in deep thought. From the moment he sat down he felt calm and at ease with the world. He felt as if he was in a private dinner hall with her. All of a sudden, the environment flooded back. He looked about as the sounds and cries and clammer returned to the front of his mind. It was then when he groaned and lent back into his seat. "I don't think it's a good idea to say. Not anywhere public in any case."

"I'm sorry?"

"Look. I get that you want to know about the past, and I really encourage it myself. The thing is that I kind of don't trust a lot of the other races. You read about all the stuff they did wrong and you get a bit…what's that word?" He stared past her. "What's the word the humans use? To mean to feel very poorly about people? All cynical and that."

"Do you mean *jaded*, perhaps?"

He clicked his fingers. "Aye! That's it. I'm jaded about them lot."

"Why is that though? Do you not get on with the humans?"

"Nah. I keep my distance. I don't want anything to do with them." He ate some more of his bird and drank his beer. "Not just humans but. Damn near all of them."

"All the other folk? Why? Have they wronged you?"

"Me personally? No. But they are all quite upsetting to each other, and their histories bare that out. I don't hate on all of them. Outside of the Dogedom I only hold favour to the Archonian men. A proud order of men. I like them. All the rest of them can go bugger off for all I care."

She stared into him for a few seconds. She had no idea exactly what to make of this response. "So, you hate the races, most of them, but they have not offended you. I'm sorry, I don't quite understand." Suddenly she twitched her head. "Also, I don't know how we reached this conversation. We were talking about history books earlier."

"I'm sorry about that Ály, but for me they are the same thing. My hate comes from their history."

"Oh dear. Did they all attack us in the past? I thought it was just the orcs."

"No, it wasn't that. It *was* just the orc bastards who raided us. I hate them the most. But yeah, everyone has their own problems that I don't care for."

"Surely not the elves though." Ceannte finished off the quail when she remarked. He looked up at her pouring water into her vessel, bone stuck out of his mouth. "The immortals are not prone to hatred or violence I think." A moment had passed. Nothing happened. He simply stared at her. She continued to look back to him for reassurance, and when it did not arrive, she became wary and concerned for him and herself. "Right?"

After another second, he began to laugh. The bones fell from his maw, and his mirth was loud. "Oh lass!" He shook his head. "What little you know. The elves have an entire history of violence to their name."

"They do?"

"Dear God, yes. Killing each other to no end. Wars against belief and the right to live however you want. Each clan secretly hates each other I reckon. I mean when you read about the sort of stuff they did, holy hell! It amazes me they haven't started harassing each other again."

She groaned quietly and continued to eat. "I suspect you're right."

"I'm sorry?"

"Perhaps it is no good idea to speak of such things at a dinner gathering."

"Ah." He nodded in affirmation. "I'm didn't mean to upset you about that stuff."

"Oh, I never said I was upset. It's just best to let the past lie, I think. Also, I'm no good about the past, let's not spoil the night with ugliness." He was amazed at her, the depth of her ignorant wisdom touched him in such an unlikely way. Ceannte could not help himself but smile, her goodness managed to trump his knowledge. "Attaboy! Shall I get us more grog?"

"No. No. No." He raised his hand at her. "Let me get the next round. For a lass with such clarity to pay for a bloke's drink, I won't have it. I insist please."

She fell backwards into her chair. "You surprise me Mister Cean."

"Nothing doing miss, but you are one of a very few people that can enjoy my company after such commentary. Certainly, the only lady that knows not to press into devilry. You show much restraint, I appreciate that." He turned about and hailed at an errand porter. The man made his way to the table. "Two more beers please. On me." He uncovered a collection of gold coins within his raised hand and placed them into the open palms of the porter. The man bowed his head and promptly left to fetch the ale. "Seriously, I get into a whole mess of trouble when history gets brought up. Oh!" He pointed upwards. "I never properly answered your question. I reckon a good book to start is Stevington's book 'the River Empire'. It's a cracking good book about us. That's definitely worthwhile. Really anything about us lot or the Archons is a good book."

"The River Empire, was it?"

"Aye. You'll learn all of it there. First meetings, island expansion, outsider tax, General Hobbiton; we even had a pirate at one stage."

"No way! There was not!" Álainn protested in shock. "There can't have been!"

"Oh yes. His name was Shortfoot and the poor sod was totally rubbish." They laughed into the night, Ceannte carried on entertaining her with the tales of old; stories of Shortfoot Bradach the halfling privateer, of the rally of the Sheriffs during the Great War, and of past doges exploits about the world.

The moon was high, and the night was late. Not a single man or woman remained on the streets, and across the town the remaining rabble exited from all corners to return to their homes, they stammered and tripped and spilled out. Within the stream of the slightly drunken crowd both Ceannte and Álainn too left the Sheriff's Serpent. They were not so affected by the drink, but all the same they chatted some more. "So wait, the Sheriffs used to ride on horses?" She asked.

"I know right? Full grown, big, proper horses. The sort of animals you see humans ride on."

"I can't imagine that." They carried on to a more secluded alley away from the populous. "I mean I just cannot picture it."

"Aye, I know. It's weird that." He paused. In the dim light he saw her smile again, brightening his mood. A grin crept over him. "I'm not really sure why they stopped. I'd reckon you'd get a great view for up on one of those things."

"Horses are about twice our size, surely. I can't imagine mounting such beasts as a simple exercise."

"Nah. It's probably not." Candles lit the side street, their small light shone over not much more than the stone surfaces of the buildings about them. In spite of the windows, chandeliers still lit in outside, they too bore little more light in the night. The shadow did not do much to dampen Álainn's features. Ceannte found her cheeky smile and curiosity quite attractive, the fringe of her hair enticed him even. He felt very calm and safe near her. The two stood for a moment, they each stared into themselves. He decided to embrace her and took her close to him. The cloth of her dress felt very smooth and tingled his nerves. He was close enough to smell a perfume, a sweet scent. Almost strawberries, yet not quite.

He let go of her. "Um, okay." She replied.

"Oh." A sense of embarrassment suddenly appeared. "Was that not right?"

"No, I would not say that, but it did feel somewhat awkward."

"Huh, alright." He slowly nodded. "I'm sorry, I've never really courted a lady before."

"I assumed that if I'm honest. That is not a bad thing though. Everyone has their first." She held him by his waist, her touch gave him comfort. "For a first dinner mister Cean, you were quite lovely."

"I was?!" He asked incredulously.

She laughed at his tone. "It was not perfect, but no first meeting ever is. No Cean, you were charming. A tad judgemental sure, but you're endearing, and I must say, quite intelligent. I enjoy listening to you talk of the past." She stared into him. The light was so dim the smallest glimmer tinkled his eyes. "I enjoyed myself tonight. I quite like to do this again."

"I'd like that too." He leaned over and kissed her cheek softly. "I'd really like to see you again."

"Shall we arrange for week's end then? A proper day together?"

"Please." She chuckled at his eagerness, he joined her shortly after. "Here would be nice."

"That's fine by me." She returned the favour and kissed his cheek just as she let go of him. Álainn began to walk into the moonlight. "I will see you then mister Cean. Goodnight."

He waved her off. "Goodnight Ály." With that she made her way into the night and out of his view. He was about to head home himself when a new feeling suddenly washed over him, a warmth filled his body with an odd glow, a strange sense of excitement. A sense he never experienced before. *What is this?* He thought to himself. He patted about to locate where the source of this might be, but after a few seconds he thought nothing of it and began to return home. He prevailed into the pale moonlight with a confident stride, a man with purpose and will. An odd confidence that was foreign to him.

It was a night to remember.

Chapter 2

The night turned, and a new day began. Slowly the town woke up to the dawn glow, a bright golden light shone over Béal na Habhann. The early risers were already carrying on about their business. Eventually Ceannte too woke up. The morning light invaded his bedroom and cast itself on his eyes. He stammered himself awake, he rubbed his eyes and stretched his arms until they became sore from the movement. Sat up in bed and now more or less awake, he left the comfort of his sheets. He shuffled about barefoot. He made himself a very quick breakfast, a nice toasted bread and some jam. He found his shoes after the repast and prepared for the day's work. He opened the door to his shack. It was a rickety thing, wooden exterior with barely fastened foundations. It was perfectly safe, but it did not look it. It did not sound safe either, every door or window or opening squeaked and screeched in pain. Again, he stretched his arms and unstiffened his body. He examined the sky – it was overcast, yet it promised a clearing. The rising sun diffused its shimmering gold into a more natural, blue sky. Suitable temperature, a gentle breeze moving up the river. A perfect day for a spot of fishing. He returned inside for a few seconds, a clatter of metal and wood could be heard without and stepped outside with his fishing kit. His trusty wooden rod and a small metal box. He set down his equipment and went around the back end. The façade of the little home was plane and common, it was nothing but wooden walls with an occasional window. Eventually, he emerged with his pony, his faithful beast of burden. "Come on Ualach." He beckoned his colt with a carrot. Ualach reached his master's hand and took the carrot, the pony munched on his treat. "Good boy." He patted him as he ate. Ceannte made his way to a keg beside his shack, he carried it to Ualach, and fastened it to his saddle. He promptly put his kit into the keg, mounted his brown colt, and with a swift kick they both left to go to work, the perfect spot for a fish.

At the edge of the city, the western most bank where the river bends outwards, Ceannte trotted towards the slope. It was a small hillock, short and smooth running down to the bank and levelling off at the water. He stopped his pony at its peak and tied him to the single tree. "You know what to do," he addressed the pony, "you stay here and have a meal." As his master unloaded his equipment Ualach grazed on the grass under the shade. He disembarked the quarter-keg and rolled it down the slope. The barrel sailed down the hill and it slowly stopped just at the edge of the river. "Perfect!"

He leisurely strode down the slope and caught up to his barrel, he righted it and emptied out his rod and box. He sat at a comfortable spot at the river's bank, opened his tackle box, baited his hook, and tossed the line into the water. It was a spot he enjoyed the most, he sat at the very edge of the city limits, beyond the bussle of the harbour and markets. Every day he would watch the ships pass by him along the river; boats, sloops and merchantmen of all kinds sailed into the city. Many of them were traders from the island of Midgard way out into the Western Sea. Humans were always keen to visit and purchase from the halflings.

Time passed by Ceannte. He whistled a small ditty to pass it quicker. The barrel slowly filled with trout and salmon that all swam around the half-filled keg of water. Another fish caught his line and he stood up. He gently directed the fish towards him. *Give 'em some play but keep it close*, was his own advice. The fish fought against him and dragged the line out to sea, but eventually the line stopped tugging. "Got 'em!" He yelled and yanked on the rod. Suddenly the kipper pulled at him again. The man fought the fish for a half a minute, Ceannte struggled to it reel in. This fish had real fight in him, so much so that he managed to break free from the line. The rod snapped back, and he fell onto the grass. Irritated, he sat up and threw the rod at the ground. "Piece of rubbish," he growled. He peered into his box for some more bait when a bell rang out from the river. Off in the distance a sloop had passed by and witnessed the defeat. One of the mariners rang the bell onboard, and the men jeered and laughed at him. He noticed the ship and the hecklers and responded in kind. "Bugger you ya bastards," he screamed, the halflings continued to mock his antics, "piss off!"

"Oi!" The captain appeared on deck and quickly dispensed his authority. The raucous rabble returned to their duties at once, and Ceannte continued his toiling. He skewered another worm and threw the line back into the river. After a few moments nothing was biting, and the recent battle deflated his mood, He decided to distract himself and take in his surroundings.

He sat on the edge of the city and saw the main thoroughfare into and out of Leath Langa. It was on the near side of the town as the Foirceannadh River meandered out to sea. On his right was the harbour of the city. It always bustled with activity and noise. Bells, calls, shouts and the marches of all manner of merchants rang out. Cargo was traded, officers transported, and ships sailed. For the halflings the harbour and the marketplace were their meeting points, chatter and gossip flew far between themselves and visitors. Ceannte sighed. *Business is getting too slow,* he thought to himself, *the fish are getting more slippery and wily.* He turned to see the hills beyond the river in front of him. Halflings love nature and do not care for large buildings or cities of stone. He was no different, he spied the hill beyond and daydreamed of settling down in it. He pictured in his mind's eye the hill house; a Teachcnoc. The interior of his hill seemed subtitle and rustic. The grand hall entered into his study and bedroom. The dining room was large enough to entertain guests, just beside the kitchen. Outside, the hill was brightly decorated with flowers and gardens of colour. Bright pansies, tulips, daisies, and all sorts of flowers in circular patterns. Gardens he tended himself to his personal colours. A few errand thoughts for his future. *Good thing I know what delta is!* Or did he? He quickly turned to the ground beside him and drew onto the grass with his finger, '$\delta = 3.1415$', he trailed off at the end, unable to recall the next digit. "Or something like that. The Diameter Constant," he uttered. He then took a quick peak to his left and saw the mouth of the river. The islands beyond were colonised by the halflings, the outposts have their own unique islander charm that they have made into their own. Along the river was a geyser that sprayed water up from the earth however, it was no simple geyser. It was the Water Node Sruth Dé, a site of arcane power. Water Mana spurted high above and caught the wind, it fell back into the sea. It glistened under the sun an eerie blight blue and contrasted the darker hue of the sea. The mysterious wonder entranced Ceannte for a moment, the magical power that coursed through the node held a beauty he could not quite identify. Suddenly another fish snagged the line, he broke his gaze and again played with his prey. "By God!" The two fought for a few seconds, he pulled at the fish, and the fish tugged back into the river. Eventually the fish gave up and he reeled in his catch. "You bloody beauty," he laughed when he saw what he caught; A Marinus Trout. A shimmering specimen – dull blue iridescent scales, fins and a tail slightly marked a bright yellow and a long body for more meat. "You're going to make me a bundle of gold." He gently placed the fish into the barrel, and it joined the school of fish. His catch of the day!

He turned around to continue but he noticed something in the water, something – maybe a fish – laid on the floor just by the shore. "What the?" He muttered to himself. The fisherman dropped his kit and walked over. It was an arm's reach from the shoreline, he stepped into the water and bent down to have a look at this thing. It was a fish. It was another Marinus Trout! It was a *dead* Marinus Trout! "What the hell?!" He immediately grabbed the fish, brought out of the river, and up it to his face. It was totally lifeless. "How did this happen?" He was genuinely puzzled at the sight. "The magic node protects these things, how can a Marinus die in water? This doesn't happen!" He shook the fish about and eventually noticed the bulge the fish had. He felt around the fish's body and discovered a mass within it. He felt it move as he pinched under it and squeezed it out of the fish's mouth. A large ploop splashed into the water at his feet, he looked down and could not believe his eyes. "How the?!" He leaned down and grabbed the object. The water revealed it to be a large disk made entirely out of gold. It was so large he was barely able to hold it in his hand, yet it was remarkably easy to handle. The disk was almost entirely uniform in its shape except for two features; one side had a very large number 6 embossed on top if it. *Is this the top side?* The other face had a shape etched into it, two lines meeting at an apex. He had no idea what it meant, just some random thing, but then he had an idea. He dropped the carcass into the keg and kicked up some grass beside him. His leather boots exposed the wet soil underneath. He crouched down and pressed the gold into the dirt. The etched symbol squelched the mud as he pushed it in harder. He uncovered the gold and revealed a dirty brown circular imprint with a large number 7 enclosed in it. "Ah," he exclaimed, "I thought so." Ceannte stood up and continued to examine the gold. For its size the piece was lighter than he thought, his tiny hands made it difficult to hold easily. Suddenly it occurred to him. He immediately dropped his rod and ran up the hill. "I'm rich! I'm bloody rich!" He untied Ualach from the tree and hurried the pony down to the keg. "Get down there, will you?" Hastily the pair returned to the bank. He jumped off his steed, took the lid and sealed the barrel. He lifted the container and strapped the barrel on the side of the pony, the colt protested the weight. "Ah, quit ya whinin'! This might be the last time you'll haul anything." He then reached under the pony and pulled a flap of material out to the other side. He secured more straps to the beast, took all his equipment and lifted himself onto it. It was little more than a piece of hardy leather, yet he stood on it in comfort, and with it controlled the beast. The weight did not counterbalance the keg, but the pony settled down. "Hyah!" Ceannte took the reins and Ualach trotted back around the hillock. He whipped the colt some more and the trot turned into a gallop. He wanted to get to the market as soon as possible, sell off his fish and get to the money changer, his payday finally arrived.

Chapter 3

Day turned to night. The time for toil was over - the time for leisure began. Again, the town revelled in festivities and celebration. Ceannte passed by the night merchants and spotted his destination. He waved past the last trader and briskly walked up to a small inn sandwiched between similar structures beside it. 'Airgead & Sons Trading' read the banner as it swung in the breeze. He spotted something new however, two heavily suited men appeared to guard the door of the shop. This puzzled him. He reached the guards and stood in front of them, he observed them for some time. He took in every detail of them, up their helms to down their suits, the length of their spears, and the colours of the decorations pinned to their clothing. "Excuse me sir," one of them asked, he caught his attention, "move along please."

"Aye, sure," he answered, "except I have business with Mr. Airgead. Top priority stuff. Nothing can prevent this transaction from taking place, not even whatever it is you lot are keeping safe."

"Sir, whatever business you have may occur at another time. The Dogess Uisce, Keeperess of the River, is transacting with the proprietor of this establishment."

"That's all well and good, I have no problem with that, but does that mean I have to wait out here in the cold? Surely, I can wait patiently inside and keep warm and quiet. I don't understand why I can't."

"It is her will, sir," the other guard explained, "and it is law. You must respect it."

Ceannte raised his hands. "Well, if it's law I'll abide," then he dropped them and pointed back at the guards, "but I don't respect stupid laws. And that law it thicker than a bloody stone."

"It is her will sir." The guard repeated. "Do not cause a fuss."

"I'm causing no fuss, I'll comply." He backed away and they relaxed their stance. Seconds passed by. He looked about him. The town was less active tonight than the last. No large tables for feasting, no shouting from rowdy folk. Couples wandered about the streets, the light from the buntings gave a magical glow to the stone and the wood of the buildings. Candlelight fluttered from within the homes nearby. He looked down at his feet. A loose pebble sat by shoes. He kicked the the rock along the road, it clicked and rattled into the distance. Eventually a rumbling emerged from the building and broke the silence. Ceannte focused on the door, a dark wooden door with no embellishment. He could hear a conversation but could not make the words. He barely heard Óir through the wood, his moderate sound appeared to be raised. He then heard the faint sound of a second voice, the Dogess no doubt. The Merchant Queen's sound was almost imperceptible through the door, what he did hear was a shrill and painful tone. He could not be sure of it, but he thought he heard his friend protest *'Be reasonable,'* or something of that effect. Then the distinct sound of a person exiting crept from behind the door. He took a step back, the door rattled open, and the little bell over it rang happily.

The Dogess left the store. She wore an elegant dress of marigold and mild blue patterns around the hem, a breastplate of gold over her garment, and she was not at all as pleasant as her attire. Some sort of earring dangled and shook about in every direction as she strode. "I do not have the time for your nonsense demands Mr. Airgead. My fair manner does not accommodate strong wills with stubborn minds."

"It is not fair to ask for a contract?" he inquired.

"It is certainly fair to negotiate a contract sir," she prepared her guards as she carried on, "it is certainly *not* fair to enforce harsh terms upon a contract that injure my country."

"Harsh terms?!" He shrugged in bewilderment.

"Enough of this. Good day Mr. Airgead."

She was quick to leave him in the cold, but Ceannte interjected. "Excuse me, ma'am? What's going on here?"

"Halt." She held her guards and turned about to him. "Master, you would do well to flee from this establishment. Mr. Airgead trades in nefarious dealings and seeks to fleece you from your pounds!" Suddenly she turned back and moved away faster, as if she were retreating from a ruinous defeat.

"Nefarious?!" They were both surprised, but he personally was affronted by the insult.

"Ah! Leave her be." Óir shooed at her. "Better to just leave it alone."

He turned back to his friend. "Leave it alone? She just insulted you like that, and you want to bloody leave it?"

"What can you do mate? You against two armed men? You'd be cut to pieces long before you could ever get a swing in. Besides, you know me much better than that."

He took a big sigh and turned back, the Dogess was now almost completely out of view. "Aye, I guess you're right, and you're right."

"Well?" Ceannte turned about. "Don't just stand out there then. Come on in." He hastily hopped over a stone in the road and made his way into the store. Once inside he closed the door behind him, and the bell dinged again. They both strode to the front end of the building. The trading house was dimly lit and full of treasures, clocks, telescopes, and ancient maps of Mundus. They stopped in front of a simple wooden counter. "Right, so what's this thing you have for me?"

"Nah nah, hold on a minute. Would you mind explaining to me what just happened there? Why did our queen just go mental at you?"

"Ah, it's no big thing." He lifted his hand at him. "Nothing a good deal of honest work can't cure. Don't worry about it."

"Don't worry about it?! Nah. I reckon I will. That load of nonsense can't just go unpunished! I wouldn't take such abuse, not even from her. And I like to think I know you well enough. You raised your voice back there. You hardly ever do that unless you get into some sort of argument."

"Gee, I wonder where I get that from!" He replied with incredulous sarcasm.

"Don't start with me now. I know you're not at all what she was banging on about. You've never rorted me out of anything right? You give me my dues."

"It ain't often, but I do."

"Aye! So, what the hell was she getting so upset about that got you to bark back then?"

Óir sighed. "Well, the last afternoon sort of got to me a bit. I decided to arrange an audience with her again about the contract. She seemed pretty easy enough."

"So that's what was going on then, just rehashing the thing?"

"I figured there was no harm in working out what I needed to finalise the deal. Money is easy enough to get. Worked out the property lot in the big city. Banker seems happy to invest. As far as I could see, everything was all lined up. She came in, gave me a whole story about economics and instability. A load of rubbish I think, no one ever told me I was entering a lull in business. I called her out, and then she got very angry, like I've never seen her so irate. I tried to calm her down, but she bloody flew off the handle. She just screamed and carried on about ruining the country and called me all sorts of terrible names. I guess I was lucky you were around to fight her for me when you did."

"Hardly. Sounds like you have had a shocking night. Sorry I wasn't there sooner."

"Ah, I'm tougher than that. If I can get on with you at your worst, I can handle anyone I reckon."

Ceannte chuckled. "Aye, I guess so."

"I feel like having a scotch. You want a drink?"

"Crikey, was she that bad? Yeah I'll have one."

"I'll fetch the drinks. You show us this thing you found." Óir made his way around the counter while his friend rifled about his vest. He lent over into one of the many shelves and display cases and produced a steel tray equiped with a flask and two glasses. He removed the top and poured a sliver of the maroon scotch into each glass. The tray rattled and he took the glasses back. When he returned, he noticed his friend waiting at the desk, he gestured to the gold coin that now laid upon the wood. He handed him the glass but was fixated on the gold. "Is this it?"

"Yeah, I know. I still can't believe it myself." Óir took the gold and began to examine it. "I've been fishing for five years and I've never seen or heard of this before. I still don't understand how a fish could eat a bit of gold that big."

"Holy hell," he whispered for a moment. He then laughed as he rotated the disk, "I know fish'll eat anything, but this is ridiculous!"

Ceannte began to grin wide. "First thing I'll do is get a deposit for a Teachcnoc. I've been spying a hill not far from where I fish for a while now."

He looked back at his friend, his face draped in concern. "Come with me, Cean. There's something I need to show you."

He began to move off, but he was confused. "Is everything alright?"

The trader beckoned him. "Just come 'ere, will you? It's important."

He sighed and walked around the oak counter. "Alright, but I better not be getting stiffed. I want my fair share."

"Cean, no offence or nothing, but I really don't want to hear that right now," Óir grumbled as he directed him to his office, "I reckon I've had my fill of aggravation for one night."

"Aye, fair enough, but I'd like to know what's going on."

"I know you do," Óir stood aside the doorway and beckoned, "get in then. Have a seat."

Ceannte entered the room and took in the sight; it seemed to be a large study. Across the wall was a shelf full of books about metals, minerals, and precious jewels. The desk under it held all of the trader's equipment: microscope tools, a scale, and a number of monocles made for spotting the details of a metalwork. He saw two wooden chairs padded with cushions and sat himself down on one. "I haven't been here in a while," he said quietly, "did you get more books?"

"Yeah. Nothing important." He sat opposite him and gave the same look as before. "Cean," he held up the piece of gold between them, "this here bit of gold is not what you think it is."

After a second of silence, he responded. "What do you mean? It's gold, ain't it?"

"Yes and no," he answered. "It is gold, yes, but it's not from an ordinary mine, mate. This came from a forgery."

He jumped up from his chair. "My gold is Fake Gold?!"

"No!" Óir briskly shook his head. "Not Fake Gold. I told you, this is gold. We call it Fool's Gold instead."

He grunted and threw his hands in the air. "What the hell's the difference?!"

"Sit down, Cean!" He sighed and fell back down onto his seat. He threw the trader a piercing look of frustration. "And just listen, will you?" He sighed with deliberate force. "Alright," he handed back the gold to his annoyed friend. "So, Fool's Gold is quite rare in this world because of where it comes from. By any chance, do you know much about Mana crystals?"

"I don't care about magic!" He declared in a huff.

He shrugged. "It's your loss, mate.' He stood up and turned to his desk. "Judging by your answer, you know Mana comes in different forms then."

"Yep."

"Well then, I won't be borin' you with stuff you already know." Óir opened a draw and produced a pair of gloves. "We're used to the Mana coming out of the Water Node not far from here, the liquid stuff," he produced an item from the draw, "but most Manae are grown into a crystalline shape and mostly look like this."

The trader turned back to Ceannte and revealed his personal shard of Mana. The crystal was mesmerising. It was a long, hexagonal thing which tapered to a point at both ends. It was just long enough for him to handle with his leather gloves. From all the lights in the room, the crystal glistened and shone, but it was translucent, and a faint light pulsated within. It had a certain gleam despite its transparency, as if it were a brand-new steel pipe or an unsheathed sword.

He stared blankly. "I genuinely don't care, Óir."

"Oi! Have some respect," he scowled the luddite, "this ain't some ol' bit of Mana you get from some bloke! This is Quork Mana. I paid a pretty penny to get a hold of this here." He waved the Mana about as he explained. "I paid seven quid for this!"

Ceannte leaned towards him in amazement. "700 dollar-pounds?"

"Yep, quite a lot of gold moved to get me this. Even handed over one of my platinums for it. Now, I'm showing you this because another type of Mana is Crysx Mana." He returned the crystal to the drawer. "Crysx is especially rare. They say it only comes from three mines in Mundus." He returned to his seat. "Crysx Mana is more powerful than Quork and all other Manae. No one knows why those two are so potent. Some say it's divination, but really, the only difference is the chemical makeup; that Quork crystal you just saw is an alloy of Adamantium and Silver." He leaned forward and pointed to the gold piece. "Crysx Mana is an alloy of Adamantium and Gold."

He raised his eyebrow. "Gold, you say?"

"Aye." Óir paused for a moment. "I guess you can work the rest out yourself."

"Yep. This gold had its Adamantium stripped from a dwarf somewhere."

He chuckled. "Well, I don't know about the dwarf bit, but yes, you get the idea. The origin of that in particular came from a shard of Crysx Mana that's been reforged into their chemical metals. We call it Fool's Gold because it's half gold's value in weight."

"Half?" He pondered at that thought. "Eh, I'm fine with half. It's still a decent sum. But I have to know how you knew what gold it was?"

"How I could tell? You didn't feel the gold?"

Ceannte stared blankly at him.

The trader pinched the bridge of his nose. "The weight, man. It didn't feel light to you?"

"Not really, no."

"Huh." Óir relaxed back into his chair and extended his hand again. "I guess you're too used to small change if you thought that was reasonable." He once again handed the trader the gold piece. "So, like you saw in my shard, Mana crystals have this hollow middle part where the power lives. When the crystal is reformed, the Adamantium is pure, but the other metal has a curious property. I'm not sure about the Alphyscis myself, but that structure ends up full of tiny air bubbles around and inside it. The metal is very light compared to the regular stuff." Ceannte nodded as he explained, but otherwise remained silent. He suddenly frowned, "Hang on, are you seriously telling me it never occurred to you the gold was light for its size?"

"Gold is gold to me," he shrugged, "for something that big, I wouldn't care how heavy it felt. It's all pounds and quid for all I care."

"That's dangerous thinking," he pointed at him, "you need to think more about the world around you and the things that affect you."

He scoffed. "The world around me? You think I don't know about the world around me?" He again jumped out of his chair and paced about. "Elves killing elves, humans ruining the world, goblins terrorising dwarves, and you call me uninformed? I know more about the world than just about any halfling there is here, mate."

Óir shook his head. "You read about the past, Cean. That's not the same thing."

"It may as well be the same thing!" He lunged at him, although neither lost their nerve. "I don't stay here because I like the scenery, Óir. Not even the people. I live here and want to stay because just about every other nation is so screwed up, I can't stand it. I can't go to any of the elf lands because they hate each other for the stupidest reasons. It's mind numbing."

"They don't hate each other today." He interjected.

Ceannte laughed. "Don't listen to what they say, mate. Watch what they do. I've seen some Eldar folk pass by, and they joke about the wood elves and the dark elves. They don't see them as equals. They still think they're above them and maybe even above us all."

His brows narrowed somewhat. "What was it you just said a second ago? 'Don't listen to what they say,' was it?"

"It's more than that, they're total hypocrites!" He stood up straight and started to imitate mockingly. "They act so wise, and just, and all-knowing about everything. They pass judgement on everything because they're the first race and they 'oversaw' everything rise from the ground. They're so bloody repressed in denial, it pisses me off. I can kinda respect the other clans since they don't bother with all that, but they have their own problems, too. I just can't stand the lot of them; I hate the elves!"

"Wow. You, dear Ceannte, are the only person I know that hates the elves." He looked both disappointed and bewildered at the same time. "I'm genuinely impressed."

"Don't get me started on hati–"

"Enough of this!" Óir rose from his seat. "Cean, stop this. You have to let these things go."

He took a deep breath and closed his eyes. He sighed slowly and calmly. "I think I'm alright."

"Good, cause I've got more to tell you about that gold. Give it 'ere!"

"What now? What could possibly be wrong now?"

He sighed. "Fine! Just have a close look near the six." Ceannte grunted and brought the gold piece close to his face. "You're looking for a nick on the left."

He scanned the gold face until eventually, he saw it: a tiny six-pointed star. "This is it?" He pointed at the star.

"Aye. That's no scratch - it's a maker's mark. Those tell you where wood and metalworks come from."

He stared at Óir again. "It's the Star of Beacon. So what?"

His lips pursed. "Well, anything with that mark is protected by law. You're not allowed to trade it in."

"Excuse me?!"

"Yep. It's a really obscure law, part of the Goodwill Policy in the Council's Mandate. I honestly never thought I'd ever have to enforce it, especially not to you mate."

"This is bullshit!" He tossed his arms into the air, and the disk clattered on the wooden floor. "This whole thing is total bullshit. You're telling me I can't sell this thing?!"

"You can't sell it, you can't trade it in for any gold, you can't destroy it, you can't mutilate it. All you can do is return it to Beacon."

Ceannte gnashed his teeth. "And why would I want to do that, exactly?"

"I'd pick that up if I were you," he pointed to the coin, "you're going to have to keep it on you until you get to Beacon."

He scowled in response. "Hey, wait a second, I never said I was going to Beacon!"

"You have to, mate, it's the law."

"It is?!" Óir nodded back. "Well that's another stupid law!" He protested against the apparent conspiracy against him. After a moment he calmed himself slightly. "Are you sure? I mean, this actually sounds made up."

"I can get you my Tome of Practices if you want. I'll show you the law."

"Please do." Out of energy and breath, he calmed down fully as his friend shuffled towards a bookshelf and reached into it. Ceannte was defeated – the best day of his life had turned into a nightmare. All his dreams seemed to slip through his fingers; his little house in a hill, his chance to bring up a family and rest, his golden years in home and hearth. He fell back into his chair, deflated by the weight of crooked justice. Óir extracted a large brown book and flicked the pages for a time. He then handed the book to him and pointed at the passage:

> *16-4 ~ the Beacon Embargo. By the law set about at the Council's Mandate, all objects, possessed or discovered, bearing the Star of Beacon are hitherto seized as the property of All History and Beacon. The person or persons found to have possession of a property of All History must return the object to the Council of the Earth immediately and relinquish said object to the Council. Said objects are not subject to bartering, transaction, destruction, or any similar dispossession. Persons who return the property of All History are to be given free passage to Beacon by the fastest possible means available with neither personal nor financial cost.*

There it was, written in black and white. The trader remarked. "It's a damn shame too. Even if it were Fool's Gold, you'd get a pretty penny for it."

He closed the book. "How much is it worth?"

"Well for that size the regular value of gold puts it at 100 platinum-quid, and Foo-"

"100 quid?" There was a change in him. Ceannte was sombre and tired, the rage in him was gone, yet it took on a different form. A benign, quiet menace. "You're telling me some made up law is scamming me out of 10,000 gold pieces?!"

"No, Cean, I was going to say that Fool's Gold is half of that. You've lost out on 5,000 pounds."

He sighed in frustration, placed his hand over his eyes and muttered. "I'm out five grand, and even worse is I have to go to bloody Beacon."

"You're not out five grand mate. You haven't lost anything. You just aren't getting any cash. In fact, you don't get to pay a thing to get there."

"If I get there."

"If? What do you mean 'if'? You are going, aren't you?"

He sighed once more. "I don't know if I want to." A silence emerged, a rather long silence. Óir folded his arms and stared him down. Ceannte did the same. They each attacked the other with piercing looks and concentrated thoughts on the other. "You know why I don't want anything to do with that place."

"Aye. I do. But I reckon you'll be assailed by the law, a law you don't like at that."

He shook his head. "I don't think so, not this time."

"Really?" He raised an eyebrow. "You'd break a law because of your hatred?"

"I might just. Gees, I really don't like the sound of that idea." He held his chin and contemplated. "I mean I obey the law, sure. I was stood out in the cold only a few minutes ago, waiting for your business to finish. I get that the Dogess would want some privacy, so even though I don't like it, I wait."

"I figured. I heard a commotion outside. I thought it was you."

"Yeah yeah." He sighed. "But see, I don't want to deal with them leaders. I know I'll just badger on about the past. I'll get right up to their faces and just mock them."

"Have you thought about not doing that?" He asked incredulously.

"Of course I have. I just notice these things here and there. Elves joking about the wars. Sometimes, when they work with dark elves, I see Eldars wince a bit. They still think little of them, like they shouldn't exist or something. Or another thing! Goblins poking fun at the dwarves, when those two have seriously bad blood. Like they want to just kill each other. And the humans are the worst of them lot."

"This again." Óir rolled his eyes.

"Yes! This again!" He hyphenated his words. "I can't stand men and their science. All balderdash and misery. If it weren't for them, we'd be a lot happier."

"Aye. *We'd* be a lot happier." He pointed at himself and Ceannte. "But all that bad blood would be running around, causing anger and hate and death. Humans gave as science, reason, diplomacy-"

"And orcs," the interruption caused Óir to sigh in frustration, "don't forget the orcs! Those bastards out there," he pointed to some direction, "there in that desert. Wrecking terrible havoc and causing grief. Those ferrel mutants. A real scourge if there ever was one."

"Ha! Now who's racist?"

"Oi! Don't start with me."

"I'm not bloody starting nothing!" He yelled.

"It's no good for elves to call anyone freaks of nature, or two nations to fight over something stupid or petty. But orcs are demons. Murderous hulking beasts that pillage towns and attack innocents. They fucked us up, and they ruined a lot of us small folk. So, the powers came together to stop them from pillaging and attacking, but not soon enough! I hate the orcs, and I hate the humans for ever getting involved in making magic. Damn them and their curiosity! And I tell you what, I'm sure I can get along with a man after some time, but you'll never see me accept an orc with any friendliness. Never ever! They are scum of the earth." The rant took much of his energy. Ceannte panted slightly to catch his breath. There was one more silence that was interrupted by his breathing for a few moments. "So yeah. I have to deal with that as well."

"Indeed." He scanned about the floor for the gold. "Well if you don't do it, I'm going to have to." Once he found it, he made his way for it. "Because someone has to turn it over the the authorities, and if it's not you it'll be me." He stared at the piece in his hands. "I wonder what reward they'll hand to me for it."

"Reward?"

"Yeah. What, you didn't think they'll just take the thing and not compensate you did you?"

"Huh. I guess I didn't."

"Gees, Cean. Really? Of course they will." Óir walked up to his friend and handed the gold over. "Look mate, have a think about it. Take a day or two to decide who should take this thing up. If you genuinely don't want to do it, I will take it from you and you don't have to worry about it again, fair?"

He looked into the gold, the light reflecting along the straight edges of the sides and impressions. The cursed gold of misfortune and penury. Ceannte sighed and looked back up. "Fair."

"Good man." He patted his arm. "I reckon it's time for bed, all that pent-up anger must've gotten you pretty ragged."

"Aye, I am. I better get going." He turned about and they both left. Out of the study they rounded the wooden counter and reached the door without a word or a noise.

Óir opened the door and presented the exit for him. As he left, he called out. "Oi Cean!" He turned to see him. "Have a good long think about it. I've been to the city myself. I won't deny, it's a beautiful place, and the people are amazing. But don't let this upset you, it's all up to you if you want to do it."

"I appreciate that Óir." He waved him off. "Hooroo!"

"Cherrio." He walked off, and the trader shut up shop. He pulled down a blind over the window of the door. Upon it read the message 'If you see this, we are CLOSED'.

The moon was high when Ceannte returned to his home. He spent much of the night wandering about the empty streets, deep in his own head. He was busy weighting the good and the bad of his dilemma, imagining himself setting out for the great city. He could not hold a vision of Beacon in his mind, or really any large settlement. Béal na Habhann was his home, his shelter. His entire world. He hastily strode around the shack to check on Ualach. By the dim light he observed the pony sleeping, he laid about on his side. As he slowly approached him, he noticed very minor movements, his free ear swivelled, slight jutting of his head, a very weak sound. The sort of utterance one would make while in a dream, faint yet comprehensible. The sight made him smile. He knelt to him and ran his hand over the lean body. *"Pleasant dreams."* He whispered. The pony stirred briefly and very mildly, only producing a short neigh and slight wriggle before he returned to his adventure. *"Sorry mate."* He slowly rose and tiptoed away from Ualach, once he was safely away, he regained his speed and returned to his home properly.

Inside the shack Ceannte entered. He closed the door and employed the lock to secure it. The dwelling was just as small as it appeared on the outside. The entrance led straight into the common area, the living room, kitchen and laundry were all the same space. He struck a match and lit a candle in a holder to see. The area was semi-organised, yet chaotic at the same time. At a glance, things appeared to be in order, but they were actually grouped into piles of related things. Stacks of books, piles of clothing, loose bits of parchment; the living space was very much in an untidy state. He sighed at the mess, he was too tired to survey the room and reorganise himself. Instead he walked to a random placement of books, took the topmost one without seeing what it was, grabbed the candle holder, and went upstairs to his bed. He shuffled up the steps and across the hallway, the light flickered with each movement. He entered the bedroom and planted the candle down upon a bed table. Ceannte dropped himself onto the bed and sighed again. He checked the book in his hand. 'the River Empire: the Known History of the Halflings and the Emergence of Mercantilism.' "Ha!" He laughed at the coincidence and opened the book. "Why not then?" He read it once again at night, a bedtime story of the rich past.

Chapter 4

The next day was unlike others. The sky was still blue, the routine was the same. Ceannte fished in the same spot however, he was much more cautious of the water. He was spotting more burdened fishes laying about on the riverbed. His concentration was not on the task. He cast lines into the water, he occasionally pulled them out, but he took no notice of others that were catching. His barrel was much smaller than his normal catch. The afternoon was just as unusual. After a hearty lunch he normally travels to the market by the docks and unloads his toil for some profit. Today was quite strange. He arrived at his stall and did what he always does; unload his pony, set up shop by the market, and sold his fish. The crowd of barters and sellers shouted and yelled for the attention of any buyer across the boardwalk into and out of the docklands, the grand meeting place for the halflings. For whatever reason however, Ceannte was not as robust as his rivals. He would interject only to those who saw his produce and approached or passed right by the stall. Customers beyond this quite small field of his influence he did not bother to conflict with the other fishermen about.

Hours passed and the sun floated atop the water. With his small cargo he sold everything save for one Aquiline Pilchard. It was the time of the day when everyone was returning home for the nightly meal and recreation. He leaned onto the table and sighed. The whole day was a blur to Ceannte, the whole time he was preoccupied with the dilemma of last night. The potential hazards of his personal hatred and bigotry, against the potential benefits of this seeming artefact of history. His dislike of the bigger countries and the arrogance his sees in them. His interest in history and being part of it. His fears of the unknown. He was living inside his own head today. He vacantly watched the people walk by, away from his reach and into their own worlds.

"You alright there, mate?"

Out of nowhere a familiar voice woke him up. He turned slowly and replied. "Oh, kind of." It was Óir, he walked over to the stall. "I've been a bit out of sorts today. This whole Beacon thing has been on my mind all day."

"I can imagine. Have you come to any decision?"

He took a deep breath, followed by a long sigh. "Not really. I keep thinking about it over and over in my head, but honestly I'm no closer to any real decision." He looked out past the dock and to the river. "There's no reason for me to go, not with my attitude anyway, yet there is also no reason not to go."

He grunted lengthily and nodded to the merchant's response. "I see. I can understand that. Perhaps I can help you along with that."

"How?"

Óir pointed down. "I'll take that pilchard off your hands. Let you shut up shop early."

"Ha! You want some seafood aye?"

"Why not? I haven't had any in a while."

"Fair enough, 10 pounds please." He rifled around the pocket of his jacket and took 10 gold pieces. Ceannte took the fish and handed it to him with one hand and felt the clatter of coins that fell into the other. He looked to make sure, each of the ten coins were thin golden disks with writing engraved on it. '1DP' shone in the fading sunlight with '20SC' in smaller writing under it. "Thank you mate. I may as well pop off to the Last Stand. Figure I'll have a ponder there."

"A pub? Really?"

"Yeah, I think better in a pub."

"Some would disagree." He scoffed.

"Yeah, well that place is still pretty decent. I haven't made an arse of myself there yet."

"Don't be trying to start nothing, aye?"

"Nah, just have a drink, see where it takes me."

"Alright but make it just one drink." Óir waved him off. "Cherrio mate."

"Have a good night." They parted ways again, and with a huff and a sigh he began to deconstruct his business for the day.

Night was still descending, the sun fell into the ground, yet its red light was still captured by the clouds. The brightness overpowered the sinking dark. A tall structure close to the dock emanated light and noise. Outside was a very long door and a signpost that hung off it, the shape of a man carrying a spear and riding a horse as if it were charging into battle. Ceannte strode quickly down the main road and without missing a step opened the entrance and made his way into the inn, the Last Stand. He shut the door behind him, the door was so tall that two handles were on it, one at his level and one much higher. He walked into the familiar scene, halflings and men drinking by the bar. Tables and chairs of various height scattered about the room, with a few of the folk eating meaty dinners. He headed towards the bar, the massive counter and the stools a good deal taller than what he was used to. It was the sort of tavern that accommodated for the humans as well as halflings, everything needed to be so tall for their longer counterparts. He reached the bar and grabbed a hold of the seat, he lifted himself up onto the stool. Ceannte looked about, he sat next to a human man on his right and a few further down, but he could not see past the first man. He found the barman polishing glasses by the far side of the bar. He called out to him. "Barkeep?" The human spotted him and walked up to him. "A pint of your house lager please."

"Stout glass or regular pint?" He asked for the size.

"I don't have the stomach for the big stuff right now. I'll have the stout."

"Alright. You after dinner as well?"

"Uh." He thought for a second. "Alright, yes. Lamb Shanks with Shamrock Weed and Mash please."

"I'll get your drink and then message the cook."

He slapped the bar. "Legend! Thanks."

The barman laughed. "All good mate." He moved over to the back of the bar. The wall was lined with kegs full of ales, wines, lagers, beers, and all sorts of drink. He found the keg labeled 'In House Lager', clasped the glass under the tap, and poured the beverage into it. The brown alcohol rushed into the miniature glass. Just as quickly the barman closed the tap and returned to Ceannte with his drink. "15 pounds." He produced a small sack from his belt and dropped it into the bar. He tripped out some coins, counted the value and handed his dues. "Alright, I'll inform the cook of your dinner."

"Thank you." The barman left, leaving him to return to his thoughts.

The man beside him had other ideas. "Shamrock Weed aye? Awfully spicy isn't it?"

"Nothing wrong with a bit of spice, I prefer food with a bit of kick in it."

"My word!" He laughed. "I don't think there are many halflings such as yourself to be so interested in spice. Now I've seen everything."

"When you've eaten it for so long you get used to it." He shrugged off the man's mirth "The trick is to have something quite soothing with it like potato. I don't know the science about it, but it just makes the heat less aggressive. Plus, I wouldn't mind a bit of luck right now."

"Been a bad day has it?" The man continued to drink his alcohol.

"Well, not really bad. Just-" he paused to think for a moment, "confusing."

"Confusing, you say?" He placed his glass on the bar and turned to Ceannte. "Do tell."

"Aye?" He looked to the man; he clearly had an interest in him for some reason. The human was not notably dressed, a simple vest and tunic, no colours that exposed his profession. His face was gruff with stubble, circular spectacles framed his hazelnut eyes, and his blonde hair fell about his neck. Strands of silver intermixed with his golden locks. They gave a sort of shimmering awe about him. The only object he noticed was a smoking pipe in his pocket. The man then had affluence, but he did not seem to show it. All the while he noticed that the man observed him as well, he felt the same analytical eye cast upon himself. "Nah, I don't want to bother you. To be honest you'd have to know a bit about history to understand the problem, and if I'm honest I still don't get it."

"Then your day has become fortuitous, for I know a good deal about the history of many things."

"Ha!" Ceannte laughed. "That's a laugh. There's no way you know anything about our history. Humans don't care about us lot."

"Actually, I know quite a bit, as well as much of academic Midgard. There's a renaissance of interest in the cultures of the minor races."

"Academic Midgard?" The term confounded him. He looked this character up and down. "What are you? Some sort of Professor or something?"

"Indeed, I am!" The man chuckled at the question and extended his hand. "Doctor William Stevington. I suspect you may be familiar with me, or rather my writings."

"Steving- bloody!" He grabbed his hand and shook it vigorously. "God, this is such an honour sir, I mean wow. I had no idea you were here, or even go to this place. Are you enjoying yourself here?"

William delighted in the sudden friendliness. "I am quite fine, yes. I must admit, I have not come across a halfling that has taken any interest in their own history. I'm pleased to finally see that changing."

"Aye, but it goes further than that. I've been riveted by your other books. Mundus' history interests me a great deal."

"My word! You mean to tell me you have read all of my work?"

"Every last one." He was blown away by Ceannte's interest and dedication. He needed to quickly obtain his beer and take a rather large gulp.

He turned back to the halfling. "Even the theses?"

"They were a bit dense, but yep, those too."

"And I assume you are not an academic, right?"

"Nah, fisherman by trade. I went to the schoolhouse here but no further. We simply didn't have the money for it."

"That's a terrible shame. You would make a fine academic. Quite frankly the Dogedom requires more intellectuals."

He laughed. "Indeed! If only it brought in any gold." He held up his glass, William agreed with a clink of their glasses.

"That's why I write books." They laughed further as the barman returned with the halfling's meal. "I must say, mister…"

"Macántacht, Ceannte Macántacht." He answered while he grabbed his cutlery and tucked into the meat.

"Mister Macántacht, if you have read my books and understand them, then perhaps indeed I may not be helpful to you or your predicament."

"No no no. Hang on." His lips smacked with each chewed word. "Let's give it a try first. No sense in bringing it up and then just abandoning it. How versed are you in modern history?"

He raised an eyebrow. "How modern?"

"The Council of the Earth, the Race Against Peace. All that."

"Oh! Oh, well I am very familiar with all the documentation of the period. Just about everyone is familiar with the Great War. Tell me your problem."

He was in the middle of mushing a bite of the potato mash. He rose a finger and the man patiently waited. After a moment his mouth was clear enough to respond. "Okay. I found a bit of gold a day ago now, somehow it got caught inside a fish. No idea how it got there. Anyhoo, I went to the moneychanger to exchange it. It turns out this thing has a mark on it, and I have to go to Beacon to do stuff with it. Have you ever heard about this at all? Some weird law about taking things to Beacon."

"Huh." William was confused by this. "Well I'm afraid my knowledge of law is quite limited. You would have to go to a legal expert in my opinion. That said, no. I have not heard or come across anything like that before." Ceannte nodded along as he answered. "Still, any excuse to go to Beacon is a good one. Historical purposes would be even better."

Suddenly he shook his head. "I don't want to go to Beacon though. I was hoping you could give me some information about the city and the races there."

He grunted. "Well the city is excellent. Clean and colourful. The idea of a unified world is indeed encapsulated within its walls. There's plenty there. Taverns, schoolhouses, markets, assembly halls. All manner of activity lives there." He finished his beer. "And as for the races, well. Everyone is highly friendly and considerate. Why would you ask such a question? Have you not met many elves or dwarves?"

He looked at the historian squarely in the eye. "Well, my experience with the races don't line up with that description. Elves in particular. I see them casually refer to their black skinned fellows as unholy freaks, or the eldars as far too intolerant. I hear jokes from some dwarves wanting to bury their axes into the heads of some random goblins. Maybe it's just japery, I don't really know for sure, but from reading your books, I get the impression that all the races seem to hate each other still. Certainly not as openly as before, but still."

"Hm, I see." He took a moment to observe the halfling and consider his words. "Mister Macántacht, you strike me as an intelligent person. You read and understand a lot. I feel that given a better circumstance you would make a fine historian." William sighed. "I see that you have clearly understood the past. However, while I completely appreciate your sensitivity, I feel that perhaps you may be projecting these attitudes onto the very people you read. I cannot speak for your personal conversations, so I will not. That being said, my companions and colleagues from other lands do not agree with your description of them. Many do openly discuss quite confronting periods of history such as the Reformation Wars, and they have demonstrated neither anger nor malice. I will admit I wonder the sort of people you find in these waters; they may well be different to you and me. I can assure you that you will find no such character in Beacon, they are good people who seek nothing more than contentment in themselves and the betterment of all Mundus."

A smile trickled across Ceannte's face for a brief second. The thought of the betterment of the world was a comforting one. "Well, I guess I can never be sure until I go there, but I appreciate the answer. It'll give me something to think about."

"Mister Macántacht- may I call you Ceannte?"

"Please, my friends call me Cean."

William smiled. "Cean. How quaint. Cean, I strongly recommend that whatever business you have there, please let yourself go to Beacon. You may find it a far better place than even my own account can ever conjure. Truly wonderous things dwell there."

"You don't have to oversell it." He laughed.

The historian scanned his pocket for his pocket watch. "I'm afraid I must depart. My squire is waiting for me as we'll travel about your land." He promptly leapt off his stool. He noticed the halfling's plate was nearly empty. "Consider coming outside for a brief moment, I'd like to give you something."

"Wha- really?" He continued to leave the tavern, all the while Ceannte hastily devoured the last of the potato. He scurried about the contents of his coin sack, dropped several coins upon the bar beside the plate, and fell from the stool. He landed safely and sprinted across the wood floor without so much as causing a ruckus.

He exited the pub where he came to two tall figures, one he knew was William, the other must have been his squire charged with his duties to the doctor. Behind them was a horse, a great looming beast that still managed to frighten him if only a little bit. There he saw the doctor write in a book which, upon finishing he noticed the halfling and made his way towards him. "Cean! Excellent. Allow me to give this to you." He knelt to meet Ceannte at his level and gave him the book. 'Humble ϕ? – the Lessons of Improper Mathematics by Geoff Keeper' was the title.

"Maths?" He turned up to him. "Really?"

"Indeed, consider it a gift. I know Geoffrey personally so there is no need to return it. Have a read, it's not so dense as to deter unfamiliar readers. Very intriguing information." This seemed so sudden and out of the blue. He briefly looked at both covers and tried to observe the finer details in the low light. The men returned to the horse and they both mounted, one after the other. "Cean! Turn to the opening pages. Have a read, will you?"

"Aye! Of course." He waved them off and they strode out into the blackness. He was quite perplexed at the gift, some random book. Ceannte opened it and flicked the pages as he turned back to the tavern. He found the page and manoeuvred about to shine light upon it. When he read the message, he chuckled to himself. "Ah. I see. Very clever." He returned into the pub, book in hand, ready to explore a new world.

Every once in a while, when the world is dark and you find yourself low, pick up a book and read something completely different.
Dr. William Stevington PhD.

* * *

The new day rose. Tèday, the middle of the week. The same activity buzzed about Béal na Habhann however, it was no longer a similar day for Ceannte. He packed his essential supplies into a few bags and sacks, attached them to Ualach by rope and belt, and rode about town. Many passed by him and stared. Some whispered, others stopped him for an explanation. His response was always the same. "Sorry lads, I'm on an adventure. No, I don't know when I'll come back. If anyone needs me send a messenger up the river, but I shan't be too long I think." Always this statement, or a variation thereof. It left some satisfied, while others were upset at the vagueness. He never told his destination to anyone, and this worked well for him. He had no interest in anyone's business.

After some time, they reached the moneychanger. He commanded Ualach to halt and dropped off him. "I'll just be a jiff mate." The pony grunted a response. He strode up to the door and knocked several times, he knew his mate would take some time. He grabbed a canteen and quickly took a drink of water. A few more seconds passed in relative silence until Óir opened up with a groan. "Uh, we aren't op-," he was cut short by the sight of Ceannte, dressed in his regular attire and jacket, carrying a bag of supplies, and the brown pony behind, standing tall and proud with its own resources. "You look like you're about ready to go on a journey."

"I am, more or less." He turned to quickly glance at the colt. "I'm not really sure what to expect but I figure I'd bring Ualach along. We can explore a new land."

"Uh Cean, just where are you going?"

He sighed, and for once he smiled at the thought. "I've decided I'm heading to Beacon. I'm going to sort this thing out."

"Crikey!" His surprise was masked by his groggy, half-asleep state. "Really?"

"Yep. I had a good think and chat, and I figured I should really get out and see new things more often. Not just stick to routine."

"Huh, alright." Óir messaged his chin for a second. "I'm curious, who convinced you to go?"

"A stranger, a got into conversation with a random human."

"Some human? That seems a bit odd to me."

"Aye, I know. I forget the details, but we chatted about culture and eventually Beacon came up. I'm actually kind of glad I had the chance, he seemed quite knowledgeable."

He was more awake and began to scrutinise this turn of events. "A stranger? A *human* stranger as well. You, and a human stranger? Something's not right here."

"What do you mean?"

"I've seen you in pubs Cean. You get drunk as a skunk and fire insults whenever someone doesn't agree with you. You get all aggressive like and get into barroom brawls because of them. You've been bloody expelled from five different taverns. I'm amazed you still have some patronage."

"Well I am working on that you know." He interjected. "I haven't been so rowdy, nowadays have I?"

"Actually, I'm glad you mentioned that. You have settled down for a bit so that's a plus. But see, you still get upset easily. So, I can imagine a stranger still getting under your grill. Also, you're not the most mailable character, you are very suspicious about things or people you don't know well. I reckon then that this stranger must have been very agreeable, or he wasn't so strange to you after all."

"Well I reckon he was quite agreeable, yes. He was an excellent chap and yes, he did not agree with my concerns, but he was very happy to explain himself. It was perfectly fine."

Óir looked him up and down, he put together the story with all his experience he had with him in his life. "Alright. I suppose that's fine." He immediately pointed. "But I want to make absolutely sure, are you certain you want to go to Beacon to resolve this?"

Ceannte took a breath and sighed. "After the talk I went back home and thought a lot. I looked about my books, all the stuff I learned from them. I'm tired of reading the same things over and over again, not learning anything new. I want to get out, see the world a bit, really come to understand the places I see in my literature. Aye mate, I want to go to Beacon." There was something very different about him that Óir noticed. The man was neither irritable nor angered, no horrid affect unsettled him. Instead he smiled, not one of greed or scheming, it was a genuine sense of happiness. It shocked him. It was so rare a time to bare witness to his friend's contentment.

Once the realisation passed, he nodded and finally replied. "Okay then. Give me a few minutes and I'll change into something acceptable."

"I'll wait out here then."

"Righto." He grinned, finally seeing something he had not seen in a long time and closed the door for privacy. Ceannte waited outside, upon his horse, prepared for a trip to a foreign land.

Chapter 5

The gentlemen walked down the main road of the town; Ceannte upon his faithful pony, and Óir escorting him to the docklands. They continued to chatter amounts to themselves over the uncommon nature of the day, the edge of a journey into an unknown world. All about them the people were quite active, running about, talking with others, building with wood and metal, working on their tasks in one form or another. They carried on about their discussion. "Who's this ferryman bloke then?" Ceannte asked.

"Aye, I've known him for a long while. Near four years I think now. He takes me to Beacon and up the river on business."

"For your network no doubt."

"Pah!" Óir noticed his friend's derisive chuckling and dismissed it. "You scoff at networking, but I'll have you know I have made excellent inroads with the dwarves and the men. I reckon I would not be so fluent in the intricacies of the Mountain Gold without dwarf tradesmen to mentor me of the finer details."

"Do you often trade with the dwarves? I don't see much of the mountain folk down this neck of the river."

"Aye, dwarves rarely leave their abodes in the mountains, you have to go to them yourself. Good thing about Beacon is I don't really have to trek to the Great Wall unless it is of the utmost import or concern."

Ceannte sighed. "How is Beacon? I've had images in my mind about what it might look like from my history books. Is it as glorious as writers say it is?"

"You tell me. What do you think it looks like?"

He took a moment to stare out to the town in front of them, his memories formed a vague mirage of the great city. "Grey. Very grey. Full of stone and cobbled roads. Huge buildings, like the pub last night. The great tower reaching up to the clouds. Stoned walls around the settlement." There was a pause. He continued to look out and tried to find more detail in the vision.

After a few seconds however, Óir turned to him and asked. "What about the people?"

"What about them?"

"Well a city isn't a city without people. Surely you know what to make of the people don't you?"

"I'm having a think." They carried on down the wide street. He visualised some folk, mostly halflings along the road. He very easily imposed the men and women on the road into his vision. Suddenly some humans emerged, jaunty men took appreciation of the small folk. The halflings sang and danced merrily and the men applauded. Archons entered his mind, high men from the golden coast. These fellows began to discuss philosophies and science things with their modern counterparts, while others blessed those about them, men and halflings all at once. There were quite a lot of the male gender in Ceannte's mind, such is the patriarchy of these nations. The Eldars disturbed this. The high elves appeared dainty in the scene, crowded by men of all kinds, chaplains and high priestesses impressed upon his imagined city. Heavenly things as pure as goddesses upon the earth. They did little more than engage deeply in rituals and spiritual communion, any other activity was no more than their own blessings. He found this to be a most agreeable scene. No foul mouthing nor ill will or the like. Certainly, no violence. It was a friendly if rather distracting affair. Dwarves made little difference to this arrangement. The mountain dwellers streamed into the fantasy, gambling with their halfling companions, discussing engineering with manly scholars, and transacting runestones with the elf dainties. Ceannte even visualised elves and dwarves counting with each other, such exotic mathematics was beyond him.

Then the darkness began to descend. Elves from the woodland appeared in his vision. Spritely, friendly creatures with tanned skin and gleaming confidence. The folk made merry about the other races with japery and open confession. Most of the prior races were friendly and quite open themselves to these good people however, the high elves began to take umbrage to the cavalier nature of themselves. Such immodesty was unfitting of an elf, it was irresponsible. Some of the

Eldar folk made arguments against these wood elves with raised voices and frayed tempers. The peace was unsettled. Suddenly again, the goblins emerged from over the hill. Similar in colour to the wood elves, goblins performed their own disarray and foolery to the other races. They stole from others their purses and shiny ornaments. Their earthly mother demands her bounty returned to the rock from whence it came, and their fervour is absolute. They upset just about all others in Ceannte's mind, their pockets picked clean of all metal, but no one was so exclusively outraged as the dwarves. Their wealth is the earth. They bark and scream at the ferrel thieves for their possessions. Many give chase and flee past him, axes in hand. Lastly, the dark elves appear. Creatures with the greatest history of adversity it is beyond belief. Elves slain by war, revitalised by the earth itself into undeath, as the other elves tended to see them. Some of these do try to exchange their knowledge of magic and the power of Mana, but just about all of them are chased by both other elf clans. Horrible freaks of nature. Things cannot live after death. It is an abomination. They *are* abominations! The scene devolved from a vibrant city of colour into a red light of fire and blood. He was surrounded by it. Anger, violence, hatred, death. The world cannot coexist, it would sooner consume itself into a flaming ball of unrest. All of a sudden, the people were not these. They were no longer elves nor dwarves nor goblins, they were something much worse. He saw orcs. Loathsome mutants with the desire to kill all, and without any ability to quench their bloodlust. Vile beasts. Mistakes. Orkrage!

"You alright there Cean?"

In an instant the image was gone. He was no longer in that feverish war, that damned siege. His mind returned to Béal na Habhann, he never left his home. "Uh. Yeah." He turned to Óir to see him visibly concerned. Wide eyed and sweating from some reason. "Sorry. My mind was elsewhere."

"Really? You looked like you'd seen a ghost."

"Nah, not a ghost." He stared out again and contained his fears within. The mortal danger he estimated out there, the rampant anger that compels the baser instincts of survival, by destroying all threat and opposition. All to preserve what is most dear, the ability to live. "Phantoms maybe, but not ghosts."

He slowly nodded to his friend's absurdity. "Right, sure. Cean-"

He was cut short by Álainn who presented herself down the street. "Mister Cean!" She shouted as she crossed the road towards them.

"Ály." He stopped Ualach and they waited for her.

As she made the final few steps she asked. "I imagine you're heading to the docks now, are you?"

"Aye, I am."

"Hang on." Óir paused her questioning with a raised hand, then turned to his escort. "You told her already? When was this?"

"In the early morning. First thing I did actually. I popped down to the bakery just as it opened and spoke to Ály in a private corner."

"Indeed," she interjected, "I won't deny I will not like the idea of Ceannte going elsewhere for a time, but I appreciate he took the time to let me know."

"Well I should say so." Óir replied, the shock still present in his tone. "If he has any sense of dignity at all he would inform his closest friends first. I'm glad he did then."

After a brief moment she smiled. "Thank you. I just have one small question. Cean, are you sure you don't know when you'll be back?"

"I'm afraid so lass. I haven't a clue."

Óir shook his head. "Aye. In fact, I went down to the library last night and took a gander at the historical records. I looked up the embargo, the Council's Mandate, and anything else related to this thing. Cean, mate. As far as I can see, you are the very first person to get caught up in this. Since ever." He patted his arm in an attempt to comfort. "You are going into uncharted waters here, there's no sayin' what'll happen."

"Fantastic." His voice rank of sarcasm. "That'll lift my spirit!"

"What's this about 'embargoes' and 'mandates'?" She asked.

"Oh I wouldn't worry about that if I were you lass. It's all obscure nonsense really." He turned to his friend and chuckled quietly. "Besides, don't be like that now mate. That's not a bad thing really. You like your history reading aye? All them stories about the heroes and the battles and that. This time you'll actually *be* a part of history. Now you can't tell me that's bad right?"

"Huh." It suddenly occurred to him. "I haven't considered that if I'm honest." Up to this point Ceannte's mind mulled over the hostilities he read about, the sheer scale of the city he heard about, and the imposition of city life itself upon him he felt in the past.

"Seriously?" Óir laughed again. "Now that's a laugh. You; mister greedy guts, 'oh, I like learnin' history, these blokes are amazin'', didn't think that you yourself will be one of those very same?"

"No. I honestly didn't!" His escort continued to laugh. It infected Álainn as well, she covered her smile with her hand and tried not to chuckle. "Yeah yeah, go on. Have a laugh. I will admit though, I quite like the sound of that." His mind cast back to the previous evening. "I wonder if he'll write a book about me."

"If who will?" She asked.

"Oh, nobody. Some bloke I met in a pub yesterday." The three chatted and laughed and went about merrily towards the dock, and the Foirceannadh River.

* * *

The sun was still rising, yet morning was fast turning into noon. The docks were less busy today than other days. By the middle of the week all the important merchants had either anchored before or were in transit in the great sea. Only a few domestic sloops and boats travelled the great river. Between one of the piers that lined the bank Óir and the party chatted with a captain to one of the ships while sailors loaded the provisions. Bright white uniforms with stark blue trim about their collars and jackets, the decorated men stacked the bags and stored the food and drink for the voyage. He handed the captain a sack of coins. "The full payment is there. Count it if you wish."

"Nah, I trust ya enough Óir. It feels right." The captain grinned. "Although, I must say, I ain't used to haulin' little horses on water. Does it get seasick?"

"Uh," Ceannte quickly checked on Ualach, the pony stood on the wooden pier in line, awaiting his master's presence, "to be honest I haven't a clue. He's never sailed before. Will that be a problem?"

"Ah, it's a colt horse. I see. And not really. Sick is sick, so I guess we'll give 'im a bucket in case all goes badly."

"Well that's a lovely image!" He moaned.

"The guest room is close by to the storeroom so ya can keep an eye on 'im if ya want."

"That's fine."

"Mister Guest sir," a sailor interjected from behind the group, "we're preparin' to load up yer horse now, so ya best be boardin' the ship now."

"Ah. Righto then." He lifted his bag off the ground and turned to Álainn. "Well, I better be off now."

"Indeed. Please write letters to me, will you?"

"Of course Ály."

"I hope you enjoy your trip, and good luck with whatever it is you're doing."

"Thank you." She took the opportunity to lean over and briefly kiss his cheek. The experience left him all giddy and fluttery in his heart. He looked back at her as she returned in front of him and grinned widely. She chuckled at his rather goofy expression but composed herself again and smiled back. A few of the idle sailors noticed and they whistled and awwed. As she walked away, he turned about and barked. "Oi, shut up will you?!" They replied with a sniggering laugh.

Óir stepped in for a few words. "So, you didn't mention the coin to Ály then?"

"Not really. Figured if it turned out to be something, I'd tell her via letter, and if not then all the better for her not to know. No sense in talking about something that might be nothing."

He grunted. "Alright. Fair enough." They shook hands. "I'll see you later, then."

"See you mate." Ceannte parted ways with his friends, made his way to the pony, and stood there waiting until the crew came to them and shepherded them over the step bridge and onto to the deck. Óir and Álainn watched him move over along and descend out of their sight.

She sighed. "Mr. Óir," she looked at him, "do you know what Cean will be doing there."

He replied with his own sigh. "I'll be honest with you lass. If I had any idea, I'll tell you by now."

"Lads," the captain yelled suddenly, "prepare to raise the anchor, how far are we?"

"Two and a half ahead of schedule, cap'ain." One of his crew cried out as a bell rang out from the ship's mast.

"Fantastic! Hoist the anchor! We sail as soon as we can." The last couple of mariners sprinted up the bridge and retracted the wood. A metal chain that dangled into the water started to clatter and churn, the anchor was pulled back up. The mast unfurled the sails, the sloop was ready to embark. The bell rang again, and the sailors all ran to their stations. "Tighten the sheets! Let's go!" The captain marshalled the crew as he climbed the stairs and made his way to the wheel. "Come on! Step lively! Get this boat movin'!" Everyone scrambled the deck, they tightened, pulled and tied the sloop together. The sails caught the gust of wind and slowly the ship began to move. At first it jutted away from the pier, then it swam away from the city, and finally it rounded a bend and sailed away from sight.

As they descended to the lower decks the porter pointed about and informed Ceannte of the ship. "The galley is under your feet there, down the lower deck. Chef makes a decent meal for lunch and dinner, but I'd avoid brekky if I were you. Down 'ere's the guest room. Make yourself comfortable although, even in calm waters the ship knocks about a bit, so if you're seasick let us know." He gestured at the door in front of them.

"I'm good thanks." When they arrived, he pushed the wooden door open to see his lodge. It was a cosy room, quite spartan and small. A small, plain looking bed, a chair beside a deck, and a wardrobe for clothing. However, the room was lit by a large and ornate window with a view of the hills and the river that sailed past. The window was carved into the shape a water lily. The petals were detailed exquisitely, the carvings were smooth and deliberate. "This is lovely," Ceannte couldn't help but utter his delight, "can I get some lighting for the night? I have some books I want to read."

"I can arrange that. Is there anything else?"

"No, that'll do." He waved away the servant and was left to settle into his accommodation. The sailor closed the door and left the guest to his privacy. Ceannte strode up to the window and looked back at the world he knew, the rolling hills, the friendly neighbours, the fishing, the good times. He wore his jacket again, a green cotton garment. Thick and quite comfortable, with lots of large pockets. He produced the gold piece from the jacket and examined it more. Beyond the investigations of the last few days nothing new occurred to him, it was the same bit of gold with a 6 on one side and a 7 on the other and the small star to ensure he got nothing out of it. "You better damn well be worth this," he spoke to the gold, "I'm getting my money one way or another." He turned back and made his way towards the bed, he sighed and laid down upon the mattress. The preparation to leave wore him out that he nearly fell asleep. Instead, he flicked the coin onto the desk, leaned over to his bag he plants beside the bed, and extracted two books. He fell back again and opened Humble Phi. The sloop sailed onward.

Chapter 6

Two rather uneventful days passed by, the ship crawled along the great river at a steady pace. Apart from passing a bigger human sloop a day before hardly anything happened. Within his room however, Ceannte enjoyed passing his time reading. While he did bring his own book of naval history, he was fixed to this new tome of random oddities in mathematics. Some of the truly abnormal accounts in the book entertained him roundly, he often found himself laughing at preposterous arguments and documents the author referred to. His recent mirth was sparked by a tale of piracy and a terrible misunderstanding.

Ponderous Plundering

It is amazing to find such absurdities around the continent. Mathematics is a complex, ethereal creature that periodically thrusts and parries with scholars, however, remains simple and neat for the average man. Yet, even at the basic level maths cheats the common folk.

One profession I genuinely never thought I would ever have the duty to inform in this book was that of the pirate: the swashbuckling water rat whose very livelihood was the unlawful hijacking of gold and supplies. In the modern view one tends to see a pirate as a fowl reeking luddite with barely presentable attire and hoarse speech. This is far from the truth. Pirates were rather well-dressed chaps, often confused for sirs of the upper class. It seems that the image of the swarthy buccaneer was largely influenced by fiction work, as is often the case for historical matters. However, you would think that, as the collectors of large quantities of plunder, it should warrant the need for simple arithmetic skill on the part of the pirate captain. After all, how else can one manage all the skulduggery to maintain a life of crime?

This is the story of a rather obscure privateer in history, nothing like the Turncoat Bill's or the Saint Jerry's you find in regular history books. This man's life was short-lived and buried by the relative success of his contemporaries. He lived a fast life of raiding and pillaging the coast of Midgard and was cut down by a simple maths problem that just happens to be one of my favourite types of error.

Jeremy Matthew Eaton is arguably a rather unique character during the Golden Age of Piracy. Unlike virtually every other Midgardian pirate and his dog, Eaton originally hailed from Beacon. Like others at the time, Eaton's background was naval. His father is said to have been a retired captain however, records seem to be a bit light on the documentation of Captain Matthew Eaton. The family established a trading company up the Foirceannadh River, regularly transacting with halfling folk and Archonian men. One day, perhaps trying to escape the threat of orcs during the Great War, Eaton decided to flee Beacon. At the age of just sixteen, he stole one of his father's trading vessels and sailed it out of the city. Not exactly subtle, is he? From there he travelled up the river and out to the open sea, he reached the Archonian coast after a couple of months and begun his own quest for piracy. He quickly rallied a small crew and set sail from Nkremós towards Midgard. However, he had no idea where Midgard was, just a vague direction of where to go.

At first, he failed. He spotted an island unusually quickly and declared they reached Midgard. It was Bancroft, some 400 miles away, and at an angle that would have nearly missed Midgard completely. Had he not found the island who knows what terribleness would have befallen Eaton. That said however, it was a great fortune he did find Bancroft. We know today that Bancroft was a former Pirate Haven, a hideout for pirates to evade the authorities and plan their next attack. The haven was that of Saint Jerry, who was out plundering himself at the time, and was therefore completely unguarded. Ripe and ready for someone to just come in and plunder the plunder. And that's exactly what Eaton did! Him and his crew allegedly looted gold from Saint Jerry and smuggled it onto a caravel in the haven's port. He helped himself and upgraded his kit!

Eaton also found a map of Midgard and the archipelago, which made things significantly easier for him to navigate his way there. He finally reached the port of Carrington, and truly began his career as a pirate captain.

I will not bore you with pointless history. While Eaton is largely forgotten, there are plenty of reference books that describe his tale fully. But that is not what this is about, this is a maths book! So, we will cut right to the end. Eaton and his crew looted for three years and amassed booty to the value of 148,267 gold by the time he decided to retire and divide the wealth with his men. He had a crew of 74 gruff underlings and himself. Unfortunately, 148,267 is not the most malleable number to divide. However, Eaton had a brilliant idea. Why not physically divide up the gold into 75 piles? Excellent! Expect Eaton made a fatal flaw which appears so many times that we mathematicians have given it a name. We call it the Fencepost Problem.

The problem is called this from the metaphor of a fence; if a 50-foot fence has a post every 10 feet, how many posts are there? Most people might divide 50 by 10 to reach the answer of 5, but you forget the first post at the 0-foot mark. There is always one extra post! Eaton correctly pointed out the prime factors of 75 – 3, 5 and 5, and divided the loot three times, splitting up the piles using long rocks as physical barriers. Unfortunately, he used five stones to divide the loot and failed to realise he was dividing incorrectly. What was worse was when he did realise his mistake after one division, he tried to overcompensate. The divisions he ended up with were 6,

4 and 3, these numbers produce the product 72. When he distributed the loot and realised three of his men ended up with nothing, all three drew their swords, angry words were exchanged, and they all killed Eaton on the spot.

"Bloody hell!" Ceannte gasped.

Jeremy Matthew Eaton was only just twenty years old when he fell. For most people reading this it is nothing more than another tale forewarning the life of piracy and its dangers. To me and other mathematicians however, it is a lesson in making sure you get your divisors right, your life might just depend on it!

He laughed again. He held in his mind the picture of just what such a scene would be like. He saw the rabble sat around a large table with many rather full sacks. One by one the men took turns taking a random packet of coin. They shuffled forward, and the gold vanished. As the last of the men approached the table, they noticed a problem. They seemed not to be enough purses for the crew. The last man claimed the final sack, and there were left three poor fellows with three years of toil and nothing to show for it. Ceannte imagined the mess play out, some flared tempers boiled into rage. The destitute men took up their arms and demanded payment. The threatened youth panicked in his mind, and in the heat of fury they leapt at him and plunged their steel into his flesh. He laid back and relaxed onto his bed, slowly he nodded off. The halfling dreamed of a life at sea, nothing exciting like a pirate, but the thought of the open water and the rocking of the boat pulled him into an excellent state for fantasising. The peace of his accommodation was enough to settle his mind.

The crew maintained the ship in the morning, the sun hid behind a blanket of cloud, the grey light shrouded the hills in a misty solemnity. The captain steered the vessel around another meander, he looked up to see the crow's nest. A sailor spotted the land ahead for any sign of their destination, a house, a farm, anything. If there was anyone that could see Beacon first, it was him. As the sloop rounded the curve a familiar house appeared ahead. "LAND HO!" He declared the approach of the city and the crew cheered.

"HAZZUH!"
"At present speed we should be at port in an hour's time sir."
"Ya better rouse our guest then," the captain jeered, "hop to it." He jumped out of the nest and landed into a barrel which started to fall. The barrel was secured by a rope and pulley, the sailor flew down the mast of the sloop. He was so fast he was already three quarters down, another half a second later the barrel suddenly jolted and stopped a few feet from the deck. The other end of the rope was attached to a large crate, far heavier than any halfling can ever be, never mind carry. He calmly climbed out of the lift and jumped back onto the deck. As soon as he landed, he ran across the deck and down the stairs.

Under deck the sailor slowed his speed at first to a jog and then a walk by the time he reached Ceannte's door. He took a moment to catch his breath and knocked the door. "Mister Ceannte sir. The ship is an hour or so away from Beacon." There was no response, instead the room rattled behind the door. He knocked again. "Are you alright sir?"

"Yes." His voice travelled through the door. "I'm just getting up now."

"Ah, very well then. When shall we prepare your pony to disembark sir?"

"Five minutes before docking, he hates the water."

"Very well sir." He turned about and left him to his privacy. The sailor passed by Ualach, he noticed the pony was quite calm and not at all upset by the rocking about. He smiled and petted the creature. "We don't get your kind around much. I reckon you don't mind the sea." The pony grunted slightly and shuffled about to be closer to his touch. "Aye, sure. You're nearly out mate." Ualach neighed softly, and after a brief moment the sailor left him as well and returned to the deck.

Sometime later Ceannte emerged from the deck below, he arrived at a bustling scene of mariners who ran and shouted orders to keep the sloop on course. He turned and continued up the stairs to meet the captain once again. "Morning." The captain greeted him.

"Good morning," he uttered, "I hope I haven't put you out with my pony. He's usually an amenable fellow."

The captain laughed. "Not at all mate. Ya horse is a fine creature. We don't get a lot of horses as cargo on this here boat, a lot of the men have taken a fancy to your pony. I reckon it was a nice change for them lot."

"Indeed." He ended the conversation. For a moment the men looked ahead in silence. Ceannte observed the passing houses and buildings, they were all so tall. They were just as he imagined them, except even larger in every dimension.

The captain tried again. "You see that house there?" He pointed out past a hill as a cottage slowly came into view. "We're about ten minutes from port."

"Right." Again, Ceannte stopped the small talk but the captain would not have a bar of it.

He noticed his guest's face; he was awestruck while concerned at the same time. His frown was quite visible and despite the twinkle in his eye, there was clearly a pressing matter that occupied his mind. He seemed to have no interest in the majesty of the river or the beauty of the hills. "You really don't want to come here, do you?" He finally asked.

He sighed. "Not really, no. I just want this thing sorted and be done with it."

"What are you doing then that's so important?"

He sighed again. "Apparently, I found this thing that I can't trade it in for gold, so I have to go here and return it. That's about all I know. I bloody better get a reward out of this. This whole thing feels so surreal, I just can't imagine anything like it."

"Well I can understand that, but this is Beacon. It's the centre of the world mate. It's one of the best places in the world I think."

"I've never been, this'll be my first trip there, and truth be told I don't want to go."

"Ah!" The captain laughed at him. "You've no idea what you're missing out on-"

"I know full well what I'm missing!" He interrupted him. "Bigotry, hate and judgement."

"What?" The captain was taken aback by the sudden attack. "Nah mate. It's a wondrous place. All the best things from each race are there."

He scoffed. "Yeah, like what? Elves killing each other? Humans making more mutants? Humans blowing things up? Dwarves and goblins ruining the ground? I don't want any of that."

"Wow!" He tutted at the guest. "Mate, you have no idea about the races."

"I know enough, I've read about them."

"HA! No wonder you're so wound up. You've been reading too many books mate."

"I know about them."

"You know bugger all!" The captain laughed. "This trip'll do ya good, actually interact with them."

"I've met some of those bastards." Ceannte refuted.

"Oh, I have no doubt you've met a few bastards by now, but if you start thinkin' they're all the same you'll go mad. You'll think they haven't changed at all."

"They haven't changed!"

The captain rolled his eyes. "Blow me! Listen," he waved his free hand and landed it upon Ceannte's shoulder, he looked into him with a genuine sincerity, "I've been travelling up and down this route for getting on to thirteen years now. I've spent a good deal of time both in Beacon and with all kinds of folk. Elves, men, dwarves, even the odd goblin who doesn't mind the water so much. I'm not saying everyone is all good or decent people, I've had my fair share of shifty blokes too, but there are some proper, decent people in the world. Sure, they come from places with a bad history, but that's not what defines them." He let go of his guest. "In Beacon you're going to see all the good things in life; Eldar wisdom, wood elfin japery, the arcane power of the dark elves, Archonian philosophy, Midgardian science, the beautiful engineering of the dwarves, the deepest faith of the goblin religions," The captain turned back to the deck and shouted, "and a decent halfling pub with beer and song!" The sailors cheered at his declaration, sailors appeared from under the deck with Ualach, his supply bags fastened on him. "Have a look around mate," the captain ordered Ceannte. He looked about him and saw that the city crept in further, more houses and inns and buildings started to stream through. The noise and clammer of the people surrounded the sloop. The harbour of the city was now in plain view and the vessel passed by the docks for larger ships. He was truly in Beacon now, "be honest with me now, how many elves do you see dying? Bleeding to death by the blade? How many freaks of nature aye? Humans mutilating others maybe? Goblins with axes buried in their heads? What do you actually see mate?"

Ceannte saw a whole community, elves chatting with other elves, elves talking to humans, halflings trading with the rest of the races, wood elves playing tricks with goblins, Archonian men teaching young elves of all kinds. There wasn't a hint of malice, no ill will nor injustice, no scorn nor hatred. "I don't know what I'm seeing," he finally said as he scanned the surroundings, "but I'm not convinced. I think this is all a sham."

The captain sighed. "Sticking to your story eh? You're a stubborn one."

The sloop neared their wharf at the dock, he turned the captain and continued. "Look, I know what you're trying to do, and I get it. I just need more than fancy talk. I see what people do and I don't always see the good in it."

"I don't know you well enough mister Ceannte, but I think you think too much about the negative stuff. You bang on about violence and hate and all that, but we haven't had a proper war in a century, and everyone is good, friendly folk."

"Mister Ceannte sir," another sailor interrupted, he shouted from the deck, "it's time to prepare to disembark."

"You better get down there." The captain pointed to the sailor. "I'll let ya go."

"Righto then." He began to make his way down to his pony.

"Drop anchor!" The captain ordered. Two burley mariners lifted the massive iron anchor and dropped it straight into the water. It splashed, and the chain rattled into the drink. "Rig the sails!" Sailors hastily pulled ropes down, one by one they slowly curled the canvas up. He reached Ualach and by the time the crowd of sailors helped him mount his colt the step bridge was retrieved and placed over the gap off the boat. "Oi! Before you go," the captain hurried down the stairs and made his way to Ceannte, "I don't want to leave you on bad terms or anything. I get that the world's been pretty terrible in the past, but that's exactly it – the past. I think you're a decent enough bloke to see it eventually. I still don't know you well, but I can tell you're honest enough to say whatever's on your mind, even if it gets you into buggery."

He nodded along to the captain. "I appreciate that. Most people don't like my honesty so much."

"That's cause you bloody shoot your mouth off. You gotta be more level mate."

He sighed. "I can't promise anything, but I'll try."

The captain slapped his back. "Attaboy!" He encouraged Ualach by the reins and he moved off, the colt clopped over the deck and slowly shuffled over the wood and onto the docks. As the pony trotted along the captain declared. "Men, shore leave!" The sailors cheered and disembarked the sloop in a single file, they chatted about their day of merriment and celebration to come.

* * *

Ceannte slowly made his way along Beacon still atop his pony. He was amazed at what was around him, a mess of people and chatter and events, so many things to see and hear. He just trotted up the road not two minutes before a crowd of children ran past, all manner of child as well. Boy, girl, pale, brown, poor, wealthy, elf, goblin, human – there must have been at least six or seven little people. A few saw Ualach and cooed interest at the animal. The halfling smiled and waved at them. They were kind enough to wave back, someone even said goodbye. Another moment passed by before he noticed something different, he caught up to a group of men in front. He was not able to tell exactly but he could see two tall figures beside two even taller ones. Two humans and two elves, and they were speaking in another language. It wasn't Common but it sounded human. Curiosity took hold and Ceannte urged his pony to move a bit quicker and overtake the party. As Ualach walked forward he turned to see the men, indeed it was two Eldars conversing with an Anchonian and a Midgardian. One of the elves waved about as he spoke, he made a clear point in his argument. He still did not recognise the tongue, but he assumed it was Archon and carried on. He remained in awe of the people, Ceannte was not entirely sure if it were real or if he stumbled into a dream. Over the crest of the riverbank he saw the rest of the city, a maze of cobblestone roads, grey inns and stores and buildings. Streets filled with people of all sorts. It was nothing at all like home, not the quiet hills or even the active night the halflings enjoy. People were everywhere. Merchants and buyers, priests and alchemists, politicians and scientists. The city was truly a melting pot of ideas and races from all corners of the known world, no hate or malice, no hint of the past.

Then, as he dove further into the city, he saw her. She was an extraordinary elf, one he never imagined before. Her tanned skin was the colour of an oak tree, it shone through her garments. Her long flowing hair shimmered in the sun with a certain allure and charm. She wore the garbs of an Eldar, a plain white dress with barely any embellishments. Ceannte recognised that she was a Chaplain and part of the religious order of the High Elves, incredibly unusual for her kind. Despite the attire her figure betrayed her modesty. She had the characteristics of a wood elven maiden. She was divinely beautiful, and she kept her beauty to the divine. He negotiated Ualach towards her. "Excuse me, miss?" She stopped and looked about her, she searched for the voice. As he approached, she loomed over him, he reckoned she was about twice his size. "Down below."

She complied and followed the voice by her feet. She saw him on his pony, stood right beside her waist. "Ah!" She knelt down to meet his level. "Good morning master halfling. Tis an excellent day for a stroll is it not?"

"It certainly is. I can think of few better days back at home. Chaplain, may I ask you a question?"

"Of course." She smiled back at him. Her hazel eyes glinted faintly.

"I'm curious, how came by you this profession? I've never seen or heard of a wood elven maiden ever consider becoming a priestess, never mind a Chaplain of Xihe."

Her grin broadened. "I have been asked that so many times I have lost count. It is true, most women of the forest do not see much of faith nowadays. I chose this path because I want to help the impaired, guide the lost and heal the injured." She paused to look above the man, she watched the life of the world about her move, and the people go about their business. She saw the energy of Mundus flow through every living being. "I have a light I wish to give to this world, to protect those from the darkness."

"No," he interrupted the moment, "I mean why the Order of Xihe? It's such a strong symbol of the High Elves given your history with them."

"My history?" She asked and paused to think. "By any chance do you mean the Reformation Wars of ages past?"

"Aye, indeed."

She could not help but laugh at the thought. Her sudden mirth caught him off-guard. "Now that I have never been asked." She gently reached over to his shoulder. "Master Halfling, may I say it is refreshing to see one who is not either an elf or a human remark on elf history." He chuckled to himself. "However, it is history. We have all become better people than our ancestors."

He found the sister very calm and wise however, he was not satisfied with the answer. His grin fell as he replied. "My apologies Chaplain, but not everyone has. I've met a few ba-," he stopped before he disrespected her, "I want to say, 'unsavoury elements'. Is that right?"

"I know what you're trying to say master Halfling." She sighed. "Yes, there are those who seek to profit from others and bare ill will, and yes some are wood elves, some are Eldars. I pray for their souls to change. I am no such person, I treat all as if they were my own brothers or sisters, mothers and fathers. All folk are my friends, even you." She again placed her cool hand upon his shoulder. "As for the Order of Xihe, it is an excellent school of the forces of Life Magic, especially with the

Elfinqueen's interest in healing. My mother was herself a High Priestess of Xihe, and my father deeply appreciates high elven culture."

"Oh! Your mother was a wood elven priestess then?"

"No, she is an Eldar."

He was shocked. He scanned her bare arms and face once again. "You're a half breed?" He squeaked.

"Indeed." She laughed at his reaction. "She visited the forest on a mission with others and found it quite remarkable. Have you visited the forest master halfling?"

"No, but I hear it is very splendid."

"Indeed, it is. You really must see the wonderous life there. Her mission stayed in one of the canopy houses high above. It is a wish of mine to see it myself. One day, not long after the end of the Great War my father met my mother, and they fell in love instantly."

He was flush with embarrassment. "I'm sorry, I didn't mean to make it sound that way. I swear."

"Tis fine master halfling, I take it as a compliment." The Chaplain laughed some more and stood back up. From Ceannte's view she shone like a goddess of wisdom. The sun's light cast a halo about her crown and gave an aura of divinity. "I really must carry on with my morning breather. Care to join me?"

He grinned with excitement. He felt a force pull him towards her. "I would be delighted to. I am Ceannte Macántacht, from the Dogedom of Leath Langa, just up the river. But please, call me Cean. My friends do."

"Cean. Very well. I am Chaplain Kamino sa Utsukushi. I live and practice here. Please, join me."

She gestured her hand and moved forward. The halfling and his pony trailed after her.

"So, mister Cean. What business do you have in Beacon?" She led him further into the city, passing a rabble of merchants trading many things. They bordered the marketplace, a loud cacophony of noise and trade and gossip the likes of which made Ceannte frightened at the sheer scale of it.

"Erm. A bit of a-," he was not entirely certain, "a bit of a financial thing. Sort of. I'm actually not sure."

"Not sure?" She was puzzled and turned to him. "How so are you not sure?"

"It's a bit complex. I guess it's more legal than commercial."

"Perhaps I will understand if you explain the matter to me."

"Aye. Sure." He sighed rather more forcefully than regularly. "So, I found this bit of gold one day when I was out fishing. This big thing that looked solid. So, I went out and tried to get the thing exchanged for coin." He cupped his hands in the shape of the disk. "A bit of gold, like this." Kamino gasped slightly at the size. "That bit of gold would have made me a bundle of cash. But it turns out it's something else. It's a thing I can't get money out of because of some stupid law."

"How so? I do not understand."

Ceannte forced a singular laugh. "Beats me really. I don't get it myself. Apparently, it has a mark on it, and that means it's protected by some nonsense." He mocked its providence with air quotes. "The law says it's 'the property of All History' and some other rubbish. That, and I have to take it back here. And I don't get anything for my trouble."

She replied with a concerning grunt. "That is quite odd certainly. I have never heard of such a thing."

"Nor have I. I have a friend at home. He tells me that this in particular has never happened. So I reckon there's nothing I can do to determine what to expect from this. The only thing I know for sure is where to take it."

"And where is that, if I may ask?" Ceannte pointed to the great tower, the tallest structure in Beacon. The building that defined the city with its delicate architecture and reaching height. "The Council of the Earth?"

"Aye." He sighed his answer. "Except I'm not quite sure that I want to so much." She turned back to him. "I mean, of course I ought to go and sort this mess out. But the uncertainty colours my attitude, and in fairness so does my knowledge of other races. I fear what is there." Kamino observed the halfling's demeanour, his face was sullen. Clouded in a fog of unease and dread. He seemed innocent. The sun reflected its light from his eyes. Yet now a deeper, more complex nature emerged from his company.

She smiled and again crouched to him. "Mister Cean, fear not." Her hand reached the back of his head. She gently massaged his hair and calmed his wearied mind. "The Council is a goodly place. The leaders are most wise and proper. I have spent some time there myself, blessing new kings and queens and performing rituals for festivals. I can assure you that there is no need to fear them. They have neither ill will to you, nor that to each other, despite their past. As for the people themselves, well, again I concede that some are disagreeable folk, and they do stain the reputation of their forebears. But to simply believe that all the elves hate each other, for example, is no more reasonable than hate itself. Mister Cean, would I be wrong in assuming you know of much history?"

"No, not at all. I have quite the collection of history books. I mean, I don't consider myself an expert of any capacity, but any book that describes past ages interests me greatly. And please, don't take me wrong. Warfare and conflict are nothing I take interest in myself. It is learning about the wider world that stirs my want of knowledge. I find it frustrating though that a good deal of our past seems to be full of bloodshed and fury. Protracted war over small, petty things that make me rage. Belief, rights, existence. Things that seem so important in our world that for some reason make others want to take life from those that simply want the same. Simple, basic, honest-to-goodness freedom. Freedom to live." He paused. He only just noticed the warmth from the Chaplain. Her touch, her aura, her very self affected his mood. Ceannte spoke but he did not rage, he was not the same stubborn fool who attacked with his words. He was a better version of himself. He made a slight grin with his open mouth and continued. "Freedom to be. And while it is not that often, I do see the occasional elf man make insensitive japes of the dark elves, or a dwarf grumble about some religious types and blame goblins for a reason." He sighed. "I wonder sometimes, can the world truly heal itself after so much bitterness and hatred, that which still lingers today?"

"No." He was shocked. Here he spoke to a saintly being with such a passion for aid, and she declared with such conviction and confidence the world is broken beyond repair by its own inhabitants. "Not unless all life; every man, woman, child, elderly folk, from all nations, all cities, all races, everywhere, believes that violent conflict is sinful. That war is undesirable. That regardless of the conflict, be it over land, knowledge or people, the taking of life is neither the first nor the last resort, but the forbidden resort. An action so unthinkable as it would never be considered. Then, and only then, can I assure that the world will heal itself from its past. For if but a single person holds within themselves the darkness, the fire of hatred, they will spread it, as belief often does. They will act with suspicion and discrimination and create for themselves the conditions of hate. They will conflate reasons to anger over others, and let that anger swell into rage, and then into violence. Others may find themselves in one's own darkness, either by belief, or by occupation of one's self, and expand the reach of hate. And thus, a new threat to one's life may rise now, or in the future. No mister Cean. Not unless all life washes itself of anger to each other, and the hate that that oppression fosters, can the world truly rid itself of war and balm the wounds war has created." Kamino's clear voice watered his eyes, her speech resonated with his heart. "Master halfling. I fear that some darkness does indeed reside within yourself. But do not fear, for I see also a great sense of clarity and honesty. All life has within itself great light, and great darkness. All beings have the capacity to give life, and to take life. It requires a great knowledge of one's self to understand what causes either and most people never get the chance to know these things. However, your character tells me of an interest in truthfulness. A want to understand all things as they are. And while I have not met you for longer than this visit, I sense a greater halo of justice about you." She leaned in and kissed his forehead. The sudden action caught Ceannte off-guard, his face was flushed. "I feel a great sense of destiny about you Ceannte. Something extraordinary dwells in your soul." She stood up. "I may not be able to guarantee haven from your fears, but I can promise you this, the city is peaceful. The folk are pleasant, respectful, and not at all what you read about in books. Beacon was created as a place for Mundus to emulate. The harmony that we all have an interest in achieving. Consider taking a day or two in this place, explore the divine districts and converse with other holy people. Perhaps acquaint yourself with other histographers and discuss more of the past. Or simply find other avenues to entertain yourself. In any event, please allow Beacon and the races therein into your heart. We may yet quiet your apprehensions."

"I will." He was smitten by the unconditional openness of Kamino.

"Excellent! I hold a mass every day at 7:00 in the Chūbu Hikari, I would like to see there you tomorrow."

"I very much like that."

She smiled and waved goodbye. "Xihe bless you."

"Bless you too. Enjoy your day." He waved back and giddy-uped his pony. She carried on her way while Ceannte continued down the road. He could not get the Chaplain out of his mind. Her beaming face, her wisdom and grace, her unique story, and her honest opinion. She was quite uplifting for him. Even though he was dreading this meeting at the Council, Chaplain Kamino gave him a renewed sense of happiness and contentment about the world. *Perhaps she's right*, he thought to himself. He smiled again traveling the streets of Beacon.

Chapter 7

For most of the day Ceannte did just that. After his encounter with the fair Chaplain, he explored the many quarters of the city. He and his pony firstly traveled to the religious district. He familiarised himself with the many shrines and temples to various gods and goddesses of the major faiths. Most importantly, he located the Chūbu Hikari monastery in order to visit the priestess the next day. The most ornately decorated buildings were the temples dedicated to wood elven gods. Their gardens and broad wooden architecture fascinated the halfling. His wonderings were blessed by the divinity of nature. From there he made for the Great Campus, Beacon's prestigious collection of academic institutions. He ventured in to and out of houses of chemistry, mathematics, the alchemical sciences, philosophy, and engineering and made himself available to lectures of the great advances in thought. Amongst these meetings he learned of the pleasant beauty of reality in complex maths, the glimpse into the future with the emerging technology known simply as *the Potential of Mana*, and found himself embroiled in heated debate of the value of δ in the world and whether to replace it with ρ. All of these from human and elven folk. He entered the artisan's quarter, and the gardens of the gods were replaced in his mind with the beauty of constructed art. Sculptures of smoothed stone and gleaming metal, paint works in and out of homes, beautiful people from all about the continent travelled the roads, many with such elegance in their passing speech. Ceannte reckoned them models for artworks, perhaps artists themselves, or actors in dramatic plays.

He then turned to the centre of the city, the business district. A vast market of all types of traders. Food and drink, materials, tools, luxuries, glasswares, literature, paints, incenses, Mana crystals, scrolls, Runestones, amulets and rings, swords, armour, animals. Quite literally anything and everything was available for purchase in Beacon. He entered the markets as the sun set slowly under the city walls, and the great mob of passers-by and merchants overwhelmed his sight. He encouraged Ualach to move slowly about the business. He kept careful attention on where he was going and not impeding others about him however, the loud ruckus still made for interesting listening every so often. At one stage the halfling overheard part of a transaction. "... finest silk in all Mundus. The silkworms of the Forest produce such a delicate thread, that make Elder silk feel cheap and unkempt. Expensive stuff this. But you seem like..." the tanned seller proclaimed.

Shortly after, another booming voice declared its treasure. "Stones from the Mountain! If you be searching for enchantable stoneware, these Runestones provide blessings from the earthly gods of the Dwarven folk. Polished and charmed these are, at a reasonable…" the dwarf bellowed. As he carried on further no other voices rose above the background noise. Ceannte looked about, through the forest of legs and chests. He quietly found an open forecourt that was much less dense in activity and people. Buyers lined the stalls about the square. Homes and storehouses bordered the market, with colourful buntings and lanterns decorating them. He took the chance to search for a proper establishment, something away from the hubbub and chaos. It took a minute or two of siting and turning Ualach, reading signposts and shop fronts about the square, until finally he found a place. Down a bright alley and away from the marketplace was a Board, an inn that houses one's horse or boar or unicorn, a person's private beast.

He trotted his way to the board and passed by one last merchant. "…however, the weed is 20 gold. You cannot obtain the spices, the pig's meat and the weed for less than 75. That's absurd!" The buyer seemed to try to barter a shorter price, or that was what it seemed to Ceannte, but he did not hear it. He simply slipped past them and rode onward down the road. The noise slowly decreased the further away he made. They reached the board and the crowd was much softer in the distance.

He leaned forward and petted his pony. "Sorry 'bout that mate. We're out of that now." He made a noise of acknowledgment and flicked his tail. "Aye." He dismounted the colt and led him into the stable beside the inn's entrance. The clacking of cobblestone changed into the clopping of wood. They entered the stable and found it quite empty apart from two other horses. The air was thick with the aroma of horse and the slightest whiff of manure. It was dimly lit and designed for the comfort of the animals.

The stable hand emerged from a dark corner. "Good evening. Just the pony is it?"

"Aye, just 'im. I'll be lodging for a few days."

"Right then. Head 'round to the inn and we'll sort that out for you." Ceannte handed him the reins and headed inside through the stable's door.

After some time, the halfling descended the stairs. He returned to the entrance of the inn and passed by the innkeepers. He entered the dining hall, a large open space for having dinner and a drink. Upon arrival he was taking aback by the sheer size of the room. *Bloody hell,* he thought to himself, *this place must be at least two, maybe three times as big as me home.* The room was bright and full of various folk. Tall, short, skinny, fat, broad, lanky, pale, tanned. There was too much variety to note. Ceannte looked on for an empty table or seat to have a quiet meal. At first all he could find were the stools and furniture for elves and men, long seats he could not hope to reach by himself. Even without the height most of these were occupied, groups of elves and men sat and ate and drank and discussed amongst themselves. The tables in front were better suited for his size. He found a solitary seat away from the crowd and made his way there. Despite the fullness of the room it was quiet for a dinner hall, some light chattering and none of the loudness. He reached the table and took a seat. He kept an eye out for an idle servant running about the room.

Beside him was a table full of well-dressed men. A group of halflings and dwarves dined and chatted amongst themselves. They were loud enough for Ceannte to overhear them. "This meat is excellent! This makes up for the last week." One dwarf commented.

"I'm sorry for the trouble Klage. I didn't expect such a thing to happen." A halfling replied.

Ceannte was interrupted by a tall waiter. "G'evening sir. I'll take your request sir. What'll you have for dinner?"

"Oh. Actually, I'm not sure. I'm not familiar with the menu here."

"No trouble sir, I'll get that for you. Would you care from some water first?"

"Aye. Sure." The human left him for a moment.

Ceannte waited patiently while the men beside him continued to talk within earshot. "I mean, what kind of person doesn't want to promote new business? I found it most unreasonable."

"Comhbhrón, you've got to talk with her." The other dwarf begged. "For a woman who leads a country of merchant men, her stance on this matter is very counterproductive."

The moment he heard the statement Ceannte looked at them. *A woman leading a country of merchants?* He asked himself. *Is this about the Dogess?*

"Aye, you're not wrong." Comhbhrón stated. "But that's the thing with monarchs. They can do whatever they want in the end, so they usually do. The question isn't why didn't she approve of your deal; it's what does she gain from rejecting it?"

"Gain? *Gain?!* She gains nothing from it! She seems…"

"Here we are sir." Again, the waiter interjected. He brought to the halfling the water, a glass, and a slip of paper. He set down the glass and the menu by him and poured water into his glass. "I'll return in a minute for your order."

"That's fine, thank you." He stepped away, and Ceannte examined the menu quietly. He looked at the options, but his thoughts were distracted. They turned to the conversation beside him. He no longer had the concentration to listen in on the merchants, he forgot about it for now.

The waiter returned. "So, what'll you have tonight sir?"

"I just have a quick question first. What exactly is a Tsurai Peasant?"

"Ah, it's a special bird from the Udoerufu Forest. Its juices add a curious spicy taste to the meat without any addition of spice or herb."

"Oh wow. I'll have that then." He handed him the menu. "I'll also take your house ale if you've got any."

"Excellent sir. It won't take a jiff." He left him with his water, and with dinner sorted the halfling returned his attention to the gentlemen.

"…even ruin their own family if it suits them." The other halfling commented.

"My beard! Has that happened?" Klage asked.

"No, never. At least not in our neck of the river. Our Merchant Queen is quite timid actually. Still, we aren't without our scandals here and there. It's just not as dramatic as all that."

Aha! Ceannte thought. *They* are *talkin' about our Dogess.*

"I see. But still, that's the problem with your Dogess. She isn't borne of merit or achievement like our Mountain King. I wager she was given the role by her birth right."

The halflings were confused. "Well, of course. She's a monarch." Comhbhrón replied. "Isn't your king divinely atoned?"

The second dwarf laughed. "Good grief no! Our leaders are wise and proud. They have to be! We value advancement and betterment over nonsense like that. Ever since Tall I our Doges have been given the right to govern the Dwarf nation by their accomplishments prior. Any dwarf lucky enough to gain fame and success can become the Mountain King or Queen."

I'm sorry, what?

"I'm afraid I don't follow."

"It's quite simple really," Klage took a rather large sip of his grog, "see, our Doge Smeltet V came into power when he discovered a large vein of Adamantium Ore in his hometown. It was the first time in our history that we found such a thing. Before then Mana Forging was our only source of the metal, now we don't need to pull apart Mana to get ahold of it."

"Indeed. Our Smeltet made the lives of the mountain folk better with his discovery. He was invited to the Mountain Hall by Doge Kunnskap to be offered the crown by the end of that year and he accepted it. So sits Doge Smeltet V of the Dwarves, King of the Mountains."

"Indeed Utstilling! It is a tradition that started with Doge Tall I who is renowned with creating our numbers. Tall made our lives better with something as simple as Two-Handed Counting, and so he decreed that should there ever be any man or woman with a history of technology or advancement, that they must be given the right to lead the Dwarves. And it has been ever since our entire history."

Holy cow! Ceannte's face lit up with sheer surprise. *That's pretty impressive. I quite like the sound of that if I'm honest.*

Utstilling raised his pint. "May the gods bless Bragdregel!"

Klage did the same and clinked his with his friends. "Gods bless Bragdregel!"

"Bragdregel? What's that?" Comhbhrón asked.

"Ah. I believe the Common tongue calls it *Meritocracy.*" The dwarves finished their drinks, they each sighed in delight. Klage carried on. "But in any event, your Dogess holds no interest in your folk. Or at least she does not have the same motivations as our kin. There's little doubt in my mind of that. Whatever business she has that would make her destroy a perfectly good contract for commerce cannot possibly be for the betterment of small folk."

Hang on, she's done this to another person? That seems a bit odd, Ceannte took a moment to think more deeply, *but I guess it's only been two people so far. It's a bit of a leap to just assume something's up.*

"Now now. I think you're being a bit too…"

"Your Tsurai Peasant," the waiter arrived with Ceannte's food, "and the house ale. That'll be 82 gold sir, please pay the innkeeper at the entrance when you are ready."

"Ah. Fantastic." The aroma of the cooked bird was full of spice and roast. His mouth watered at the thought of such a meal. "Alright, thank you lad."

"My pleasure sir, enjoy your meal." He left one final time, and the halfling dove straight into his dinner. He cut a piece of the blushing meat and took a bite. The heat of the spice was unlike any he experienced before at home. The taste was slightly sweet in his mouth, but the acid overpowered the quirk, yet remained quite docile. He felt the heat immediately on his tongue, but the spice was not alarmingly hot. It was pleasant and unexpected. He ate the pheasant happily. He turned to the group beside him for more information, but they were done with their meal and prepared to leave.

He quickly finished a bite of meat and projected. "Gentlemen." They each turned to him one after the other. "Forgive me sirs. I don't generally eavesdrop, but I could not help but overhear your conversation. If I may."

"Bah!" Klage started. "It is not a concern, given nothing is moving forward in any event. Are you a trader of any kind?"

"Sort of. I work as a fisherman back down the river and sell my toils. However, I have a money changer friend at home. He recently approached the Dogess himself for a capital venture, and she felt it was necessary to reject his contract."

"Money changing?!" The second halfling was shocked. "That's our primary business! And she ·wantonly rejected it?"

"It would appear so. Now he can't expand outwards."

"By any chance mister halfling, would this be Airgead & Sons Trading?"

"Aye, the very same."

The merchant halfings were amazing at the news. "Is this a problem?" Klage asked.

"Airgead & Sons is one of the most profitable businesses in all the Dogedom." Comhbhrón explained. "That business is ripe for enfranchisement. I reckoned a shop front in the capital city would be the best possible move for the company, so much so that I met the erstwhile Óir Airgead and advised him to do so. I helped him organise the paperwork and meet the conditions to produce the contract. You tell me it was denied?"

"I was there at the time. She made quite the kerfuffle."

"Aha!" Klage pointed out. "You see that? She undoes her own kin! What sort of Merchant Queen does this?"

"There is more to this than meets the eye I reckon." The other halfling argued. "We are but one company, and so is Airgead. We cannot draw a reasonable conclusion one way or another just yet, but I thank you mister…"

He stood up to met them at their level and shook their hands. "Macántacht. Ceannte Macántacht."

"Mister Macántacht. Thank you for providing this information. We are to journey back to our homes tomorrow. I will return to the capital itself and investigate this matter myself in case there is more of this taking place that I am not familiar with."

"Well then. I hope I have been useful to you."

"You most certainly have good sir." Comhbhrón added. "Carry on with your meal, I shall pay for it."

"Oh no no no, I can't have that. Please. It's fine."

"Nonsense! I must insist. Our combined net worth is over 28,000 gold. I can part with some cash for a helpful chap." He placed a single piece of platinum, the most highly valued coin. Worth as much as 100 dollar-pounds. "That ought to cover it. Keep the change mate." Ceannte discouraged him further, but the merchant was adamant. He saw the intent in the stranger's eyes, and he relented. The merchant and his gathering left the hall. They left him behind, surprised at their unusual charity, but only for a minute. He swiftly took the coin and sat back down to his half-eaten meal and drink.

"Alright," he cut a new piece of pheasant, and with a mouthful of meat he continued, "suit yourselves."

* * *

The next morning saw Ceannte keep his promise with the Chaplain. He arrived early at the temple for mass. A small crowd gathered by the steps of the building. They all talked amongst themselves under the cover of the threshold, the shelter was supported by large columns of polished rock hewn from the mountains. The sun slowly rose behind the temple. Streaks of golden light shone past the stone, and all about the district was covered in the warm glow. The wooden doors opened, and the parishioners entered the delicate structure. He entered the temple, it seemed to stretch towards the heavens themselves. He filed within the crowd and saw the majesty of the building. It was simple and traditional, and yet immaculate and beautiful at the same time. The gallery was humbly decorated with paintings and stone statues of the great goddess Xihe, the mother of all life. In most depictions she was a simple elven woman in plain robes, white or golden or a sky blue. She always wore a crown of some kind. The size varied but the shape was the same, a golden pronged adornment that presented her with a sort of divine aura, a halo of godliness. Priests about the group lit candles and burnt incense as they all left the gallery into the altar.

Inside, the altar was an amazing sight. The pews were a polished dark wood with rows and rows of massive seats for the larger folk. Among the walls was more paintings of the goddess, and decorated windows of coloured glass. They showed more of the mythos of the Eldars and their deity. Xihe fashioning the first man and woman, giving them wisdom and knowledge, and the spark of life. The sun's light slowly crept into the temple through the glasses. Suddenly the pews grew smaller. They were still bigger than what Ceannte was used to, they were more the size for humans. He looked up and noticed the great chandeliers. Large golden circles of light hung upon the roof, lit by many candles about the place. The colours and the light from all places and the stone and the incense, it was such an alien world that for a moment he forgot where he was. He felt as if he teleported himself into another place elsewhere, a world of a bygone age of mystics and ancient wares. He reached the front side of the altar where the pews were small enough for him. He walked all the way to the very front row and took a seat by himself. Others combined to fill the seats behind him, but he found himself to be the only one seated so far forward. It did not matter however, the sight and the smell and the thought of what was to come filled his soul with great energy and gladness. As he waited patiently, he looked about the space and thought, *Blimey! This place is massive! It's so shining and ornate. I wonder if the churches at home look like this. I'd go to mass more if they were.*

A moment later, as the last few parishioners settled into the temple, more priests and priestesses entered the hall. They shrouded themselves in veils and simple attire, plain robes twinkled with golden trim, they carried lit candles of a fragrance he did not know, a spiced sweetness of some sort. Earthy, yet quite charming. The light as well was especially interesting, the flame was deeply golden instead of the reds and oranges. The clergy precessed along the edges of the crowd, and up along the walkway. They all converged onto the altar itself. Ceannte looked about for her, he eventually noticed that the Chaplain was at the end of one of the precessions. In front of the altar, and the first thing in front of him, a wooden podium sat. It was empty and he thought little of it. As the priests reached the altar, they placed their candles upon the podium, one by one they slotted their light onto it until the podium was lit as Kamino placed the final candle. They then carried on past the podium, past the altar, and out into private areas of the sanctum except for the Chaplain and a few of her kin. About the walls of the altar were decorated walls as high as the elven body, it could hide all of their form save the head. The priestesses proceeded to these nooks, while she approached the lectern in the centre.

"Xīhé shēng qile. Jīntiān, tàiyáng zhùfú women." She spoke in a foreign tongue, but her tenor was the same as yesterday. The sound of her clear and calming voice gladdened Ceannte. He did not understand a word of the Eldar language, all the same though he heeded her sound. She was steady and confident in her speech, the words flowed through her like a gentle river babbling in the breeze. Occasionally she would lift her hand and make a motion, she would provide a visual stimulus to her preaching. For the halfling there was no saying what exactly Kamino was talking about. He did try his best to infer the sermon from the tone of her voice, her mannerisms and physical movements, but to no avail. For all he knew, she might as well have been discussing military tactics during the Great War, arguing against

some petty tax she had to pay, or describing the biology of the delicate Luminous Butterfly.

I could listen to her all day, he thought to himself. *Although, I wish I knew what she's talkin' about. I'd hate to miss out.* He briefly looked around to watch the audience. Many seemed to be quite happy and engaged with her words. They were just as entranced in her sound as he was. The odd man or woman that was not transfixed to the Chaplain appeared to whisper quietly to their friend. *There's a load of people in here. I wouldn't have thought faith would be so widely practiced by this mob.* Much of the crowd were indeed typically religious, the high elves and Archonians and goblin folk. However, in amongst them were also the more faithless races. A group of dwarves in very decorated armour and shining trinkets also attended Kamino's mass, Ceannte reckoned them to be Runemasters. Midgardians also appeared to take attendance, as well as the odd wood elf in respectable dress. He returned his attention to her. She suddenly began to speak in Common.

"Xihe has risen. The Sun blesses us this day. The Goddess gives life to all things, and we, as her children, give thanks to her divinity. O Sun, mother of all, giver of life. She who breathed into all the flowers and trees and animals her divine gift. She who created Er and Yi, man and woman. We praise you this day, for the Sun returns to us once more, to bless us again with your great light. So begins today, the three hundred and forty sixth day of the one hundredth year of the fifth age. From the very first day of the ancient age, we give thanks to you, as we do so today, for the continued peace and longevity of all Mundus and its people.

"My brothers and sisters, the year is ending. In more than two weeks time the world shall pass into a new year. This year has seen much, from the orc sightings about the halfling lands, and the fears of mishandling Mana, to the unchecked terror of goblin rebels. Much of this world seems to frighten us into a state of a settled panic. An anger that persists unseen. The fears of the past appear to be creeping back from the shadows. Those fears are moving good and well-mannered people towards extreme belief, some are good and just, while others are dark and deathly. My dear friends, all of these are terrible. Every one. Even that which you may think is holy, is not more than a powerful weapon of malice. For the belief is not the cause of the fear and anger. It is they who use it for their designs that sully belief. If there is but a single lesson the past can and has taught us folk, it is that all men, of all race, is fallible. From the greatest mind to the keenest merchant, from the most righteous of saints, to the dastardliest villains. All err.

"Upon my reflections of the year, I reminded myself of a period of history that seem to describe this quite well. The Reformation Wars, of my own ancient past. The account is well known, recorded by many great writers and orators. There is no point in reciting common knowledge. However, while the stories recall the sorry state, of the elves great sorrow, and the schism amongst us, I feel that the truest moral of the story has been lost to common knowledge. That while we know the characters and understand the conflict, we have failed to uncover the great truth of the matter. That we elves still believe, in one form or another, that we are no mistaken. That we do not err. That our personal wisdom is absolute." She shook her head slightly. "It most certainly is not. We fault. We are not immune to poor judgement. Some of my kin are troubled by the story, its meaning and morals challenge the very nature of our belief. The Eldars are taught at a very young age of the importance of truth, that deception is a fallacy. One that will ultimately advantage no one. They are told to inform what they see, to speak only the truth, the facts of the matter. Because what we see is the truth. Taoyan represents the devil, the evil that grew from within. He is the creature who allowed his hatred to fester under a guise of unity. He spoke of spreading tradition yet acted with furious rage.

"It is a part of us we were not familiar with in that age. A blatant superiority. A belief that we are above others. We are above this attitude today, at the cost of the lives of many elves. In that decade of madness, we lost our very nature, our devotion to life, and the living. What is more, the aftermath of the fighting wrought more of the unfamiliar to us. In hindsight, it should have been seen as a blessing, as if Xihe herself graced the earth and returned the gift of life to the fallen. But instead the resurrection of these elves, and then the creation of the dark elf nation, was met with even more fury and hate. Suddenly the creatures were fell beasts that distorted the law of nature. Unholy freaks, they were called." She paused again and focused on the back of the temple. She saw the final rows of the crowd and smiled. "Every time I look upon a person I smile. I think of how history tells of ancient hostilities between each other, and the great lesson these things teach us. That is it well for a person to question their teaching. That a person can live outside of one's own belief. That all peoples can unite and achieve a common goal. Even now I see a few from the wastelands and I smile. The dark elves history is a remarkable tale of oddity, fervour and survival. I welcome you all, with open arms, just as the Eldars of this very sanctum allowed me into theirs many years ago.

"My friends, my message is simple and clear. Love all. Love your fellow man and woman. We today live in an age of peace because of the wisdom that the many kings and queens of the world allow each other into their hearts. The ancient fire of the past has been in check since at least the past century of this Fifth Age. Yes, some violences are present, but they are no match for to the formidable shield of friendship. Go!" She reached out. "Spread love. Spread life. Dispel the perils of hatred. For the more you create friendship and merriment about you, the more you will ward the fires of fury and violence. History lives in the past. It should not dictate your present. I wish for a world without hate, and I believe many of you want the same thing. I believe in fact that all peoples want a life of peace. So make it so. Make the world the heaven you wish to live."

Somewhere within the temple, behind the altar, a low gong reverberated about the hall. As soon as it did the audience stood up from their seats. Ceannte looked about the people for a second, he stood also, after understanding what had happened. The gong continued to chime periodically, the metallic sound was slow and rhythmic. The Chaplain and her companions met about the front of the altar and slowly proceeded down the hall. As they passed each row of pews the parishioners followed them as they slowly exited the temple. Again, it took the halfling a moment to work out what was happening. When the idea occurred to him, he walked briskly to the forming queue and quietly inserted himself to be just trailing behind the Eldars. Ceannte followed the elves out of the hall, and out of the temple.

Shortly after the mass, when the crowd departed, and only the halfling was left, he reacquainted with Kamino at the steps of the temple. They sat there and chatted. "It was stirring." He remarked. "Soft and gentle, yet very clear-eyed."

"I am glad you appreciate it." She was as kind in her voice as she was the day before, as she was moments ago.

"You know, it's funny." She looked to him. "I've read about the wars a few times now. I never really saw Taoyan the way you have. He always struck me as a bad guy, a real low life."

"He was a bad person," he met her gaze, "however, it was an evil that possessed his soul. An evil that caused him to forget who he was."

"Who he was? I'm sorry Chaplain but I don't agree with that." He turned away to the street. He watched the people pass by. "I mean, I don't remember seeing anything about him being all that interested in letting live. He seemed much more interested in killing and squashing heresy."

"Many books of man indeed tell of Taoyan as a tyrant king, and for what it is worth they are not wrong. He most certainly created the first armies of the elves. However, our literature speaks more of his upbringing, his teaching."

He raised his eyebrow. "What difference does that make?"

"A world of difference. You see, as far back as the beginning of our people, elflings are taught the truths the Eldars learned from their infanthood. Much of what has survived today are the very same teachings at that time. The lessons of the world, its truths and life were then, and have always been given to the youth. It is those lessons that Lian Jie questioned, and then rejected. However, while these were also passed down to Taoyan, the king then showed much the same rebellion. But he was more dangerous. Lian Jie simply wished to live a free life, to experience all that life offered and the Eldars forbade. Taoyan held a much darker view of the wood elves. He resented Lian Jie's separation, so much so that he held a hatred of him and the forest. When he came of age and was coronated, his most immediate actions were to rally a militia, train an army, and plan a campaign. He encouraged open hatred of the wood elves, and thus the nation fell to the fire."

Ceannte nodded along to her recollection. "Now that's starting to make a lot of sense."

"He is a stark contrast to Lian Jie. He never wanted to take life, nor praise anything other than the sun and life. He held no ill will to his teachers or the Eldars, or the elves at all. He simply wished for a life more befitting, more available. That is why he left. It is also why he helped other elflings onto his path. He believed he was not the only one of our kind to feel similarly. Instead of furious anger, he let live his opposers and made a new life for himself. That, my dear halfling, is the great truth of the Reformation Wars. It exposes our capacity to hate, an emotion we were not at all used to in the First Age. Our intolerance towards things that are not what we believe. First it was against the rite to live freely, then it was the right to live beyond our comprehension. For the most part it is something we are aware of and mitigate for the betterment of Mundus, the elves, and ourselves however, not all choose to do so." He was speechless. He read about and knew of everything she said, yet he never once made any of the connections she was pointing out. All the facts and records of all the world was trumped by her speech, in a manner that seemed to preserve the echos of voices that passed out of this world. It was not a history. It was the world itself talking back to its children. He was so moved, he wanted to comfort her. He reached out and placed his hand upon her, despite his best effort he landed on her leg. She smiled. "You are quite a curious fellow. I know of no other halflings with such an interest in history, much less the history of others. I know only little of your past. Please, tell me of your history Cean."

"Eh. There's not much to say really. We're not so grand as the elves or the men. Really our story is just expanding, getting wealthy, and getting overlooked by the bigger nations."

"I do not look for impressive stories master halfling, I merely wish to hear your past."

He chuckled lightly. "Well, it'll be a short one then." She also chuckled at his quip. "Honestly, there's not much to it, but I'll try to stretch it out a bit. We don't really know how old the halflings are, we kind of guess that we are as old as you lot, but we have no clue. We've lived on the hills the whole time, built up a few cities here and there, nothing special. Then the Archonian men found us first, even before the elves. They were about for a week, but then they really invested in better relationships with the elves so they just up and left. Personally, I would have thought there would have passed on the fact that they found us to you lot but I just that didn't happen." Kamino started to giggle, Ceannte's recount had been giving her mirth. "Then the Midgardian men showed up, and really the same thing kind of happened. Except they were more interested in halfling friendship then the other lot, even if they did leave again. Anyway, the humans finally opened up contact to the world for us. Gees. He had a right start when the Doge saw how big elves were. They met, they traded, they left. With little more than a hello and a goodbye. At around that time, while elves and men and all them made leaps in science, our corner of the world expanded up and out the river. We colonised up to the islands just past the delta."

She could not contain herself. The Chaplain's laugh grew louder over time, until eventually she interrupted him with such delight. "I'm so-. I am so sorry master half-, halfling. Your manner is just so funny. I'm really not used to it." She continued to laugh for a few more seconds.

"Oh." He smiled again. "Well that's fine. I reckon you'll need a good laugh from that."

"I sincerely apologise." She quieted down, and her charming smile lingered.

"That's fine ma'am, cause the next bit's going to be horrible." Her smile disappeared. "Now we're hitting the Fourth Age. The point where the real action is." He turned again to watch her. "Full of orcs and steel and blood." He paused. He stared at the Chaplain. He watched the shine of her eyes dull. Her face seemed quite sad and sullen. "Uh, yeah. We don't like to take about our history really. It brings up very bad feelings for us."

She slowly nodded back. "I see. Are there many survivors of the attacks?"

"Today? No, this was all two thousand years ago now. Right at the very start of the whole thing. Only stories." He looked off into the middle distance. His face was solemn, aged by grief and fear. Kamino saw the pain in his eye, the quiet shadow that muted his tongue. He bowed his head down, his mind was made heavy by the thoughts that entered his head. Thoughts of a distant relative, and the Great War. She reciprocated his gesture. She reached over and grasped his back. Her hand straddled the width of the halfling's back.

"I understand," she started, "not all tales are easy. Some strike us at our very soul. They plunge themselves into our hearts and infect our very nature with their narrative. I will not push you for my curiosity."

"Oh, thank you. I understand why you'd want to know, it's fine really. It's just-." He took a deep breath and sighed. "I lost me great grandpa to the war. I never had a chance to see him." He paused for a moment. "You know, a lot of halflings today have been affected by the war. We're really not very upfront about our past because of that. I just hope we're all over it now. I quite like the peace we have, and I don't reckon we wouldn't be interested in another fight."

"Master Cean, no one is interested in war. No one person seeks to engage in mortal combat, unless there is no other way to resolve a matter. Only the truly evil amongst us favours bloodshed and death." He turned to see her once more. "Think of the past century. Our world has experienced peace for its entirety. If any one of the kings or emperors were so interested in deathly conquest, we would be again fighting to stop his or her advances. We would not have peace if one such evil persisted in the halls of the Council."

"Ah!" Ceannte stood up. "I think I understand now."

"Master halfling," she stood up after him while again she crouched to meet his eye, "you are a truly remarkable character. For such a man to contain so much knowledge of the past is impressive, yet I can see it has infected your soul with fears and preconceptions. May I ask you, how was your time here in Beacon?"

A smile crept back onto his face. "In truth, eye opening. I've been pleasantly surprised by the people I've met and the wonder I've seen."

"I'm glad." She raised herself up and looked back down. "What do you plan for the day master Cean?"

"Well, I'm here." He turned around to the tower, the great building in the middle of the world. "I may as well finish what I set out to do."

"Then we shall part ways. I must return to the temple for my duties. Farewell master halfling." She waved him goodbye and walked up the steps.

"Hooroo." He watched her leave. The graceful angel reached the top and entered the ornate temple. He sighed again and turned back to the tower. He took a few moments to think through the past two days in the city, and what he might expect when he reaches the Council building. "Well, I better get a move on then." He walked down the steps and proceeded towards the great tower. *It was a nice diversion,* he thought, *but it's back to business now.*

Chapter 8

The Council of the Earth stretched high above the city, the tower was the tallest thing for miles around. The stone staircase spiralled around the building, it wound all the way up. High above the city the leaders of Mundus gathered at the convention hall, a large open area at the top. Hewn into the stone circle were thrones for each king or queen. Behind the seats was a nondescript slab of grey stone, a blank adornment. Columns rose from the floor. They held the peak of the structure. All else was open space, a truly bird's eye view of Beacon and the surrounding lands. All the leaders discussed matters amongst themselves, trade deals with the elves, cultural exchange with the men, scientific breakthroughs from the dwarves. All manner of chatter ensued.

"Good morning Council." A voice rang out.

Many turned to see a tall hooded person at the steps, a lanky creature whose features were barely visible at all from the contours of his attire. The voice was familiar, and they all knew immediately who it was. The Midgardian king addressed him first. "Welcome Necromancer." The king beckoned him in, and he stepped towards him. "Is the Khan not with you?"

"My master will arrive shortly." His features were not made any clearer. He was a looming elf shrouded almost entirely by his black cloak save for two red eyes that glowed through the blackness. "He and I have to tend to a small matter first. Is there a free wall I can borrow?"

"A wall? What would you want a wall for?"

"I dare not ruin the surprise. However, it will be for a demonstration I intend to display today. All I am willing to disclose at this time is that it is an advancement in Darkness Magic."

The man lit up in delight and wonder. "An advancement in magic, you say? There hasn't been progress for years. Are you sure Necromancer?" As the king inquired the mysterious elf reached into a pocket hidden in his robes and produced a long blue crystal whose light within it pulsed and danced.

"Quite so, sirrah."

The king turned about and called out. "Empress?"

He saw two women at one end of the hall of thrones, a goblin sitting at her seat and a high elf stood beside her. They both turned and the goblin answered. "Yes?"

"We require your skill for a moment."

She sighed and jumped off her throne. She was unnaturally tall for her kind, nearly as tall as a young human. Her attire was distinctive and ornate. She wore a suit of armour and a crown over her discoloured flesh and dirtied hair however, neither of the them were metal. The crown was a rock fashioned into ornamental headwear, a simple band to fit her head with a flattened triangle shape at its front. The breastplate was something else entirely, it was a chiselled work of art. She wore an entire piece of solid iron ore with two images on either side of it. The front side emblazoned the image of what looked like a divine female. Perhaps it was the Earth Mother. The back side bore the face two gods, the Protectors of Royalty. "You asked for me sirrah?" She reached the men.

"Could you please cast a stone wall by this gap here?" The king pointed at an open gap overlooking the city. "The Necromancer wishes to demonstrate a new magic for us."

"Oh joy!" She too looked back at where she was a moment ago. "Elfinqueen!" The goblin's voice cracked through the crowd, a few of the other looked about distracted. Her partner not a minute ago was still by the goblin's throne, she reacted to her call. "Fetch me my satchel! It contains my Mana."

The Elfinqueen leaned over the chair and found the empress' personal items. She took a bag and rose back up. "This?"

"Yes! That one!" She made her way to the rest of the gathering. The Elfinqueen contrasted the empress' grandeur, her dress was simple yet elegant in its design. A humble blue dress with a pattern of white triangles about its edges and a dainty lace at her feet. Over it was her own plate-mail, a steel breastplate depicting the sun radiating its rays onto the earth. Her crown exposed itself through her hazelnut locks, a golden band with spires from her scalp. She had an aura of wisdom about her, a blessing from highest heaven. The Elfinqueen approached the group and handed the goblin her satchel. "Thank you!" The empress opened and quickly rummaged about the bag. She produced a green rock. It was unlike any other Mana crystal; it was almost totally opaque yet light still flickered from within it. The crystal was decorated in a marble pattern, streaks and swirls of all shades of green.

She approached the gap with mana in hand, she overlooked the south of the city and the hills in the distance. She tightened her grip and the crystal began to break. The energy sparked through the cracks, a glow of light shone from the brighter hues of the mana. She snapped the mana in half and the energy of the crystal fizzed all around her hand. Eerie green lightning crackled and arched all the way down to the broken pieces of the crystal. She closed her eyes for a moment and concentrated. She focused her energy and her mind. The arcane energy soon engulfed her, and she was empowered by the lightning, the pieces on the ground began to lift and hover as more energy imparted back into them. The goblin opened her eyes and they glowed a shining bright green. A clap of thunder rang out as she, with her right hand still clenched, looked down at the ledge and aimed her fist at it. Instantly the broken pieces shot towards the edge of the floor and more intense lightning streamed from her arm. The energy now directed itself to the ledge, intense arches of lightning poured from her fist towards the ground, the pieces of mana, and the columns beside the open gap. Overflowing in magical power she screamed over the noice. ***"PATTHAR KEEDEEYAAR!"*** The mana transmuted into small stones in the blink of an eye, energy continued to fizz and crack onto the ground. She suddenly pulled her arm upwards. ***"VRDDHI!"*** Just as quickly a wall of stone emerged from seemingly nowhere. As she moved the energy arched and sparked even more than before, it appeared to drag the rock face up to the ceiling. The energy began to die down, the empress no longer glowed, and the lightning did not arch anymore. Her job was done. She blinked and her eyes returned to their normal hue. She unclenched her hand and the final sparks of magic were gone. A round of applause burst from behind her, she turned about and bowed to the leaders. "Professor King! You don't need a stupid piece of paper to prove you know Earth Magic!" She quipped.

"Quite so milady," the human responded, "I have taught many students in my time, but you are indeed a master."

"You should meet my sister empress." the Elfinqueen added, "Shenghuó feels as strongly with Life Magic." She turned to the king. "Why are we in need of a stone wall?"

"It would appear that Muu Neg will be demonstrating a new spell of the Discipline of Darkness."

"Oh wow, how interesting. I thought we discovered the entire branch of the discipline."

The Professor King looked about him and beckoned her. A little confused, she obliged. They moved off to a quiet corner of the hall and he encouraged her to stoop to his word. Her ear lowered and he whispered. "To be entirely honest with you that was my thinking as well. According to what we know, each of the eighteen Disciplines of Magic appear to have twenty-four practical applications. The spells you and I were taught bare out these applications. What the Necromancer appears to be suggesting is that a twenty-fifth spell has surfaced." Her ear pricked slightly. "If this is true and the Sage's Guild and other institutes of knowledge can verify this, it might very well spark a new era of magic, a second golden age perhaps."

"Oh my! That is exciting." She giddily whispered. "Will I need to return to the guild?'

"Only if it is confirmed, and in honesty there won't be a need. If this really is a new development, I'll just tutor you myself." She laughed at the prospect, and he joined in her mirth for a moment. "Oh, Zhìyù Zhe. I do miss teaching, I thoroughly enjoyed it in my time. You were my best student in fact, respectful and curious. That's the best kind of student."

"It is our way to respect the wise." She responded.

"It also was the way of the Eldars to never question what is told to you. I'm glad you have the good sense to defy such a trait."

In the hubbub of charter and gossip, Ceannte rose from the great stair with a squire behind him. He stood upon the great hall for not more than a second before the human bellowed behind him. **"Hear ye, hear ye!"** The kings and queens all turned about to the squire, the halfling shuddered at the volume. "Here stands the halfling, Master Ceannte Macántacht of the great river land of Leath Langa. He seeks an audience with the Council of the Earth."

The Professor King queried. "What is the nature of his business?"

"Tis the ninth degree, mine king. It is of the utmost importance."

"What?" The halfling turned about. "No, it's not."

Many of the leaders gasped. Some murmured, others talked softly their concerns. "The ninth degree?!" The wood elven fellow repeated. "That has never been declared before."

"Muu Neg." The human addressed the Necromancer. "Is the Khan nearby? He is required for this assembly."

"My master the Khan will be present shortly however, I must press that our magic must take precedence on order for him to arrive."

"Magic can wait for a threat to our security." The Elfinqueen rebutted.

"Ordinarily I must agree milady. The reason why I protest is that in order to bring the Khan to this hall, I must conduct my magic."

"Excuse me!" Ceannte raised his voice. "I'm sorry. I'm sure there's a good reason for all this, but what the hell is going on?"

The king looked about him, first to the halfling by the steps, then the Necromancer and his unusual protests. "I must admit, I am not quite certain myself.

Thank you, Harold. You may go." The squire bowed and turned about down the stairs. "Master halfling, come, please. Address yourself and your business." He turned back to Muu Neg. "Do as you must to bring the Khan here. An agenda of the ninth degree requires the presence of all of Mundus to address the concern."

"Aye sirrah." The Necromancer stood in front of the newly created wall. "Sovereigns, master halfling, please take your thrones. My demonstration shall commence." They all retired to their seats about the hall as Muu Neg began. "Originally this was meant for the ceremony of the centenary of peace about our lands, but due to recent events I will be as concise as possible. It has been a century since the Great War was won. On the day of the signing of the Council's Mandate the world changed forever. War had no place here. We offered the Orking our hand so that he may prove himself to be above such treachery. He begrudged, yet he accepted the terms. A small mercy perhaps, but it was a mercy, nonetheless. All the Races of Peace could have easily smashed the Orcs to the ground, yet we did not. We chose not to give into our history. We did not choose the easy path to peace. Elfinqueen," he outstretched his hand to her, "you have my eternal thanks as well as that of all dark elves for taking such a righteous act." She bowed her head to him as he continued.

"The year before this we travelled far from our home from the mountains. We were headed for Beacon. We were headed for the Council for the very first time. Three weeks of trekking an environment no dark elf had ever seen for millennia. We arrived, and it was the first time in an age anyone had heard our tongue. My master then and now Khan Urjil Shimgui greeted the Council. 'Bid khoosorson irsen baina. Bid Kharankhui ger Ongontsny ni Khar Mönkhiin amid baina, bid Zövlöliin chuulganyg khaikh.' We have arrived from the wasteland. We are the Dark Elves from the Khanate and we seek the assembly of the Council. Immortal words of history. Today marks a new era for Mundus." The Necromancer turned to the wall and brought a mana crystal to it, he pressed the tip of the shard against the stone and began to score along the surface. As he drew the energy in the crystal flashed with every move and the powder it left slightly sparked. He drew a very large oval, enough for himself to fit through. The shape sparkled and fizzed with the little energy it received. The leaders looked on with interest and curiosity. He rubbed the etched end of the shard onto his hands, the powder again sparked with some of the energy of the crystal. He gently placed the mana on the ground and rubbed his hands, when he was ready, he placed both hands onto the surface within the oval. Immediately the shape and his hands reacted to each other, everything began to spark with energy. He pressed hard against the rock and the tips of his fingers shone a bright purple, in a meditative state he chanted *"Od khaalga,"* several times. Streams of energy stretched from his hand to the edge of the shape, the whole oval shone the same violet colour. The light became brighter and brighter and brighter, everyone shielded their eyes from the display.

Ceannte sat in amazement. *Is this magic?* He asked himself. *I've never actually seen it before.*

Muu Neg let go of the shining light and as he did it faded away. The shape transformed, everything inside the shape revealed itself as a swirling maelstrom. Cloud and lightening and energy and magic. He took the used mana crystal and rested it on the storm. The wall was still there, it still held the same substance and texture as before. Lastly, he said, *"ordond, neelttei baina."* Suddenly the mana fell into the wall, the storm was no longer a shape on a wall. The Professor King stood from his seat, dumbstruck by what had transpired. The electricity of the storm attacked the mana, it held it in place as the energy was released from the crystal. The magic poured out of the mana and the storm began to destabilise. The storm was angry, the clouds became choppy and more electric. The energy overflowed. Soon the entire structure of the maelstrom subsided and cleared a vision through the shape.

No one could not believe their eyes. Every single king, queen, emperor, empress, and the odd halfling was shocked, speechless or unable to understand what had taken place. Many of them gasped in awe, the Archonian king was especially taken aback from the show. "By Apollo!"

The goblin empress herself let slip her thoughts. "Is that what I think it is?" The Elfinqueen stood up beside the Midgardian king. They both left their seats and strode towards Muu Neg.

"You may wish to stand back. The Khan will be entering shortly." He warned the approaching leaders and raised his hand to haunt them just behind him.

"Bi orognonoosoo salj chadna!" A voice proclaimed.

"I come from the wasteland." Nuu Meg began to translate.

"Bi boi Kharankhui ger Ongontsny kharankhui negen."

"I am a Dark Elf from the Khanate."
Suddenly a man stepped through the wall into the hall. He stood right up to the group and proclaimed himself. "Bi Zövlöliin chuulganyg khaij baina!"

The Necromancer turned about to the king and queen behind him. "I think you can work out the rest of that."

"It's a spatial tunnel!" The Elfinqueen responded. "I have always believed such things were possible. Seeing it now I am-," she, the king, indeed everyone saw amongst the beauty of the city and the hills beyond a portal within a stone wall the size of an elf that linked to a dark, dusty world with such humidity the heat fell into the hall, "fascinated. Enticed by its curious beauty."

"Our sages and physicists call such objects wormholes." The Professor King added. "We have studied the concept for decades and virtually all fields of study agree wormholes cannot exist. I would never believe the stories if I wasn't here to see it myself."

"Excuse me." The Khan waved his hand about, he tried to return their attention.

"Forgiveness Khan." Zhìyù Zhe apologised.

"How long have you known about this Khan?" The Professor King asked. "Such a spell has the potential to affect the very nature of our world."

"A week sirrah. This development has surprised many of our sages. Necromancer Muu Neg announced his discovery and his strange practice in front of the ministry. Can you believe it? I've emptied my coffers for more scientists and research, and my good friend finds a new spell for free like that." He clicked his fingers. Behind them the wood elf Emperor and the dwarf Doge both laughed at his quip.

The human and the Elfinqueen approached the portal. "Is it stable?" She asked.

"Quite stable milady. It has been tested since its discovery amongst many of our men and no one has suffered at all from it. More experiments must be conducted, but in theory these gates can exist anywhere. A gate can open up from the ashes of the Khanate to the tropical forests, from the peaks of the highest mountain to the depths of the Bhoot. In theory of course."

The Midgardian king raised his brow and turned to Muu Neg. "What do you call these gates Necromancer?"

"Astral Gates we call them. I thought calling them *Star Gates* might be rather unusual."

"No more than Astral Gates I'm sure." The wood elf jeered behind them and some of the others chuckled.

"Let me get this straight. I could, say, go to the Khan's palace and take a piss?"

Everyone turned to where the voice came from. Ceannte leaned back on his seat and watched the gathering. "Cause to be honest, I'm kinda bustin' to go right now." Most of the leaders were aghast at his foul tongue. If they did not gasp in distress, they uttered their disgust. Most of the leaders. Not all. The wood elf laughed in delight of the man's frank humour.

The Professor King did not react, he stared at him as the commotion happened about him. "Excuse me master halfling, this is quite a feat of technology. One must be curious surely."

"Oh, I'm curious, sure. But I don't really care much to be here. I mean it's a lovely city and all, the people are excellent folk, but this place here annoys the buggery out of me." He swung his finger. "See, I'm here because I have a thing that's apparently a very big deal, and I need to give it to you lot because of some stupid law that makes no sense." He reached into his jacket and once again produced the troublesome coin. "I'm out ten grand because of you, so I expect a reward for this."

Once again, the leaders gasped. As he showed the other kings the gold, they also expressed their shock. The wood elf stood from his seat. "Is that what I think that is?"

The Khan approached the halfling as the Necromancer remarked. "Master, is that a Piece of Eight?"

He knelt to Ceannte and extended his hand. "May I, friend?"

"Oh, I ain't your friend mate. Give it back to me, will you?"

"Of course." He reached over to the enlarged hand and dropped the gold into the Khan's palm. He grunted as he felt the metal. It felt old and worn, it felt very familiar. He grasped onto the gold and with his other hand he searched the coin until he too found the makers mark. "There is no doubting it," he turned to the rest of the Council, "I hold in my hand a genuine Piece of Eight. This stranger has recovered a piece of our weapon."

Many of the leaders whispered amongst themselves over this new development. The Khan returned the gold back to Ceannte. "Master halfling," the Professor King walked to him, "it would appear that you have in your hands an important piece of history." He turned to the elves that stood by the gate. "Come, leaders of all Mundus. Make yourself known to this man. He requests an audience." They all began to return to their thrones.

He sighed. "Fine. But I'm not leaving without compensation!" He surveyed the assembly. The nine diplomats were arranged randomly about the table.

The Khan arrived at his seat at the extreme left of the halfling and proclaimed himself. "I am Khan Urjil Shimgui of the House Id Shidiin Mod. I rule over the Dark Elves, the Khanate at the very south of the continent, where the sand is pitch black and rivers of lava flow across the Wastelands." His plate mail clanked as he sat down and he took off his helm, a steel pointed hat lined with fur and a cloth to cover one's neck. His grieves and gauntlets were thick with metal and muscle, his breastplate however was ornately decorated with the face of a terrifying deity. His features were hard to see past his black skin even in sunlight. Ceannte saw only the eyes and the hair clearly, his eyes shone a silver hue in the sunlight and his striking violet locks brushed against the wind. He was short for an elf, yet still quite imposing.

"Pleasure to meet you sir." The halfling replied. "How was your experience travelling through the wormhole?"

"Eh, think nothing of it. It was not any more novel than a person stepping into their house."

"Good grief!" The man beside him tutted. "He speaks as if it were common to project a portal from one world into another." The man stood up. "I am the Emperor Mokuzai of the Forest, and the Wood Elves who dwell within it." His attire was also interesting. The tanned elf wore a green tunic the colour of the wild plants of the woods, a bright emerald shade. Over the clothing were his own protections, his arms and chest were shielded by a suit of armour made of the bark of a tree. Ceannte had seen enough of the woods to recognise the bark. Oakenshield, the toughest skin around. All of the Emperor's features were brown, his skin, his hair, his eyes, yet unlike his kin he was a portly fellow. It was his crown that stood out the most for the halfling, a large piece of wood that encircled Mokuzai's head and stretched outward beside him.

"Afternoon to you sir." Mokuzai bowed and returned to his seat.

"I'm Empress Prthvee VII," the goblin proceeded directly after the elf, "sovereign of the Goblins under the ground. We live with Earth Mother herself in the Bhoot, the great caverns of Mundus." She remained seated next to the wood elf, the caster the stone wall.

He took a good look at her unusual attire and posture. *Crikey! She's a bloody small thing.* "'Allo ma'am." He managed briefly.

Beside the empress the Elfinqueen returned to her seat. "Good day master halfling. I am Zhìyù Zhe, Elfinqueen of the High Elves. Matriarch of the First Race, the Eldars, and the keepers of all Life upon Mundus." She sat upon her seat and smiled. He felt her regal grace from her greeting. A very faithful compliment.

"Aye. Good afternoon." He paid her respect and bowed. She was delighted by his manner. Beside her the seat in the middle was still vacant. He noticed this chair was different, all the other thrones were simple stone chairs with their own style. But this one was raised, polished steps led towards a much more ornate throne. The same stone was carved perfectly into a tall throne with broadened corners atop the rest. The back rest of the seat depicted a picture of the Council of the Earth building and the standards of each nation under a shining sun. *I reckon that's for the Midgardian bloke.* He thought to himself.

Left of the throne sat a familiar face. She stood up upon her chair and proclaimed. "I hardly need any introduction for you sir. I am your queen. Dogess Uisce of the River." Just as quickly, she sat back down.

"Aye. Now that's interesting ma'am." He read her face; she seemed stern and sounded prompt. Her manner was quite closed off. She stood tall yet was eager to return to her seat. *I'm not sure,* he speculated. Not a hint of recognition seemed to register. He pointed directly at her. "You look as through you don't know me."

"Should I?" She tilted her head.

"But of course! You had the audacity to discredit my good friend. I wager you blurted it all about town with that racket you made."

"I'm sorry, I don't know what you mean."

He noticed a change in her voice. It had the slightest hint of mockery. Condescension. He furrowed his brow at her. "Óir Airgead. That bloke back in the Habhann. The moneychanger you weaselled out of a shop in the capital."

"Ah! Mister Airgead. I recall now. Grotty little thief if ever I saw one." She raised her finger and glared a menacing look. "You would do well, sir, to distance yourself from that leech."

"I beg your pardon?!" He rose to her challenge. He could feel her words get under his skin. Ceannte grew angrier by the second. "Óir is not a crook! He's never once done any shady dealing."

"All the same, he seeks to-,"

"SILENCE!" The Midgardian King hollered, seated at the great throne in the middle. The halflings turned to him, and he in turn directed his words to each at a time. "There are more pressing matters at work than your arguing and your disagreement." He attacked the Dogess' manner first, then the guest's tongue. They each cooled down and saw each other. "Doge, please." He asked the next king to present himself. While he did Ceannte noticed the Merchant Queen's reaction. At first she relented to the human's command however, as his attention turned and they caught their gaze, she smiled slyly. A devilish grin, she seemed to project an odd confidence.

"Yes, certainly." Next to the petulant halfling the dwarf stood upon his own seat. "I am Doge Smeltet V, King of the Dwarfkind, the Mountainfolk of the East, at the edge of the world." He adjusted his monocle to take a good look at the halfling stirring up trouble. He sized up the Doge himself. Much of the Dwarf's appearance was impressive, his beard was large and decorated with plats and threaded beads. His breastplate was a simple piece of gold, it was lined along the bottom edge with gemstones that seemed to sparkle the same luminous colour as the metal itself. One detail was the Doge's shoulder plate, his right shoulder was adorned with its own armoured decoration.

The last of the sovereigns greeted the halfling seated. "Gia sas, I am King Ilios of Árchontíkó, Grand Archon of the High Men, from the land of the Golden Coast." Of all the leaders he was the plainest, he wore no crown nor distinctive attire, little more than a light blue robe and a bright yellow belt to affix it. Atop of the clothing he wore large epaulettes over his shoulders, silver plates to broaden his stature. The Archon stroked his beard while he observed Ceannte.

"*Gia sas?* What does that mean?" He asked.

"It is of my language. It means 'hello'." Ilios' accent was more pronounced, the halfling noticed a particular emphasis on vowels.

"Ah, I see. Good morning sir." The Archon nodded slowly.

Then, to his extreme right he saw the one other dark elf present. "I am unlike the other folk here." He stood up, his tall, lean figure was both imposing and unnerving. "I am the Necromancer Muu Neg. I do not hold a seat of power. I am a servant and advisor to the Khan Shimgui. Rather, my role is to play the Orking in matters of policy. I do so by-."

"I'm sorry, what?" Ceannte interjected. "What do you mean 'play the Orking'?" He saw Muu Neg's eyes pierce through the cloak, the fray cloth moved in the breeze. The Necromancer wore his ceremonial armour around his neck, a broad leather suit as black as himself.

"All races are represented here," the Midgardian man replied, "it is arrogant to impose our wills onto an entire race without representation."

"Aye, true. It would be wrong to, say, force a nation into submission by imposing sanctions so they stop killing people. You wouldn't do that right?"

Mokuzai laughed at the observation. "Well said sir!"

Smeltet chuckled smugly. "The moxie of this one."

Some approved, Ilios nodded in agreement and even the Khan was compelled to applaud the insult. Others were not so humoured, Zhìyù Zhe sighed and held her head in frustration, and the goblin empress simply sat back in amazement, her arms folded with a sly grin across her tiny face. The human was much less reactive than the others. The halfling noticed the king remained unmoved by his sharp tongue. Ceannte saw something odd about him. His shining blue eyes, his scruffy head and ginger beard. The Midgardian attire was simple, yet maintained a strangely present aura, as if he could see into the soul with a third eye. It was Uisce who eventually defied the halfling. "What would you have us do? Just let the orcs destroy us all wantonly?"

"Oh no, I'd kill 'em. But see, I'm not hypocritical about that. I don't pretend like what I'm doing is going to make us all 'happy, fun time, peace' and all."

Zhìyù Zhe was aghast. "You would annihilate an entire race of people to preserve peace?"

"Without a second thought ma'am." His frank attitude upset her even more. "I would kill off anything that threatens me and my home. If that's a race of mutant killer men, then so be it. I'd feel no regret."

"Careful your tongue master halfling," Muu Neg started, "you say this now because you've never seen such things in front of you-."

"Oh, and I suppose you have then?" Ceannte interrupted.

"Indeed, I have." He gestured to the other side of the table. "As have my lord and Emperor Mokuzai. We have all fought in the Race Against Peace, each of us have slain many orcs and while I cannot speak for either, I can say from my own experience it is not well. They are tortured creatures. Ferrel bands of men with such a desire to end life, the very thought shrivels the soul."

"Hang on. You're a Necromancer, right? You're not adverse to killing."

"That is not entirely true. Necromancy is not an interest to end life, such ideas are common misconceptions. My role before the great war was not to actively kill to preserve my power, necromancy is the preserve of the soul once its mortal vessel cannot be mended, it is a ritual to keep one's self eternal. I channelled power through Death Mana in order to extract an essence from the body of the fallen, I granted them honour in death. Therefore, when my master compelled me to use my powers against the orcs, I was most upset. I told him it was a dishonour to myself and necromancy to thrust death to the unworthy."

"I must apologise again for such an imposition Necromancer," Urjil intervened, "it is not my place to dishonour our traditions so aggressively."

"It is all well Khan. It was a necessary course of action. I am grateful for the Midgardians to provide our people with skilled apprentices to learn from. You see, despite all our appearances we are averse to warfare. Khans fight each other as a ritual to power, the Reformation War disillusioned our kind from violence and hate. Necromancy regains honour from death. We are not a culture of death master halfling, but a culture that embraces death as a reality. All things must end; therefore, we must live our lives well enough to be honoured." Muu Neg sighed. "The days of the war were without honour. We clashed with the Orkind, metal on metal, blood on steel. Men were cut down like felled trees, sent to their graves without names and stripped of their distinction. Shamen and dark artists all threw their magic behind our army. Dark bolts, deathly rays and hexes everywhere. War is not the business of a necromancer, yet we too cast our lot at the orcs.

"Rarely an orc slips past our forces and threatens us. I remember one occasion, there was a rather large opening in the battlefield. I cast my bolts at stray enemies and conjure hexes to disable others. This creature must have noticed me and thought me an easy target, I saw him charge at me in my periphery. He was much too close to cast anything without injuring myself, so I drew my staff and fought him off physically. He was a mongrel beast. I still recall seeing his eyes ablaze with fire and rage. He was so uncontrolled and unaware it was disconcerting. The poor soul kept swinging his axe and throwing his fury at me, he never saw where I was going. I kept running and dodging out of trouble and soon I saw a number of Bladedancers charged at him." He sat back into his throne. "I am an elf. I was at least two feet above this orc, and he filled me with such dread I had never experienced before or since. That day I truly appreciated the gravity of the war, how it could turn giants into weaklings. I had no armour, no real weapon to defend myself, and that orc had a mind to gut me without any other thought or second guess. I feared for my life, not because it would end but rather that such conflict would dishonour my name. I saw no honour in that man. I saw no honour in myself. So no, master halfling, we do not conflict. There is no honour in ending innocent lives to stop a madman. War is an evil that must be averted at all cost." A silence descended over the council, many of the kings and queens were in their own minds, contemplating the Necromancer's words and the stark images of battle.

"I'll be honest with you mate," Ceannte began, "I'm all for ending war and peace and all. I mean I'm a halfling. I love a peaceful day of just sitting by the river and listening to the world go by, reading a good book and spending time with my lady friend. The last thing I'm interested in is battle strategies or combat. But see, I can't really trust anyone who won't be straight with me. I know I can be annoying or rude or just an idiot sometimes, but I am who I am. I make no pretence for anyone. I am straight up honest all the time. Now I trust you mate. I've never been into war and I doubt many others here can really talk about something like that so openly. I respect you for that." He paused to observe some of the other leaders. He saw a few nodding to his words and smiling at his admission. "It's just the fact that this place doesn't live up to its claims sometimes. I often wonder about the kind of things that happen here, why laws and things happen the way they do. And why people are the way they are. Sometimes it's just bloody baffling to me."

The Midgardian smiled. "Master Ceannte." He stepped around the end of the table and upon reaching him he knelt down to his level. "You are indeed a fresh breath of air in this house. I see you're quite blunt but noble as well, and genuine. You are truly a unique character." He reached out to him. "I am King Cairbre of Midgard, the Professor King of the land of Men, upon the westernmost island of the sea. I speak for the Council and uphold much tradition in the place however, I reckon all of that is quite meaningless for you." He hesitated for a moment but eventually the halfling shook his hand. "What is your occupation sir?"

"I fish. Mostly trout and salmon. I'm right by the edge of the delta, just as the mouth starts to open."

"Well Ceannte, it would seem that your life is about to take a very unexpected turn. I won't lie to you, it will be lengthy and troubled, but you will earn your name into history."

He raised his eyebrow. "What are you on about?"

Cairbre rose and slowly he walked about the hall. "In order to understand the Pieces of Eight, you must first understand the story of the Great War. A story that has remained hidden from this world, and one that will very likely unbalance the peace of this fair land." He returned to his throne and sat as he retold the story of ages past.

* * *

"Our books recount the previous age thusly; that the Age of Destruction was brought about by a terrible accident of alchemistry. Having discovered the first seventeen Disciplines of Magic, an experiment was conducted in the desert to find the eighteenth. Every known possible combination of the Elemental Magics were discovered bar one, the fusion of Fire and Deathly Magics. The process was simple, a cauldron of molten Fire Mana was poured into another cauldron of Death Mana crystals. That damn heat. The molten mana affected the crystals in such a way it caused the test site to explode, the raw power escaped and affected the elves and men the same. Some died that day, but most experienced a fate worse that death. By all accounts they changed, their skin burned a sickly green colour amongst bloodied scars. Their minds too transformed. The Orkrage was born, called so because of their unique characteristics. It was not a simple hatred or malice one sees in others; it was pure, indiscriminate bloodlust. A desire to kill as if it were a need to breath or eat. Indeed, we did discover Explosive Magic, the last and most recent discipline, but the cost was unimaginable. Unpredictable.

"That day sparked the Age of Destruction, a period of horror, fear and needless bloodshed. It is a blight in the annals of Mundus. I will not discomfort you with the early years of orc terror, nor shall I condescend to you with lectures of halfling raids. The Great War appeared when the Orking Mudammir I declared war with the rest of Mundus when the other races allied with the dark elves. The declaration sparked my forebear King Dalton III to assemble the kings and queens of all the races and form a united front against the orc-men. After much trial and tribulation his plans for peace took form and this city was built from it. However, his final plan to end the war was a much larger problem. This is where the pages of history differ from what is known.

"The taxing process of agreeing to a consensus is as it is written however, it was not so easy to compel the Orking. In truth, the war was not ended by mere unity alone. Mudammir's thirst for elf blood was not quenched, he continued his fighting and for a while we were all at a loss. But we hatched a plan, a safeguard of sorts. An alchemist from Midgard discovered a way to tap into the power of Mana crystals. The energy stored in them can be harnessed directly. This news reached our council, and it was the Necromancer who formulated the plan." Cairbre gestured his hand to Muu Neg.

He stood from his seat and continued the tale. "Aye, indeed. I recall that time well. I smuggled a very large shard of Crysx Mana from a magical node within the Khanate. It was the most powerful form of mana. Me and a caravan of sages brought it to the Council, and we applied a technique to introduce more energy into the crystal. We were creating a weapon never before seen. It took our best chemists three days to find and export the energy from seven lesser crystals into it. We called it War Ender, the Destroyer of Chaos. The intention was clear, to release the energy at the heart of the Orcs, deep in the desert.

"War Ender was prepared, and the plan was in motion. I was again given the Mana shard and was tasked to place it as closely as it was possible to the Orc 'capital', or whatever passes for the nucleus of a nation they have. But before we were able to set it off the Orking caught wind of our plan. He was able to see the position he was in. A bomb of such cataclysmic proportion as to annihilate an entire race aimed directly at his honour. As soon as he realised this, he approached the Council and laid down his arms in surrender. He yielded to us not by reason but by might. We negotiated with the Orking soon afterwards and we reached a mutual agreement. We granted him the ability to live peacefully and to restore his honour by omitting the information we must now oblige to give to you, in exchange for immediate disarmament and cooling off his warmongering. History tells that we block all trade with the Orcs, but this is not true. We allow a special treatise for merchants to transact with Orcs, for the

Council to study and observe them and ensure they do not mean to attack us again.

"Finally, it was arranged that War Ender would be dismantled. The stored energy of that crystal was fed back into magical nodes all about Mundus, and the remaining shell melted down and transformed. From the Crysx Mana eight golden medallions were made, fashioned just like the one we have before us here. Each of the Pieces of Eight were given to each member of the Council to distribute as they saw fit. We each knew our own piece but not the rest, and inso doing no one alone can recreate War Ender. We all pledged never to remake it, to keep safe the home we have made. For if such a power were forced out of our hands, the destruction would dwarf the fallout of the great mistake from an age hence." Quietly Muu Neg returned to his seat. His eyes reminded affixed towards the halfling.

Chapter 9

Ceannte was dumbfounded. The air was cold and still. His slacken jaw and widened eyes painted the picture, his breathlessness mimicked the sound. Sheer, utter disbelief.

"And there we have it. The truth revealed." The Professor King pointed at the coin on the table. "That, sirrah, is a Piece of Eight, a part of a warhead never set loose. It is a ghost of a past unknown, and it haunts us today."

"Aye, it is quite true," Mokuzai lamented, "I too was present at that meeting. I find such business quite upsetting. Thinking of it still angers me at the hopelessness of it then-." He was cut short by his view. The Emperor stared out, past the city and over the river. Beyond the hilly banks, to the very edge of the horizon which the smallest stretches of sandy desert could be seen so far. "I am forced to see the Orkind as not so dissimilar to myself. Of the struggle of my own people, and their right to exist. You see, the orcs are very much like the woodly folk. We are both born from diaspora; ours were a difference of belief, and theirs a difference of physical mutation. Our lives were threatened by outside forces, and we each fought to defend ourselves." Zhìyù Zhe was so moved by the elf's somber story she reached out and laid her hand upon his shoulder. The comfort soothed his anguish. "Elfinqueen, I appreciate your care."

"I'm sorry." Ceannte rose his voice and from his seat. "I mean no disrespect or nothing. I mean, I've read enough history to know about the sketchy past of the elves and whatnot, but are you serious? Did this really just happen?" The halfling started to pace about the hall, taking the attention of the Council by force. "I mean, if what you lot say is what really took place, then this building, this city, all of it is built on a lie. Unity, friendship, solidarity. You didn't get peace from that, you won it with a massive bomb. You're no better than the Orcs!" He pointed defiantly. "The only difference is you don't want to fight, so instead you come up with some sort of insurance. Some kind of thing that makes sure you can obtain victory, as if we can blast hatred out of existence! Well guess what. That's not how people work! People don't appreciate their oppressors. Any kind of history can show that. You sit on your lofty chairs and talk about friendship and all that bullshit, but you don't do it, do you? I bet you all hate each other behind your backs." He began with Empress Prthvee. "I bet you bitch about the dwarves and all their wealth! How they murder nature with their digging up the earth." Then to Khan Urjil. "You probably get angry every time the elves call you a mutant or a freak of nature. Because they can't accept the very idea of death."

"You know, I always thought this place was just nonsense, but I had no idea it was this messed up. I don't really care about politics. So, when I learnt I needed to come here I was upset. The thought of all the fighting and the hatred just burned a pit in my stomach, but gees, I thought that was mental enough. Still I made the effort to come here, got me to explore a bit. Once I made it and had a walkabout and met a few people, I warmed up to the place. There are some amazing people down there." Ceannte turned the the Elfinqueen. "Ma'am, I got talking to a lovely Chaplain. She's a positive creature with a devotion to the Goddess I find quite admirable. It makes me seriously consider adopting the faith. She is a wood elvin maiden." He paused to observe her, he noticed she smiled back at him. *She knows her I reckon.* "A wood elf Chaplain. I had no idea such things existed. I thought those fey creatures were more interested in pleasure and happiness rather than tradition. I thought they all ate and laughed and pursued the meaning of life. It was so refreshing to see a religious forest maiden, it made me think about the world more. It made me think people were not just the products of history." The halfling walked up to the table and reached overhead. He pulled himself up and climbed upon of it. He wanted to look at Zhìyù Zhe squarely. "She's a unique flower that needs to be preserved. For fuck's sake, don't ruin her or I swear to every single god there is I'll kick your guts in." He saw her smiled drop slightly as he added. "And I don't make threats I don't intend to keep!"

She nodded and replied, "You will have my word master halfling." She began to shiver with nervous tension.

"I don't know you well ma'am, but right now your word means bugger all." He spat back and lowered his finger. He took a moment to stare into her. His eyes pierced the Elfinqueen, and she was made uncomfortable by his rage. She quivered a sigh, an effort to relive her nerves, and he decided to break his attack. "The beauty of this whole thing that you still don't trust each other, not really. You see, because you don't know where these Pieces of Whatever are, and you all have a piece with you, you've created a perfect system to ensure security. Not by making everyone promise never to use it, but to make it impossible to try to without everyone's consent. It achieves exactly what you want without worrying about someone going 'gee, I really want to blast the dark elves into oblivion. Let me get my bit of bomb!' The idea is so perfect you don't *need* to trust each other." Ceannte was spent, tired from the hate and the anger and the fury. He laboured his breath, turned about and slowly climbed down from the table. Eventually he landed back on his seat and just breathed for a few moments. The wary warrior was no more. Everyone was silent, the leaders all simply looked at each other in shock and amazement.

Zhìyù Zhe was the most affected, she saw in him perhaps too much. In between his pronouncements she thought much about him. *Such fire,* she internalised, *such a sharp tongue with indignant foresight. His argument is impossible to defeat, yet the alternate is beyond even this ideal. This man must surely see the folly in his speech, he certainly has the intellect to understand the intricacies for polity. What has done this? What foul thing has caused this capable man to be so unsettled to make better this world?*

Ceannte leaned back onto the backrest, slowly he panted towards calmness. "Well. What now then?"

King Cairbre addressed him. "Well, we can't simply leave the piece here. Even though it's just one, the fact it was discovered in the first place is a serious breach in security."

"I'm surprised they weren't destroyed!" Empress Prthvee interjected. "Melt down the gold."

"It was an oversight. We should have done that immediately."

"Perhaps we should collect our pieces and pledge to destroy them." Doge Smeltet suggested.

"It is not possible," the Professor King shook his head, "I must inform that I do not possess my Piece of Eight. The treasury has been under siege by pirates this past year and it was lost to the raiders."

"Surely we can undo the others though. Without all the pieces they cannot be remade." Zhìyù Zhe added.

"In theory that is a sound plan. You forget your studies though, Crysx Mana has a much larger electric capacity for a reason. The structure of the crystal makes a small shard of it still quite potent. A medallion that small can still cause terrible damage. However less powerful such a coin is, it too must be destroyed."

"This was never resolved?!" Uisce shrieked.

"Of course not. Whose piece do you think that was?" Emperor Mokuzai heckled.

"Bickering will not solve our predicament," the Professor King declared, "complaining about the past is wasting the time we have. What we need is to find all the Pieces of Eight and destroy them once and for all. Exactly what we should have done in the first place. Ceannte," the halfling lifted his head. "We need someone to search and find the missing Pieces of Eight scattered about Mundus. As the only other person here we, the Council of the Earth, must ask you to carry out this quest."

He took one deep breath and sighed in frustration. "Yeah, I figured you'd ask me that."

"This is a voluntary quest. You are free to refuse, and we can make other arrangements. Do you understand?"

Everything was crashing down. *All I wanted was some gold,* he thought, *not even a lot. Really just something to be a bit better off. A nicer place, or some fancy things.* "Yep." His responses became monotonous, robotic, prepared.

"Very well. Master Ceannte, do you agree to take this quest?"

"No!" He stood up and continued. "I'm no hero, I'm a fisherman. I spend my day relaxing by the river and catching my dinner, not fighting and questing. And I am sure as hell not going to clear up your mess, I have better things to do. You're on your own."

Cairbre raised his hands. "Are you certain master halfling? We would certainly not wish to find another Hero and further spread this conspiracy."

"Well what about this conspiracy then, huh? What about the fact that you stuffed up this bright idea, and now you have to fetch some random bloke to do your dirty work? Did no one here seriously think this was going to happen? Someone loses these secret things for another person to stumble into them. You genuinely didn't see how this could have happened?"

"Master Ceannte," Zhíyú Zhe leaped from her seat and addressed the room, visibly quaking and audibly breaking, "your concerns and declarations are correct. Your clarity is blunt yet remarkable. Your words move me and hurt me deeply. I cannot address the issues you raise. My mother was complicit in the creation of this terrible event. However, she told me much of her own concern. Beyond your foul speech I can hear my mother's anguish through your words, she too could not reconcile the actions with the intent." She watched him carefully, his flaming rage and powerful stare. She ensured not to arm him with even more darkness. She sighed. "I will not ask you to accept this quest, you have made your position well known and I personally agree with your protest. However, this question is a matter greater than virtue, I must admit. It was an impossible choice, and the decision to create War Ender was not at all taken lightly. Trading lives is a deeply imposing confrontation, a truly evil precedent, yet it was decided to take such a measure to afford a peace that lasts. That was the justification then, and despite both mother and my protests of immorality, the Council agreed it was necessary for the good of the peace.

"Why the Pieces of Eight were not destroyed, I do not know. I can tell you that no one in the High Palace wanted anything to do with it. And so, the destined talisman was cast out into the wild and protected by a powerful magic. We washed our hands of such blackness. We let the matter lie dormant, waiting for the right time to finally resolve it. Because ultimately, we knew then what you denounce now, that like the talisman, such an evil is not destroyed but merely rested. It sleeps in shadow and breeds in fear, and that a toxic cloud of hate and death will signal the return of the great evil. That monster of blood and steel." She could see his face loosen. His grimace was less pronounced. She reckoned he was relaxing to her words, and the thought relaxed her into a steadier stance. "And, master halfling, I see in you a firebrand righteousness. A furious compulsion of justice. A highly defined sense of rightness. Perhaps rather too much profanity, but it seems well placed and deliberately chosen." A smile crept across her face. "Good sir, you are what is required to fulfil this task. I feel your strong will and sense of goodliness is what is appropriate to gather the talismans and destroy them. Again, I will not ask you to accept this quest however, I encourage you to reconsider your disdain, for if there were ever a time for the right hands to collect the pieces, let them fall into yours and not into any others that have more sinister agendas." Her confidence restored, she sat back into her seat.

The silence briefly returned. Ceannte considered the Elfinqueen carefully. "Ma'am, I'm flattered by your words. Quite frankly most people can't seem to get past mine. My personality is just too blunt. I say what's on my mind, people don't always want to hear it. So it always makes my day when someone says things like that. I appreciate it, so I do appreciate and understand the things you say." He paused to think for a few seconds. "But I just cannot accept this. The whole idea is just so morbid and strange. It's so hard to not think about this as just doing dirty work for some sort of villain. Almost like there's a sinister agenda itself. And don't get me wrong ma'am, I can tell from your speech and your manner that you're no villain, and honestly no one here really is from the little time I've met you all. But this whole history and quest stinks of skulduggery and intrigue that I have no choice but to decline. It's not something I'm prepared to do and just drop everything because of my dumb luck." He took one final look at the elf, this time a much more open stare. One devoid of fire, a look of sincerity, sad yet calming. She was no longer afraid of his eyes and peered into his soul now undefended by rage. "I'm sorry, but the answer is no."

Zhíyú Zhe bowed to him. *There is more to this man than he cares to express. It is a shame he will not aid his countrymen. However, I must grant him his courage and his will.*

Cairbre nodded. "Very well. We thank you for your time and patience." He stretched his hand to the exit.

The halfling rose from his seat. "My time here hasn't been in vain. I have a better appreciation of this place now. The Great Experiment works here I reckon. Bringing people for all races into a city of peace. I came here a sceptic; I leave here seeing it with my own eyes. This place works." Many of the leaders bowed and nodded and all demonstrated their own acknowledgement to Ceannte. He promptly took the Piece of Eight and made his way towards the exit. Every step he took he was true to his conviction, assured in his belief. His confident stride took him right up to the steps and, without a moment's hesitation he descended the tower. The warrior, the fighter against the dishonest and the unfair, left the Council of the Earth with their thoughts, their past and their future.

Chapter 10

The halfling carried on down the stairs, he slowly encircled the tower as the broad view of the city constantly changed. He was high above the canopy of the urban land. The roofs gleamed a strange yellow light from the sun. Ornate buildings drew Ceannte's attention the most. Interesting shapes and detailed steeples scattered about the ceiling of the city. Too many to count or examine in any detail, simple symbols of life, learning and magic. He approached halfway down the great tower when a stray memory entered his mind, a distant memory of his youth. He gazed over the yellowness, and his third eye conjured the thought.

The sound of rushing water trickled past his ears. The smell of fresh grasses filled his lungs. Wet and crisp. The air was still without a cloud in sight. Ceannte was a childling, barely ten years old. He returned home from the schoolhouse, the first week of spring did nothing to lighten his mood. He strode calmly back home, to the same shack he resides today. The house appeared more stable in his mind, the wood seemed cleaner and the foundations less rickety. The glass of the windows were clearer than his own, and there appeared to be more of them. He was terribly upset, volatile and fragile. His eyes were blurred by tears and reddened by injury. Outside he saw a figure tending a garden of marigolds. He knew Pa would be out now. He quickly ran towards him. "Pa! Pa," he shrieked.

A gristly figure peered over the flower bed, broad and bearded. He caught the cries of the child. "Boy?" He called out to him, but by the time he did Ceannte already made it home. He ran around the garden side and snapped himself onto his father's waist. The child desperately hugged him. The comfort of his father's form soothed him if only slightly. "Son," he was taken by the boy's sudden appearance, "what troubles you?"

"The others-," his crying interrupted, "the other boys. They beat me up again."

"Again?" He hushed the poor soul and kept him close to his heart. Slowly and with gentle hands he coaxed the boy to show his face. He was aghast at the sight. The youth's face was ruined. His cheeks were scuffed, dried cuts scored across his face. Eyes bloodshot from pain, his left eye was black, bruised and swollen. Blood dripped from his nose and lips. The ravages of war.

"They called me a poor kid. A stupid, smelly tramp. They called you an idiot with no money. They took me, and just kept hitting me all the time,"

"Well what about the teachers? The Headmaster. Was no one there?"

"No. School was over, so we all went home. They just came from somewhere and beat me up." The thought of the attack drove the child into his father more, a futile attempt to restrain his sadness.

"Damn snobs. What kind of mongrels do we live with?" Father was getting angrier by the second, the thought of his son bullied by thugs every other day upset the man to no end.

"Why are we poor Pa?" The question broke his temper and he looked down to his son. The shattered soul looked into his father's eyes. He saw in his child a broken spirit. "Why can't we live in a big house?" A will made weak be constant and extreme pressure. The gaze of the boy sank back down, and he continued to sob into his father.

"What? Where's this coming from?"

The child's wail was muffled, he yelled into his father's chest. "I just want people to like me!"

"Oh son." The man hugged his lamb, shaken and frightened. The warm hold washed over the young Ceannte. The familiar embrace slowed his heart and granted him some security. His hold on father loosened. Fear still negotiated its way through the comfort, the pain had not yet dispersed. Disquiet still raged inside him. Suddenly, he felt a strange force compel him. An upward force appeared to lift him into the air, as if his soul wished to leave his despair. He found himself again close to father, this time he floated into his shoulder. Eventually he noticed what happened, father carried him off the ground. "There's a lot of things going on 'ere. A lot of stuff you're too young to really get." The child fell into father. He continued to cry. However, the man *noticed his sniffling began to slow down. "I don't know why them other kids pick on you. Maybe they just want someone small to bully, or maybe they really do think we are beneath them. In any event, the important thin-."*

"What's beneath them?"

Father smiled and lightly ran his free hand into the child's hair. "Social status son. That's stuff you will learn about later. Really all you need to know is that those kids probably just want to be bastards."

"But why?!"

"I don't know son, honest. I was not like that when I was a youngin'." He sighed and peered again into his son's eyes. Ceannte was not shaking anymore, yet the fear lingered. Through the tears and the redness, he saw in the child's eyes a glimmer, a twinkle of himself. "You know, you look up to a grownup like me or your ma, then you turn into a grownup, and there are still things you don't know." He chuckled at the final thought.

"Like what?"

"Oh, big things. Hard things. Things that make grownups scared. Things that they think about all the time." He sighed again. "Things that someday you'll know about yourself."

The child laid upon his father. "I don't want to do that."

"Ah, you can't help it. You cannot run away from your problems all the time, son. You must beat them. Fight for yourself. Get tough-."

"I don't want to fight." He interrupted his father. "I don't want to hurt people. I don't like it."

"Sometimes you have to, son. People do things they don't like a lot. People are not always like me or your friends. Some people want to hurt you. And if you don't fight back, they'll just keep getting you again and again." He saw the boy sink his head, the child thought deeply. *"And I reckon you're a strong kid. You can stay tough and fight these bullies."*

He shook his head. "No. I don't want to. I don't like it. I just want them to leave me alone."

"Well, you don't have to this time." Ceannte looked back up to his father. *"I'll have a word with the Headmaster tomorrow. This sort of thing is turning into a real problem. But son, know this; you must deal with your problems head on, but sometimes not all problems must be fought. You need to have a sharp eye to spot these things. You have to know when to fight, and when to use a bit of deft cunning. If you can't beat 'em at their own game, -."*

"You fight dirty. You get even!"

The words of his father echoed in his mind. A fork had now presented itself. At the foot of the tower the halfling stood. He brushed his cheek to feel the scars of his past, made smooth and fresh from the passage of time, and weighed his options. He remained there for several moments, carefully he envisioned the choices and the implications they would leave. Eventually a cheeky grin sprang across his face. The thought could not have been any better. "Oh, that's good," he uttered to himself. "I like that. A lot." The devilish idea gave him the good humour and the energy to turn about quickly and run back up the steps he only just walked down.

Each sprint and leap up the stair well gave him more resolve to return to the Council. He made light work of the ascent.

The Council of the Earth remained atop, they carried on about their business. "The orcs remain mobilised milords," Muu Neg explained. "There is much animation about the desert however, it is not more than the usual business. It continues to baffle me how they find anything worth mining there. There seems to be nothing but sand and stone."

"I just have one question."

The kings and queens turned to the stairs, and the familiar voice provoked a smirk on the face of King Cairbre. "How much does a quest like this pay?" Ceannte asked.

The Midgardian raised his eyebrow. "The quest? You mean the search for the Pieces of Eight?"

"Aye. What sort of reward can I expect?"

"The price is negotiable."

Slowly a wide smile spread over the fisherman's face. He walked back into the great hall with a newfound confidence. His stride returned him to the seat he sat before. "I'll take the quest under one condition, I set the pay."

The leaders murmured, it was clear from their tone and whispering that they all noticed his sudden change. "What do you have in mind?" Smeltet asked.

"A thousand platinum pieces. Each."

"One thousand platinum?!" The dwarf jumped off his seat in disgust. Others gasped and groaned at such a cost.

"We don't have gold to pay!" Prthvee protested.

"I don't really care where I get it. A hundred grand is a hundred grand."

"You intend to capitalise from this quest?" The Doge question him. "Compound our grievances and bleed us dry?"

"Well, I figure I can extort you all. People would pay sacks full of gold for a story like that. You don't want me to tell anyone about this do you?"

"You wouldn't dare!" Urjil slammed the table. "You dishonour us with such a threat!"

"Me? Dishonour you?" He laughed at the thought. "That's rich. I'd reckon you all dishonour everyone with hypocrisy, making a bomb while you preach peace and unity." The dark elf recoiled back into his seat. The comment left a lasting disgust on his face.

"Quite so Ceannte." Cairbre then turned to Urjil. "And Khan, I believe he would indeed leak the story elsewhere. He is clear eyed and honest without a hint of pretence. He is nothing if not a man of his word I think."

"Too right!"

The only person who applauded the defiant display was the Emperor Mokuzai. "Good show. What a coup! Excellently played."

The Midgardian sighed. "Very well Ceannte, if you agree to accept this quest, we will pay you a finder's reward to the value of one thousand platinum pieces for each Piece of Eight you recover. Do you agree to these terms?"

"Absolutely!" He grinned cheekily.

"Then we will draft a contract for you and all of us to sign, you may use it at any time as a warrant for any business relating to the quest."

"That's fine by me."

"I object!" Uisce sprang from her chair. "This scoundrel is asking for such a high price merely to punish us for the actions of our forebears. I hardly see the benefit in agreeing to such a contract."

"Benefit? Why should you benefit from this?"

"I must agree with the master halfling." The sage King Ilios spoke over the hubbub and drew everyone's attention. "What kind of world would we live in if we did not allow the common man to rightly punish another of their crimes? What fell nation discourages justness? Are we now to admonish citizens for our own missteps? Employ imperial rule to do as we wished without any regard for legality or consequence?"

"Yes!" The Dogess answered. "If it is for the benefit of the nation, let no man tilt at titans."

Groans from all about the tower echoed the open space. "By Apollo woman. Do you regard yourself as such a thing? Divinity amongst the rabble? What possible rite do you have to even think of such things?"

"I am the people. The law is my will, and all must obey it. I am Queen of the River, Lady of the Halfling folk. That is my rite."

"Oh, piss off!" Ceannte grumbled.

"You, ma'am, are also quite outnumbered." King Cairbre interjected. "You, Queen of the River, stand alone in this matter, and this is a hall of free thought where a majority is heard. I say we shall put it to the vote. Are we agreed?" Everyone uttered their own noise of affirmation. Even Uisce herself. Even Ceannte. "Ladies and gentlemen, you've heard the arguments. On the one hand speaks of a terrible wrong whose making right requires the world itself to pay its due, a rather handsome one at that. The other hand speaks of the absolution of the past and the consignment of blame to be buried there. That is the crux of the matter. If you side with the master halfling, raise your hand and declare aye." One by one the monarchs all showed their support for the fisherman.

Many did exactly as the Midgardian asked; arisen their right hand and proclaimed their backing, with the notable exception coming from Muu Neg. "Anything that grants the Orking his security is a motion he supports unreservedly."

"All who side with the lady halfling, raise your hand and declare nay."

A new silence was cast onto the great tower, a wave of change rather than fear, a wave cut short by the Dogess' futility. "Bloody nay!"

"I believe the aye's have it." Cairbre announced. "Eight councilmen to one, let the record show. If you don't mind my saying master Ceannte, I find it quite amusing that your country refuses you, as it were, yet the world accepts you."

"Heh, indeed." He found it difficult to find the humour.

"If there is nothing else master halfling, then that concludes our business. You may go from the Council Hall, but please remain below for the contact will be signed and delivered to you there."

"Righto then." The halfling again got up from his seat, strode triumphantly out of the hall, and marched down the stairs. He beamed a confidence unknown to himself, a strange relief, a conclusion that was beyond his own expectation. He just swindled all the leaders of Mundus into paying him an unimaginable amount of gold. He entered the hall a nobody and left it a practical millionaire. He left such an impression that not one of them reacted for a few moments. They all just stared blankly into the scene, they tried to understand and process what just happened. The man, the attitude, the truth, the confidence.

Eventually King Ilios pointed out. "I must say, the man has such a terrible manner about him."

"He doesn't need manner," Uisce explained, "he just became the second richest halfling in all Mundus. At the end of this he'll buy all the power he wants."

"He's not after power," Emperor Mokuzai interjected, "he's after justice, a fitting punishment for our past. He is smart enough to know what is wrong and has enough of an ego to call it out. When he knew he had the high ground his greed took over, and that is where the plan came from. He wanted to send a message against our conspiracy, and he knew how to hurt us. Just how many of us even have such wealth?"

"I must agree to that." Zhíyú Zhe added. "The man is quite clever, and quite mischievous."

"I too concur." The dwarf conceded.

"Perhaps it is a good thing *he* found the piece." Cairbre observed. "It takes a stranger to fairly judge the guilty from the innocent. In the end perhaps we may all be judged treacherous fools in our futures. Primitives who live only in a time of baser desires and challenge threats with destruction. Fearful and savage." He looked to each of them. He noticed them contemplating his words privately. "Kings, queens, let us challenge our fate. Set the past as a bar upon which we must surpass. Build upon ancient ruins and create a legacy. Let us make the world better, actively." Many nodded, some applauded his thoughts. The Professor King produced a sheet of parchment and an inkwell. "Let us prepare this contract. We must all sign the document to give our halfling friend the ability to clear our mess. Honour the contract," he quickly shot a glaring look at Uisce, "accommodate him. Pay him for his dues, no matter how egregious." He saw the look on her face, she was not at all pleased at the prospect. The lines of her skin accented her frown and stern eyes. "Once your name is set into this document, it becomes international law. You must fulfil it." He took the quill and began writing the agreement, the agreement the Council of the Earth must grant Ceannte during his quest.

* * *

The halfling returned to the board, the night was ending, and a decision was looming. He entered his room and shuffled towards his bed. He flopped onto the bed, the sheets puffed out around him and slowly settled down like a fluffy mist of comfort. He mumbled into the bed for a moment and turned over. The spent halfling stared up into the chandelier. *What am I going to do?* He asked internally. The flickering light of the candles captured his mind. "Where am I going to go?" He asked the room. The oscillating light entranced him. A soft warmth appeared within him, some calmness entered his heart and radiated across his body. His eyes were feeling heavy, he yawned loudly, and slowly he drifted into sleep. He breathed easily in rest, the gentle rise and fall of his chest was the only movement in the room. The light continued to stir, yet all was still, silent and calm.

WAKE UP!

Suddenly Ceannte blurted out a noise of alarm. He immediately woke up, and for an instant the same warmth began to fill him again. Instead, he climbed himself up and sat on the bed. "I have to sort this out first before I doze off." He rummaged his hand into a pocket and produced a piece of folded parchment. He opened the paper and the instant he saw its contents he folded it again. "Ah, not that one." Again, he searched his pocket, deeper the second time, and he extracted another folded leaf. He opened it and set it down beside him upon the bed. It was a map of the continent. The Nine Realms of Mundus were open to him. The great mountains to the east, the glades of the forestland, the Western Sea towards the kingdom of men, the forbidden desert beyond his home, and the impressive wasteland of ash at the southern end. *I don't want any of those bastards near me,* the halfling vowed, *or at least not yet.* He quickly realised by scanning the map he had only two options that he was happy to go to; up the road from the Dogedom towards the Golden Coast and the land of the Archons, or go back the way he came, visit the capital city of his world, and get his payment now from the Dogess. "Bugger it! I'll get my money now. No sense in waiting around." He folded up the map and put it back into his pocket. Ceannte looked about and grabbed the other bit of parchment. He played with it for a time, spun it in his fingers and sighed. He again unbound the paper and reread the contract.

We, the Council of the Earth, bind the halfling Ceannte Macántacht to complete a quest of great import and the utmost confidentiality. Under Article VII of the Hero's Code of Conduct, the Hero's Binding is active and recognised by all signatories. This contract binds the signatories to compensate the halfling to the value of 100,000 gold pieces, or goods and treasures of the same value, upon the recovery of artefacts of All History. The Hero's Laws apply to the halfling, and his actions are bound by the laws of the country of Mundus he is present.

I hereby bind myself to this contract;

Emperor Mokuzai of the Forest

Elfinqueen Zhúyú Zhe

Professor King Cairbre

King Ilios of Árchontikó

The Mountain King Doge Smelter V

Khan Urjil Shimgui

Empress Prthvee VII of the Bhoot

Dogess Uisce

"Well, I guess I'm a Hero now." He stared out into the room for a few seconds and sighed again. "I don't feel all that different though." He fell back onto the bed again, with contract in hand he read and reread the words several times. *I wonder what'll happen,* the thought ran about his mind, *this quest will take me many places I like to see, but also people I'd rather not.* Eventually the warmth passed over hum once more. He closed his eyes, dropped the paper about him, and as he descended into his dream, the words of the Council whispered echoes in the darkness.

"*Well Ceannte, it would seem that your life is about to take a very unexpected turn...*"

"*We were creating a weapon never before seen... War Ender, the Destroyer of Chaos.*"

"*... the orcs are very much like the woodly folk...our lives were threatened by outside forces...*"

"*... your word means bugger all.*"

"*This was never resolved?!*"

"Your words move me and hurt me deeply...I can hear my mother's anguish...I will not ask you to accept this quest...however, this question is a matter greater than virtue...trading lives is a deeply imposing confrontation, a truly evil precedent...it was necessary for the good of the peace."

In his sleep, an errand thought escaped his lips. "Shit."

* * *

The halfling remained atop his bed for the night, unmoved from his position the whole time. The sun shone into the room. Its light was cast onto his body, slowly it crept across the covers of the bed and towards his face. At first the light struck his mouth, the warmth did nothing to rouse him. The room was peaceful. Nothing stirred save for some errand dust that exposed itself to the sun. Specks of whiteness in front of darkened wood and cloth. A minute had passed, and the light had covered his nose. Ceannte rubbed it while he was still in his dream, the sun was yet to enforce its will. He yawned randomly and rolled himself into the mattress. More time passed and the sun reached his eyes. The blackness of sleep transformed into a sudden red light that shone through his eyelids. He groaned at the colour that streamed in, and after he turned away from the sun, he opened his eyes to the new day. The halfling stretched his arms and unstiffened his legs. His vision was blurry, and his mind was still groggy. The strain of the muscles, and the dullness of the senses caused him to groan and make noise, a mild pain darted up his limbs with every move he made. His arms were warm, his legs moving, his sight clear, and his mind awake. The halfling was satisfied, so he sat up, relaxed himself, and breathed a sigh of relief. A final yawn escaped Ceannte, he then got up and left his bed. Unburdened, he made for the door and quickly exited his room.

He left the board with a mouth full of bread, upon leaving he grabbed his meal and continued to eat breakfast. He idly walked into the markets. They were much less busy than before, the bakers were selling their breads and pies, but little else moved. Many stalls were empty and barren, frames and wooden stands with nothing more than the scratches and stains of ware. A few of the artisans were crafting, bead ware and cloth, etchings of wood and metal, simple craft of small things. The halfling wandered about the strangeness of a quiet centre. The cold stone way normally made warm by the people. The smell of fresh bread rose alone in the air that typically competed with aromas of incenses, wines, and hot air. The sounds of idle chatter were scattered about him that would usually fill the space with great terror. The market in the morning could not be more opposed to itself in the evening. The peace pleased Ceannte, the charm of the morning light peeking through the modern city fell into his mind. "Master halfling." A warm voice cast itself into the wind, and he looked about to find it. By the northern entrance of the square, the familiar queen waved at him. The Elfinqueen Zhíyú Zhe beckoned at him. "Good morning to you."

"Oh." He responded in kind and hollered back. "Morning ma'am. Surprised to see you here if I'm honest."

"Indeed. I make a habit of taking a moment to see the city in the morning. Visit the sellers and discuss matters. Care to join me?"

"Oh no. I-," a sudden thought interrupted. *For the more you create friendship and merriment about you, the more you will ward the fires of fury and violence.* "Actually, alright. I don't mind your company."

"Ha! Well I suppose that's better than naught." He made his way to her. The stretched creature grew taller with each step.

"Crickey! You're a tall lass." To the halfling her crown reached far, as high as the sky itself. The clouds seemed to scrape the tines of her golden halo.

The Elfinqueen laughed heartily. "I am rather tall. Mother tells me I am a clear foot higher than most of my kind."

"How high, if you don't mind the question."

"Eight foot, nine inches." They began to walk slowly. "I am indeed one of the longest of the elves alive."

"How did that happen? Do you know?"

Zhíyú Zhe laughed again. "I'm afraid I haven't a clue. Biology is not a subject I know very well. However, I have a theory. Perhaps my father contributed to my growth."

"Huh. Why is that?"

She turned to him. "You can't tell?"

"Tell what?"

She stared at him for a second. She felt a strange shock, an uncanny curiosity. "Well, now I am surprised. Have you not seen many Eldars before?"

"Oh I have, yes."

"Well, have you not noticed their appearances?"

"Not really, no. They seem like mostly decent folk, if a little insensitive, but I don't pay much attention to people's looks."

"Insensitive?" She asked, and after a while she nodded in reply. "Interesting. It sounds as if you have met some traditionalists. Some of my kin still see themselves as superior." She saw him return his own nod. "I am all too familiar of their ilk. However, to return to my point, many of the high elves have a similar physique. Often, we are fair skinned and golden haired. I, however, do not share these." She grabbed ahold of her hair, and his eye followed her. "See? Short, brown hair, and hazelnut eyes. I have my father's looks, and I suspect his height yet, I know from mother he was not so tall."

"Wait wait. Hang on." Ceannte stretched in front of the Elfinqueen and she stopped to his command. "I'm not quite sure what you're getting at ma'am. You seem to attach a lot of yourself to your father. Who is he?"

"The philanthrope Evimería. An Archonian man."

"An archon?!" The idea forced a sudden yelp from him. "You have a mortal dad?"

"I did. I don't know how it affects me, but I can only assume my parentage has moulded my features as they have my upbringing."

"Oh wait." He fell quiet from a sudden thought. "I'm sorry."

"For what?"

"I only just realised; I'm guessing from your speech that your father might have passed away."

"Indeed, he has. But I'm not upset." She looked at him and smiled. "I hold my father in my memories. He is not with me now, but he lives in me. He dwells in my thoughts, and thus he does not truly perish. His spirit shall live on."

He softened to her. "That's very poetic. I like that."

"I learned much from him as a child. You see, Eldars are very religious folk. Mother taught me to believe; in Xihe, in the power of life, and in our traditions. Every waking moment the elves are taught to venerate as if it were the breath of life itself. The sun is divine, the animals are creatures of divinity, and that we are the divine children, descendants of the Goddess. Philosophy is surprisingly limited on our world. Therefore, father taught me to think. Think of things no elf will ever think. Morality, the concept of social law, the family and the government, the gods- well his gods really, but gods all the same."

They approached a stall at the end of a street. A bright-eyed elf sat behind it, she was unloading her newly made foods atop. "Master halfling, I'm feeling rather peckish. Do you care for a fresh bread?"

"Oh no, I've had my breakfast."

"Very well." They arrived at the stall and Zhíyú Zhe addressed the maiden. "Ni hao. Qing, a Miànbao."

"Qing, gatoa geijīn." She then produced a brown coin purse of hessian, and the Elfinqueen paid the seller five gold coins from it. "Xièxiè." The elf handed her a soft bun.

"Xièxiè." She continued her walk, and Ceannte followed. She took a bite from the warm doughy thing, and the taste of a lightly seasoned, crusty bread caused a slight gasp of delight.

"That seems so strange," the halfling finally replied. "Yet, I'm not really that surprised, now that I think about it. It explains a lot. 'Ere! I can recall one time I overheard a couple of merchant elves in a pub. They were banging on about darks and how they make their skin crawl just looking at them. They called 'em freaks and the walking dead and the like. They turned me off me beer. I had crossed words with 'em. I didn't like their slander."

"What happened?" She asked in between bites.

"I got myself into a right brawl with them. Ended up with quite a few stitches in me head and all sorts of bruises."

"Your head? You suffered blows to the head?" He nodded. "I imagine these were…roughly twice your size. And quite possibly four times your stature. How on Mundus did you manage to survive?"

He laughed at her horror. "I haven't got a clue, but it sure felt like death after a day. Went to the infirmary and everything."

She watched him recount his battle. He laughed and smiled and poked fun at himself and the assailants. *How does someone just decide to enter into a deadly fight without a care to themselves?* "I'm curious master halfling, why-."

"Please," he interrupted her. "My friends call me Cean ma'am."

"Alright. Mister Cean, why would you beset against someone with much more strength than you? Why gamble your life over a quarrel?"

"Bah!" He swung his hand about. "I couldn't care less about the fiend. He could be a common urchin, or the Great Khan himself for all I could notice. It's the word ma'am. It's some free-floating insult that really upsets me, something uncontested and corrupt to the soul." The halfling paused for a moment. Memories of the past began to flood his mind. Visions of playground hijinks with boys and girls of all sorts. Large boys kicked about, round kids milled upon the grass, fast children played games and races. Then he sighed. "I've had to deal with a lot of bullying as a kid, some real nasty stuff." She noticed he was handling his fists, rubbing the knuckles of his worn hands. "Got into my fair share of fights as well. It was different back then. It was all about being a fisherman's son. I used to get beat up quite a bit, so I had to get a thicker skin. But not before my Pa knocked some sense into the headmaster."

"Your father assaulted the headmaster?"

"Oh on, I don't mean that. I mean he went there and gave him a lecture about it. He was right upset I got such attention. I was singled out as the poor kid. All the other lads were from the rich folk, traders and lords. Things died down after that, but really the damage was done. After school I took an interest in the history of the wider world. I learned about the Reformation Wars, the delicate balance of the Treaty of the Bhoot, the Accident at the Desert and the orcs, the Race Against Peace. I learned about every one of the petty nonsense reasons races wanted to annihilate each other, and all I can think is just 'why'? Why can't people just be better to each other? Is it really that hard to just listen to others and not act so insensitively? It really makes me upset when I see a random moron blurt out freak or hobgoblin or some other insult. So nah, every time I hear any snide word, I'd always go back to my former self. That fragile ten-year-old. Getting beat up for no damn reason, some callus fool who thinks he's better than someone. But this time I'd fight back, I'd give 'em what for and not be afraid. Because I don't want any more of that, some bloke forcing hate into the people around them, just like it was beaten into me."

By Xihe! It suddenly occurred to the Elfinqueen, her eyes grew wide at the thought. *That's what I felt! This is no rightness, but a righteousness blinded by fury. A volatile danger if left unchecked.* "I see." They carried on in silence for a time. Ceannte simply followed her absent of mind. Zhíyú Zhe however thought deeply about this creature, the troubled man permanently destabilised. As they entered an open street, and she knew it was clear of traffic, she took the time to look to her halfling companion and stare. *His mind is both simple and intricate. He values kinsmanship and unity with friendly banter, all the just things in life, yet would strike and a moment's notice at insurrection, and feel not so much as a second thought of such action. He holds dear the warm hearth of friendship and destroys that which does not pay him the same kindness. This man is fire. A smouldering warmth of the one hand, and a consuming fury of the other. He will turn as soon as a threat presents itself. And he tells of a damaged past. A child trapped inside a man, acting before thinking. Reacting before knowing.*

"You alright there?" He asked.

The question snapped her out of the realisation. "Oh yes. I'm fine. Thank you." Again, a silence appeared, but then. "Master Cean, are you certain you want to complete this quest?"

"Aye?" Her question distracted him. "What do you mean?"

"It is not one to be entered into lightly, nor taken by unprepared folk. It is something, I suspect, that is well beyond your scope of vision. Perhaps even your understanding. I cannot know. But I am not sure if you appreciate this."

He watched her present her concern. He noticed something about her that only now occurred to him. The great leaders at the Council of the Earth all have their personalities amongst each other. The confident woodland Emperor, the wise manly Kings, the vain Khan of the wasteland, the shrewd Dogess of his own kind. What was present then, as was present now, was a clear honesty. The giantess' eyes were clear and shining in the light. Her brows bent themselves and framed a sense of worry. Her head subtly wrinkled under her hazelnut hairs. He felt that there laid an active mind, one that learns and thinks and understands a great deal. And her speech was transparent. Nothing then and nothing now was distorted into another foreign meaning. She was him. She spoke exactly what was on her mind, only manner separates them. She seemed much to proper and gentile to stoop to his crass nature. At this time, he knew she was worried for him. "Truth be told ma'am, not really." He finally responded. "I have better things to do than chase after the past. God knows I've read plenty of that by now. But see, I reckon that for all the buggery and strife the past caused, it's always necessary to get past it, if you'll forgive the wordplay. I don't believe in the whole 'sticking to tradition' idea and really placing the past on a high pedestal. Especially before Beacon. It's good to know about history, sure, but it's too dark a force on people. It gives people an excuse to hate on others because they look weird or think different."

"Master Cean," she interjected his thought. "I fear you are confusing the bias of others with your own bigotry."

"What?!" He reacted immediately.

"Your observation of history is certainly an interesting one, however, history is not entirely warfare. Indeed, violence has shaped the minds of folk, but it is not the only thing history is. People are made by many things, the people about them, the world they live in, the forces that act upon them. History is more than the battles fought, the blood spilt, and the fallen victims."

"I don't disagree with that, but what has a more lasting effect on people? I argue that war is the great mover. The force of evil that curses all things to live in pain, torture or suffering, or if none of those things, not at all."

"That is not wholly true." They found themselves entering a public space, an outdoor area with many decorated things. Ceannte recognised it when they arrived. They reached the cultural space, and the Elfinqueen seemed to carry on through it. A circular pool sat in the centre. A quaint, ornate piece of stone carved with much detail and care, brimmed with water. Around the pool they passed many sculptures and buildings. Historic people, creatures of beauty, abstract things, works of chiselled and polished stone, set to a background of marbles and golds, shaped delightfully into pleasant appearances. Galleries enclosed the space; the entire square reflected a pristine radiance all about it. One beautiful thing beside another. As he walked about it, he felt the square was casting visions of inspiration and delight upon him. Zhíyú Zhe continued her argument. "Consider this promenade. An entire place dedicated to the visual arts. A collection of Mundus' gifted artisans and painters. Their vision is in many respects the vision of us all."

"I doubt that." He scoffed. "Most maybe, but not all. Some are just too stupid to get it."

"Perhaps." She led him to one statue. It was itself visually striking. It appeared to be a young elven woman with arms shortly outstretched, as if to embrace a loved one sorely missed. She loomed over, looked down to them and smiled subtly. The statue was entirely golden save for the crown upon her head, which seemed to be fashioned from pieces of Life Mana. The glowing yellowness of the crystal shone upon the metal and gave the installation a curious aura. "What say you of this one?"

In the presence of Zhíyú Zhe, the statue seemed even more imposing to him. A giantess' giantess. Its beauty was there, but it towered over his head. "Xihe herself."

"Indeed. Allmother herself."

"I feel quite…threatened, yet safe near her."

"Threatened?" She turned to him. "Why threatened?"

"Well, she's at least twelve foot tall. I've never seen any statue or anyone at all that big. But looking at her, I do feel a bit calmer. More content I suppose."

"The statue has that affect on its audience."

"But she's so big though. She's like a terror almost, a great big inescapable force. Like she's something you cannot free yourself from."

The Elfinqueen took note of the halfling's demeanour. A slight dimple near the corner of the mouth, a lowered brow and wrinkled head. A quiet concern surfaced upon his face, a defence to an imagined threat. She looked back at the statue and taking his view into her own she saw the subtle difference. The glow now seemed a little unsettling, the statue's pleasant face appeared to glint a menacing glare. Her eyes were focused, not relaxed. Her mouth smirked, not smiled. Her open arms invited a trap, not friendship. In that moment Xihe was not the protector of life, but a harbinger of something sinister, unseen. Eventually Zhíyú Zhe blinked and undid the harsh vision in her mind, she restored the image of the solemn Sun Goddess. "I can see how that may be the case," she replied. "However, try as I might, I will never truly appreciate your vision Master Cean. It is too far removed from my own." She turned back to him. "That being the case, do you think the theme of war is present in this work?"

"War? Certainly not, no. But I can see the idea of Xihe as a symbol for war."

"The idea? A symbol of war? I don't follow."

"It's quite simple really. Any religious thing is a good enough symbol to incite violence. Xihe is a Goddess of Life, right?" She nodded in reply. "Okay. So, you find a clan or a nation or a group of people that is the complete opposite of what Xihe represents. Someone that does not represent life, culturally or physically. Some sort of bad interaction happens, some crossed words or a bad transaction or a careless imposition. Something that can make clear that people are different, sometimes for the worse. People talk, get annoyed by these things, and start to draw divisions between themselves and others, sometimes within their own clan. Hateful crowds make these divisions known. They don't simply tell others; they proclaim that the evildoers are not at all like them. They make their *anger* known. Anger that's attached to small interactions that probably mildly upset one random person. But that fact doesn't matter anymore. It's a much bigger thing now. Now the others must be excluded for their difference – the colour of their skin, the way they govern, the things they value, whatever it is – either socially restricted, or as is the way of history, physically killed. The angry mob might organise into some sort of group, something that they think represents the clan, which may or may not be true. They would use a symbol to represent themselves as a standard." He gestured out to the statue. "In this case, Xihe could be the shining light, the protector of the good and fair. The bane of all else that dares encroach the good people with its darkness. And *that's* how you can make her a symbol of war, as the idea of the good overcoming the evil."

"I understand the point you're making, and I do agree with it. However, I must protest." The Elfinqueen also implied the statue with her movement. "You're conflating notions that are outside the scope of this piece. Yes, everything you say is correct, but what does any of this have to do with this statue? What is the hatefulness here? Where is the symbol of evil?" Ceannte prepared for a reply, yet the moment he opened his mouth he stopped himself and turned back to the object. He quickly scanned the golden figure. There was no suit of armour, nor great sword. No grovelling subjects following her. She was not stood above anyone besides themselves, nor was she posed into a position of domination. Her face was not as menacing as he first noticed, she seemed content with him. Satisfied with his reaction, Zhíyú Zhe continued. "This is why I believe you are governed by your own hate. You claim to be above it, and I feel that you certainly can be, but you are yourself just as fallible by the very thing you revile. You attribute other meanings into things that exist elsewhere, and I suspect you may be overly sensitive to such things. Young master," he felt the large palm of the Elfinqueen rest upon him, and he turned to face her charming manner. She had knelt slightly, enough to reach his shoulder. "Yesterday, I found you quite intriguing. I wondered about your character and concern, what it was that made you so threatened. Our chance meeting has been most illuminating. I understand you better than before." She stood again, now more assured of the halfling.

"I guess I can see your point ma'am," he eventually responded, "but I'm still unconvinced. I'll concede that I have some growing up to do still however, a few pleasant conversations won't undo the years of racial hatred."

"Such things rarely do unfortunately." She produced a timepiece from her dress and remarked. "I'm afraid I must leave you here Master Cean. I must away and return to my home, as I suspect you must as well. Is that so?"

"Yep. I'll be sailing out today."

"Very well then. I should leave you to your travels. But before I do, promise me one thing."

"Oh? What exactly?"

"When you do reach the North, please come and visit me there. I would like to see your progress."

"Oh, I reckon you'll be seeing more of me ma'am. I wouldn't worry about that."

She laughed at his remark and waved to him. "I'm glad. Fare well young halfling. May Xihe bless you."

"Hooroo!" He waved back as she turned about and left the square. He watched the great figure slowly shrink into the distance and turn a corner, out of view. He stood there, contemplating his interaction. *I'm no bloody bigot*, he told himself, *I've seen enough of it myself to know not to go round insultin' anyone. Sure, I get into a fight here and there, but I don't look for trouble.* He then turned to the great statue once again. The gold sentry remained as unhindered as she appeared last to him. The statue was just as open and inviting as she was with the Elfinqueen about him. *Why did I think about all that? Even I'm having trouble finding that malevolence again. If anything, she looks as if she's seen a friend.* He was lost in the shining detail of the metal. The strangely flowing garment, the delicate petals and leaves about her ankles, and the stray strands of golden hair lifted by a breeze unfelt. Despite its great size, Ceannte felt a new calm flow through him, the effigy's glow was much more pleasant than earlier. *I don't see a lot of good art a lot, but I really enjoy this one. I don't know why but watching her makes me feel good. She looks calm. Peaceful even.* He smiled. *I reckon I'll be alright.* He also grabbed his timepiece and checked the time. *Ah, bugger. I better get going myself.* He looked back up to Xihe's face. He took one last moment to imprint her image into his memory, the calm contentment and pure happiness. An unfamiliar feeling he wanted to maintain. He sighed and, satisfied with his newfound delight and his experiences of Beacon, turned to leave the square. As he left, he noticed the artist space slowly filled with visitors and the creative residence of the surrounding galleries. The Goddess' smile found its way onto the halfling's face. The city left a lasting impression on him. The sudden warmth of the people, the honest wisdom of the elf maidens, the grandeur of the Council of the Earth, and the novel beauty of its buildings. Ceannte was leaving the city better than when her arrived.

Chapter 11

Two days passed since Ceannte arrived at Beacon, and two days hence he travelled down the great river. The sloop anchored upon the dock, and he returned to the Dogedom. As soon as he disembarked, he was met by two armoured men. They were mariners, protectors the river's ports. "Afternoon sir."

"Hello gents."

"We're part of the Merchant Queen's force charged with the security of the river. We will not disturb you greatly however, we have heard rumours of a possible racket in the piracy business. Would you care to answer some questions and let us examine your possessions?"

Piracy? Here? "Aye, sure." He dwelled on the idea. *Aren't all the pirates dead? I haven't heard of any piracy ever.*

"Thank you, sir. Súile." Mariner Súile approached him on Ualach. The second man began. "Alright sir. Where have you departed from?"

"Beacon." Ceannte unclipped and handed him the baggage.

"What was the business of your vacation?"

"I was required to address the Council of the Earth. I've been called to complete a quest."

"Ah! A Hero then." The mariner remarked. "Should I assume you are crossing through to Bunaitheach to Dogess Uisce?"

"Yes sir."

"Alright."

"All is well, Sir Cluas." Súile began rearranging Ceannte's belongings into the bags. "A few books, clothing, food, dollar-pounds, no contraband. Nothing of particular note."

"Excellent." Cluas said. "All seems to be in order so far. Mariner Súile will replace your baggage onto your pony. Now, have you travelled to Midgard or the Western Sea at all?"

"Never." He shook his head.

"Have you ever made any dealings with pirates, privateers or criminals in general?"

"No."

"Do you know anyone who is a pirate, privateer or criminal?"

"No one."

"Alright then. Lastly, do you have anything concealed on your person?"

Ceannte lifted his jacket. "I have some gold and a contract for my quest. Do you need to see that?"

"Aye, we do." He took the document and handed it to the guardsmen. Cluas read it hastily. "A hundred thousand gold? That's mighty expensive."

"Oh, I know. It's a rather important quest."

"It better be for that price." He folded the parchment and passed it back to Ceannte. "Well, everything is fine, mister Macántacht. Thank you for your cooperation."

"If you don't mind my asking, what exactly is happening here? What's with the piracy?"

"We can't disclose too much information," Cluas answered, "all we can say now is that we are aware of rumours of a black market somewhere in the city. The Dogess has since declared a search to be placed on all cargo and persons coming in and out of the docklands."

"That's fair enough. I won't trouble you." Ceannte waved off the guards and began to leave. "Hooroo."

"Enjoy your stay, Hero." They looked on as he left them on the docklands. They fixed their gaze on him until he was out of sight. Súile turned to the other mariner. "He's the man she's looking for."

"Indeed. I found his manner quite casual as well. Very open and amenable."

"Why do you think she didn't want us to arrest him?"

Cluas folded his arms. "Well, my best guess is that she wants to trap him up there rather than here. I imagine it would look quite silly for us to bind a seemingly innocent man here for all the public to see. Without any evidence or contraband, we would have certainly appeared foolish. She warned of the lack of evidence and advised us to let him pass unimpeded."

"Still though, to let a pirate in one of the richest cities in all Mundus is quite a risk."

"Indeed, I told her the very same. She says she is aware of the risks." He turned to his subordinate. "Mariner Súile, make haste to the palace. Inform the Dogess her pirate has arrived."

"Aye sir." Súile immediately left him and followed Ceannte's path out of the port.

∗ ∗ ∗

He landed on the port of Cnoc Gorm, the great trading hub. 'The Doge's Vault' as some call it. Cnoc Gorm was the richest city in the halfling nation. It was nothing like home, the city was full of grey. He became bothered by the lack of nature. *It's stone and wood, it's all just stone and wood. There's no nature in this place. I mean, I like the cobble road and all but at least there's trees and a few parks at home. There's so little homeowning here. I love passing by all the gardens, the bright colours of the rainbow blossoming. Purples and blues and yellows, colours you don't see a lot down here.* Above the crowded buildings Ceannte saw the strange horizon. *Even the damn hills are stone! Grey hills! That's just not right. This whole city is unnatural. No trees, no grass, no flowers. Beacon was alright though. It was full of stone sure, but there were parks and gardens and colour. It wasn't bland. Even the people were different. But nah, there's no colour here. It's nothing but grey and wood and cold. Just one big bland city of stone.* He was not bothered for long, he and Ualach were passing through the port town to get to the capital. He had never travelled so far northeast to visit Bunaitheach. In truth he never left home much at all before, and it was never far from the outskirts of Béal na Habhann.

He clopped over the roads and through the crowds of gentlemen and dames. *Gees*, he kept to himself, *look at all these people. There isn't an honest bloke for miles. They're all in their fancy dress and big bloody hats.* Cotton attire, ornate jewellery, top hats of all things, his attention was constantly taken. The halflings and the humans all looked posh and wealthy, not the sort of people he was used to. Crowds of elegance and fashion splashed about him and his horse. He made it over the first hill, and he noticed the rows thinning out. *Ah! Good. The riff raff is clearing off the road. Mind you though*, he looked about what he could of the city. *I can't see the frontier at all. This place seems to go on and on forever. I have no idea where it ends, it all looks the same.* After an hour of patient trotting, the stony greyness gave way to the familiar colours he saw of his home. He saw the farmlands. Fields of wheat and produce sat atop the familiar image, perfect hills of green. "Well this is different now," he muttered to himself. "Aye, Ualach, I bet you've never seen these before, aye?" He rubbed his neck and the beast neighed softly. Shades of green and gold and purple and white, all the colours sprang out of the hills in patches. Ceannte encouraged the colt and they stayed on the road, but was totally distracted by the unique nature around him. As he passed by, he could name many of the plants. Barley, wheat, hops, sugarsprout, shamrock weed, bloated pumpkin; he counted off each crop he could as he passed by them.

The flowers were especially beautiful. Scarlet tulips, marigolds, Nimue's eyes, nightshade, bluebottle brushes, velvet roses, opalescent wattle. Some were completely new to him, rare colours of brown and even mildly translucent flowers captivated him. He entered a sea of colour and perfume, a wash of sight and smell. The stuff of dreams and enchantment, moving colours and sweet smells of glad memories.

The sky turned bright red above them. The sun was setting in the east the light cast a golden hue onto the clouds. Ceannte was close to the edge of Bunaitheach, the fields were gone, and the land levelled into a plateau. He passed by shanties that sat about the city's frontier and saw the capital in the distance. The sun's halo shone over the city and the mound it sat upon, Bunaitheach was awash in golden splendour. As the pony carried on towards the city the halfling turned to the sun, and with one hand shielding it he determined the time. The blight yellow disc edged closer to the horizon. *Just about sundown*, he observed. He turned back and leant down to his horse's ear. "Mate, I don't want to be here when the sun's down. Can we pick up the pace a bit?" Ualach grunted a response. "Hyah!" He clapped his legs onto the horse and Ualach galloped faster. They stormed up the rise and reached the city walls just as the sun sank. Shadows stretched over the city as he arrived at the gates. The guards took one look at him and without query the doors parted to reveal Bunaitheach, the great jewel of the Doge.

Inside the city was an amazing spectacle. Buntings and lanterns zig-zagged over the streets, polished sidewalks and roads built out of carved stone blocks, quaint buildings and establishments, a decent crowd of halflings – not empty, but not overcrowded. It was the image of a city Ceannte expected, not the vast mass at the harbour side. Beautiful, tasteful in fact. Understated yet distinguished. He wondered the streets looking for somewhere to retire. There were plenty of inns to bunk but he was running low on cash. *Have I got the time for the Dogess?* He checked his timepiece. *Nah. It's too late for that. Plus, I reckon Ualach is getting a bit hungry. Actually, so am I.* Randomly the pony shook his head and whinnied. *Huh, I guess he's tired too*, he added. He made his way to a board some way into the city. He reached the stable and dismounted, gave the reins to the stableboy, and entered the building. He had just enough for a night's lodging and a couple of beers.

* * *

The next day he arose from bed. He found the accommodation so like his own home that he decided to forgo breakfast and catch it himself. Ceannte eventually remembered where he was. He exited out of the board and reclaimed his pony. "Boy, where exactly can I find the Dogess here?" He asked.

"Mate, you're looking for the Teachóir. Just keep riding to the centre of the city. You can't miss it."

"Righto." He gave the stableboy a few dollar pounds for his trouble. "Thanks for the tip mate." He and his pony left for the palace. The stableboy hollered something back, but he paid no attention. He passed by more crowds of chattering maids or debating gentlemen.

Amongst the hubbub Ceannte found a familiar sound. "Mister Macántacht?"

He looked about to find the voice. He found a man waving at him. "You!" The man shuffled through the people. "You're the bloke from Beacon. With the dwarves at the inn."

"Quite so." Comhbhrón shook his hand. "I'm glad you've arrived. There is much news since our last meeting. Are you due anywhere soon?"

"Uh, not really, no. I am heading to the Teachóir, but that can wait. What's happened?"

"Well, I fear it is too dangerous to discuss such a matter here. I can take you to a less public street."

He raised his eyebrow. "Sounds rather serious. If you feel it's necessary, then sure."

"I shall lead the way for you." The businessman cut across the stream of halflings, he made way for Ceannte. "In the meantime, I don't think we have properly met. I am Comhbhrón Soiléire. I deal in the trade of luxury items about the continent."

"Aha. Like what exactly?"

"Furnishings for the home. Candelabras, polished tables, satin sheets. All the refined things of a stately house."

"I see." He paid little attention.

The merchant directed him into quieter, less active streets until eventually they turned a corner into a rather dim road surrounded by stone buildings. "Ah This will do quite nicely." They halted in the middle. "Now, mister Macántacht, I have some news about the Dogess that you will interest you a great deal."

"Alright. What's happened?"

"I have been inquiring with my friends and advisors to the Dogess. It would appear that Dogess Uisce has been making a habit of upending contractual obligations. At first, I thought she merely stymied financial ventures however, I discovered she also stopped major investments into other companies. For whatever reason, Uisce is hording her gold and granting small payments while withholding against larger sums."

Ceannte raised his eyebrow. "What do you mean by *other companies?*"

"Well, beyond financial investments, which I will add is suspicious on its own, she has denied the commission of new structures, scientific advancements, levying the armies, and constructing new trade ships."

"Gees, all that?"

Comhbhrón nodded. "She isn't even considering short term investments into markets with a known potential to return wealth. Windfalls are being passed up here. I raised the issue with her when she returned yesterday. She gave me no reason for her frugality. Only unsatisfying excuses. She kept raving about keeping the coffers full of gold." He sighed. "I'd dare say she's obsessed with it.

"I can see that," Ceannte nodded, "but why though? Why go to such lengths?"

"I haven't a clue. It makes no more sense to me than it does to you."

He rubbed his chin. *So, she doesn't want to spend a lot of gold. A few ideas spring to mind here; the obvious one is she's hoarding the money for herself, or maybe a big purchase in the future. She might have a similar attitude to traders as she had back home with Óir, just distrusting everyone, and the fact that no one's trading is a consequence. Oh! The piracy rumour is another thing to consider. Maybe she's shutting down business to flush out the naive. It's a unique idea, but I reckon it is worth doing to undo a criminal.*

"You seem to be deep in thought." Comhbhrón said.

"Aye, I am. I've been reckoning her motivation. There's a lot I'm trying to understand here. The Dogess hoarding gold, and also this piracy business. Do you know about it?"

"Ah, I am aware of the rumours. The word around town tells an agent of the Sea Wretch may be operating somewhere in Cnoc Gorm. Nobody knows where exactly or how."

"I'm sorry, the *Sea Wretch?*"

"Aldora. The last pirate. It appears that she is the only one left in the Western Sea, probably plundering ships and raiding towns."

Ceannte widened his eyes. "Wait, so there *is* a pirate around?"

"It would appear so. I don't think there's ever been piracy this far south." Ceannte scratched his head. "Mister Macántacht, I would advise caution with dealing with the Dogess. Given all of this news and intrigue, I would expect neither any friendliness nor ease when negotiating with her. In my dealings with the Dogess, I can tell you she is a shrewd businesswoman with an interest in only her own profit. She never accepts a deal that leaves her with less. Therefore, you must be prepared to give something she desires in order to transact with her. However, I can no longer guarantee success in your venture anymore."

"I appreciate the advice, however, I am not proposing a deal. I'm fulfilling a quest that she must pay."

"A quest you say?" Comhbhrón held his chin. "That may be a concern, however, a quest is significantly more important than a transaction. Do you still have the contract upon you?"

"Indeed, I do."

"Then you are protected. Contracts of such a nature are upheld with the utmost confidence. That contract will secure your wealth." The merchant patted Ualach. "Mister Macántacht, I wish you luck with your quest, whatever it be. However, the times are changing, and I fear they are not changing towards betterment. Uncertainty is a powerful force. Be prepared for the unexpected and the unusual." Comhbhrón waved at him. "Good day, mister Macántacht,"

"Goodbye." They parted ways, and Ceannte carried on to the Teachóir.

Soon he saw something in the distance, between the people and the shops was a light. It was right where he needed to go. He carried on, and slowly the light changed. It was more of a shine, like a light reflecting off something. "What is that?" He muttered to himself. Ceannte advanced further. He reached the last row of stores when he saw it. Before him, a circular building of white adorned with windows. The roof shined, a hemisphere of pure gold. On the grounds outside, the garrison patrolled. "I bet that's the palace mate."

They rode right up to the entrance of the palace gardens until the guard halted them. "'Scuse me." Ualach stopped right in front of him. "Who are you and what business do you have with the Dogess?"

"The Dogess is expecting me, I have a contract she needs to fulfil. I am-," he took a moment think. *"I'm Ceannte Macántacht, Hero of the West."* He proclaimed himself with all the grandeur he could muster.

The guard scoffed. "Bugger off! We get that all the bloody time."

"Oi! I mean it!" He opened his coat and pulled out a bit of folded parchment. "My contract." The guard made his way to Ualach's side and grabbed the document. He unfolded it and read its contents, mouthing the words as he looked over it.

As he read, the guard's face turned to worry. A sudden tension fell. "Just, uh-." He hastily and quietly fumbled about his suit. "Just a moment." He took out an object from a satchel hidden under his armour, a glass lens. The guard read the document a second time, the lens held up to his eye.

Now that's interesting, Ceannte thought, *the other soldiers didn't use a glass to read the contract. The writing isn't that hard to read. Why did he do that?*

He started to nod and returned the parchment to Ceannte. "Where exactly did you get *Hero of the West* from?"

"Uh, I kinda made it up on the spot." He let slip a cheeky grin.

He shook his head. "Yeah, don't do that. It makes you look like an idiot. I'll escort you into the palace"

"Thanks mate." They continued forward, Ceannte followed the guard inside the grounds. He saw a wondrous sight. The palace was surrounded by a moat, a lush garden of shrubs and verdant flowerbeds. More guards circled the building itself, but they were more accommodating. He dismounted by the steps of the Teachóir and guards relieved him of Ualach. "You mind caring for him please?"

"Of course, sir." He handed them the reins and they all walked off. He turned back to the guard by the stairs, and they both walked its lengthy slope. The guard opened the great door and ushered him in.

While the outside of the Teachóir was wondrous, the interior was audacious. The great hall was enormous, three granite tables, the length of the space, stretched all the way to the throne, flanked by delicate wooden chairs. The width between the chairs of each table was wide enough to fit a troop of Sheriffs. *Crikey! Óir was right,* he thought, *this place is massive! Just how big is this place? These gaps are so big. Maybe those spaces are made for the Sheriffs. Regiments lined up in the hall.*

"Who enters?" A familiar voice echoed from deep within.

The guard boomed. "The Hero, Ceannte Macántacht, has arrived to obtain his payment."

"Excellent. Send him in."

"Yes ma'am." They started the long walk along the hall.

"You know I was quite surprised to see you so late. I expected you to arrive the moment I made it back and demand my wealth." Despite the echoes of the great space he detected a tone, the slight sound of aggravation.

"Oh well. You know what they say, better late than never." He still had a way to go, but the image of the Dogess finally formed in the distance. Uisce stood on a stage of sandstone. The flames of the torches flickered upon her auburn hair, the light illuminated her powdered yellow dress and reflected a striking golden gleam of her breastplate.

"Better *never* than ever, I say."

"I'm sorry?" He asked. Finally, he reached her. *Gees! Up there she looks like she can loom over everyone.*

She walked towards them. "Capall, you have reviewed this man?

"Aye, I have." The guard addresses her. "He possesses a contract that bares a claim upon the treasury."

She turned to him. "What did you say?"

"Mister Ceannte has a legitimate claim of payment, one that some scoundrel has attempted to deny him by trickery."

"What?" Ceannte said. He extracted the document and read it once again.

Uisce's hands clinched. "What do you think you're doing Capall?"

"This is an outrage!" He found the name of the Dogess Uisce missing. He read, reread, and read it again, looking for some reason why it disappeared.

"This has gone on long enough, Uisce." Capall replies. "It's one thing to shortchange lords and men of wealth. I couldn't care less about the intrigue of the rich folk. But I cannot let stand the same tomfoolery to a Hero. This is a clear violation of the Cooperation Agreement."

The Dogess reacted in disgust. She twitched and barked back. "Oh, spare me that nonsense, Capall. My name is not on that contract. I am not paying that man a penny."

"Are you serious?" Capall asked. "Are you really going to gamble war with the Heroes over a petty dispute?"

"I saw you." Ceannte said. "I *saw you* at Beacon. I *saw you* write your name," he pointed to the vacant space, "here. I *saw* that name as soon as it was given to me. I saw it a second time when I retired to my board. And then a third time travelling back home. I. *Saw!* It. I know exactly what I saw, and I know that I don't have to prove anything, because I *saw you* signing this."

"Oh piss off, you country bumpkin." The words cut deep in Ceannte. The memories of youth bleed into his mind. The sharp taunts. The childish fights. The fragile emotions. "What kind of a Hero are you? You're a rank fisherman with a foul mouth and an ill temper. Heroes are noblemen, highborn into the service of the king and queen. What do you know of nobility?"

His anger turned into sadness. *She's right. What am I doing here? I'm no adventurer. I don't fight monsters, save people, travel to far away lands. I'm a nothing. Nobody important. No one worth anything.*

"Heroes are mercenaries," Capall interjected, "we aren't nobles, we're fighters. Hired swords and spears. We go where the gold goes. We stay in a city that welcomes us with open arms. If we aren't wanted, we leave. Simple as that. We do jobs, and we get paid. We keep you happy, you keep us happy. It is a mutual agreement."

"I am subject to no one!" The Dogess spoke slowly, with anger.

"You are not a subject." The Hero raised his voice. "You are an equal. A partner, whose interest is to maintain the peace. Do you not wish for a time of prosperity in peace?"

"Why should I wish for something I already have? We are at peace, and we are prosperous. I have other sources of protection about me. I will not jeopardise my wealth for any reason. Not to you. Not to this urchin. Not to anyone. My wealth is my own."

Capall fell silent. He considered her words, and his response. "What other possible protection is there against the evils of this world? What force can sabotage militias, entrap criminals, gather information, suppress dangerous creatures, with the same effect as the Order of Heroes?" He paces around Ceannte. "The Templar Knights perhaps, but they do not serve the monarch. They preserve the peace with selfless piety. A total belief in maintaining divine virtue. Fighting for peace when evil attacks, with no regard for wealth or politics.

They are our contemporaries in battle, and our rivals in principle. Therefore, I know for a fact the Templars are not your protection. Templars do not serve leaders. They are the holy champions of Mundus. Who then can protect the Dogedom?"

She pointed at them. "I have my sources. I don't need you, or the Heroes."

"Well that's fine. We will leave you with your wealth and your peace." Capall gestured to him. "But you are still charged with paying recompense to this man. Your trickery cannot stand here. You are risking peace and prosperity over a petty dispute."

"Aye!" Ceannte said. "Pay up, will you?"

"For an exorbitant price? For a seeker quest? For a past I have no responsibility to? Nonsense! Ridiculous! Begone from this place!"

"We aren't going anywhere!" Ceannte barked.

"Bugger it!" Capall turned about. "Let's just go. She won't change her mind." He encouraged Ceannte to go with him.

"But what about my gold?"

They walked briskly down the great hall. "We'll get your gold, don't worry about that."

"I'd be very careful if I were you." The Dogess said. "I had planned to arrest you here for piracy," they stopped and turned back to her, "but it would seem that my guardsman has forced my scheme to take a different turn."

Capall sighed. "Let's go."

"Pay heed, Capall. You leave with that man, and you will be treated no differently."

"Who do you think you're talking to?" He pointed his thumb to himself. "I'm Capall Beag. Champion Pony Rider, and a general of the Dogess' guard. I trained under the legendary jouster Impéar. I can handle anything you throw at me." She said nothing, his defiance surprised her. "We'll be off now, but we'll be back, and Hero Ceannte will get his dues. It is the least he deserves."

"The least he deserves is the knowledge of the person who commits him to a life of suffering and destitution." Capall sighed and continued to the great door of the hall. He pushed open the doors, they swung with force and clatter, and they both left the palace. The Dogess looked about the hall for the remaining guards. "That man is a felon and a pirate. He is never to be trusted, and must not return here under any circumstances, under pain of death. Should anyone aid him, the penalties of the law will fall upon your head just as it has to him." Uisce secured herself with one final thought. *No one challenges my authority. No one.*

* * *

The doors flung open, and the two halflings left the Teachóir in a fog of anger and frustration. Capall huffed and grunted. Ceannte was confused and irritated. The Hero sighed. "Well, that went well." He turned to Ceannte. "I'm sorry about that mate. She had always done this to big businesses and whatnot, basically anyone that asks for huge sums of gold. If her name is not on the document the contract is void, that's the law here. I saw she was trying to pull the wool over your eyes, and I needed to intervene."

"This happens often?" *Wait a minute,* Ceannte's mind worked it out. *Óir had this problem, and so did those blokes back at Beacon. She knocked them back too. She refused them, and me.* "I had no idea she was so corrupt. I mean I figured she'd moan and complain about it, but I didn't realise she'd go to that length."

"Oh mate, I've seen it so much it's nothing to me now. But this is a Hero's Contract."

"So what?" He queried Capall. "What difference does that make?"

"Well, aren't you a Hero?"

"I'm a fisherman. From Béal na Habhann, just down the river."

"A fisherman?!" He was taken aback and sized him up. "You were given a Hero's Contract? *You?*" He suddenly burst into laughter

Ceannte sighed loudly. "You don't have to be that way about it."

"Oh, I'm sorry. That story just sounds so ridiculous."

"It *is* ridiculous! I find a bit of gold in a dead fish that I can't sell, I found out I had to go to Beacon and give it to the Council, I get pegged into a quest I can't even complain about, and now the damn Dogess decides to renege on giving me my pay." He counted off his problems with his hand. "I've got no gold, I'm nowhere near the river to fish, I'm in the most expensive part of the Dogedom, and I just now realised all my stuff is with my pony. I bet he'll be impounded for ransom!"

Capall nodded along to his story. "Well, we're in a bit of a pickle now. She's basically declared a hostility against Heroes now. Business is one thing, but this is too damn far."

"You'll have to forgive me mate," he raised a hand to the Hero, "but why should I care about you? I'm out a hundred thousand gold, without my pony, and no where to go. I've got my own problems right now."

"Actually I reckon I can help you with that. The Eight Arms is not far from here. We can lodge there and plan our next move." Capall descended the steps. "Come with me, I'll take you through what you need to know as a Hero."

Ceannte followed him. "The Eight Arms? Is that a pub or something?"

"Aye, an inn, but a special place. It's a safe house made for the Order of Heroes. Come now. There is much to learn and little time to act."

"What do you mean by *safe house*?" They quickly reached the gardens, and left the palace in search for a place to scheme.

Chapter 12

Somewhere within the capital city, amongst the decorated houses of stone and wood, stood a plain, humble building of little detail. A wooden structure with windows, a door, and little else. Above the door hung a sign. An octagon of wood, with nothing else upon it. A dark, unmarked building designed to blend into its surroundings. A perfect space to hide. Inside the inn were just three residence, Ceannte, Capall, and the innkeeper. The innkeeper tended bar in the background as the other two discussed in a quiet corner. "So, this is a place to go whenever you need to strategise, is it?" Ceannte asked.

"There's more to a safe house than that, but yeah, it's a secure spot for Heroes. Unless something big happens it's usually this quiet. Actually," Capall turned behind, "hey, Seangharda, are we the only ones here?"

"Aye," the innkeeper replied. "It's just you two."

"Righto then." He turned back to Ceannte. "So yeah, this is an inn that protects Heroes whenever we're in a jam. It's much better to be here than in just any old tavern."

He shook his head. "I still can't believe I can just lodge anywhere for free. I had no idea that was possible."

"Aye. It's brilliant, ain't it? One of the perks of being a Hero. It's a bit more complex than that though. Heroes can stay in any lodging for free for a week, or use all the services of an inn freely for a day. It's more of an honour system. We keep the people safe, and the people treat us well during jobs. We present our contracts and declare what we want."

"Sounds like a good deal to me."

"Of course, *you'd* say that." He sighed. "Look, the good news is we can clear up this mess pretty quickly. We'll confront the Dogess when we can. We can't do that at the moment. We'll have to cross into Cnoc Gorm and catch up with a colleague of mine."

"Why," Ceannte moaned. "What can he do to help? And why do we have to go back there? I just came from there."

"Gees you don't stop moaning, do ya?' He sighed and relaxed back into his chair. "Look, it's a small deviation but I promise you, your pay, your horse, your honour, all that's going to be fixed. This isn't a light matter, and we are going to someone…I don't want to say *outside the law,* cause he ain't, but he's certainly not a royal connection. I don't mean to hassle you honestly, I've got better things to do than catch a civilian into this mess, but now this is suddenly more important. You'll have to trust me on this for now mate."

Ceannte stared the Hero, he saw all the frustration and anger he built up over the last week in himself, and the balms of the Chaplain, the Elfinqueen, and now the Hero shielded him from it all. He bowed his head and sighed. "I'm sorry. I know I can be a pain in the arse. It's just so damn annoying what's been happening to me. It's like I'm in some nightmare that keeps getting worse and I can't get out of. I really don't like knowing I have to take a step backwards."

"No one does." The Hero replied. "And I gotta tell ya, that story you told me is pretty incredible. A fish swallows a bit of gold, and suddenly you take on a quest. No one'd believe that without that contract you've got. Frankly, Mister Ceannte, you've had a rotten bit of luck this whole trip. Be sure to tell people about it whenever you can, they will understand in time I think."

A brief silence emerged between them. "You're forgetting the confidentiality clause."

"You don't have to be specific about it. Just say *the quest is most vexing*, or *it concerns me no end!*"

"*Most vexing?* I'm not trying to sound posh."

"No, but you'll be amazed how effective using those words really are. Shall we head off?" Capall stood in anticipation.

"Actually, I have one question I've been meaning to ask. I know the signature was missing because I saw it there when I got the contract. How on Mundus did you know the signature was missing at all?"

"Ah," the Hero again produced the lens, "this thing here. It's no ordinary lens. It's made of pure diamond."

"Okay, so what?"

"Well, diamond has this interesting property. It's the only material that can uncover illusions that magic conceals. You can see the truth through diamond. It's pretty amazing ain't it?"

"I'm not sure I know what you mean." Ceannte scratched his head.

"Pull out your contract, I'll show you." He also stood, grabbed the contract and opened it onto the table. Capall placed the lens upon the space at the bottom. They saw it, a glowing blue shape dazzled through the crystal. The 'Dogess Uisce' shone clearly, as if it were there the whole time. An azure mirage.

"That's amazing!" Ceannte was mesmerised by the magic. "Actually, could this have been used to confront the Dogess?"

"Not really, no. Anyone could just write her name and cast magic onto it. And add to that, she has no idea about the lens. I wasn't going to give up my foresight like that. Nah, this was always the plan. Anyway, we better be off." He took away the lens, and Ceannte removed the contract. "It'll already be late by the time we get there, let's not dwell over trickery." They replaced the chairs into the table and moved towards the innkeeper. "Seangharda, send word to every Hero in the city." Capall leaned over the bar. "The right honourable Dogess Uisce has decided to renege a Hero's Contract, and Hero Ceannte here demands his pay. Rally everyone Hero here. When you see a white tipped spear, send them all to the Teachóir. Either this man'll get his gold, or the Order of Heroes will leave this place and convene an emergency council."

He nodded. "I shall get the courier."

Capall slapped the bar. "Excellent. We'll be off to get some aid. We shan't take long."

"Safe travels Capall." They left the safe house immediately.

A moment later they both emerged from the safe house on top of a pony, Capall led the party, spear in hand and patted the grey beast. "You sure your horse does it mind me back here?" Ceannte asked.

"Nah. Chapaillíní is a tame little thing, she's a friendly filly." They galloped away from the inn and the city. The streets were unhindered by persons.

Day turned to night again. The heroes made their way out of Bunaitheach to the outskirts of Cnoc Gorm. Ceannte again saw the coloured hills, this time they were dulled by the ever-present blackness of night. The reds seemed to be blackened maroons. The blues were deep navy colours. The yellows appeared almost white, while darkened into a vague grey. The only light came from the moon above, and the starlight of the town. Homely and warm. Ceannte yawned and drifted in and out of sleep.

Capall sniggered. "You don't do much traveling, do you?"

He yawned again. "No, never really so much. Beacon is the furthest I've gone."

"You really should get out more. There's a whole wide world out there. It'll take a better stamina to appreciate it all."

"Bugger that." The darkness of the night lulled him. "Give me a warm home and thick walls, and I'll be happy and content."

"Bah. City folk." After some time, they crossed the hills and arrived at a block of houses. The Hero spotted something ahead and roused his guest. "Oi, we're nearly there."

Ceannte looked over his shoulder. "The house over there?"

"Yep." Capall pointed his spear in front at a stone house lit by lights, and the silhouette of a person working inside. "That's the place."

He grunted. "Seems pretty ordinary from here."

"Oh no mate, just wait until we get in." They approached the dwelling and Ceannte saw more its detail. A couple of wooden tables sat beside the door. One was bare save for some writings and a weight, the other was covered by a thick canvas. A gap under the canvas revealed tubes and beakers filled with substances. On the wall behind the tables a board hung over the workstations, but the light was too dark to read it.

Huh, what a mess, Ceannte thought, *lots of stuff left out. Clearly this bloke's a scientist, but do they all do that? That seems strange.* They arrived at the door, and both dismounted.

He leapt down first, and then gave the Hero his hand. "Thanks mate." They landed on the dusty path and strode up to the door. Capall knocked on the door. Ceannte noticed he knocked particularly. He knocked once then paused, knocked four times hastily then paused, and finally knocked once again.

Huh, that's code for something. They waited patiently.

"Ah," they startled the man. "Well this is a surprise." His voice traveled through the stone wall, and the silhouette moved across the window. The door opened and the man greeted them. "Ah! Capall, it is excellent to see you again. Now who is this fine chap?"

"Mister Ceannte, allow me to introduce Doctor Tintreach Thoirní, the premier magician in all Leath Langa." The fisherman's eyes immediately lit up. He knew exactly who this was. "He is our own true-blue hero of academia here."

"Pleasure to meet you lad." Thoirní extended a hand and he shook it vigorously.

"Aye, it is. I've read about you. Your struggle to learn and teach magic here is quite amazing."

"Indeed, I'm glad to see those days end. Do come inside." The Doctor stepped back, and the guests entered his home. Immediately Ceannte noticed something different. *What the? What is that?* Instead of candles, the Doctor used little glass chambers housing some sort of brightly burning metal. He could not help but stare into these. "Careful there, don't stare into the light for long. You might go blind from it." Thoirní warned.

"Wait, that happens?" He turned to the Doctor.

"I guess so. I mean the sun can if you stare into it, and I think the same thing can happen, but no one's game enough to try." He laughed. "Besides, you look strange staring into the light like that."

He laughed with him. "Fair enough." The group made their way to the Doctor's rumpus room, a large space with cushioned chairs enclosed around tables of experiments and notation, and shelves full of scholarly literature. Ceannte glanced past a few of the titles; *Albiogenisis: Origins of the First Summoned Creatures*, *Ingenuity: Humanity's Effect on the Nine Realms*, and *Evolution of the Study of Magic* to name a few. One book caught his eye, *Splitting the Crystal: Theories on the Electrostatic Charge of Manae*. "Doctor, what does it mean, *splitting the crystal*?"

"Aye?" He followed the guest's finger to the book. "Oh my! You've got a keen eye there. Take a seat, gentlemen." They all found a seat to relax and converse. "That book is an interesting read, it's all about hypotheses about Mana crystals and their electric charge. See, most other stuff has an Astrapí Limit of only 40 milliamps before discharging, but Mana can maintain an extremely high electric charge before releasing its energy. Some say it might even be infinite, but that's a load of rubbish, I think. No material can contain an infinite electric charge, it's impossible."

He heard the Doctor carry on about the subject, but Ceannte became visibly confused. His brow furrowed and his mind strained under the dense knowledge. "I'm sorry. I don't know the first thing about any of that." He smiled broadly to hide his shame.

The doctor chuckled. "You're not the first person to say that. Basically, it's about how and why Mana seems to have a lot of electric energy. It seems to baffle a lot of us smart types, and with good reason. It's the only thing we have found in nature to have any kind of electric charge outside of lightning. But I bet you're not here for me to prattle on about alphysical properties."

"Indeed not," Capall said, "we're here on more serious business. It's a bit of a long story, so you better tell him Ceannte."

"Aye, sure." He then retold the story to the Doctor, from the very beginning…

* * *

"Well, Mister Ceannte, that's a mighty fine pickle there," Thoirní proclaimed, "but I have to be honest with you Capall, I'm not entirely sure why you've brought him here."

"It concerns the Dogess," Capall answered, his voice low and soft, "she has foregone a contract with this fellow."

"That's not exactly news," the Doctor retorted. "Uisce's protection of wealth is known amongst the lordship however, this man never mentioned a financial business in his story. What concern is it of mine?"

He signalled Ceannte to produce the contract. He retrieved it and handed it to the Doctor. "His business is that of a heroic nature. Ceannte is protected under the Hero's Law. She has dishonoured the order with her greed."

He examined the parchment itself. "I assume this was where her signature was?" He fingered around the end of the document, the copious space underneath the remainder of the signatories.

"I checked it myself with your diamond lens. She has bewitched the ink into concealment from the naked eye. He may be a fisherman, but he is a declared Hero." Capall took a deep sigh. "This is the first contact broken in several hundred years. Last time that happened, the Order of Heroes sparked a skirmish with Árchontíkó. I hope such an event does not happen here."

Thoirní carefully examined the ink. His lips pursed in thought. "Let me fetch my diamond. I wish to see this myself." He stood up and took the parchment to the one of his decks. He rummaged about the strewn mess until he found the jewel, and he held it to his open eye. Through the crystal the empty space of the document was no longer blank. "There we are." A dim shadow of blue magic shone through in the shape of the Dogess' signature. He addressed Ceannte. "May I say Mister… Macántacht, you truly have a gift of skullduggery to produce such a fee for your services. I would doff my hat to you should I ever wear one. How on this earth did you manage so steep a price?"

He shrugged in response. "I'd love to tell you, but there's this confidentiality thing that stops me. Sorry."

"That's a shame, but also rather a good protection." He set down the diamond and returned the contract to Ceannte. "It's a shame Uisce decided to renege on her deliverance. However, I believe I can shed some light on the matter."

"I was hoping you'd say that," Capall replied. "What do you know?"

"I will furbish our guest with information about our dear Dogess Uisce, but in fact Capall, I have more information that even *you* are not aware of. Gentleman, prepare yourselves of the story of the money hungry Queen of the River.

"Our splendorous Dogess Uisce is a curious character. She imposes her will onto her subjects by encouraging business and wealth, while at the same time, her intense greed and fear of tyranny compel her to adopt corruption. She is a mad-woman, and the best part is, no one saw it coming. She's only been Dogess now for thirteen months after her father had a terrible case of the Shakes and died. She helped make new connections with the more distant races like the high elves, but her biggest win was the dark elf routes. Doge Bain traded through the dwarf land, and them dwarves made a pretty penny with their tariffs. The orcs down south didn't do much good either, so Uisce helped her dad skirt the mountain passes. She built ports along the coast and established direct trade with the elves. Bloody brilliant idea that was! She's clearly a competent saleswoman."

"Bah!" Ceannte scoffed. "I don't reckon she's all that good. What kind of merchant reneges on deals?"

"One that's desperate," Capall interjected. "One that calculates risk and reward on a penny. One that understands the difference between power and honour, and plays moves to strengthen themselves."

"Aye. She's playing a game of survival, everything she does keeps her power." The Hero nodded, but Ceannte did not. His face remained mindful, eyebrow raised and frowned lips. "Anyway, then Bain got his illness and carked it. Eighteen is too young an age to give someone a crown. Anyone! When I was eighteen, I was roughhousing with my mates in school and working out what I wanted to do with myself. She was ordained and quickly enforced her position. She upheld much of her trade routes, but she was also very forward thinking. She can see any kind of financial threat a mile away and shoots it down." He paused for a moment. "I know this is true," and lowered his head, "for I have also suffered from her reactive nature. After I acquired my doctorate, I became a minor celebrity of sorts. I spoke with many businessmen about how one could make money from magic. Doge Bain was my biggest patron however, Uisce wanted none of it. She would always speak harshly and dissuade him from committing to major investments. So, I expected her to be critical of my proposals when she became Dogess. Good grief, she was *horrible!* She ripped apart my papers. She told me never to waste her money again. I fought long and hard to build a centre for alchemical knowledge. She just threw it away like it was nothing at all. That did not stop me though. Soon after, I learned from others that she had been canceling investments elsewhere. They all had one thing in common: a large sum for investment into something that could reduce her power. And for her money *is* power."

Suddenly, the Doctor chuckled. "I guess that should be expected. We halfing folk prize wealth too highly, I think. It's all about the coins in your pocket." Ceannte concentrated on the man's speech, as if it addressed him personally. "But that's not true. Huge pools of wealth don't make you happy, they make you greedy. I get by on a few quid a week and I'm not complaining. I don't think you really *need* more than three or four hundred, but some people chase after the cash cow."

The words had a strange resonance with Ceannte. Memories of his childhood resurfaced once again. Memories of the wealthy boys at school, showing their disposition to the poor child. Memories of the affluent lords and noblemen who pass by him without a care. One image stood out above the rest, Óir. Memories of his good friend returned to him as well. *You know, I reckon Óir is my only good mate. I can't think of any other posh bloke that'll give me a chat and a beer at a pub.* Ceannte smiled at the thought. *Indeed, wealth doesn't buy you happiness, but I reckon wealth isn't as bad as all that. Óir's living proof.*

"Anyway, that was all I could find out about the Dogess, until last month." As he spoke, Thoirní noticed Capall looking about the place. "You better start listening, Capall," the Hero snapped back, "this bit I haven't told you yet. I took a brief detour just beyond the outskirts of the city and spotted a port I didn't know we had. I did not go to it, but I had a *very* good look. It's a shady building, very plain and basic. Unlike any other port in the Dogedom, with a single small pier. There were no roads leading to it, which I found most suspicious. Eventually I heard and saw the crew from a docked ship." He raised his eyebrows swiftly. "It's a pirate ship."

"What?!" They gawked at the discovery.

"Aye, as clear as I see you now, I saw a human ship with a pirate ensign. It was unmistakable, the port is a Pirate's Haven. A safe harbour for privateers and pillagers."

"What's a Pirate's Haven doing so close to the capital?" Ceannte asked.

"What's it doing up the River at all?!" Capall followed.

"If you'll let me finish," the Doctor pointed, "I think I have an idea about that. See, it's one thing to *find* a Pirate's Haven, it's another to *understand* why it's there. I stayed in the distance and espied the place. Now I don't know a lot about seafaring, but even I know that only one pirate still exists, and her reputation precedes her."

"Aldora?" Capall asked. "Is she still operating?"

"Indeed, she is." He nodded. "Aldora the Sea Wretch. The bane of the Admiralty, and the greatest pirate in history. What us halflings don't know is the second half of the Fourth Age was the boom-time for the Age of Piracy. Sometime after the turn of the age a new scoundrel took control of a galleon and began to hunt down every competitor. Slowly but surely, Aldora destroyed all pirates and stole their loot. Her supremacy is unmatched. Some say otherworldly but that's a load of rubbish."

"That's great and all," Ceannte interrupted, "but what exactly does this have to do with the Dogess?"

"I'm getting to that!" Thoirní huffed. "See, she's the only pirate left, and there's no sport in raiding the same cities over and over. She's so quiet right now, I reckon hardly anyone knows she's still out there. Just look at Capall!"

Ceannte nodded and Capall replied. "That'll be right. There's been no chatter of pirates here until very recently."

"Aye, I've noticed that too. I can't help but think she's using some new way to plunder in disguise, although for the life of me I have no idea why. She's too gregarious for that sort of thing. But it is the only reason I can think why the Pirate Haven is there, and why Uisce doesn't want to fund big projects. Maybe Aldora steals the Dogess' wealth, but that's just speculation. We'll need to see for ourselves."

"I see, and how do you suggest we do that then?" Ceannte asked. Capall and Thoirní just stared back at him. "What?"

Chapter 13

A new day shone in a clear blue sky. A rather large ship docked at a single port, surrounded by the quiet of the river. The crew loaded their vessel with barrels of a large mass. Something heavy and plentiful. Beyond the foot of the hills, a broad thicket stood at the crest. Hidden in the underbrush, the three halflings observed the shady business, covered by the slight shade of the canopy. Thoirní scouted the landscape ahead upon his pony. Capall and Ceannte stood behind upon the Hero's steed. "Good news gentlemen," the Doctor said, "the ship is a simple sloop, a normal sized one at that. It's a skeleton crew, so there's only about eight or nine of them down there."

"Why a skeleton crew though?" Ceannte asked

"Most of her fleet is somewhere in the Discovery Archipelago. This is probably just a trade vessel made especially for this place. I'd say she's on the move right now, keeping her crew with the big ships."

"Still though, nine burley blokes are hard to defeat with just us three. Plus, I'm not armed."

Capall turned behind. "Can you fight?"

Ceannte scratched his head. "Not with swords or all that, but I can pub brawl."

He tutted and shook his head. "That won't do at all."

"Come now Capall." The doctor turned to them. "Surely you are skilled enough to combat four or five aggressors by yourself."

"Yes. Four, *maybe* five, but not nine. Not in close quarters."

"Aha!" Thoirní shuffled his hands on the reins and pointed his quarterstaff at Capall. "That's where I come into the fray. Mister Ceannte, do you know what you're looking for?"

He nodded. "Aye. Anything with the brand."

"Do you recall its shape?"

He acted the image with his arms. "Heart, cross, weapons."

"Crude, but correct." Thoirní turned back and prepared his pony. "We will attack from two fronts. I shall charge forward and cast a maelstrom. It'll destroy the building and much of the ship. Capall will dispose of the others should fortune favour them. Ceannte will, in secret, hide below deck, barring any resistance, where he will search for material evidence. Do we understand ourselves?"

"Aye." Ceannte said.

"Yes." Capall followed.

The Doctor nodded. "Capall, wait here for the signal, and whatever you do, stay the hell away from the storm." He struck his steed and bolted towards the port. The others stayed atop the hill. They saw the Doctor charge at a remarkable speed.

Gees, Ceannte thought, *he'll reach the port in no time with that speed. He's already at the foot of the hill.*

He held his staff ahead of him, the stone at its top began to shine a bright white light. At full speed the Doctor chanted. **"CIOCLÓN DRAÍOCHTA!"** His staff pulsed. A sudden surge erupted from the stone. A strange tunnel appeared to arc from it down to the ground in front, it sped forward.

"Now!" Capall shouted, and they also flew into the fray. The tunnel grew quickly into a new shape. Clouds formed, and the swirling mass began to crack with electricity.

Far behind the magician Ceannte and Capall followed his trail. *So much is happening all at once.* Ceannte's mind raced. *I've never moved so quickly before. I can barely take in where we are all the time. I do hope Ualach is alright. But blimey, this magic thing is something else. Gees, it's all too much too quickly. I'm not cut out for this business.*

It had now transformed into a torrid maelstrom channelled through Thoirní's staff. The few clouds above him began to follow, one in particular started to fall closer to the ground and twist. He encouraged more speed from his overworked pony. He held his staff aloft as the cloud continued to descend, the vortex cracked with fury. He swung his staff down and quickly snapped it upwards again. The vortex flew from him and the cloud caught it, free to terrorise the pirates, and he eased his pony down to a calm trot. He patted its neck. "Good girl. When we're done, you'll get a cool drink of water." The sound of the vortex dimmed as it propelled onwards, the sound replaced by the others charging towards him. He oriented his pony out of their way as they continued their pursuit. As soon as they could hear him, he gave one last bit of advice. "Mark the vortex and stay away from it."

"Aye!" Capall shouted.

Ceannte screamed behind. "Can't you control the bloody thing?!"

"I can't!" He yelled.

"It moves randomly!"

By the port, the men formed a queue and rolled barrels over the gangplank onto the deck. The building was a small, flimsy overlook that barely obscured the bank from the hillside. Not a single man noticed the impending attack. The foreman prepared the next barrel for departure when he noticed a sudden gust pressed against him. He carried on and sent the barrel to the next man. "The wind's changin'," he advised. "Might wanna start preparin' to go."

"Nah," a nearby sailor replied. "Bring it all on, what have we got left?"

"Three or four more I reckon, but I dunno. It just doesn't feel right."

"It's probably nothing, just keep goin'." It was not long until they could hear the storm, the winds whipped flags and sails, and the sound of thunder boomed from behind the building. The men stopped and saw the clouds looming behind it, but for a moment that was all the saw. The structure was cracking from the stress of the gusts, and then **SMASH!** The vortex crashed into the building.

"MAELSTROM!" Everyone dropped their cargo and hurried about to take cover. The storm ripped through the port and made its way to the ship.

Behind the storm, keeping a safe distance, Capall and Ceannte approached the ruined structure. "It's looking pretty clear!" The Hero said. "Do you remember the brand?!"

"Heart, cross, weapons!" Ceannte kept on repeating the words.

"Sounds like you do! Jump off when you're ready!" They reached the other side of the port to see the vortex had passed over the ship and continued over the river. The ship was mostly intact, but the wear of a violent storm was present. Lightning strikes ignited spot fires. On the deck, a few scattered pirates were waylaid by the force of the attack. They reached the ship, and Ceannte leapt off. He fumbled onto the deck and staggered down the stairs to the lower decks. Once he was stable, he turned to survey the surroundings. The ship was dark, only a few beams of light cast through its windows. He appeared to be in a storeroom, crates and kegs were strewn about the floor. He looked about and saw no one, he then began his search.

Capall circled around the ruined building back to the ship. He noticed some pirates had fallen overboard, while others laid onto the deck in piles of rubble and smoke. *Looks like we won't be seeing much trouble from them*, he thought. The pony slowly walked back towards the ship. The Hero stood guard atop his beast for his companion. He saw the vortex continue out on the river, it seemed to carry on to the other side. Then, he heard a groaning. One of the pirates close to him had awoken from his trauma. *Aw, damn. Why couldn't you be dead?* Capall dismounted his pony and pursued him slowly.

I can't bloody see anything here. The lack of light disoriented Ceannte. The sounds of creaking wood and shuffling steps were the only things clearest in his mind. He searched the ship's galley, and the columns of hammocks where sailors rest. Nothing yet. He found himself outside a doored room by the end of the ship. *This seems important.* He tried to open the door. It was locked. *Huh, why would there be a locked door on a ship?* He lunged his shoulder into it to no avail, he did this three times without success. "Ow! Bugger! My shoulder'll be sore tomorrow. Ah!" He held his bruised joint and kicked the door. The wood bounced the foot back to him. "Stupid thing."

"Oi!"
Ceannte turned to see a silhouette, a man obscured by the light behind them. *That doesn't look like Capall.*
"What'cha doin' down 'ere?" The man simply stood in the light. Hearing his foreign sound, Ceannte engaged him at close quarters. The man fought with the blind fury, while Ceannte was *very* adept to the skirmish. He

dodged the wild swings, knew to block when he could stop the man's fist, and when the opening presented itself, he landed gut punch after gut punch followed by a cracking right hook. He felled the man like any other brute. He landed into a small patch of light, Ceannte examined the poor fellow. He was a pirate, some crewman that perhaps heard his whining or sensed his presence or saw him in the dim light.

"None of your bloody business." He felt safe enough to claim. The distraction ended and he carried on his looking about.

The pirate screamed pain. Blood and cuts littered his attire. Capall stalked the injured man, like a tiger watching its prey. He creeped behind him. The pirate's wailing muted his approaching steps. He stood behind the pirate and lifted the spear. The blade loomed above him. Then, Capall plunged the spear into the pirate's thigh.

The pirate yelped. The intense pain shocked his entire body. "Ah! Fuck!" He cried.

"Oh, that's such a poor sight. Let me help you there." Capall twisted the spear out of the pirate's flesh. He screamed a horrific sound, blood trickled from his gashed leg. "Yeah, a hole in your leg'll do that."

"Gazza!" He heard a shout from behind him. The Hero turned to find two more pirates rise from the deck. They were enraged by the attack, yet themselves also wary from the storm.

Bugger, he thought. *Two of them is a lot trickier than one. I'll have to take one out quickly.* The blade still dripping blood, Capall threw the spear straight into one of the pirates. He was impaled through the chest with such force that the pirate was pushed into a railing. Unlike his other victim, the pirate whined a small huff and grunted his final breath. "Bullseye! I've still got it."

"Jez!" The remaining pirate called out. "I'll fuckin' gut you, you little prick!" He advanced towards Capall and produced a sword with a curved blade.

"Bugger." He whispered to himself. "Alright. I'll go you." The Hero charged towards the pirate, he swung his sword and Capall dodged the strike cleanly. The dance began.

Ceannte still tried to break into the room. He searched the rest of the ship and found little of note. Nothing of what he seemed to be looking for. He continued to kick at it, each time he did the wood creaked. "Come on. Just. Break." His last kick snapped the door open. Splinters flew from it, and the door flapped freely. He saw the lock twisted out of shape. As the door slowly rested open, he noticed the rend in the wood, a bent curve moulded into the door itself. "Open." He then saw into the room. A candlelit chandelier, shelves full of scrolls and fine equipment, a deck with more parchments upon it. The only room without any windows around it, a proper bed sat in the corner of the room, and upon the back wall hung a black banner with a stark image. A red heart, under two white weapons crossed over it, a flintlock rifle, and a curved sword. *The Brand of Aldora!* "Jackpot!" Ceannte dusted himself off and stepped inside.

Capall dodged and sidestepped his way around the deck of the sloop, leaping over the debris and loot, avoiding his attacker. Eventually he made his way to the spear, still buried in the dead pirate, blood continued to leak from the wound. The pirate again slashed at the air, Capall ducked and limboed under the shaft of his spear.

"Fuckin' fight!" He snapped.

The Hero took a second to realise what he moved under. "Well, if you insist!" He grabbed his spear and extracted it just as the pirate pulled back to strike again. He swung his sword, and it was met with a loud clang. The blade of the spear struck. He gave the pirate a cheeky smile. The pirate continued his attack. However, Capall demonstrated his skill. The Hero's ability with the pole arm, and his close grip to the blade caused the spear to act the role of a staff. The thump of the wood interrupted the clang of the metal. Every move his opponent made he countered perfectly. He managed to dislodge the sword from the pirate's grip. Stunned, the pirate reached for it as it clambered onto the deck. "Oh no you don't!" Capall launched the spear into the pirate's shin.

"AHHH!" He collapsed from the pain. He continued to reach for his blade but Capall snatched it first. "DAMNIT!" He slammed his fist on the deck. He coughed blood and began to wheeze. His energy spilled out of the spear.

Capall returned to him. He pointed the sword at the pirate's head. "Right. Now, why are you here? What is this place?"

"What's it look like?" The pirate barked back. "We're just loading up supplies. Food and shit. We're sending food back to Midgard."

"Okay. First of all, your ship is way too small to ferry anything out to sea. That's no merchantman. No manly port'll believe a word of that. Also, even for a boat this small, there's hardly anyone around. This sloop is made for a crew of twenty-five, thirty sailors. There's barely ten people here."

"Yeah, well you chucked us off with that bloody maelstrom out there."

"We're not idiots. We took a good look before we attacked."

"What d'ya mean *we*? There's only one of ya."

"I'm no magician mate." The pirate looked about, he groaned as the pain shifted and stung in new ways. "Anyway, that's not important. You've still not answered my questions. Tell me why you're here, and just what is a Pirate Haven doing up the river?"

I reckon I'm in the captain's quarters. Ceannte sat at the deck and searched about the nooks in the lit room. Many interesting things caught his eye. *This is brilliant! It's all here. Letters, contracts, a map of the city, even a bloody handwritten journal of Cnoc Gorm.* He picked up a document. *What's this?* He quickly read it. "Oh shit!" *This is a whopper! A letter for the Dogess from the pirate herself. This Aldora character seems to keep contact with our Uisce. And yep, all these letters and diaries and whatnot all say the money's being looted. The Dogess pays pirates.* "This is unbelievable. The gall of it!"

Ceannte took the letter, some other documents, and a journal with him under his jacket. Suddenly, he heard a smash from across the room. He stood and moved to the shelving to investigate. He saw a broken mirror, sat on an empty shelf. He looked about. *I don't see anything that might have smashed the mirror. And I didn't hear something fall to the ground. You'd think for something to break a mirror, it would be enough to slam it down, or at least bounce off and land somewhere close. But nope, the looking glass just shattered by itself.* Ceannte approached it further. It was not anything special, a simple circle mirror with a copper frame. Now its only embellishment was a single crack that cleaved the surface in twine. *Hang on.* He noticed another object. The mirror sat upon another map. He lifted the broken mirror and took the parchment for a closer look. It was a map of islands. *Well, I'm not sure where this is. But it seems far off. The Western Sea perhaps, but I haven't a clue.* Ceannte saw no names nor writing, except for a single term on one of the islands. "What? *The Republic of the Pirates?* What is this?" He continued to examine the map but to no avail. He added it to the rest of the documentation he took from the quarters, and quietly exited the room.

"I ain't talkin' no more!" The pirate tried to stand on his ruined leg, but the pain was too much to bear. He screamed and slumped back onto the deck.

"Well that's a shame," Capall replied, "cause I'm not done with you. Some of your story doesn't make a lot of sense. You say you work for the Sea Wretch, and you work a trade route to her port. The Aldora thing, I understand, but what do you mean by a *trade route*?"

"What do ya think I mean? A trade ship. A treasure barge. I slip booty to Aldora under your nose."

"You what?" He scratched his chin. "Treasure barge? You slip booty? I don't understand you at all."

"Well, it ain't any simpler than that. I ain't talkin'."

"You sure about that?" The pirate nodded.

Capall sighed and walked around him to his spear, still buried into the pirate's shin. "What are ya doing?" He grabbed the shaft and swiftly twisted the spear. **"GAAHHHH!"** His body seized with a shock so intense that every limb quacked.

"I prefer not to do that, but needs must come first." He questioned him more and returned to face him again. "Why would a pirate want for a treasure ship? Loot is the prize, isn't it? Sacking ships and evading the law to live freely. Is that not the aim?"

The pirate whimpered. "Aye, sure. But the booty of a single ship ain't as huge as the booty of a city. A rich city at that." He paused to compose himself, breathing deeply for a time. Then, a glimmer shone in his eye. "The motherlode is a city o' gold, like that one up the hill. Them are the big scores. Here, the Golden Coast, and up the river to the dwarf towns."

"So, you plunder cities now? Why waste the time with a small fortune when the real loot is behind walls of stone."

"Aye, but there's more to it than that. I mean, we ain't raising shit to the ground, aren't we? We don't cause a big fuss. No pillaging, no burning, no looting. We do it covertly. We go out of the way of praying eyes, we settle as little land as we need, and we ferry booty out of the town before anyone suspects a thing."

Capall raised his eyebrow. "That's all well and good, but then how do you get the loot? The coffer is inside the capital, this shanty is nowhere near Bunaitheach. How can you move the treasure from there to here?"

"Who said we move the booty? The booty ends up here. We take it. We sail away. I dunno how it gets here, it just does."

He raised the sword again. "You're lying. You must have infiltrated the Teachóir."

"I swear I have no idea." The pirate raised his hands. "I reckon someone's workin' on the inside, but I don't know nothin'."

The Hero stared into the pirate, his arms shook in fear, his eyes focused on the edge of the blade, and his skin made pale from his injury. "Alright," he nodded and lowered his arm, "I believe you, but there is still much unclear. I'll let you live."

"Oi! Capall!" He turned to find Ceannte emerge from the lower deck.

He turned back. "Stay here. Don't do anything stupid alright?"

"Aye, sir." He turned away and walked to the staircase.

He quickly checked on the vortex. It had curved back to the river far out west of them. "We'll have to make this quick." Capall pointed behind Ceannte, he turned to see it. "The vortex seems to be heading back this way."

"Aye, alright." He turned back to the Hero. "So, I found a lot of stuff, plenty of evidence that this is Aldora's ship." He produced a parchment. "But I reckon this is big story."

He handed Capall the letter. "My dear Uisce, I write this letter to inform, and remind you…" He scanned the letter, and after a few moments his eyes widened. "*Pay a fee 75,000 gold pieces?!* Good God!" He began to pace. "*This fee of protection will keep my men from plundering your cities, lest you decide to do anything stupid and try to withhold your riches from me. Return this letter with your signature. A real signature please, or I shall unleash my might upon your puny boats.* Ceannte, this is unbelievable."

"I know. It's quite the read." He sighed. "If that note is to be believed, every month a ship docks here to cart away that much in gold. The sheer scale beggars belief."

"So this isn't simply an underground operation. This is extortion. Aldora has intimidated a head of state to pay her a large amount of wealth to essentially do nothing. All the while we suffer from it. Businesses can't expand, soldiers can't get paid. A nation that can't grow." He stopped. "It's starting to make sense now. The renegade behaviour, it isn't wanton hoarding. She's trying to pay off the pirates. She's making sure she can meet the value of this arrangement."

"By the sound of things, you're right. She really is desperate." Ceannte said.

"Aye. It's a different desperate though. It's not a fear of poverty, it's a fear of violence." Capall waved about the letter. "Threats like this here don't sit well. And from a notorious killer no less."

He sighed again. "Well, we have this, plus some more stuff I've got on me. What do we do now? This isn't just proving that pirates are here anymore."

"Indeed. This by itself is enough to dethrone Uisce. We should gather the Doctor and convene here to work out our next move. You monitor the fiends and I'll bring him here." Capall left him on the ship. He made haste to his pony, mounted her, and trotted away.

Ceannte kept guard upon the deck. "Oi," one of the pirates shouted, "you don't wanna get in it with Aldora. She'll skin ya alive and clean ya guts out."

"Shut up you!" He pointed at the fallen pirate and stared him down. *So, I've noticed a couple of things. The bloke behind me hasn't moved or made a sound since I've came upstairs.* He turned to him. The man was slumped over, with a pool of blood about his legs. *Wait, is he dead? I can't be sure. Can a hole in the leg kill you?* He looked back to the other one. *He's surviving though. He doesn't look very hurt. I reckon he must be hiding something.* "I'll just check on the other bloke, see if he's alright." Ceannte still stared at the pirate for a moment. *I've got an uneasy feeling he's playing us for fools. He's got the look of a criminal.* He did not reply, he glared back at the fisherman. He had the rugged face of a crooked past, and the scarred skin of a toughened will. He walked backwards while still seeing him, he moved slowly and with great care. He gave the pirate all the attention he could afford, until Ceannte needed to turn to the other man.

He inspected the body. *Nah. He's not dead, but I reckon he might still if that wound ain't treated. Still though, that's quite a lot of blood.* He lifted one side of the body. *Aye. His skin has colour. He's alright for now. I'm guessing he's just unconscious. Not a real surprise if I'm honest.* He let the body rest and examined the wound. *That's a very odd place to get injured. I wouldn't think a hole in the leg'll cause that much damage. Judging from its size, I reckon tha-.* Suddenly, Ceannte was knocked off his feet. He felt the force strike his back and fell upon the body. He turned and saw the remaining pirate behind where he was, he stood on one leg and had kicked him down with the other. "What the?!"

"That's for Gazza." The pirate stomped his foot. The man was a muscular beast, broad and shaped for battle. He pulled Ceannte to his feet and held him while he slammed his powerful fist into his stomach. "You damn Heroes think you can fuck around with Aldora?" He landed a blow to Ceannte's head, and he flew out of the pirate's grip. "She'll hunt ya down and kill ya the moment she sees ya. She has no mercy."

Ceannte was rattled by the attack. He faced the pirate. "Well then," he lifted his fists, "she'll have to come get us." He launched into him, and they both fought each other.

* * *

Not far from the site, Capall and Thoirní discussed Ceannte's findings. "A mole operation." The Doctor read the letter. "I cannot say I'm totally surprised if I'm honest. With the way she handles large expenditure, people are bound to think it's all going somewhere else. But to a pirate? I quite certain that's treasonous."

"Do you think she'll forfeit her life?" Capall asked.

"Oh no. She's much too clever to let herself get hanged." He folded the parchment. "I'm sure she'll just pay off the guards. Buy her way out." And handed it back to the Hero. "The real question is, what'll happen next? This sort of thing has never happened before. There's no precedent to recall here."

"Not only that, and I might be wrong about this, but I don't think there's any kind of procedure for deposition. At the very least there's never been any thought of unseating a ruling monarch." He stroked his chin and sighed. "There's dangerous times ahead, I think. Uncertainty's abound."

"That's not a concern of ours. The lords of the land can sort out the politics. Our path is uncertain, but our action is clear. A General Audience is due to take place tonight. Along with some of the mayors. We must regroup and away to the Teachóir, present our materials to the electors, and let the chips fall where they may."

"Very well. You should be aware that I've also sent word to rally the local Heroes as well. This whole debacle has triggered my rite of summons."

"You have? I wouldn't have expected that action from you." Thoirní began to trot.

"Why not?" Capall followed him. They headed towards the ship to their companion. "Payment is a serious matter for us Heroes. We don't simply go around and do any odd job for some layabout king for nothing. When we take on a quest or fulfil a task for our patron, we expect to be compensated for our labours. Indeed, it may or may not benefit us to complete the task. However, it is often dangerous to our lives, or our reputation. All these laws and drafting contracts are the insurances we need to not burden ourselves with a fear of becoming indentured. If a patron decides that they would much prefer not to maintain their end of the bargain, what is to stop them from just getting free services whenever it suits them? That's the purpose of payment mate. It keeps everyone in check."

The Doctor laughed. "If I were a Templar, I would argue that your greed has overtaken your sense of duty."

"Oh don't give me that pious nonsense." Thoirní continued to laugh. "I mean, who here really wants to place their mortality at risk? I don't, and I reckon you wouldn't either."

"That is well and good however, it raises another question. If you feel so strongly about the value of life, why are you a Hero at all? It strikes me as uncharacteristic to want to live in peace yet charge yourself into dangerous environments."

"I'm a skilled soldier mate. I've trained under captains, mentors, commanders and other Pony Riders to become a master of the spear. To me, there's no danger in a battlefield. That stuff down there," Capall pointed to the ship, "that's easy for a veteran like me. Guard, parry, thrust, block. That's not a risk. I'm taking about the unknown here. The stuff that can't be predicted. When you don't know if you're up against an army of footmen, or a bivouac of fairies, or an aggressive dragon, and there's plenty of them out there. I'm a good footman, but I'm no commander. I can't cook up a new strategy at a pinch." *Wait, how did we get to me now?* He realised and sighed. "My point is, Heroes do the job of questing and keeping the peace. The payment is the closing of the contract, it unbinds the Hero from the charge of the patron. When the patron doesn't pay his dues, we are still bound to their charge, and they can do to us whatever they want. Surely you can appreciate that."

"Indeed, I do." They were close to the ship when they saw them. "Steady on."

What? Capall panicked. *How is that man still standing? And fighting?!* "Gees! I shouldn't have left him there."

"You'd better get over there!" The Hero did not respond, he galloped away towards the fight.

Ceannte was still fighting, but he was losing strength. He dodged and blocked the attacks, yet he was still struck, and as time passed, he was hit more and more. His face was bloody and bruised. A right hook knocked him off his feet, doubloons fell out of his jacket. He was losing his senses and his head pounded. As the pirate came towards him, he tried to think. But the trauma burned with such intensity that he could not create a thought. Nothing was in his mind. The pirate grabbed a hold of his hair and pulled him up. Ceannte used what little energy he had left trying to break free, but his efforts were futile. He was in the air, a worm on a hook. "Here's a free lesson for ya," the pirate spoke, his voice was icy. "Don't go stickin' ya nose in business it doesn't belong." He clinched his free hand.

Fuck! I'm going to die. Ceannte's mind overflowed in despair. He shut his eyes. *I can't do this. I can't fight back. I'm out of energy. I can't stop the pain. I'm going to get pummelled to death. All over some stupid bit of gold. What's the point?*

"AH!" Suddenly the pirate shrieked, and he dropped Ceannte onto the deck. He opened his eyes and gasped.

"Here's a free lesson for you." He saw the blade of a spear pierced through the pirate's chest. The blood-soaked metal pushed further out. He sunk to his knees and fell over dead, revealing Capall behind him. "Muscle is no match to metal." Ceannte panted in relief, he was just able to express a smile. "Are you alright mate?"

"I. Can barely. Move." He panted out of breath.

"We'll fix you up." Capall pulled him up onto his feet, then he dragged both him and the spear off the ship.

Ceannte's mind continued to process. *Well. This is something, I've noticed Capall is quite different to the people I see. He isn't the type of person that gives in. He just keeps on going when things are rough. Even when I gave him a worry. I can't think of anyone I know that does that, not even Óir. He'd sooner bend to the will of any crook that crossed his path. But right now, I can't think much at all.*

Capall unloaded the wary halfling and sheathed his spear into the ground, then he ran to the side of the derelict building, his pony beside him. "All clear!" The Doctor rode down to him, and Capall came back to Ceannte. "The doctor's coming over, he's got some remedy for you. You'll be right."

He slowly sat up. "Thank you. I thought I was. Going to die then."

"Aye, I know." He sighed. "Sorry about that, but I had no idea he could stand up with that gaping wound, never mind brawl like that."

Thoirní trotted up to the men and dismounted. "Excellent work, gentlemen. That'll be the last of them lot."

"Can you get us a healing flask?" Capall requested.

"Indeed. Are you alright Capall?"

"Not for me, Ceannte's knackered." The Doctor produced an oddly shaped bottle from his robes. It looked more a scientific implement than a drinking bottle. The liquid itself had a curious blue glow. He uncorked the bottle and passed it to Ceannte. "Here, drink this. It'll heal you."

He ingested some of the drink spat it back out. "Is that bloody Magic Water?!"

"Aye," the Doctor cheerfully replied, "Hydro-Adamantium Hydroxide. Straight from the node, that."

"Bleh!" He took a moment to drink more of the elixir until he grew accustomed to the metallic aftertaste. He felt the magic work its way. The energy swelled in his belly, then suddenly he felt the effects surge about his body. He was awash in a newfound energy, his head felt clearer and more precise. The bruising and scars receded to nothingness. The magic water reinvigorated his muscles and his bones. "Wow!" He addressed the Doctor in amazement. "That stuff is amazing!" He stood and turned about, ensuring he was alright. "I don't believe it! I feel fine, like I just woke up from a good night's sleep."

He grinned widely. "Yep. Magic Water'll do that to you. Most healing potions use it for a base, certain weeds and stuff can improve the result, but I reckon that's fine for a quick journey like this one." He turned to Capall. "Where's the storm right now?"

"Off to the left." He casually pointed to the vortex. "It kicked off that way after it blasted through the ship. It kept going for a while, but I think it's staring to come back. I'm not sure when it'll get back here though." The Doctor steered his pony to where Capall pointed. The funnel appeared to point towards the mainland, but also appeared to remain still in the distance. The storm still struck lightning occasionally, the low rumbling of thunder rolled.

"It'll come back." He took out his pocket watch. "Give it five minutes and it'll be barrelling down on us. But luckily, in that time it will also dissipate into the clouds."

"What do we do then?" Ceannte walked to the Doctor.

Capall chased after him. "Oi! Steady on mate. Are you okay?"

He chuckled. "I'm fine. It's like nothing happened."

"If you don't mind gentlemen," Thoirní spoke over them, "a question needs answering. Are there any survivors?"

"One." Cappal answered. "I've incapacitated him on the deck. The rest got flushed out the water, and I had to kill two of the bastards."

"Actually, there's a second one." Ceannte interrupted. "I found one below deck and I gave him what for."

"Did you now?" The Hero asked.

"Aye! I'm not completely useless. That bloke caught me off guard."

Thoirní grunted. "Well at least you didn't kill more of them. As much as I respect your skills, Capall, I never condone violence."

"Says the man who cast a giant magic tornado." Ceannte replied.

The Doctor sighed. "It was a necessity. Nine pirates would easily overpower us, and they would take no hesitation in murdering us all. You of all of us here know that well."

"Aye, I don't deny that. But I can admit to myself when I have to do dirty work."

"Can we not bicker right now?" Capall pleaded.

"I must agree, I don't agree with your tenor mister Ceannte, but we must not linger for long." He gathered his thoughts and sighed. "Two survivors is plenty. We can take them with us back to the Teachóir and confront the Dogess there. Besides, our materials are much more plentiful. We must reach the palace before sundown. But we can't bring everyone with us quickly enough. Our ponies cannot charge with the speed we need. We need to find a faster form of transport."

"Well what the hell do we do then?" Ceannte asked angrily.

"Oh, I have a plan, but it'll be a bit risky. Mister Ceannte," Thoirní turned towards him, "are you any good with flight at all?"

"Flight?" He raised his eyebrow. "What do you mean by that?"

* * *

The sun began its descent when a sudden beastly howl pierced the air, the sound of large wings flapping soon followed. On a quiet and secluded hillock a creature rose, broad and intimidating. A supremely large dragon. It was grey, but its scales gleamed iridescent of purple and violent. Its belly was lit with a whitened glow that occasionally dimmed periodically. The body of the dragon was sharp and abrasive, and a stark span of its wings with claws. Upon the creature, the puny halflings sat. "Wow! Settle down boy!" Doctor Thoirní uttered.

Ceannte screamed vulgarity. *"SHIIIIIIIIIIIT!!"* He barely kept a hold of the dragon.

Capall was elated at the thrill. "I didn't know you could ride a bloody dragon!"

"All summoned creatures can become beasts of burden," the Doctor explained, "they serve their master with complete obedience."

Ceannte paused briefly. "I had no idea dragons were summoned creatures. I thought they all live in the mountains."

"Yes and no. Some of the hardier breeds live up with the dwarves, while the gentler sort roam freely up north with the ancient races. But above all, freed dragons first and foremost are called forth by mages to do their bidding."

"Aye, you should head up to the land of the high elves." Capall added behind him. "Báilóngs move about up there."

"What?!"

"Báilóngs, the White Dragons," the Doctor continued, "they are a breed of dragon local to the Eldar folk. Docile things, but just as huge. Let's not sit about now though, we have a queen to depose."

"Hang on. Wait a minute." Ceannte tried to balance himself and ask more questions.

"Go forth, Slatintreach!" Thoirní commanded the dragon. Slatintreach took one great sweep of its wings and launched into the air, a stream of lightning flew from its gapping maw. Tied to the tail of the beast, the two captive pirates flew with them back. Their screams were diluted by the noise and chaos. The storm was headed for Uisce.

Chapter 14

In the Teachóir the Great Hall was filled with a gathering of some of the wealthy townsfolk from the whole of the Dogedom. Uisce sat upon her throne, and two others sat on either side of her. Men of some repute. All the denizens were entrenched in discussion and business. "Mayor Teorainn, can we please move this along?" Uisce groaned. "I see little merit in granting such a frivolous loan, if any at all."

"My Dogess, it is most important for the island to prosper." The bloated, balding man from her left defended his case. "A mining operation at the water node will be a profitable venture. It is an untapped resource of revenue."

"Magic has no use here. It is a total waste of time."

"Who said anything about using it? I propose we siphon the fountain of its rich elements and sell the contents at high prices. There is a market just outside our doorstep of customers waiting to obtain our enchanted water."

She shook her head. "I am not convinced Mayor Teorainn, I cannot grant such a ridiculous proposal."

He grumbled in his seat. "Ridiculous? Frivolous?! What total nonsense this is!"

"Your displeasure amuses me." She leaned over and glared at him. "The magic does more than just enchant our waters. It enchants the creatures within it. We have a reputation amongst this world of some of the finest and exotic seafood, fishes that cannot be found anywhere else. Extracting the mana from Sruth Dé may be a most lucrative venture, and I have no doubt you will repay your loan. However, you must also consider the industry you will hurt in the process. No, mayor. I cannot allow such destruction to our economy."

He leaned back into his chair and tutted. "Nonsense! What rubbish!"

"Is that all?" Authority rang out in her voice.

After a moment of silence, he replied. "Aye. Tis all."

"Excellent. Our next order of business."

A crier stood before them with a long parchment that fell to the ground. "Item 31; A charter for a settlement on the Riasc Islands beyond the frontier, proposed by the honourable Mayor Leathnú."

Uisce quietly muttered. "Good grief, we're going to be here all night." She relaxed into her chair. "Mayor Leathnú, that's quite a proposal. You want to fund a new city, is that right?"

"Not really a city, but a little hamlet." He stood above the mass in front of them. "Right at the very edge of our influence over the sea." They continued to discuss the matter.

* * *

The dragon approached its target. "We're not far now," Thoirní pointed out in front, "we've just reached the outskirts of the capital, and the palace isn't long from here"

"Set us down a half a mile before." Capall pointed to a vague street elsewhere. "We'll send the Heroes with us to the palace."

"If you insist however, are you sure your dispute is relevant at this time?"

"The Dogess can't pay for the protection of the Order of the Heroes because she is siphoning her treasures to a pirate. I reckon that's pretty relevant!"

"Very well."

"Are you sure this'll work?" Ceannte asked. "I mean, what's to stop her from just denying everything?"

"Oh, I fully anticipate she'll deny everything," the Doctor answered, "that's a certainty. But if what our prisoners say is true, and I reckon it is, all we really need to do is just expose her connection to Aldora." He turned his head to him. "In truth, mister Ceannte, your evidences are the most valuable materials in this enterprise. Our fellows over there are just an added insurance."

"Down there!" Capall called out to them. They all leaned over to see a narrow stone road, and a small crowd flanked by the buildings about them. "The safe house! Set us down at the square ahead."

"Aye!" Thoirní compelled the dragon to fall towards the ground and control its landing. In no time the beast zoomed towards the stone, righted itself, flapped its wings, and stood in the space just wide enough for a dragon. Not a person was present to see the greatness of the shining beast, save for the crowd of Heroes.

"Where is everyone?" Ceannte asked as he dismounted carefully off the dragon's back. "Isn't it a bit odd for a city to not have people about? I'd reckon we'd alarm the guardsmen or some poor soul if they caught the sight of a great big dragon looming over a city."

"Aye, you'd be right on any other day," Capall remarked while he followed the fisherman, "but the General Assembly's on right now. Everyone important is at the Teachóir, discussing and planning for the next year to come to pass. Everyone else is back the other way at the Gorm, finding some excuse to have a drink."

"Capall, how exactly does one safely enter the palace grounds by dragon without alerting the Royal Guard?" The Doctor asked.

"The Guard's got these things for just such an occasion." He quickly buried his free hand into a pocket and revealed an object, a sphere set on top of a sort of pyramid shape, all in a navy-blue colour. With his arm wrapped about the spear, he fiddled with it for a second, then the sphere was lit. He set the piece onto the blade of his spear, he held it aloft with the blue light atop.

"Is that a beacon?"

"Indeed, it is! That light informs the men a friendly Hero is approaching. Just point it in front of you when you reach the grounds. The guards are trained to observe and care for Heroes with respect." He handed Thoirní the spear.

"Genius! I shall head to the Teachóir. I will expect your presence shortly then."

"See you then." The Hero waved him off.

"Hooroo." Ceannte added.

"Safe travels." The Doctor launched Slatintreach, and they flew towards the golden dome.

Capall and Ceannte turned about and walked towards the group of halflings. They saw a small crowd of Heroes cluttering the street outside the safe house. "Oi Capall," one of them called out, "what's all this business with the summons?" His query roused the attention of the other Heroes.

"It's a rather important business mate. There's grumblings in the Teachóir." They stopped, and Capall greeted the fellow with a quick salute. "There is much of this story that'll take too long to explain, so I'll brief you quickly. The Dogess has suddenly gone renegade." Gasps sprang from the bystanders. "She has openly expressed hostility to the Order, she has placed me and my companion under arrest on pain of death, and we have returned from a battle which exposes her inability to maintain our contracts. Uisce no longer wishes to remain under the umbrella of the Order of Heroes, and she lacks to capacity to do so."

"Aye, right. That's a big problem there. We've not had a head of state turn down Hero protection in a very long time."

"Indeed. I was thinking about the Templar Conflict myself at the time."

"Yes, but it wasn't quite as serious as you're currently proposing. A merchant queen that's incapable of paying her soldiers is a volatile reaction just waiting to explode. No wonder you rallied us." The man turned to the fisherman. "Say Capall, who is he anyway?"

"Ah! This is Hero Ceannte." Capall patted his back. "He's a conscript, but he has already proven his worth in battle. He needs a good deal more training, but I reckon he'll do us proud."

"G'evening sir." The man shook his hand. "The name's Cosantóir, Garrisoneer in Command. I hope the fight hasn't deterred you from heroism."

Ceannte laughed. "I don't mind a bit of rough housing, but I reckon those pirates can really fight."

He raised his eyebrows. "Did you say *pirates*?"

"Aye. With a bit of help from our wizard friend we smashed up a syndicate. It turns out that the Dogess had colluded with the pirates in a secret deal."

"The details are a bit scattered," Capall added, "but from what we've learned it would appear that the Dogess Uisce would ferry the treasure to the Pirate Haven, the pirates arrive, load their vessel, and sail away. All without detection of the guards and sentries. Or at least that is my understanding."

"The Dogess? Colluding with pirates?" He shook his head. "Nah mate, that claim is just too far fetched without real evidence."

"Take your pick." The fisherman reached into his jacket. "I have notes, letters from Uisce and Aldora, journals about the big cities about the Dogedom, doubloons from the ship itself." He took and letter and handed it to Cosantóir.

He opened the parchment. "What the? 75,000?"

"Indeed." Capall added.

"A protection fee?!" He stopped and turned back to the other Heroes. "Brothers and Sisters-in-Arms, we are to disperse tonight."

A cloud of confusion and curiosity flew about the Heroes. "What are we here for," one asked, "what is the cause for this summons?"

"Skullduggery. Treason in its highest form. A serpent hides in the Teachóir."

"What must we do?" Asked another.

"We must communicate with our Brothers-in-Arms at Midgard, they are the most capable to aid our cause however, right here and now, there is nothing we can do. Go to your homes, keep healthy and wise."

"Wait a minute!" Capall saw the band disband and murmur to itself. "What do you mean *nothing we can do?* The evidence is right there, we can fix this right now!"

"This fight is not ours to take, Capall. It is one thing if Uisce simply hoarded her wealth by her own cause. It is quite another if the Dogess has had her coffers emptied by an outside force. You will have my full support in this unseating you seem to want, no ruler should be the puppet of a swindling thief, but ultimately the problem is not here. It's out there," Cosantóir pointed behind, "somewhere out at sea. That is a task that we, the protectors of the River, will not do independently. It is lucky for you that our network runs across the entirety of the continent. Our Midgardian comrades will be more than accommodating to you. You will have your help in time, but it will not come from us." He returned the letter to Ceannte and joined the rabble of Heroes. He turned about and began to walk. "This is your battle mister Ceannte, not ours. You have your weapons, use them." All the Heroes left them on the road. He too disappeared, a shadow of strength and duty.

They stood idle for a moment. A mild silence entered their company. Ceannte turned to his hero. He saw Capall jut his head and look to some thing in the distance, nothing he could identify. "What do we do now?" For a second nothing happened, Capall did not appear to have heard the question. He seemed to have remained within his mind.

He suddenly smiled. "We go to her now." He turned around and left him on the street.

"Wait!" Ceannte caught up to him. They both started to run. "What about the Heroes? Aren't they going to help us?"

"No. Cosantóir's right. When we first started this, I summoned the Heroes, thinking that she was holding onto the money and just being greedy. Now that we know the truth, the problem is much bigger. It's not a petty dispute anymore, this is a proper scandal. We have to let the natural course of action take place, we have to front up the Dogess ourselves and get her off the throne. And don't worry about it. We have all we really need to do that." They passed the familiar roads and streets. They saw the Teachóir in front of them, this time with Slatintreach perched atop of the golden dome, breathing lightning into the greying sky. They continued their pursuit.

* * *

"Madam Doge, I must protest!" Comhbhrón stood above the audience. "Business has been waning in recent time. Many lords and barons have sought to expand themselves into larger markets, and to capitalise over foreign competitors. Business partners have come to me to advise and establish themselves about the land. Yet, they return to me and tell of a quarrelsome Merchant Queen who seems not to have a care for growth or taxation. Why, not more than a week ago a conglomerate of bankers intended to create a branch in the harbour city of Cnoc Gorm. In the last month I have orchestrated the establishment of this, of the Airgead trading family, the business of Sir Kosmímata's finery and metalcrafts, and even more recently than the bank, a coalition of dwarven blacksmiths intent to supply the river with bronze and steel." He became animated, he rose and waved his hands. "There is no shortage of willing investors keen to trade and give wealth to the Dogedom. What possible reason is there to prevent such prosperity?"

A silence fell upon the palace. Comhbhrón remained upstanding, he waited for her response. For a moment, Uisce did nothing except stare into him. A battle of will was at hand. She raised herself off her throne, and after a brief second of more silence she replied. "Business is not stagnant. We of the river folk are indeed prospering already for our great wealth-."

"Pardon my imposition milady," Comhbhrón interrupted, "but I never said business was stagnant. I said it was waning. As best as my guess can be, we are producing wealth that is less than before." His comment stirred the crowd. They murmured quietly under him.

"That is a lie." She replied a low grumble.

"That is an estimate."

"Then your estimate is faulty. I cannot speak to your mathematics however, I can both assure and prove to you that our coffers are full. Our trade and treasures provide more than enough of the precious gold and platinum to maintain our lovely country and its people."

"Sit down Uisce." She turned behind her to the mayor sat on her right side. "Return to your seat, and let cooler heads prevail."

She turned completely towards him and came so close that she spoke in a low voice. "I will not be made a fool of by a commoner."

"You already *are* a fool," the man whispered back. "Sit down and let the man speak. He isn't wrong anyway. What exactly is the harm?"

She sighed and subtly nodded. She turned back to Comhbhrón. "Mayor Amhras is correct. Perhaps it is wiser not to act so impulsively." Slowly she returned to her throne and sat back upon it. As she did a rumble swept the great hall. The walls of the palace shook about, and the ground was not stable. A few shrieks flew about the audience, yet just as suddenly did they appear, the tremors stopped. Despite the uncertainty, not one halfling panicked. "Do not fear, citizens. It is nothing to worry yourselves about." The Dogess called a guard over to her seat. "Would you mind checking to see if anything or anyone has caused that?"

"Aye ma'am." The guardsman left them upon their stage and quickly marched to the great door of the palace. He opened and closed it with speed. In that brief period, she saw the weather had turned grey. A bolt of lightning struck somewhere behind the building. It lit the sky in a flash of white light.

"Ah, you see?" Uisce gestured to the door. "It is nothing to fear. Just a bit of stormy weather. Perhaps we should proceed forward and let time elapse a bit slower for the storm to pass." She moved her hand to him. "Mister Comhbhrón, please continue. The court may yet seek your consul, though I fear it may conflict with our interests."

"I seek only to improve our condition, Dogess." Comhbhrón carried on his proposals. Uisce turned to briefly look to Amhras. He continued to scratch his beard, he remained oblivious to her glares. She gave in and returned to the merchant's proclamations.

* * *

Ceannte and Capall reached the palace grounds. The great dome of the Teachóir dulled, reflecting the grey dragon and the clouds that formed about it. They rushed across the gardens towards the stairs. "Alright, things are about to get serious," Capall said. He slowed down and stuck his arm out to halt his friend in front of a bed of marigolds and tall grasses. The flowers appeared to float over a sea of green. The halflings crouched below until the grass concealed them. "This'll be the only place in the city that's guarded right now," he presented three armed guardsmen in front of their path in the distance, "and the Doctor's got my spear. I need to nick one from one of the guards."

"How do we do that then?" Ceannte asked.

"I work here mate. I know where the armoury is." He pointed out a stone hut nestled in a back corner beyond the gardens. "Just gotta sneak our way there."

"Hang on now. Are you sure we should divert away and not just storm up the palace?"

"You what? Two unarmed blokes? Fugitives, no less. Remember? We're outlaws here now. Try to ambush a heavily guarded building without a proper plan?" Capall raised a finger to him as he spied the grounds. Apart from the front guards, he saw a number of men patrolling the gardens, and the regular watch secured the armoury with its own men. "Question; how good are you with the pole?"

"What?"

He turned to Ceannte. "Lancing, are you any good with a spear?"

"No. I can't harpoon to save my life."

"That's not lancing mate, but if you're rubbish with a throwing spear, then I reckon you're not much better with a holding spear."

"Aye. I stick to fishing."

"Alright, just one then." The Hero nodded as he spoke. "Right, just sit tight here. Stay low and out of sight. If you need to, hide in the flowerbed." He gave

Capall a thumbs up. The Hero left the fisherman behind and began to creep about the gardens.

Ceannte kept his eye on Capall. *Crikey. He moves quick*, he thought. *It's not been long and he's already much of the way across.* He observed the Hero's actions. *It's like he's got a map of everyone in his head at all times. He's not checking where the guards are at all, and he can find a lot of cover about the grounds. That seems like a bit of a security problem now that I think about it. Even with so many guardsmen patrolling about.* Capall fell out of his view. *Well, the waiting game's started.* He turned about to spot the closest soldiers.

All about the gardens were beds of fragrant flowers and forests of grasses and reeds. The colours and smells were pleasant and inviting. Behind a bed of vibrant purple flowers, Capall hid from a guard a few meters ahead. He kept himself fully covered, only his eyes peered through. The guard took time to survey his corner. He scanned the scene and the sound, nothing moved. The guard walked down the stone path, he passed by Capall unaware. Once he was far in the distance, the Hero sprang up from his hiding spot and continued towards the armoury. *I'm not far now*, the Hero reckoned. *I have to work out how to slip past the patrol. There's normally four men guarding each side of the building, they see the entire perimeter so that no one can approach it unseen. If I'll get inside then, I need to distract at least two of them. And the garden ain't good for things to distract with.* The armoury was close by and Capall hid behind another flower bed. *Right, what am I going to do? Wait a minute.*

He quietly rose again. *No one's here! No front or side guard.* He looked around. *There's literally no footman at all that's in a visual range of the armoury. What on Mundus is going on?* He confidently strode towards the building, the long house of stone with a smoking chimney. The Hero creeped around the corners of the armoury and returned to the front side of the building. *Nope. No one is guarding this place. Why though?* He again looked about for any clues. Something, anything, that could account for such a lapse in discipline. Capall heard a deep growl from the roof of the Teachóir. The dragon remained perched atop the gold. It pawed its feet closer to the top of the roof. Faint shouts followed, the sounds of familiar commanders directing their men. He did not hear any them clearly save for one word, 'drake'. "Cheers, Doctor," he smiled and turned to enter the armoury.

Ceannte checked the time on his pocket watch. 6:21, it read. The sky was a mix of red light and grey cloud, the sun just hid under the horizon. He sighed. *It's been a good fifteen minutes now. I hope he's not been caught.* He checked his side again and saw Capall return into his view, carrying a spear and moving quicker than before and with more confidence. He gestured to him and whispered. "Get down!" The Hero crouched into the flower bed and continued to move as quickly as before. They reunited under the very cover they arrived in. "Careful with that thing! You'll have my eye out."

"It's good to be back." Capall replied. "Mate, everything is going to be fine. Finer than I originally thought."

"What do you mean?"

"Well, I expected the armoury to be fully guarded and I'd need to sneak about to get there. Turns out some numpty pulled out the garrison, probably to deal with the Doctor's arrival with the dragon."

"Well, I figured that might be the case," Ceannte shrugged. "I mean, it is a dragon after all."

"Aye, sure."

"Oi. What's that?" He pointed to a gathering of guards surrounding a man, Doctor Thourní. Shouting from all sides drowned each other out into noise. The Doctor appeared to have his wrists bound and escorted up to the palace.

"I reckon he's been arrested. Damnit."

"I thought you said he'd be alright." Ceannte's whisper became faster and louder.

"I did! It always works for me getting back home. The light is meant to indicate friendliness, so I thought it ought to be enough. I guess a great big dragon was just too much of a hazard." Slatintreach roared a lightning bolt into the clouds above. The white energy flashed across the grey canopy. "Case in point."

"What are we going to do now? We can't just leave him there."

"Aye, no, we can't. But what do you expect us to do with-," the Hero looked back at the group, "eight trained soldiers, plus the other three? I can't take on a troop of eleven men. Not by myself."

"Well you have me."

Capall patted Ceannte's shoulder. "You're an alright bloke, but you're no fighter. You might hold your own in a pub brawl, but these are military trained men. Foot soldiers with the ability, and for most the experience, of an armed conflict. They will strike you down before you think to throw a punch." He examined the guards. They nearly reached the top of the stairs. "No. We need to sit back for a moment. Our time will come." They watched on as the crowd forced the Doctor to the great door of the palace.

* * *

Everyone was still discussing their proposals and policies. Uisce and the mayors reclined into their seats as the audience turned. There was a murmur of dissent in the air. While they chatted amongst themselves, the more vocal lords expressed their upset over each other. "I don't understand this. Why will she not grow the-," a question flies from one.

"-but there's no plan. No interest at all!" Another asserts.

"This is balderdash! Utter nonsense. The madness-," a third accused.

"-future in woodwork? Wood is eternal! You need a chair, don't you?" The tension from the commotion was rising by the minute. All the audience made their displeasure known, except for Comhbhrón. He saw the fury about the hall flow from the angry rabble, and feed back into itself. A perpetual loop. *Gees. This place is getting a bit too rowdy right now. She's put everyone offside.* He shuffled in his seat. The environment produced a nervous energy in him. *Someone needs to stop this before it gets out of hand. She'll have a riot if she's not careful.*

Teorainn leaned to the Dogess. "You'll have to do something ma'am. This crowd'll take over the place."

"You don't think I can see that? I have been trying to summon my garrison to return and quell this audience. Their disobedience is most unprofessional."

"The guards will only enflame the problem," Amhras interjected, "you need to address their concerns. Understand why they are upset and resolve the matter lest anyone gets the idea to rebel."

"Oh please." She waved him away. "Their concerns are insignificant to the wider world. Threats from foreign powers that are far greater than us. The troubles of a nation are more important than someone's bread, or their servitude. And on the subject of rebellion; what possible rebellion is there? They are my subjects, and they will do as I say, as they have done so before."

"Not for long with that attitude." He pointed out. She tutted him and shook her head. A great thud blasted from the entrance and the doors gave way. The jot startled the audience, and everyone hushed themselves and turned their attention.

The troop marched up the hall. The crowd of onlookers reacted one by one as he passed them by. Many gasped, some whispered to the others near them. They all seemed to recognise the apprehended. "Madam

Doge, my apologies," the lead guard said, "we have apprehended the culprit to the commotion outside."

"The culprit?" Uisce furrowed her brows. "What do you mean? Has he caused the storm outside?"

"In a manner of speaking, yes." Thoirní replied. "I have come to this hall atop a great dragon of thunderous energy. I have come bearing-."

"A dragon?!" She shrieked. "There's a drake upon this house?" The audience replied with gasps and murmurs.

"Well…yes." He chuckled mildly. "However, the drake is docile and well behaved. He isn't attacking anything, by my will. In any event, I bare news of much import, and with the assembly present tonight it was imperative to arrive as soon as I possibly could. Me and my-."

"And you felt it was necessary to endanger the royalty, and the people with a giant bloody dragon over our heads?" Uisce waved about her hands in a panic.

"Necessary, yes. Dangerous, hardly. Slatintreach is a quiet beast, well mostly. And he is controlled by me. I have no interest in upsetting this assembly with the threat of a wild dragon. Just listen to the outside and you will hear not a crash or a boom. No thunder rumbles now." The assembly fell silent, they all waited patiently as the sound muted into nothing. Nothing. Nothing produced noise. For a few seconds everyone heard the sound of total silence. Vacuous and eerie, the empty blackness of noiselessness. Until eventually a distant rumble echoed into the great hall. It was quiet and mild, yet it was enough to shift the Dogess in her seat. "Discharge, ma'am. Electricity from a lightning strike earlier."

"I'm not entirely convinced Doctor," she replied, "you may have a tame beast, but I believe that anyone who feels the need to carry themselves to me on a dragon cannot bode friendly tidings."

"You say you bring important news." Amhras interjected.

"Quite so, your honour. Me and my companions have discovered and destroyed a Pirate Haven found upon the fringes of the harbour town." Again, the citizens behind him whispered and uttered to themselves at the news. "There has been a black operation working under our very noses for quite some time."

"That's not news," Uisce slightly shook he head, "we know about the pirates and have been guarding the docklands for many weeks now to deter them."

"Ah! But you have not." Raising his bound hands, he pointed out her argument. "There's been no news of a capturing or even a sighting of any piracy within our borders. Only rumour and hearsay abound." As he spoke, the crowd appeared to agree with his argument, both visibly and audibly. "I have with Slatintreach two of these fiends who will stand trail for their crimes."

She rose from her throne immediately. Her eyes widened. Her skin paled slightly. *Two pirates? Here?* She looked to the middle distance. *Did he capture them, those foul Heroes? Has he really done my work for me?* A smile crept onto her face. "Aha. You have captured our two fugitives then. Well done Doctor Thoirní. I, the Merchant Queen Dogess Uisce, thank you for your service and duty to your brethren. Bring these miscreants here and let them pay for their treason."

"I'm sorry, I don't quite understand."

"Never you mind Doctor. You, footman," she pointed out to one of the guards, "unbind this gallant gentleman. He has performed a great service to the Dogedom."

The soldier looked about vacantly. "Me?"

"Yes, of course."

"But why?" He asked as he pulled out his knife and cut through the ropes. "He's been going about with his great big dragon, causing a nuisance."

"He's done more for the good of this land than you have in your entire service of the Royal Guard. He's a magic man. You're a trained soldier."

"Now hold on a tic!" The guard protested. The audience groaned in disgust.

"That's a low insult to the both of us!" Thoirní added.

"It matters not," she blocked them all with her raised hand, "bring the pirates to me. We shall make an example of them here." She returned to her seat. "A show of strength and defiance against these wayward souls."

"They should be here shortly ma'am." Another guard said.

The Doctor raised his eyebrow. "Madam Doge, do you *know* these criminals?"

"Indeed, I do. They came to this great hall nought one day ago now. The one plied his sly tricks to try to rob me of my treasure. The other joined his fell cause, duped into a life of hazard and strife for the sake of gold. They are poor, misguided fellows, and they must be stopped to keep the peace and prosperity of the land." Some of the audience cheered at Uisce's declaration however, the rabble seemed openly divided amongst themselves. The sound of gladness mixed with the noise of discontent. Nothing could be clearly heard over the dense shroud of utterance.

Surrounded by the troop, the Doctor did nothing but wait patiently. He looked about to see the Great Hall. The entire room was animated. The citizens argued and conversed over the news. The confirmation of piracy, the interruption of himself, the seizure of criminals. Everyone spoke over each other in a frenzy of gossip and intrigue. He observed the guardsmen, they too were somewhat interested in the events of the day. While most of the men were silent, he heard a trio of footmen.

"This whole thing doesn't make a lot of sense. She knows the pirates?"

"Nah, that can't be right. No shifty bloke's ever come 'ere."

"So what if they did though? Isn't it a bit odd that she'd just say that to the public? Isn't that just like saying she's in on the whole thing?"

"No, there's a clear difference."

"What's the difference?"

"She's not been actually out there plunderin' and sackin'. She's just known about the pirates."

"But how though? How did she know about them? Did she just greet them all casual like, or perhaps she-."

I don't have the care to waste listening to this nonsense, Thoirní was just able to hear his own mind over the noise. He turned to the thrones. Even the mayors Teorainn and Amhras engaged in their own discussion of the news. All were in heated argument about the threat of piracy, except for the Dogess herself. Upon her throne and above her subordinates, Uisce did not speak. She remained relaxed in her seat. *Now that's odd. For someone that claims to have had contact with pirates, she seems to be less inclined to talk of such things, and instead simply allows the masses to spin their own meaning. In place of clarity, she wants ambiguity. This is not at all how I would expect a respectable monarch to act.* He remained focused on her. *She seems very assured of herself. Perhaps she's prepared for this eventuality, she somehow managed to counter our gambit with some new rouse.*

Two more guardsmen entered the hall, they hauled two other men with them. "Your Highness, the pirates." One proclaimed as they dragged them towards the amassed troop.

As they came closer into view Uisce's grin turned, her sly face transformed into shock, and then into anger. "These aren't the pirate's I'm after. Who are these men?"

Thoirní kept his eye on her as they dropped the pirates onto the ground. They both screamed in pain, their injuries were still fresh on their flesh and their clothing. "The pirates ma'am." The other guard was the Hero Cosantóir. "Mister Thoirní claims to have found them upon a now ruined Pirate Haven at about the outer edge of Cnoc Gorm. We've ordered men to make some investigations into the whereabouts of this dock, and any other relevant information about any pirate syndicates operating about the area."

"Indeed, the very same pirates my associates dealt with," the Doctor said. "Are they not the men you're wanting? The scoundrels that see fit to impoverish our free nation?"

She took a moment to collect her thoughts. "Why yes, of course. Anyone who means to steal our fortunes is a pirate against the Dogedom. Rise, fiends. Explain yourselves. What dark business do you have in our hallowed walls?"

Two of the guards lifted them off the ground. When they stood upright, they shrieked at the sharpness of their injuries. "We- Ah! We work for the Sea Wretch. We're part of her crew. We've been assigned the task of ferrying gold from this place to her." The crowd reacted to their claims.

"You have been ferrying our wealth out from under us? How? And by whom?" She stood from her chair and hunched over them. Her confident stare exuded a powerful aura about her. "Speak. Who allowed you to move such wealth?"

"Why? You did ma'am!"

Uisce looked to the great door. In the pale light of the moon stood Ceannte and Capall. They set their sights on the Dogess. "Well, I assume so anyway," Ceannte concluded. They walked down the hall with strength and confidence, guided by a wind of defiance.

Her smile returned. "Aha! More pirates! Honourable men, this man is just as much a vagrant criminal as these two. I have no doubt that this devil probably masterminded this entire enterprise. Seize that phoney."

"Belay that order," Cosantóir shouted. "Let no one impede his cause."

Uisce took a step backward and placed her hand over her mouth. "Cosantóir. You as well?" She walked towards him with such slowness as if time itself moved as she did. "You too have been taken in by this traitor and his lies?"

"The Order of Heroes is a union of protection ma'am," he replied. "Heroes protect each other, as they protect their patrons. Our oaths bind us to you, and our honour binds us to the brotherhood."

"This bloke ain't no pirate," Capall added. "Sure, he's a crass, angry sod that'll complain about the smallest things, but he's no swashbuckler."

Ceannte turned to him. "You're not helping you know."

"If there is any traitor among us here, it is you ma'am." Thoirní pointed at her and threw his weight, the condemnation rushed past him to the audience.

She looked about. *I have to stop this now while I can! I need to turn the masses against them. Especially the guardsmen, they can easily end this. But perhaps a public execution may not bode well with an audience.* "Treason? You have to tenacity to suggest that I commit treason?" She laughed with a low and unsettled sound. "You come here without invitation and disrupt this session, only to point fingers and fly slurs wantonly? What do you have to gain from this display?" She then turned to Ceannte. "I know what you want. You have no claim to entreat a reward you are not entitled to. You will never get one red cent out of me." Her attention turned to Capall. "I can guess your demand. You have given this urchin far too much of your time Capall. You have filled him with ideas of camaraderie and honour. He is a fisherman. Nothing more. Your disloyalty has not gone unnoticed. If you expect to be paid, as you so argued for his worth, you will stop your rebellious crusade now and reaffirm yourself to me. As you are *paid to do*." She addressed the Doctor. "As for you Doctor, I'm not sure what your business is here. What do you stand to gain from my dismissal? Another magical institution perhaps? More nonsense!"

"Madam Doge, I am here to aid my friend mister Ceannte with his cause. Not only do we all accuse you of treason against the people but have the evidence to prove that fact."

"Ha! What evidence do you have? Two mongrels who will say anything for freedom?"

"Calm down, madam Doge," Teorainn persuaded her. "This is a serious charge. Let us hear them with whatever they have, and let them make arses of themselves should this be found untrue."

"I do not entertain nonsense such as this! Throw them out now!"

"*UISCE!*" The Dogess was startled from Amhras' bellow. "This is a serious offence they are claiming. You are subject to the same justices of this land. If you are innocent you have no need to fret. Allow them to be heard, and let God swing his sword."

She stared back at him, her eyes were sharp and icy. She slumped from her tall stature and sighed in exasperation. "Very well." She returned to her seat. "But we have no time for your noise-making, so make this quick."

Ceannte continued to walk up to the very edge of the stage. He carefully studied his audience. *That bloke on the right. No idea who he is. Some fat bastard that probably sits about all day. But he is a mayor, otherwise he'd be on the other side with the crowd. I reckon he might be the treasurer. The other one seems to be much more aware. I see a much more of a level bloke. He looks like a thinker.* "Your honours, I'll make this brief. I'm accusing Uisce of high treason. With the documents and items found in a ship that was docked, we found rather a great deal of incriminating information. She has been consorting with privateers and diverting funds from our coffers into criminal hands." The audience murmured at the wild claim. The mayors each began to scratch their chins however, Uisce remained largely unaffected by the claim. "I'll cut this story short. We discovered a Pirate Haven near Cnoc Gorm. There we uncovered the disturbing conspiracy which implicates the Dogess, and with some help we've defeated the pirates and arrested those."

"Indeed, good sir," Teorainn said, "we thank you for your efforts in apprehending these criminals. However, this conspiracy you speak of. What does this have to do with our Uisce?"

"Well, after some interrogation and searching for evidence, we discovered her treachery. By those fellows it would seem the Dogess is in collusion with the Sea Wretch."

"WHAT?!" Teorainn lifted off his seat. The audience became particularly unruly and angry.

"Aldora? That villainous witch," Amhras inquired. "How dare that vile terror incriminate our queen."

"Lies!" Uisce erupted from the throne and proclaimed in a large haller. "Lies and skullduggery! I *WILL NOT* listen to this effrontery!"

"Then it's a good thing we've got things to show as well as tell," Capall said. "He's got rather a lot of intriguing books and papers and what not, all about this dalliance. He'll hand over what you'll need no doubt."

"Aye, that's true." Ceannte quickly removed his objects from his person onto the ground about him. "I've acquired a- book about the comings and goings of the ships in the docklands of Cnoc Gorm, Aldora's personal journal of the capital here, some sort of a guidebook for attacking a city in a stealthy manner. Aha!" He produced a folded piece of parchment. "This here's the whopper. A signed letter by Aldora herself, addressed to our Dogess. Clear as day and marked by her royal highness. I suppose you'll be wanting to investigate this right?"

"No!" She answered.

"Yes, sirs." Amhras rose from his chair and turned to Uisce. "We will listen to these men, and if indeed their story is false, we will send them all away. But we must grant them an audience, they deserve that at least."

"They deserve the end of my pike!" She barked back. She pointed her finger squarely at the fisherman and turned to him. She saw the pile of books and papers and coins scattered about his feet, his uncanny delight across his face as he waved about the letter, and the other men, the Hero and the Doctor, watching her carefully. *I might yet be able to block their evidences and destroy them at a later time with some more privacy.* She sighed and turned back to her throne. "But you are right, mister Amhras. I hate it, but you are right. Speak then. Amuse us with your tall tales." She again sat in her now wary seat.

"Right." Ceannte cleared his throat affectedly. "*My dear Uisce, I write this letter to inform, and remind you of the arrangement we agreed upon a number of weeks ago now. The port of Shortfoot has been constructed in secret just beyond the fringes of your little town. The hilly environ should be ample coverage from anyone with nosy intentions. Send your cargo to this place, marked on the enclosed map. Pay a fee of 75,000 gold pieces, or its equivalent value in treasure, to this port by the twenty-fifth day of every month. This fee of protection will keep my men from plundering your cities, lest you decide to do anything stupid and try to withhold your riches from me. Return this letter with your signature. A real signature please, or I shall unleash my might upon your puny boats. Yours in trust, Aldora of the Pirate Republic.*" The hall filled with the sound of shock and disgust. The loud shouted, the offended cried, the amazed questioned. Ceannte looked about him. The Heroes near him stood in defiance, proud and tall against the rage. Thoirní was still surrounded by guardsmen, he did much the same and surveyed his environment. The men around the Doctor turned their attention to the crowd and their growing restlessness. The guards stood their ground. Their spears aimed at the rabble, ready to engage. However, upon the stage was a different tension. The Mayors beside the Dogess were both enraged and cautious. They argued amongst themselves. *Bugger! All this noise. I can't hear a word they're saying. They're waving their hands about, but I have no idea what for.* He finally turned to Uisce. *Well then, she's not moved. In all this noise and anger, she hasn't reacted at all. She's upset, sure, but she isn't raging. I wonder why.*

She held her gaze upon him the entire time. From the moment he began his recitation, she did nothing but stare into him. Those piercing eyes with such terrible effect, now felt like nothing more than a mild presence. In a great hall that rang in a loud, deep roar, she remained calm and tempered. But for only so long. After several seconds of clammer and fire, she rose from her seat. **"SILENCE!"** Her voice commanded the wailing to dissipate, and once the hall returned to peace, she attacked. "Firstly, that document is a forgery. I have not now, nor every been in correspondence with any privateer, much less the Sea Wretch. She is a terror in the Western Sea, she is Cairbre's problem! Piracy has never been a problem in Leath Langa, and it never will. Secondly, I do not recognise the Republic of the Pirates. No one does. That loose confederation of professional lawbreakers is just a cesspool of the worst kind of people. No king, emperor, doge, or wizard worth their pride would so much as consider any dealing with pirates, especially none so capable as Aldora. Lastly," she strode up to Ceannte by the edge of the stage, and again made all attempt to upset with her staring, "you have made quite enough noise, so much so that the entire assembly has been disrupted by your lie-making and rabble-rousing. I am tasked with maintaining the peace and the prosperity of our nation, and I have every intention to do that within my capabilities as the Dogess, Merchant Queen of the River. When this is over, I will personally see you and your associates be taken to the gallows for your treasonous behaviour. I will execute you myself if I find it necessary." For a moment nothing happened. Silence befell the hall. *I have control again,* she thought, *I have his life in my hand, and I will crush it when it suits me. I am the Merchant Queen. I am* the River Empire.

"Okay, first of all, I have more than a letter," Ceannte shattered the peace. "I have a journal that not only describes the city detail but recounts a discussion Aldora seems to have had with you, ma'am. I have a-," he produced even more objects within his jacket, "detailed map of both the capital city and Cnoc Gorm, and a very descriptive map of the palace grounds, so I reckon Aldora's actually been here before, back that's just a guess."

"Enough!" She demanded.

"Second of all, I'm sorry to tell you this, but I baited you." He turned over the letter and pointed at its bottom. "I deliberately read the wrong line."

She quickly read the final lines.

Yours in trust,

Aldora, Admiral of the Republic of the Pirates

"That is hardly evidence," she replied. "If I care not to phrase a country by its proper name, it is no more a signal of treachery than a bird would be in a foreign nest."

"Expect it was you who corrected me. Word for word. The fact that you *did* use the formal term tells me that it's a name you've heard before. It's not what you said, it's the way you said it that matters."

She raised her voice to him. "That still proves nothing!"

"That is technically true," Amhras stood from his seat and made his way to her, "however, given the nature of this accusation, we must treat this with the appropriate care." He turned to address her. "Let us not take extreme measures without extreme reason. Prove him wrong, don't just declare it and expect people to remain quiet." She glared into him again for a moment. She grunted and turned back to her throne. "Very well then. Good sir, may I have the letter?"

Ceannte reached over to him, but then a sudden thought entered his mind. "Oh actually, I'll give you the letter on one condition."

He raised his eyebrow. "What would that be?"

"The last time I had a written dealing with her, she bamboozled me out of payment. This whole tussle with the Heroes here is for that reason. My condition is that she does not touch this document under any circumstance."

"Seeing as she is the defendant in judicial assembly, she is not allowed to in any event."

"Excellent." He gave Amhras the document.

The mayor read the parchment. "Indeed, I recognise her signature. It certainly looks like she has at least seen it before." He looked to the two pirates, they stood about idly and without purpose. "Well, we still have to hear from you lot. What is your connection to the Dogess, and her wealth?"

"We've already said." One replied. "We work for the Sea Wretch. We sail the route from here to the 'aven, takin' the gold. We ain't part of the Dogedom and we don't know the Dogess. We just take her money when it comes to us."

"Did you say the treasure *comes* to you?"

"Aye."

Mayor Amhras slowly turned about. "This suggests a most horrid thought, that there is set in place a system of conveying treasury especially *to* the port." He stopped and stared directly at Uisce, she responded in kind. "A *trade route*, as it were."

"He is obviously lying! I do not make secret ports all over the Dogedom to pay off every pirate under the sun."

"Interesting," he pointed out at her, "that was never the accusation. Merely the transference of gold."

"I *do not EVER* deal with privateers!" She stood in defiance against him, the party, and the pirates. "Besides, this is all hear say! What physical evidence do you have of this *trade route*? How can I be sure you are not all conspiring to dethrone me?"

"There's plenty of evidence," Ceannte answered. "There's all these books and papers and what not. I really much prefer to not go through all this a second time now, it's really a lot of boring stuff, but this one," he bent down and took a book from his pile, "the stuff about Aldora's excursion in Bunaitheach, she goes into some detail about a discussion you had with her, allegedly."

"Aye, and to be completely fair, we are basically trying to dethrone you at the minute." Capall added.

"I believe she is asking about a legitimate means by which to unseat her from the title of Dogess." Cosantóir corrected.

"Mister Ceannte is right," Thoirní said, "there is rather a lot of reasonable and admittedly circumstantial evidences presently and investigating all of it will take time. But fortune favours the bold, for there is a much more provable and direct examination that can be done to show the Dogess' treachery. Aldora does not simply take new crewmen or clients by their words. She is all too familiar with the nature of lawlessness and piracy. So, she compels any new persons seeking her confederation to take a pledge, an oath of trust and companionship." He turned to one of the pirates, and the closest guard to him. "You there. I encourage you to grab ahold of either one of the pirate's attire by the collar and expose his left shoulder. Be sure to uncover it fully." The guard nodded, took the collar of the closest pirate, and uncovered his bare shoulder. The mayors were aghast, the sight of the wound startled them all. The man was branded. The image of a heart shape, crossed by a sword and a flintlock pistol, was burned into his skin. "In the most literal sense, cross your heart, hope to die."

Amhras nodded upon the sight of the brand. Uisce shifted about her chair in discomfort. She adjusted the hem of her dress and held her own shoulder. "So, such a brand is present on all Aldora's crew?" She asked.

"Not exactly." Capall answered. "Anyone and everyone who ever deals with Aldora, even a lowly trader in some backend stall in some hamlet, is branded with this image, or at least that's what these blokes told us."

"I see." The mayor turned about to the Dogess. She stared back at him, and they both tested each other's nerve. "Madam Doge-,"

"I shall not!" She answered immediately before he questioned. "I *will not* disrobe in a public space!"

"Disrobe? I'm not asking you to remove your clothing. I merely wish to see your left shoulder."

"All the same to me! I will not debase this place with such impropriety." Her outburst upset the audience.

"It's a simple request!" A man hollered.

"Just do it!" Shouted another.

Amhras opened his hands to her. "It is a very easy demand, and frankly Uisce, your reluctance is a suggestion of guilt." He walked up to her and continued. "If you want to remain at your seat, and us as your subjects and advisors, you must satisfy our doubts and ensure you have no such ties to Aldora." He stood in front of her, they again glared into each other, one final test of their steel wills.

The Dogess took a deep breath, sighed, and relented. "Stand aside, mayor." She held the collar of her dress. He saw this and obliged, he took a step away for the public to see. She pulled upon her left side, and the gathered masses, the guardsmen, the Heroes, all who was present within the Teachóir saw it. The pale skin of her bare should was tempered with the same fleshy wound found upon the pirate. She wore the brand of Aldora. Despite all the materials he possessed, Ceannte was just as amazed to see the brand upon her skin as the rest. She stood for some time, she ensured that all could see it. The Merchant Queen was exposed as a puppet of a privateer.

* * *

"I did what was needed to be done. She approached me at the start of the year. I was not aware of the piracy abound up north, but she had total control of waters of Men, or so she told me. She was not on her vessel, nor surrounded by her minions. Aldora was all alone. She was visiting the city, or so I thought. She came to me and pulled me into an empty alleyway. She told me who she was and what see wanted out of me. That baying hyena threatened me with constant raiding and looting, she said she would target me personally upon her voyages on the seas. I was so affronted by this I replied in kind and threatened her. I told her I would send the navy to hunt her down and drag her to my feet before the axe would remove her head, but she laughed at me. She actually laughed at the idea of a violent death. I was so shocked I lost my nerve. Who does this? *Who laughs at their own death?* She called me a worthless waste of time and started to walk off, but I stopped her. She wanted a ridiculous amount of gold to keep her at bay, so I decided to pay it and keep her from destroying our homes."

"No doubt this would be the seventy-five thousand gold she writes about. The protection fee mister Ceannte makes reference to." Amhras said.

"Indeed. The tribute ensures the safety of this nation."

Ceannte's mind was confounded. "That's insane! Seventy-five grand. Just how much is that?"

She sighed, and after a brief silence she prepared to answer, but a voice interrupted her chance. "Very nearly the entire net profit of the Dogedom for that quarter-year." They all turned behind them. Comhbhrón stood in the crowd. His face was stony, yet his eyes were wide and bright. "Everything makes sense now. The quarterly profit of the final three months of the ninety-ninth year was about 76,500 gold by my reckoning. That prosperity plummeted after the end of the next quarter. The Dogedom has not been making more than five thousand since then. I made inquiries about this sudden poverty at every opportunity I could, but I made no progress. Instead, I was given ridiculous excuses, some nonsense about defunct markets and what not. Now I understand entirely. There was never any more gold to invest into major works. Business was stifled- no, *paralysed*, by this threat against us. I must ask milady, how the devil did she know to nick that much gold?"

She sighed again. "Through our *'pleasant'* conversation. I kept giving her lower numbers in a plan to preserve some kind of wealth, but she was much too persistent and resolute in stealing near everything."

"I could shed some light on that matter." Ceannte reached for a second book by him. "I mentioned a book about the city. It would seem that Aldora's made some excellent observations about just how much gold flows through the nation. She's noted as much in this book."

"But a whole quarter's worth of gold? That's not possible! We would have noticed this!" Amhras stated.

"No, I was quite careful. With the knowledge of the infernal port I arranged a private transport every half-week to carry and store it. The ship would arrive, relive me of my treasure, and depart. The very ship you and your Hero friends have just smashed, Doctor. I would siphon a fraction of the gold into this hiding space and simply neglect to record it. A small loss is easy to miss. And the location of the port was also well considered, before the sight of any building, the ship appearing only in a window of no traffic to avoid detection. I rather think it was an excellent plan."

"It is of no consequence Uisce," he interrupted her. "you have tried to deceive and confound, your plan is exposed and you are now to be known as the traitor you are."

"*I AM NOT AT ALL A TRAITOR!* I did what was best for my people. I could not expose us to the horrors of battle, not again. The last thing we need is to relive those damn orcs and their insane bloodlust. I *will not* allow that ever again, if that means paying off a threat to keep her at rest, so be it! I rather that then fire and death."

"I'd rather a capable navy then your faulty leadership!" Thoirní replied. "Seventy-five thousand gold, surely that can pay of a large force of protection. A fleet of galleons and frigates to pursue Aldora."

"Indeed, it should," Amhras added. "This fear of yours has totally incapacitated your ability to think. Surely it has occurred to you to amass a fleet and deal with her. Some sort of response!"

"With our margins? We barely have enough to sustain our *current* progress right now. This *and* an armada is out of the question."

"Then don't pay it! Rush the work, recruit the finest sailors and captains. Give yourself the might to overthrow this dread queen."

She shook her head. "No, I still believe I did the right thing here. And frankly I don't care about what you think. I am the merchant queen. I am right."

"Not anymore you're not!" A rolling *'here here'* emerged from the crowd as Amhras called out. "Guards, arrest this woman!" The guards all removed themselves from the Doctor and the pirates, save for four. They rose up to the stage and surrounded her throne. She did not respond. Uisce was without power, authority or merit. She gave the men her hands, they bound them, and they escorted the Dogess away from her title. Cosantóir lead her and the guards back down the hall and out. Thoirní, Capall and Ceannte glanced at her when they passed by. She was sullen and shameful, her head bowed forward as if she could not bare to face the truth. A few strands of her hair covered her eye. There was no air of majesty anymore, she was not the golden woman in the golden house. The pacing of the men clattered and tinked in time as they made it into the distance.

Ceannte turned back to the Doctor. "What happens now?"

At first his began to respond, but as soon as his opened his mouth and pointed his finger he paused to think for a few seconds. *Actually-*, he turned to the mayors. "What does happen in an event of a deposition?"

"We're not sure really," Mayor Teorainn said. "We've never had a tyrant forcefully exit the throne. The protocol is unfamiliar to us."

"We will need to reconvene tomorrow I feel," Amhras added. "After tonight's revelations it might do us all some good to have a rest and enquire about the procedure in the morning. All in favour of an emergency convention tomorrow morning?" Every sitting representative, from the majors to the lords in the first row of the audience, rose their hands and replied with an *'aye!'* "All opposed?" An almost ritual silence persisted for a moment. "The ayes have it. We will return here at sunrise to determine what exactly to do. Doctor Thoirní," he turned to the fisherman, "good sir, what is your name?"

"Ceannte sir. Ceannte Macántacht." He replied.

"Mr Macántacht, the both of you please return here in the morning, for this requires your attendance as well."

"Righto." He turned about and intended to leave, but the Doctor stopped him.

"What about me?" Capall asked.

"For now, return to duty. You will also be apprised of the situation however, for the time being you best return back to garrison the palace."

"Very well then, but how about this whole business about Ceannte being a pirate and my being a bloody accomplice?"

"That will all be quashed immediately. Your names shall no longer by sullied."

"Excellent!" They all made for the door.

"Doctor," Amhras called out, "please help rid us of your dragon friend?"

He laughed. "Of course, your honour. You chaps go. Ceannte, shall we meet at the safe house here?"

"Aye, of course." They strode down the great hall. The Hero and the rambler succeeded in dethroning the tyrant queen and uncovered the grand ruse.

As they passed the threshold into the cold night, Ceannte asked. "Hey, I have a question. Are quests usually like this?"

"Uncovering hidden information? Often, yes. Deposing kings or queens? Not really, no."

"Ah. Good. I thought this one was kind of strange. I'll see you tomorrow."

"Aye, see you then."

"Hooroo." Ceannte continued down the stairs and left the scene. He passed by the guardsmen ferrying Uisce to the jailhouse elsewhere. At the bottom he turned back to the Teachóir. The dragon sat upon the dome, it rested quietly and curled itself on the great curve. The storm upon the hill died down, its rage had ended. He sighed. *What a night. What a sorry state we live in. Who could imagine this? A nation, a full society of people, of families, of friends. We are all just puppets.*

Dolls caught on the strings of masters. Children pulled by parents. Workers pulled by lords. Soldiers pulled by kings. Pulled by the great actors to manipulate the world into their own image. What even is power? Do actors act to keep power, or are the actors just the puppets of power itself? Who controls who here? How much control do we have? Is the world really ours to make? He sighed once more, turned back around, and left the grounds to retire to somewhere pleasant.

Chapter 15

The sun had just risen over the city and the sky turned a golden colour. The light shone upon the palace. Capall stood guard at the great entrance to the Teachóir. In the distance he noticed two men enter the grounds and making straight towards him. He stood his ground and observed their movement. As they made their way, he recognised them. "Good morning chaps."

"Morning mate." Ceannte greeted him, and Thoirní waved in response. "Any idea what we should expect in there?"

"Actually yeah," he turned to the palace briefly. "I'm not sure what the process is, but they're going to decide on the next Doge or Dogess. You better get in there." All three of them made their way up to the door.

"If I were them," the Doctor started, "I would seriously consider Mayor Amhras. I quite like his mind. He processes information very quickly."

"Who's that?" Ceannte asked.

"He was the bloke that sort of grilled Uisce for us," Capall explained. "You gave him the letter."

"Oh him! He's great. I like him."

They reached the great door and Capall opened it for them. "Good luck in there." The Doctor and the fisherman stepped through, and he closed the door behind them. He turned about and returned to his station, he kept guard of the palace.

* * *

Much time passed. The day was high and Capall remained by the door. He still kept guard of the palace, yet he sat on the steps and ate his lunch. A fine roll of bread with some cooked meat. He wiped off his hands, stood upon the steps, and returned to his post. "Good pork." Only a moment had passed when at last the door opened behind him. The Hero turned about and was surprised by the sight he saw. "Woah! Okay. So, what exactly do I call you now? Doctor or Doge?"

"If it's all the same to you, I much prefer Doctor."

He grinned. "Aye, you could be our own Professor King, like what the men have."

Thoirní stepped outside into the sunlight, he revealed his new attire. The good doctor wore his regular white robe and leather belt for his many flasks. However, he also wore a green sash over the clothing and a golden pin attached to it. Atop his blonde locks sat a cloth hat, another green garment to signify would-be royalty. "I quite like the sound of that. Professor King Thoirní of the Halflings."

"It sounds just as pompous the second time." Ceannte said.

"Oh hush! It's not as if I really wanted the title." He turned to Capall. "I made my intentions known, the mayors agreed and put it to the vote, and for whatever reason very nearly the entire council felt I was qualified to obtain the title. But honestly, I've never managed a business in my life. How on this good earth can I run a country, never mind maintain a profit?"

"I'm sure you'll work it out," Ceannte answered. "You've definitely got the head for leadership and all that. Maybe it's not such a bad idea."

"Aye, plus you'll have a number of advisors to help you out with stuff like that. Surely." Capall reached over and patted his shoulder. "You're in good company with some of the best businessmen in the country mate, you'll do fine."

"Besides, if you really didn't want the job you could have simply said no. They certainly didn't force you to do it." Ceannte pointed out to Thoirní.

"Wait, he didn't refuse the title?"

"Would *you?*"

"I have to admit that I did not Capall. Frankly, the offer to take on the most important office in the land is too big a temptation. To lead the halflings into a new direction…I'd like to think I can leave a lasting impact on our fellow brethren. Perhaps create a new world for us, one not driven by wealth and excess, but something more focused on betterment. Knowledge, or medicine, or some such business."

Ceannte smiled. "That sounds lovely." A gentle breeze rushed past him.

"Lovely?" Thoirní laughed. "I'm not really aiming for *lovely*, but I do appreciate the thought. For now, I just want to caretake and repair the damage Uisce caused. We should be able to raise a naval force and protect the river from the pirates should they ever come for us. That and her practices should generate a good deal of revenue to make some improvements."

"It's a start," Ceannte interrupted. "You're already going the right way I think."

"Indeed. Speaking of the right way, Mister Ceannte-."

"Call me Cean." He extended his hand. "All my friends do."

He promptly shook his hand. "Yes, Cean. You are due to carry out your quest and receive payment. Now I do not have to power to purchase your services however, I can provide you the recovered loot from the Pirate Haven. How do you feel about sixty thousand gold?"

He sighed. "Given what's happened here, I'll settle for my pony and several rounds of ail."

"Nonsense! I won't have you leave without proper payment." He turned to Capall. "Can you please fetch this man his transport?"

"With pleasure sir." The Hero left them at the door, descended the steps, and made his way out of their view.

"Do you mind a private chat, out here?" Thoirní asked.

"Sure." The men both took a single step down and sat beside the great golden dome. They looked out over the city, out towards the fields of green and red and yellow.

"Cean, I hope you don't mind my saying, but your story seems so bizarre, so unlikely, that even now I still have trouble grasping it. A typical fisherman, a lad of all things, gets strong-armed into a rather peculiar quest. You become a Hero by technicality, rather than by strength or intelligence." He shook his head. "I must tell you. It is beyond ludicrous."

He signed in exasperation. "Believe me, you're not the only one. Honestly, I'm like you, I'm still working this one out. I have no real idea if this is a good thing or not."

"We never truly know these things. The best we can do is look back into the past, and guess." He saw Ceannte engage with him. The fisherman nodded along to his wisdom. "Take me, for example. I am a respected scholar and alchemist. I spent much of my life fighting; fighting for my magic, my respect, my right to live how I saw fit." He sighed. "There were very few days where I was content with my lot."

"Yeah, sure," he interrupted, "but you rose above all that. You made a name for yourself. You proved halflings aren't just about money and family."

"Don't interrupt me Cean. I have a point to convey."

He lazily raised his hands in innocence. "Sorry."

"You are right to say these things, but hindsight is a tall mountain upon which to sit. It is one thing to talk about my knowledge now. It is quite another thing to experience the pressures of reaching success. As I was saying, there was little rest for me. I was in a near constant struggle to make the kind of mark I left on this world. It began with my family. My father was horrified to learn of my disinterest in farming. He threatened to disown me for not taking after his business. Mother was not much better, bless her soul. She encouraged me to choose my own path, but she had no real understanding of Alchemistry. As a result, I had no one to look to for guidance." He leaned back and sighed again. "Mother was kind enough to put me into school, but back then there was no learning of magic here. Mana was too tradable. It was just another money machine. I fought hard to travel to Midgard. Father disapproved of it, and many of my friends discouraged me. Mother helped me fund my trip, but not before I was thrown out of home and barred from returning."

"Crikey!" The Doctor's words reminded Ceannte of his own childhood. *Bugger! And I thought I had a rough start. Pa's always been a supportive bloke to me. He's given me the best education he could afford to, and helped me whenever I needed it, or make me fell better when I got hurt. I honestly can't imagine how I'd be without him. He really was a father to me. Hearing the Doctor's story has made me think about him more. I do miss him.* "That's rough. Did you get to reconcile with your dad?"

"No. We never saw eye to eye. He was pleased with my success, but he never appreciated it. He died without apologising for his treatment." Thoirní paused. He started into the distance. He contemplated silently to himself. Ceannte rested his hand on the mage's shoulder. The Doctor turned to him. He saw the man's subtle smile, and chuckled. "You know, I can't help but feel that even with my newfound confidence, I would still cower in fear of my old man. I still respect him, despite his manner." He took a long breath and sighed. "But that really was the start of the trouble. Getting to Midgard was hard, being there was wondrous, exciting, horrible, and aggressive, all at the same time. I had to deal with the prejudice of the students around me, and even some of the tutors. But I am very thankful of a few of my companions, they saw past the ridicule and knew me for who I was. I reckon you will meet some of them in your travelling, some are kings and queens now. Be sure to send my regards to the Professor King, he taught me you know."

"Wait, the King taught you? How?"

"Quite so. He was a professor before he was the Professor King you know. Where else did he get his name?"

"Ah! I see." He nodded.

"King Cairbre was once an esteemed professor of the Alchemical Sciences in the Sage's Guild. He was the legal heir to the throne, yet he pursued his own path to magic and become a lecturer. For anyone with an interest in any magic at all, they spent a semester with him on the background of Alchemistry. Unlike many of his younger kind, professor also saw in me the potential for greatness. He held no reservation in teaching me magic, and I succeeded with great ability. I proved them all wrong, my family and my enemies, I could become something from magic.

"I felt that I did everything right, that my life would no longer have to deal with such a bigoted view. However, once I had returned home and reacquainted with my former life very little had changed. People were proud of my success, but still failed to see the use of magic. I had to debate the creation of buildings for learning with tenants and mayors, and personally fund programs with little or no support. Also, you remember that story I gave you before all this business happened."

"The one where she ruined your papers?"

"Yes. I fought back against her with my own network. My success is off the back of a bent spine and a wary heart." He paused and watched Ceannte. His eyes stared deeply into the mind of the Doctor. He heeded every word of his tale. "Mister Ceannte, what I wish for most in this world is a place for all living things to be. A world of wonderment and wellness, so that all can live peacefully. May I ask what you wish for?"

Excuse me? He was taken aback briefly. "Huh? Well, I don't quite dream so big, but-," he took a moment to gather his thoughts. "To be honest, I'd quite like a nice home. Nothing fancy or anything like that, just a space to live and take a scroll about the hillside. Fish by the water, provide for my missus. To be totally honest, I don't want not much different to what I have now. Just to live with someone and settle down." He sighed. "I don't want to just survive anymore. I want to be able to live well."

Thoirní smiled and patted his friend on the back. "Cean, you don't realise it yet, but your dream is much grander than mine. You see, I want to make a difference in the world. Deep down just about everyone wants that, they see an injustice in one way or another, and they seek to make it right. However, ego always plays a part in the shaping of a legacy, be it small or large. I cannot deny that I seek to be known as the man who brought magic to the halflings, it gives me a sense of happiness knowing the title is given to me. You are a rare breed. You seek no fame, no interest in pomp. Your rage is not attention, it is truth in purest form. A truth against evil unchecked." He noticed Capall return into view with Ualach following behind him. "Ah! Your pony has arrived." They stood up and he was about to reunite with the colt, but the Doctor stopped him. "Before you go, I need to make sure we have an understanding. What I mean by *your dream is grander than mine* is that I seek something material and lasting when I perish. You seek the comfort and joy of life that only living can provide. I look for the future, you look for the present. I envy a man that can see beyond such things and find happiness in the little moments of life." He gestured to the pony at the bottom of the steps, they both made their way down and returned to Capall.

"Afternoon chaps, having an old chin wag?" The Hero asked.

"A heart to heart discussion," Thoirní answered. "Learning more about our fine friend here. You will look after him, will you?"

"Course!"

"Wait, what?" Ceannte looked back and forth at the others.

"What? I'm joining you on this thing."

"But why? I didn't ask you to come."

"Did you really think you could do this thing all by yourself?" Capall asked.

"I mean sure, I'd like the company, but it's really not *that* necessary is it?"

"I've seen you fight. It's definitely necessary."

"And in any event, there is absolutely no way a respectable Doge such as myself would ever send one of his own countrymen to complete a journey by themselves. No matter how confident one is."

"Yeah, okay, fine. But why didn't either of you two tell me about that?"

The two men briefly looked at each other. Thoirní spoke first. "Surely that was implied!"

"Because I'm a veteran fighter, and he's an expert tactician. And we both genuinely think it should be clear to you by now that this quest is *absolutely not* going to be a solo mission, you bloody idiot!"

"Alright then!" He raised his hands in exasperation. "If that's that, I'm not complainin'. I can use the muscle."

"Here," Capall handed the pony's lead to him. "I'll go get my pony, won't be a jiff."

"Righto." He waved off as the Hero claimed his own transport.

"He is right you know," Thoirní spoke and Ceannte turned about him. "If you think quests are done without help, you are very much mistaken. I can appreciate you are still quite new to this business, but given everything that has happened here up to this point, are you totally certain you can deal with issues of this kind out there, in the great unknown, by yourself?"

Ceannte shrugged. "I thought it was just finding some gold things. What's so hard about that?"

"Good grief! All quests have an underlying issue, some grand plan schemed by a mastermind. Heroes are a valuable commodity in a quest, they can provide fresh minds as well as fresh muscle. The more you have, the better your chance of survival and success. Never forget this."

"Aye, alright." He nodded.

The Doctor shuffled about his attire and produced a parchment. "Here. A parting gift for you." He took the document and read the text, but it was in a language he never seen before. Strange symbols appeared to make some sort of words and sentences, but he recognised none of it. "That is a scroll, it contains a spell." He looked up to the Doctor once her heard this. "You cannot read it. It is in a lost language known only by mages. Just be sure that whenever you need to, place your hand upon the scroll and chant the words '*A aithris*'. The incantation will cast an enchantment over you that will repel lightning strikes about your person, magical or otherwise."

"Handy!" Ceannte blurted out.

"Indeed."

"Right," Capall returned on top of his own steed, "are we ready?"

"More or less," he turned back to Thoirní. "May I be paid now?"

"Of course. Gentlemen, please come inside and we will finalise everything." The Doctor headed upstairs back into the Teachóir, Capall followed him up, still riding his pony.

"Come on Ualach." He too made his way up the steps. He towed his beast into the palace. "Did you miss me mate? I reckon after this I'll give you a fancy treat to munch on." They retired into the Golden Hill, waiting to transform themselves into heroes,

* * *

Some hours passed when once again the doors parted. The two men emerged as if they were decorated Sheriffs on patrol; dressed in military armour, and upon their ponies. Ceannte wore a nondescript suit of plate mail. The polished steel gleamed in the sunlight. For the first time he possessed a weapon, a short sword. He too wore a sash over his armour, similar to that of the Doge in material. A bright royal blue colour with a golden chevron weaved into it. Ualach trotted out with his own protection, a leather face mask. About the pony packs and bags were attached. He whined briefly at his master. "I know it's a bugger, but you'll need all that." He replied with a whinny. "It's no picnic for me mate, this stuff is damn heavy."

"Ah, you'll get used to it." Capall wore a similar suit of armour, and he carried his lance by his side. His sash was the same blue as Ceannte's, but it bore more insignia. A golden sun, a strange helmet shape, and a gear were stitched underneath the chevron, and the chevron itself was much larger than his. "It'll take a while but soon you won't feel much."

"Easy for you to say, how long have you been adventuring?"

"Getting on to five years now. Me and Chapaillíní here have been exploring a lot of the world." He patted the neck of his pony. Chapaillíní had her own metal protection instead of leather. She was a proper work horse, battle-hardened and content with discomfort.

"Where have you been?"

"North mostly. I frequently visit the Archonian men and high elves, occasionally the dwarves. Personally, I want to steer clear of the forest though. Them woodies are a really strange lot."

"Yeah, sure. I've heard weird stories about them."

"Have you heard the rumours about their promiscuity?"

Ceannte blushed. "Um, I'm afraid I have, yes."

"Well, the good news is most of it is exaggerated. The bad news is there are a few kernels of truth in them."

"Gees, really?"

"Yeah, but I don't want to scare you right now about it. We're are we going?"

Ceannte raised his eyebrows. "You're asking me?"

"Aye. It's your quest after all. I'll train you up and help you over the journey, but you're the one leading it."

"Oh! Alright." He chuckled to himself. "Well, I reckon we should head for the islands first. The quicker we get ours back at Aldora the better."

"Are you sure about that? We've only ourselves to fight her armada. Also, she's not part of the quest, is she?"

"Ah! We'll be right." Ceannte laughed. "If we have the help of the Order of Heroes, and if they are just as skilful as yourself, I reckon we can smash her to smithereens. And besides, I have to visit all the free lands of Mundus anyway, so I may as well."

Capall laughed after him. "Well, you certainly have a great deal of confidence in the Heroes. In order to reach Midgard, we first need to cross Árchontíkó and set sail." He pointed ahead and directed his companion's eye to the far distance. "We'll exit past the Bealach Isteach, then we'll make our way along the Great Western Road."

"Árchontíkó. That's the land of the Archons, right?"

"Right." They trotted out of the grounds and into the city. With the setting sun behind them, they began their long journey into the wide world of Mundus.

So ends the first tale of Mundus.
Tis a tale of time, and of history; how the individual changes over time, how the state does so, and how the world itself changes. The three actors are also examined by how each treat past events. For our principle hero, the unready Ceannte, the passing of time reveals his journey towards personal growth and philosophy. His knowledge of history has tainted his view towards the other races to such an extent that in the eyes of every elf, man, dwarf, and goblin, he sees only their past evils. Ceannte, therefore, is an example of, and an object lesson in, racism and how it can propagate, even through seemingly rational causes such as the history of the world.

The Dogedom of Leath Langa is a nation of halfling folk, creatures whose past has not been noteworthy, outside of recent war and the horrific violence it entails. In a society such as this then, it is a learned habit amongst the halflings to forget the past. The fixation amongst the halflings towards gold and profit is a distraction, an object goal to toil one's life to achieve. The Dogess Uisce is the embodiment of the pursuit of wealth above all else. In most of her actions in the story she is an arbitrator, she manages dealings with clients and has gained the reputation of being an excellent businesswoman.

As for the world itself, Mundus is a continent in a state of flux. Conflict has been a part of the continent for as far back as the Age of Schism, and hostilities have always followed closely behind it. However, amongst the death also lies great advancement. The Age of Discovery enriched the minds of all the races into new avenues of science and philosophy, and the most valorised accomplishment amongst the denizens of Mundus is the lasting peace that diplomacy had encouraged.

History is long, complex, and detailed. It is the fabric of every day, every person, and all that is the human experience. The stories by which we illustrate our past defines ourselves, potentially in ways we cannot easily predict. History is both clear and shrouded in bias. One story is no more a complete history of events than any other story, and the story of the world changes as the people change with it. A national epic to one people may be a tragic defeat to another. It is therefore necessary amongst all that the history of all the world must be understood, that a culture is defined by the past that it writes for itself and not by other actors, and that the people of today are not defined by the past, but shape them into what they can be in the future.

***

The second tale of Mundus shall follow our Heroes to the lands of men west of the continent. There, Ceannte discovers his potentials as a fighter and explores the wonder of humanity, in magic, and in science. The Heroes chase down the Sea Wretch in the Western Sea, and search for more Pieces of Eight about the land. However, along the way they run into a conflict with the Templar Knights, a friend from the past challenges the party into battle, and the sheer size of Aldora's shadows lurks in the dark waters. How shall Ceannte and the Heroes tackle these obstacles? Find out in the next book; Tales of Mundus – Treachery at Sea.

Epilogue

Inside the Teachóir, and well past the night of the Heroes' departure, the Doge Thoirní had been examining the palace with the squires and butlers of the great building. "I find it most upsetting, master Seirb, that a structure as large as this one does not seem to have any reserved space for my laboratory. I will not be parted with my things."

"Begging your pardon Doge," Seirb replied, "but the Teachóir is not exactly equiped to store magic things within the golden dome. Magic's not been any part of our heritage is all."

"Our heritage has only ever been about getting moneys and growing wealth. It's a pity it has brought about such a reputation amongst the other peoples. Well, I'll soon be changing that, for what is gold good for without a thing to spend it on. I shall build more houses of knowledge about Leath Langa. Let the gold in one's coin transform into the gold in one's mind, and one's heart."

"Very good master Doge." They arrived at a door at the end of a hallway. "This'll be the mistress's old privacy room. Uisce's private space."

"Uisce had a room just for her? Is this not simply her bed chambers?"

"No sir. This was a room especially fitted for her. She asked for the space some time ago now. Last year I think, but I forget."

Well then, Thoirní thought to himself, *if that's not an alarm, I don't know what is. I'll wager my diamond spectacles that a rather incriminating bit of evidence is behind that door. She needs no more now, but all the more skulduggery against Uisce the better.* "Well, that right there is giving me an idea. This shall be my laboratory then. If this space is indeed simply a privacy room, then it holds no purpose for me to keep it that way."

"Fair enough, it's your palace now." Seirb set down his candle holder upon a table beside him, rattled out a large circle of keys, and unlocked the door. He pushed it open and regained his candle. He stepped inside and lit the candles about to give light.

"If it is all the same to you master Seirb, I shall attempt to improve the Teachóir with electrical lighting. There's no sense in you constantly keeping lit the rooms of the palace if I can fashion a better method without all the energy."

"That'll be a great boon master Doge. I'd be much more useful in my tasks."

"Excellent then." Thoirní studied the room with great detail. He carefully observed everything in it, from the paintings of herself about the walls, to the plating of gold upon the tables and decks about the room. He saw the ornate objects within the room, the intricate shine of gold and steel and colours. Upon a desk were several necklaces of jewels, the reddest rubies, the greenest emeralds, the bluest sapphires. Each beautiful thing gleamed with a shine of exquisite light. "My word," he finally said, "she keeps quite a lot of her stuff down here. I can't think of a reason why though."

"Aye, you're not wrong. This place is givin' me the creeps."

"How so?"

Seirb looked about the room. "It appears Uisce's gone and made this a kind of shrine to herself. I reckon there's about three or four pieces of art that's all just about her, and the mirror and jewellery seem to be quite indulgent."

"Interesting thought master Seirb. I have similar feelings."

"The space is well lit now, if you don't mind, I much prefer to not be here and return to my duties."

"Carry on." The Doge gestured to the door as Seirb passed him by. When he was out of the room, he closed the door behind him. He listened carefully though the door as the squire left him. He quickly snapped back to a centrepiece at the end of the room, the mirror. Between two portraits and away from much of the decorations stood a large oval mirror. The size of it was especially unusual, it was the height of a human and much taller than a halfling could need. "I know you're there Aldora." The Doge said to the mirror. "I can see from my spectacles. This mirror is bewitched, and judging from the aura about it, I reckon you have planted a hex upon it to espies your dealings. You should be able to hear me." Nothing. He walked over the to mirror. "There's no point in hiding yourself. You've been exposed. Your treachery with our Dogess is all but void now, and we will-."

"You will what, exactly?" The mirror called back. "Add some patrol ships up the river perhaps? Send a fleet to find me?" Slowly an image was cast onto the metal, Aldora's reflection loomed over him. She was a tall, intimidating shadow. She wore an admiral's outfit and a feathered tricorne, the image of a distinguished sailor. Her eyepatch told another story. The scar upon her face told of her steely grit. The turquoise of her feather matched the eerie colour of her hair. "Your miniature boats are nothing to me. I will crush them under my boot."

"There is no need for this. I don't want war."

"Yet you threaten me with whatever nonsense your think will placate me. Pathetic!"

"I mean no offence ma'am. I merely seek to inform you of the most recent developments of our land. I trust you would care-."

"I don't care!" She interrupted. "I could not possibly care any less about what pointless news comes for your backwater homestead. All I want is our deal to remain as it has been, plus the cost of a new sloop if it is all the same to you."

"I shall do no such thing! Such a tribute for no return is nothing short of exploitation. I cannot in all good conscious continue this extortion. I will not allow it."

Aldora upturned her chin. Her image had a strange malevolence, a darkness unlike any other Thoirní had experienced. She laughed lowly. "Do you think you can stop me? Do you believe that your poultry wealth can possibly undo my will? Your small, meaningless gesture. It will be for nought. You will send your men to their graves and subject your helpless folk to the steel of my cutlass. You will ruin your home and the lives of all about you, just to stand your ground against me."

"I shall not allow it. We can come to an agreement."

"There is no agreement! There is nothing I will accept, save from all your plunder. If you think you can stop me from raising your nation to the ground, by all means, test your metal. I extracted your gold for a reason. My fleet is vast, and my crew many. You cannot raise a navy against me, and I will throw the full weight of my might against you. I own the water between Midgard and the mainland. I will loom over your very shadow, until the day I set foot on your land once again. And then, when I see it fit, I will lift my foot, I will step on you, and I will grind you into the dust."

A long silence fell between them. The Doge took his time to respond, he observed her details. *She certainly feels quite sure of herself. Not very much different to Uisce now that I think about it. But she is still different. Uisce is just a distractor, a fast-talking diplomat that spins stories when it suits her agenda.* Aldora looked down on him and gave a sly smile. *But this doesn't feel like a distraction. Aldora's seems very direct and blunt. And also quite testy, volatile perhaps. Uisce is ultimately an inconvenience, a trickster. Aldora might just be the real deal here.* "There is one slight problem with that plan," he said, "you may well have the navy to blockade our ports, and the men to sack our cities. But my dear, what would be your plan should you find yourself dead on arrival? Can your pirate fiends attack without their battle master?"

She made no reaction She still smiled her devilish grin. After some time, she laughed. "Do you fear death, halfling?" Her head tilted slightly at Thoirní. "I don't fear death. I *am* death. I am the Sea Wretch, Mistress of the Water. I have destroyed every remaining pirate before me and incorporated their loot, and their crews, into my own empire. I stalk my prey, as the vulture circles its food. And, good sir, master of the River Empire, I will do to you as I did to all those fools," she raised her hand, "and what I will do to this mirror right now." She clicked her fingers, and the great mirror shattered instantly. Shards of polished metal and glass sprayed the room. The Doge covered his face. The breaking and clammer stopped as soon as it began. He dropped his arm and he saw the state of the mirror. It laid broken on the sandstone floor. Millions of cold, sharp blades littered the side of the room where it once stood. There was no mirror left, only the remnants of what was. He looked about for any other objects under a hex, but none remained. Not even the shards of the mirror held any magic left in them. *She's gone, for now. I reckon she will come to get me now. Godspeed Cean. We'll need all the help we can get.*

Acknowledgements

It is difficult to describe the experience I have had creating my first proper story. My friends and family have been excellent foundations of support, and via conversations over the internet, colleagues have given me useful knowledge, and in some cases inspiration that have been eventually baked into the story itself. I want to personally thank those around me that have had a hand in the product of this story, as well as my fiction work in general.

I want to thank my mum and dad for always surrounding me with stories. There was always a distinct difference between my parents' narratives. I grew up with my working-class mother. She would tell tales of Greece in the 1960s, emigrating to Australia, working in a factory, and becoming everyone's favourite barista. Unfortunately, many of my early memories with my father have faded away. However, I would always enjoy talking with him. He would spin yarns about his time as a tutor in university, the antics of selling phonecards, and other various anecdotes in his life. They each made me laugh and think deeply about life in their own ways. I also want to thank my brother, who I made the lore for this story originally. A few years ago, the background and lore the narrative is steeped in was originally made for a different medium. Over time, I worked on the history of Mundus through the project. It may not be the original idea, but this project was the trigger for me to begin work towards my first professional story.

I want to thank my good friend Maree for her continuous encouragement and interest in my work. Developing and writing a story while working an eight-hour day most days has the tendency to drain a lot of my energy. Weekends are precious gifts that I spend most of the time working on this story. Ever since I began to write the story, she has been supportive and would always ask about it, and on the occasion I decide to parse the draft through someone, she would pester me to send a copy. With every read she finds more nuance and new things to talk about with me.

I want to thank my editor David, who over the initial drafts of the story gave me invaluable advice on how to expand and improve it. The original draft was much shorter, much vaguer, and almost nothing at all like the current story. While I wrote the elements of the story, it was David who coached me to understand and appreciate concepts such as foreshadowing and logical character development in a narrative. Entire chapters emerged from my work with him. This includes a device in which I must also acknowledge another person entirely.

I want to thank Gezel and the production team at TellWell for giving me the ability to produce a book, and the opportunity to publish my work for the first time. It is a dream come true for me to be able to publish a story. They have been very patient and understanding and have guided me through the process. Also, can we please appreciate the cover art of the book? The artist is amazing and that alone makes me want to work with them more.

I also want to acknowledge and thank people I have never personally met, yet still managed to influence the story in subtle ways. Specifically, they nudged me to add an undercurrent of mathematics in the narrative. I want to acknowledge Brady Haran and Tom Scott and thank them for their contributions to this story. I go into detail about this specific effect in Appendix C however, as a brief overview, I discovered a YouTube video featuring Tom as he explained the variety of counting systems within humanity. The video compelled me to seriously consider the concept of novel numeracy systems.

Lastly, I want to acknowledge Matt Parker and thank him for allowing me to stylise a section of my story to emulate his work; *Humble Pi: a Comedy of Maths Errors*. Before I ever considered it, I read his book and loved it. During the writing process the need for a foreshadowing device was raised. The idea of a book of stories centred around faulty mathematics is a direct reference to *Humble Pi*. The short stories, the humour, the title of the book, even the name of the author is a reference to Matt.

Seriously, get *Humble Pi*, it's an amazing read.

Appendix A

Etymology

I am a big believer in the idea of giving character names meaning, such as describing certain behaviours, physical characteristics, or the past of said characters. I began to adopt the notion of adding meaningful context to my character's names in an unfinished work more than five years ago. At the time I purchased a baby naming book because it was an excellent resource in learning and understanding the meanings of the names we give each other. My name, Chris Sifniotis, is Greek in origin; the first name "Chris", written in Greek as Χρῆστος, has very obvious connections to Christianity, however, in general the term actually means "King". "Sifniotis" is much more specialised in its meaning. It is written as Σιφνιώτης and literally means "of Sifnos." Sifnos is an island in the Aegean Sea. In relation to the mainland Sifnos is halfway between Attica – the state in which the capital city of Athens is, and Crete – the island of the ancient Minoans, and features in the mythology of the Labyrinth and the Minotaur. Putting these terms together then, my name can be interpreted as "King from the Land of Sifnos", however this is just one example and one can twist these terms any way they want.

In this appendix, I will establish the meaning of the names of characters, places and terms featured in this book. Each of the races of the Nine Realms are inspired in some way by real world histories and cultures, one of the clearest examples of this is in the names I give the actors and locations in this world. This book features names of the Halflings, which are rooted in the Irish language. Spells are also featured in their own section, notes in parentheses describe specific information about the use of the names.

Characters and Names

Ceannte – *ceannt te,* an Irish term meaning 'hot head'.

Macántacht – *macántacht,* and Irish term meaning 'honesty'.

Álainn – *álainn,* an Irish term meaning 'lovely'.

Eagna – *eagna,* an Irish term meaning 'wisdom'.

Athair – *athair,* an Irish term meaning 'father'.

Óstach – *óstach,* an Irish term meaning 'host'.

Ualach – *ualach,* an Irish term meaning 'burden'.

Óir – *óir,* an Irish term meaning 'gold'.

Airgead – *airgead*, an Irish term meaning 'money'.

Comhbhrón – *comhbhrón*, an Irish term meaning 'sympathy'.

Soiléire – *soil*éire, an Irish term meaning 'clarity'.

Uisce – *uisce*, an Irish term meaning 'water'.

Lámh – *lámh*, an Irish term meaning 'hand'.

Súile – *súlie*, an Irish term meaning 'eyes'.

Cluas – *cluas*, an Irish term meaning 'ear'.

Capall Beag – *capall beag*, an Irish term meaning 'little horse'.

Impéar – *impéar*, an Irish term meaning 'impaler'.

Seangharda – *sean-gharda*, an Irish term meaning 'old guard'.

Chapaillíní – *chapaillíní*, an Irish term meaning 'pony'.

Tintreach – *tintreach*, an Irish term meaning 'lightning'.

Thoirní – *thoirní*, an Irish term meaning 'thunderstorm'.

Bain – *bain*, an Irish term meaning 'smash'.

Slatintreach – *slat tintreach*, an Irish term meaning 'lightning rod'.

Cosantóir – *cosantóir*, an Irish term meaning 'defender'.

Teorainn – *teorainn*, an Irish term meaning 'frontier'.

Leathnú – *leathnú*, an Irish term meaning 'expand'.

Amhras – *amhras*, an Irish term meaning 'suspicion'.

Bradach, Shortfoot – *bradach*, an Irish term meaning 'pirate'.

Seirb – *seirb*, an Irish term meaning 'a servant'.

Terminology

Teachcnoc – *teach cnoc*, an Irish term meaning 'hill house'.

Astrapí, Limit – αστραπή (astrapí), a Greek term meaning 'lightning'.

Locations

Mundus – *mundus*, a Latin term meaning 'the world'.

Leath Langa, the Dogedom of (country) – *leath langa*, an Irish term meaning 'half ling'.

Foirceannadh (river) – *foirceannadh*, an Irish term meaning 'winding'.

Béal na Habhann (settlement, town) – *béal na habhann*, an Irish term meaning 'mouth of the river'.

Sruth Dé (magic node, water) – *sruth dé*, an Irish term meaning 'god's stream'.

Cnoc Gorm (settlement, city) – *cnoc gorm*, an Irish term meaning 'blue hill'.

Bunaitheach (settlement, capital) – *bunaitheach*, an Irish term meaning 'founding'.

Teachóir, the (building, palace) – *teach óir*, an Irish term meaning 'house of gold'.

Riasc (landmass, islands) – *riasc*, an Irish term meaning 'marsh'.

Bealach Isteach (building, bridge) – *bealach isteach*, an Irish term meaning 'entrance'.

Spells and Incantations

Patthar keedeevaar (spell, Earth Magic) – *patthar kee deevaar*, a Hindi term meaning 'stone wall'.

Od khaalga (spell, Darkness Magic) – од хаалга (od khaalga), a Mongolian term meaning 'star gate'.

Leachtú (spell, Water Magic) – *leachtú*, an Irish term meaning 'liquify'.

Cioclón draíochta (summoned creature, Storm Magic) – *cioclón draíochta*, an Irish term meaning 'magic cyclone'.

A aithris (enchantment, Storm Magic) – *tintreach a aithris*, an Irish term meaning 'repel lightning'. While a airthris does mean 'repel' in this context, the term is not used in a general sense.

Appendix B

Notes on the Halflings
and Their History

Mundus is ruled by nine nations amongst five types of humanoids. Three elf clans and three human clans dominate the earth, the halflings are grouped with the dwarves and the goblins as the Minor Races. They govern a hilly land called the Dogedom of Leath Langa, situated at the delta of the great Foirceannadh River. The nation is driven by mercantilism and good cheer. The reputation of the halflings is that of jolly small folk with a love for a good bargain. They tend to stay in the Dogedom and do not travel beyond the borders of their own experience, making them one of the more hermit creatures on Mundus. Leath Langa is surrounded by multiple nations; the golden coast of the Archons due north, the Udoerufu Forest north east of the Dogedom, Beacon – the city-state of hope due east, and the Orkland in the Tajriba Desert south of the river. They have settled on both sides of the Foirceannadh

River and the surrounding islands at the mouth of the river into the Western Sea.

As their name suggests the halflings are small folk between 4'6" and 5'4" in height, and they are generally wide people, many have a girth despite being active and eating healthily. Their common physical appearance is that of a red headed, well fed youth with bright blue eyes and plain clothes. Their occupations vary but are mostly centred around acquiring wealth. Most continue family businesses such as farming, fishing, butchery, etc. The middle class tend to transact along the local and national trade routes amongst the neighbouring races. The halflings trade directly with the Archonian and Midgardian men, the wood elves and the dwarves, and indirectly with the high elves. Others establish eateries, pubs and inns to ply more gold from otherwise peaceful foreigners at high prices. The most affluent govern important naval trade routes by operating the many harbours and docks littered across the nation. Due to the commercial nature and lifestyle of the halflings the docks are the most valuable structures in the Dogedom, they are the vital lines of both communication and trade they have and use to power their nation.

Halflings are a unique lot. They are a generally happy folk because they want for nothing and dream small. They seek fulfilment, and they tend to find it in toil and work. They live to earn a decent living and own a house, either a normal house above ground or a Teachcnoc, an underground dwelling – typically a hollowed-out hill. It is normal and well for a halfling to desire a good home, a good husband or wife, a good family of children and good wealth to deflect hardship and suffering. They often have passionate feelings towards their beliefs and opinions, but they never raise they voice. A teaching of good manners prevents them from acting indignantly to friends or strangers alike. They much prefer to laugh at a funny story or hear a fanciful tale than to upset others, halflings are therefore slow to anger. Lastly, while they generally maintain large circles of friends and a friendly relationship to all, it is commonplace for them to exploit transactions to their favour. In a culture so heavily geared towards gaining wealth, halflings themselves are shrewd salesmen and often trick strangers into handing them more gold than they ought to from regular purchases. Only tightly knit friends or partners are immune to their guile and charm.

Halflings have little interest in their history, most do not know their past beyond the Fourth Age. This is due exclusively to the orc attacks against them during the Age of Destruction however, this introduction will cover their known history. Records indicate that the halflings were first referenced late in the Second Age after the dark elves encountered the race first in the 930s and again at 1118SA however, they claim their founding further back before the Second Age. The dark elves described the folk as 'queer half men' with an interest in storytelling. The Archonian men then discovered the halflings in 1809SA after landing on the mainland

and establishing the first human presence known to the rest of the races. The high men took little interest in them as they were more intrigued by their interactions with the high elves. What was written about them was a friendly reception and 'a lyrical race of men, prone to toil and merriment'. Upon the landing of humanity and the passing of time into the Third Age the Midgardians discovered the halflings in 89TA. Similarly, the men took little notice of them due to their engagements with the Archons and the other elf clans. The advent of the landing of men brought about a new age of science for both the mainland races and the human nations. During the Age of Discovery, the halfling sovereign – the merchant king known as the Doge – discovered the other races and promptly endeavoured to open trade routes and connect the nations to Leath Langa. Their economy rose rapidly and spurred the growth and expansion of the entire nation, so much so that several settlements far from the capital declared independence from the Dogedom and the then Dogess granted it to every town east of Beacon. Of these city-states only Teorainn Abhann and Doras an Duine still stand today.

The Fourth Age is the period which places the halflings in time largely against their will. The catastrophe that precipitated the creation of the orcs is a well-documented event. In 1056TA an experiment took place in the Tajriba Desert during the expansion of the disciplines of magic. Human and elf scientists conducted a test to determine the nature of the eighteenth form of magic – what is now known as Explosive Magic.

During this period scientists and alchemists began to combine various forms of Mana to create new forms of magic, in this case the experiment attempted a direct amalgamation of molten Fire Mana poured into a cauldron of Death Mana crystals. The chemical reaction resulted in a devastating explosion killing some and mutating many of the survivors. The affected men and at the time elves suffered severe chemical burns, scorched and discoloured skin, and a terrible affliction – Orkrage, a psychological condition specific within the orc race where their thoughts boil over in rage and violence, attacking anything and anyone in their path. The mutated men chased after unaffected survivors all the way back to the edge of Leath Langa, and in doing so brought the Age of Destruction to the halflings.

Without any experience in warfare the halflings were unprepared for a sudden attack from a group of violent men. The southern hamlets were wiped off the map, the population were killed, and the buildings raised. Strangely, the orcs moved east along the feet of the hillside and after more attacks and harassment most of the lucrative city-states also fell to them. The affected towns were all risen. Oddly again, the raiders turned about back the way they came. This time, they swept the rest of Leath Langa. The aggressors initially breached a gap in the nation which exposed the capital city, Bunaitheach. By 70FOA the orcs returned to threaten the city and the heart of the halfling nation. In the decades that passed between the first attack and the current threat the folk armed themselves. They established a few military regiments and, with the assistance of the neighbouring Archons, learned close quarter combat, military strategy and organisation on the battlefield. On the day of the attack the halflings fought bravely by all accounts, and did in fact repel the orcs however, the achievement came at a great cost. Despite their valiant attempt, the army was decimated. Just over three quarters of the entire army perished: 135,000 men. The nation was crippled with every industry directly affected by the loss of life, and the Dogedom itself was scarred by the horrors of warfare. The orcs retreated from the hillside and turned their attention to the dwarves in the mountains. In fact, despite the major events of the Council of the Earth, the Race Against Peace and the Age of Peace that followed, the halflings were never again harassed by the orcs nor any other race. Within their culture, the Sheriffs are the most respected men in the Dogedom. Their cunning tactic and deft strike ensured the safety of the people and themselves, suffering by far the least casualties of all the regiments and divisions of the standing army. Sheriffs, Pony Riders and cavalry regiments are highly valorised by the halflings.

Today the halflings live only for peace, prosperity and pleasure, they eat, they chat, they buy, they sell, they toil about in the fields or the waters, they rest in their cozy beds or lively bars, they laugh, they dance – they live only to live happily, for they remember the screams and the gore and the utter destruction violence brings, and they never wish to see it again.

Notes on the Race Against Peace

The Race Against Peace is a war that took place near the end of the Fourth Age between the orcs and a coalition of every other race on Mundus. The war and the events that took place within it are the most documented and well-known events amongst all the races due to its recent history and its importance. The chain of events that led to the war began in 1452FOA with the sudden expansion of the orcs. The then Orking Mudammir I claimed the throne after a bloodless assassination of his brother Hagar Alzzuhr. Little is known about Orcish culture due to the current embargoes against them. What we do know is that they were both born into the house of Muqatil, its significance remains a mystery. Mudammir had a clear hatred against the dark elves who reside directly south of the Tajriba Desert, his xenophobia developed as a young child.

The Orking openly declared war against the dark elves the following day after he ascended – a behaviour that was totally different to previous conflicts. Surviving records before this time show the orcs as having, for lack of a better phrase, a lack of strategy. They were known as sudden aggressors and immediately harassed towns. However, analysis of orc warfare revealed a shocking lack of control or plan in the way the soldiers fought. Always they attacked, raided and pillaged with random bursts of objective and intent. One primary example of this is the Seizure of Hvelv in 225FOA, upon which the orcs attacked the dwarves and were easily defeated militarily. Unlike the halflings, they were not only refined blacksmiths and metallurgists but also skilled swordsmen. Their prowess in close combat was well established. However, while the dwarves were dominant in offensive play, they payed no mind to their defences, this lapse allowed the orcs to apply their Orkrage and breach through the defences to the city's treasury. Discovering this, the pillagers made off with whatever gold, platinum and jewellery they could get their hands on and fled, they then alerted their comrades about their luck and every raiding orc made for the treasury. Dwarves for all their armaments and plate mail were suited for sword fights, not pursuits. Traditional dwarf armament includes a thick suit of armour made of a toughened steel. The advantage of such skin gave warriors a near impregnable exterior that was heavy and cumbersome. None of the defenders had either the stamina or the raw strength to either stop or catch the thieves. While many orcs were cut down by the dwarves during the raid, they succeeded in at least looting a significant fraction of the Doge's treasure.

Given Mudammir's declaration, he still enjoyed the same furious speed the orcs were capable of. In no less than a fortnight the Orking rallied his army and formulated a battle campaign to annihilate the dark elves. Despite Mudammir's fury, the orcs still suffered from the same level of disorganisation. The additional settlements that he attempted to establish were directed off course and followed a purely random path. It took the army almost thirty years to reach the closest dark elf settlement, they reached the outpost of Khargal by 1494FOA. However, once there the orc attacks were remarkably effective, by 1500FOA Mudammir I occupied nearly all of the north of Kharankhui ger Ongontsny. During that time, despite the obvious gap between them and the dark elves, the other races quickly allied with them against the orcs. The Archonian men were the first to side with Khan Urjil Shimgui, followed quickly by the Midgardians, the wood elves, dwarves, goblins and halflings. After much deliberation and pressure, the high elves too unified and began to establish the very first united front Mundus had ever seen. However, everyone was separated from the despairing dark elves. There had to be a way to bridge the gulf and secure the safety of the Khan.

Enter King Dalton III; the Midgardian king led the push to create a tangible location for global diplomacy and to unify the races in order to spread peace. In 1502FOA Dalton sailed to the Archonian coast to call the leaders of all nations and confer over the emerging war with the orcs. At first no one entertained the idea of entering a conflict, no one felt they should enter a war that does not involve them but they also agreed with Dalton who is attributed with the quote, "idle conversation would do nothing except bring the savage Orkind to the doorstep of every man, woman and child for the slaughter."

Disappointed at the result, King Dalton III persisted. Immediately after the conference he returned to Midgard only to deputise his prince as a regent to rule in his stead, return to Mundus, and campaign for a renewed push for unity. For one and a half years Dalton travelled to all the nations north of the desert to continue his dialogue with the other leaders. He achieved that goal by 1504FOA when he returned to the surface from the underground realm of the goblins. Dalton's newest plan was to create a centralised point, a common place for the kings and queens to converge and discuss. A new city where the world would unite into a new era. The king approached the then Doge Úinéir of the halflings to purchase land and create his city, Úinéir let him the land for the equivalent of one million gold pieces. Between the years of 1505 and 1506FOA, elf, human and dwarf settlers arrived onto the site, and with the help of King Dalton III engineered, planned and constructed the first buildings of the settlement. The township was the beginning of Beacon – so named to be a beacon of hope for the world in times of trouble and hardship. Initially Dalton wanted the city to be purely a diplomatic city-state, "a point on the map that is not governed by any one nation but in fact ruled by a consensus of all leaders, for the betterment of all races," according to the original doctrine of the founding of Beacon. Over time however, with the constant interaction of all the races conversing and trading, the city turned into a commercial hub. Beacon today is used as a viaduct for global trade. The use of Midgardian tongue as a Common language emerged because of Beacon.

Dalton's final part of his vision was about to take shape, a place for the leaders to convene.

It was at this point that the Race Against Peace truly began, for the Orking caught wind of the Midgardian king's plan. King Dalton III began construction of a large building within Beacon, what would become the Council of the Earth – the meeting place for the leaders of the Nine Realms to convene on matters concerning Mundus. Orking Mudammir I doubled back from his occupation of the dark elf nation and instead denounced the other races and declared open war. He focused his attack on Beacon itself, but the orcs were, as they are still, highly erratic creatures. Once they left their roads again the troops wondered in odd ways. The Council of the Earth building took a total of five years to complete, in that time Beacon suffered its own trials outside of Dalton's control. The most damaging of such events was the abdication of Doge Úinéir in 1508FOA, the halflings were and still are vital traders to Beacon, and the lost transaction crippled their economy for months. However, Beacon also suffered military scares, fighting outside of the city took place at 1510FOA, and it was the worst assault the orcs mounted. According to several primary accounts, waves of soldiers crashed up to the defenders. Attackers of all sorts fought the orcs; halfling Sheriffs charged in front of Archonian Hoplites, who defended wood elven Ranger troops, and all gathered support from Eldar Chaplains. The best of Mundus repelled the worst the orcs threw at them, holding their position and giving Dalton the time he needed to complete the structure. By the end of the year Mudammir's time ran out and Beacon was prepared. He therefore decided to turn his men around a second time and back the way they came to harass the dark elven lands. The Orking's folly was the major characteristic of the orcs. When he turned his attention to Beacon and away from the wasteland, Khan Urjil Shimgui saw the opportunity to restore his land. He promptly pushed back at the garrison as soon as the Orking was nowhere near a position to respond and reclaimed more than half of his loss. When Mudammir learned of this he was furious to find his past claims where retaken, but the resources were spent at Beacon. Against the remaining armies the dark elves totally recaptured their lost ground by 1514FOA.

Before the end of that year arrangements were made to bring Khan Urjil Shimgui from his encampment at the front line to Beacon. By 1515FOA the first convention of the Council of the Earth took place. The focus was to address the orcs now that they were contained within the Tajriba Desert. Like the previous summit, they could not reach a unanimous decision. All three elf clans sought to destroy the ferrel band of raiders, the human races believed a diplomatic approach was more reasonable, and the minor races were split with their own desires and wishes. Dalton's dream for peace would be a far more difficult task. Compounding matters was the Khan's invading force poised to march into the desert, and that the Orking himself was preparing to respond. Dalton convinced Shimgui to maintain his army but not to launch any attack while the Council determined the best course of action, it took the leaders a lengthy ten months to negotiate and concede terms for a universal agreement and for action to finally be implemented against the orcs.

The first draft of the Council's Mandate was established in 1516FOA that allowed the co-existence of all nine races of Mundus. The assurances of the policies within the mandate established that peace was fundamentally above all other desires, and therefore all laws within the treaty must uphold peace. The laws stated that for the orcs to remain independent, they must disband their armies, repay the dwarves for their stolen treasure, and uphold the rite for peace on Mundus. Orking Mudammir I was cornered into signing the harsh terms, but the orcs were in return capable of trading exotic goods with the other races in order to raise the reparations and maintain an economy. The Orc Signing marked the end of an era of violence, suffering, blood and war, and the following year was marked as the First Year of the Fifth Age, hitherto known as the Age of Peace.

Appendix C

The Mathematics of Mundus and its Unique Counting Systems

Before I begin, I want to acknowledge and thank Brady Haran and Tom Scott. They are two men who have produced a YouTube video that has had such an effect on my work that I paused the production of the plot and immediately set about introducing not only a mathematical bend, but also novel counting systems into my fantasy work. As a result of the video, it is now my interest to think deeply about, and inject new and unique ways of counting. If you are interested in the universality of counting and how other human cultures express numbers, please search for the Numberphile video *58 and Other Confusing Numbers* on YouTube.

I am a recreational mathematician. I enjoy playing around with numbers and seeing what I can find. I have discovered an obscure proof that seems to be lost to us today; the Nicomachus Theorem, questioned the notion of prime numbers by looking into the primality of -1, and to this day continue to find and observe curiosities in numbers and puzzles. As a result of this and the video, I have decided to introduce mathematics into my story, albeit as a shadow and hidden from plain sight most of the time. This appendix will explain recurring mathematical symbology and themes in *Tales of Mundus* and feature two counting systems made exclusively for two of the races: Finger-Counting by the elf clans, and Two-Handed Counting by the dwarves.

(same, same) = dif²re²nt

The abstract nature of mathematics is universal. However it is constructed for humanity, maths is the purest form of thought. Chemistry, physics, geology, astronomy; all other sciences are either directly or indirectly rooted in mathematics. Therefore, it should surprise no one that the principals of mathematics have not changed in Mundus. Fundamentally they cannot change, even in a fictional world where the author can dictate its internal structure. The logic of numbers must exist. One plus one must always equal two. The symbology may change, a + may become a И, a 1 may turn into a <, but the core principle of addition does not. < И< x ?. 1 + 1 = 2. In Mundus, therefore, it is easy to appreciate mathematics because in this world it is not a case of absurd logic in impossible worlds, but rather a cipher in which concepts like exponentiation, factorials, and other higher order mathematics are represented. This part of the appendix will highlight the subtle differences in the symbols and characters in the language of Mundus Mathematics.

Division in Mundus is essentially the same compared to the real world. We use ÷ to inform ourselves to divide the latter number from the former number. The development of division as a concept emerged everywhere on Mundus, the earliest records come from the ancient site of Archon on Midgard. However, the symbol used in division is ∕, a single diagonal slash. In the same way that ÷ is used to represent the fraction in which the division function is processed, division and fractions in Mundus are both expressed with ∕.

Example 1.

$$\frac{314}{100} \Rightarrow 314 \, / \, 100$$

The symbology of division in Mundus is a simple change, yet it is a more consistent visual representation compared to the standard use in our own world. + and × are the same image rotated, and both the addition and multiplication functions are additive functions. They generate larger numbers. + and − are similar images, one line is omitted, yet the images represent linear functions in mathematics, positively and negatively respectively. ÷ is an image that breaks this symmetry with × and to a lesser extent −. The use of ∕ grants a harmonious synergy in the use of mathematical notation within the four fundamental operations, the simplest rules of maths. One line for subtractive functions, two lines for additive functions. Turn the image to switch between linear functions and multiplicative functions.

Mathematical constants are fundamental ratios. They are discoverable in all worlds in all universes in the multiverse. The symbols for the mathematical constants, however, are completely arbitrary. Just because everyone on Earth knows what π is does not mean the denizens of Mundus understand the symbol as being anything more than the conjunction of three lines. Below is a list of the five mathematical constants and the definition of their symbology.

Ξ = **1.414213...** Xi is more commonly known as the square root of two. Xi is the first irrational number discovered by any race in Mundus as part of Trígono's *On the Subject of Squared Triangles*:

Example 2.

$$a^2 + b^2 = x^2$$

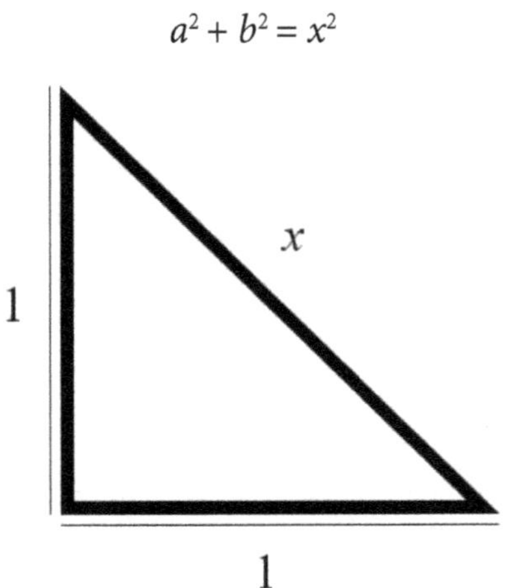

$$1^2 + 1^2 = 2. \ x = \sqrt{2} = \Xi$$

The square root of two does not have a specific character on Earth as it does in Mundus. The symbol was originally a square with a line though it but was later changed to Ξ after one of Trígono's students recognised its similarity to the square with the line. Xi is a largely underused constant in the modern era. It was used largely in roadbuilding across multiple nations. Styled roads and streets use square stones of length Ξ to project rotated squares within squares. Examples of roads with rotated squares include multiple flagstone streets across the Dogedom of Dvergmark, central districts within Archonian cities, and the Great Road leading into Nótiapóli, Xībù Chéngshì, Shēngmìng Zhīchéng, and Golyn Khot.

$\phi = \mathbf{1.618033}\ldots$ Phi, sometimes known as the Divine Ratio, is the mathematical constant of proportions. In the simplest definition, Phi appears when comparing quantities: ϕ is the ratio generated between the larger quantity and the smaller quantity when the ratio is equal to the sum of both quantities compared to the larger quantity.

Example 3.

$$\frac{(a+b)}{a} = \frac{a}{b} = \phi$$

Phi is the only mathematical constant that is almost exactly the same as on Earth, only a modification of the original symbol. In Mundus, ϕ was first coined by ancient men and used in their architecture, proportionality was observed in structures and especially in religious institutions such as temples and shrines to the gods. Modern Archonians today still use ϕ-structure architecture. Beyond mortal usage the high elves have adopted the mathematical constant into their own buildings however, the Eldars have been so enamoured by the beauty of ϕ that they also imported the concept of Phi into their pantheon. Today they assert Pi as the mortal daughter of the great goddess Xihe, mother of the earth. Ironically the Archonian alphabet does contain a character named Pi, π, that is not attached to any mathematical constant in Mundus. The use of the symbol ϕ emerged from the elves as it also represented the sun, just as Xihe is the representation of the sun in high elven religion.

$\varepsilon = 2.718281...$ Epsilon is a number rooted in exponential theory in mathematics. Discovered mathematically much later than any other constant, Epsilon represents the highest possible rate at which a value can increase infinitely, over infinite time. The number was first discovered by Professor Charles Leopold Yeoland in the Sage's Guild of Midgard. Upon attending a lecture in specialised magic casting, the instructor informed of the curious property of Mana crystals seeming to discharge more energy that they were made to hold. Yeoland became intrigued by the mystery and, with the help of his companion, set to work investigating. It took them nearly two years to analyse the crystals, and one of Yeoland's most famous observations was notated. Values in brackets are modern values based on recent experimentation.

The electrical capacity of a purely Adamantine Mana crystal of precisely 100g appeared to reach a peak of marginally under 272kW [271.8kW] of energy. A Silver-Adamantium Mana alloy of the same quantity is significantly more powerful, generating 1515kW and a half [1515.4kW] of electrical energy. By far the most powerful substance to date is the Gold-Adamantine crystal which produces an electrical output of a fraction below 161,818kW [161,817.8kW]. The testing of these materials with differing lengths, masses and volumes has concluded that the aforementioned power outputs for each form of unbounded Mana crystal is a multiplicative function of its mass to its specific power, which are defined as the earlier values...

It is not certain the kind of devices such power can be useful for however, should such a time occur in the future where electrical energy can be harnessed and extracted, the value of the natural Gold-Adamantium alloy will most certainly appreciate in value, perhaps to an extent where entire nations could not purchase such pristine treasure.

Yeoland's discovery of the power outputs of Mana crystals found the number ε in a natural circumstance however, it was not known the importance of the number. The abstract concept the mathematical constant is associated with was unearthed in a later piece of what was then unrelated material. Dwarf merchant turned mathematician Antall Hjerne worked with compound interest and wanted to calculate the best possible financial return. Using the process of the recent creation of calculus, Hjerne found the number to be approximately 272%, which was Yeoland's original power output value. Modern mathematics have defined Epsilon to 25 decimal places, and thanks to Yeoland and Hjerne modern alchemists know that the specific energy output of unbound Mana crystals is a composition of indices of ε. The specific power output of pure Mana is $100(x\varepsilon)$kW, Quork Mana – Silver-Adamantine alloy – is $100(x\varepsilon^\varepsilon)$kW, and Crysx Mana – Gold-Adamantine alloy – is again an increase of an exponential of ε. There is currently no known method for writing such an expression in Mundus. In the case of Earth, ε is the equivalent to e, often called Euler's constant. Epsilon was created after Hjerne originally wrote his undefined rate to be ε for 'exponential'.

$\delta = 3.141592...$, and $\rho = 6.283185...$ Delta and Rho are the two circle constants, each were found at the same time by multiple races. The two most noteworthy discoveries of each were the ancients work from the Archons and the high elves, and the interpretations of ρ by the Midgardian men and the Dwarves. All four methods were independent of each other. δ and ρ represent the numbers π and τ on Earth.

The development of δ first began by the Archons on ancient Midgard. The ancient men developed a simple technique for approximating the Delta as the perimeter of proportionate shapes. Schímata Kýklou constructed the Enclosed Circle Algorithm, whereby a circle was set within two shapes of similar type – starting with equal triangles – one large shape whose sides rested upon the circle, and one small shape whose corners touched the edge of the circle, and then he calculated the upper and lower bounds of δ by measuring the sides the two similar shapes:

Example 4.

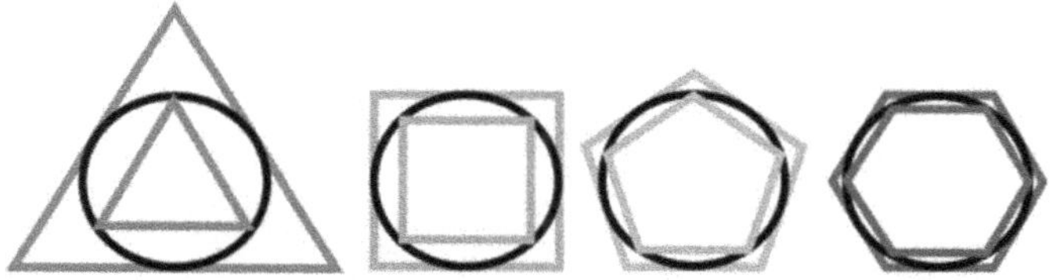

A demonstration of the Enclosed Circle Algorithm.
The function uses the similar shapes to estimate δ, in
which the range changes and becomes increasingly
smaller as the shapes increase in vertices.

Kýklou then introduced similar shapes with more sides and repeated the process. For each pair of shapes, the more sides the shapes had to the previous, the more defined the range between the upper and lower bounds became, narrowly closing in on Delta. He estimated the diameter constant to be *"nearly twenty-two seventh parts, or there about."* This popularised the notion of δ equalling exactly 22/7 for most of the Third Age until recent processes better defined the number.

Meanwhile, in isolation of the ancient men, the Eldars engaged in similar geometric puzzles. While the Archons established δ as a linear constant, the high elves examined δ as a function of area. Priestess Shuāng Bèimiànjī attempted to define Delta as the area of two regular polygons. Through an impressively genius process of division and geometry, Bèimiànjī rearranged the original circle into a rectangle within a margin of error. This process is now called the δ-algorithm. This algorithm is very abstract and tends to require advanced mathematical knowledge.

Example 5.

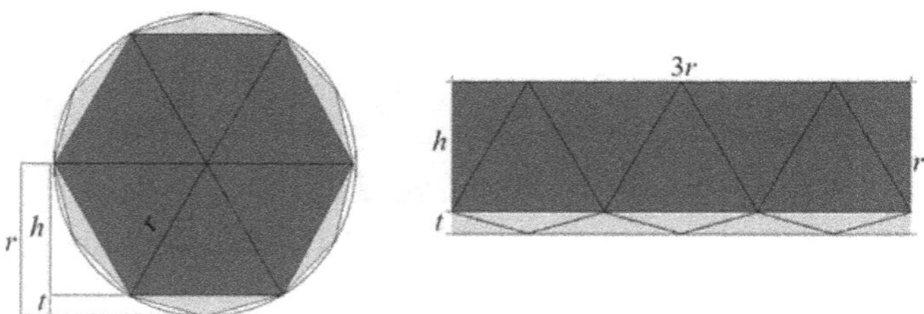

A demonstration of the δ-algorithm using a hexagon and a dodecagon. The use of the hexagon is important in visualising the area of a circle as the length of the rectangle is naturally close to δ. Through this example the hexagon can be split into equilateral triangles of r length, r being the radius length of a circle. r is also the combined heights of the triangles formed by the hexagon, and the isosceles triangles created by the remaining area of the dodecagon, having the height lengths of h and t. The resulting rectangle formed via this method creates an area of $3r^2$, which is almost the same value as δr^2 we use today.

Bèimiànjī began by inscribing an octagon inside a circle, which she divided into eight discrete parts. With the remaining space unfilled by the octagon, she then created eight triangles from each side of the octagon, tapering to a point on the circle in the middle of two adjacent corners. The act of doing so created a new shape underneath the octagon, a sixteen-sided shape – a hexadecagon. The eight pieces of the octagon where divided into eight triangles of the same shape and size, from the centre of the shape to one of the sides, and then were cut and arranged into a rectangle with a length side of four units – what Bèimiànjī herself commented as the "half circle", or semicircle. The triangles around the octagon were also cut and rearranged into a rectangle, the combination of shapes resulted in a rectangle of side lengths of the radius of the circle, and half of the circumference. Because of this area Bèimiànjī then defined δ as;

"the ratio between the radius of a circle, and half of its perimeter. Given that a semicircle is defined by its diameter and not its radius, I feel it is more logical to instead define the circle ratio as the relationship between the circle and its diameter, for just as two halves make a whole, two times the radius presents the diameter."

The δ-algorithm was not perfect, but it proved to be a tool to process Delta more precisely the more vertices the shape used. Bèimiànjī and her colleges within the Chaplaincy processed shapes into the algorithm up to an impressive 16,384-sided shape. The resulting number produced the most accurate definition of δ yet and was only updated as lately as 74FIA with the new mathematical practice of producing infinite sums.

By contrast ρ was a largely unconsidered ratio until late into the Third Age. Well into the Scientific Revolution, mathematics boomed just as much as Alchemistry or specialised magic. When the Midgardian men acquired written records of Shuāng Bèimiànjī's δ-algorithm, they were both amazed by the mathematical prowess of the algorithm and impressed at the length the priestess went to produce an exact number. Mortal scholars however noted the intriguing definition of the circle constant Bèimiànjī provided, and then began to redefine circular geometry as a result. Matthew James Parkes, a then student of the Sage's Guild of Midgard, first noticed a curiosity in the definition of a circle. It was defined as 2δ – two times the circle constant, which meant that δ was the circular length of a semicircle rather than a full circle. Parkes therefore decided to produce an arbitrary number at the time to accurately represent a constant using the radius of a circle rather than the diameter, ρ. The definition of Rho was simple; $\rho = 2\delta$. The measure was largely criticised for its lack of any apparent relevance to mathematics. Within the academia of men, ρ was a dead argument.

However, the dwarves disagreed. Guildmasters from many mathematical, scientific and engineering institutions worked with the proofs of Kýklou and Bèimiànjī to expunge new utility from δ, and as it turned out ρ. The most immediate revolution of Rho was *the Translation of ρ into Circular Geometry*, where

Guildmaster Bue codified Parkes' initial triviality. Bue redefined the original notion of the circumference of the circle being $2\delta x$ using the creation of the radius segment, the segment of the circle that is the same length as the radius. As the ratio of δ is, by definition, the circle compared to the diameter, Guildmaster Bue's measurement uncovered the fact that all circles, regardless of their size, always has exactly ρ radius segments. This redefined the circumference of circles to be ρx. Another example of the transition to ρ in mathematics is *the Curious Nature of δ, ρ, and Elemental Manae*, where Guildmaster Makt conducted similar experiments to Charles Leopold Yeoland with elemental mana crystals. She made remarkable discoveries in the power output of the crystals, that were strangely inconsistent amongst each other. Makt found that unlike Yeoland's observations, elemental mana appeared to have an exponential function of power, and that the function differs between certain mana.

In my observations, a double grouping of exponents has emerged from the power outputs of the mana crystals. Taking the same measurements of volume and mass that Yeoland placed in his own work, the crystals of Air Mana, Earth Mana, Fire Mana, and Water Mana all appeared to have a power output of 314.16kW (from crystals with the mass of 100g). However, unlike the mortal's results, the mass of the mana crystals inflated the electric energy within it. A shard of 200g of any of these materials produce an output of 986.96kW, a shard of 300g produces 3100.63kW of energy, and a crystal piece of 400g creates *a power output of 9740.91kW...using the good work from my faithful companion Lyn, we have determined the function of power that [the aforementioned] mana crystals produce $100(\delta^x)kW$, in which x is one one-hundredth the mass of the crystal.*

The other most astonishing discovery is the great power in Life and Death Mana, for while the other four manae operate with a standard base, these mana crystals operate with a standard exponent. At first the shards of Life and Death Mana produce only 100kW of power from a 100g crystal. However, a piece of mana of 200g produces an impressively high power output of 7788.02kW, furthermore a shard of 300g demonstrates a power output of 99,504.16kW. At a mass of 400g the electrical energy reaches 606,533.08kW. It would appear that the exponential rate at which the energy within Life and Death mana propagates is $100(x^\rho)kW$, in which x again represents one one-hundredth of its mass.

The oddity of numbers such as δ and ρ both occurring naturally, and outside of circular geometry validates both ratios as natural numbers of great import. Guildmaster Makt's replication of Yeoland's observations firmly justified both circular constants, and most importantly the acceptance of ρ as just as valid a constant as Xi, Phi and Epsilon.

Shǒu Zhīshù – Finger-Counting, and the Interaction of the Elves with Binary

Humans originally developed a base 10 counting system from the use of their fingers. By counting each finger of their two hands they established the common decimal system of numbers most of the Nine Realms use today, including the elf clans and minor powers. However, this tally system was not the only method of counting. Independent from mortal hands, elves fashioned their own method of counting that was more complex and led to unusual properties in how elves applied mathematics and developed solutions to complex problems. The method by which the elves count is called *Shǒu Zhǐshù*, Finger-Counting. Originally from the high elves, Shǒu Zhǐshù is a base 2 binary system in which each finger represents one of two possible states: existent or non-existent. For the purposes of simplicity, both states are renamed to mean each finger is either on or off. Unlike human tallying where the state of each finger is dependant on the previous one to generate a number, elf counting employs a system of independent combinations of fingers that in turn generate 1024 unique gestures: 2^{10}. Elves could therefore count to 1023 with their two hands, giving them the ability to convey much larger quantities via personal interaction much more easily.

One defining feature of this method is the apparent ability of elves of any clan to quickly calculate and identify natural powers of 2 as until 1024 each of the powers can be simply expressed with one finger. The Eldars took great interest in such numbers. Prior to the Third Age, the concept of prime numbers was not highly regarded, yet despite this the concept of Eldar Primes arose as a strange consequence of the elvish counting system. As a basic summery, prime numbers are whole numbers that cannot be divided into even factors apart from 1 and itself. The first ten of these numbers are 2, 3, 5, 7, 11, 13, 17, 19, 23, and 29. The Eldar Prime series is a special group of prime numbers that were the first of their kind discovered by the high elf clan. Eldar Primes were first derived by Chaplain Zhǔyào at around 295SA when, as she was bartering for provisions, she noticed a curious pattern. Zhǔyào observed that when she presented a certain prime number with her fingers, she produced a row of fingers that themselves equated to a prime number of digits. She returned to her convent and within her quarters she notated a list of the values of her fingers, and then marked off each number that was less than 1 of these, and that was *"a number without factors"*. She discovered that the numbers 3, 7, 31 and 127 were all prime numbers, and that each of these numbers generated groups of fingers that were themselves prime numbers. She quickly wrote down this discovery that has now been translated into a mathematical formula:

Example 6.

$$E'=2^p-1$$

"One can conclude from the existence of particular factorless numbers, an unusual partnership arises with other factorless numbers to create such duplicity, it confounds and enchants the mind. Such a curious characteristic about these odd numbers that they are

without factors in the simplest definition yet can still be derived from a number that is itself without factors. If it is not the work of Allmother Xihe, then at least it most likely be the creation of the fine Pi." – Chaplain Zhǔyào

The unique nature of Finger-Counting is further expressed in the language of the elves. Unlike most other tongues that produce distinct words for each number, elf numbers are themselves a binary chain of consonants and vowels. The representation of their fingers in producing a number is directly translated into how the word of the same number is constructed.

Common Numbers	Binary Representations	Elvish Words for Numbers
0	0	o
1	2^0	a
2	2^1	tao
4	2^2	gatoh
8	2^3	ragotoh
10	$2^3 + 2^1$	ragotao

In this basic construct, each power of 2 is given a sound, generally one consonant, and a vowel. If the power is required in creating the number, the suffix is -a. If the power is not required for the expression of the number, the suffix is -o. With an accurate knowledge of the correct structure for the consonants, numbers can be expressed as high as one wants in as quickly as the brain can calculate such numbers; like 1000, which when divided into its powers of 2 becomes $2^9 + 2^8 + 2^7 +$

$2^6 + 2^5 + 2^3$: shajafahakasoragotoh. Theoretically Shŏu Zhĭshù has an infinite application however, the elves have been known to use this simple method up to 2^{25}; 33,554,432.

Outside of Shŏu Zhĭshù, the binary representation of these numbers is much the same on Earth as it is in Mundus. Binary numbers are written as sequences of 0s and 1s. The example of shajafahakasoragotoh written in binary is 1111101000.

Tohåndsnummer – Two-Handed Counting, and the Exotic Numerology of the Dwarves

Just as the elves developed their system of Finger-Counting to produce a natural base 2 method of counting, the dwarves took a different approach from all else. The unique nature of dwarf numbers drills into the origin of its creation. Other counting systems account for the fingers on both hands as equal, the left index finger is the same as the right thumb. The dwarves base their counting system on the idea that each hand is itself one part of the number, that the left hand carries more *"weight"* than the right hand. Thus, the concept of Tohåndsnummer, Two-Handed Counting was born. Tohåndsnummer is a dual tally system split between the hands, where the right-hand counts in units, and the left-hand counts in multiples of five. This unusual method of counting is the only one of its kind on Mundus, it led to the development of the dwarves adopting not simply a base 25 counting system, but what is known as *quinquinary*. A quinquinary system is a method of expressing numbers as a fusion of two smaller numbers – a subunit base of 5^0, and a subunit base of 5^1 – at the same time.

Units	0 (-io)	1 (-in)	2 (-ou)	3 (-ee)	4 (-ur)
+0	0 (io)	1 (in)	2 (ou)	3 (ee)	4 (ur)
+5 (fi-)	5 (fiyo)	6 (fiyin)	7 (fiu)	8 (fee)	9 (fiur)
+10 (te-)	10 (teeo)	11 (tein)	12 (teu)	13 (tee)	14 (teor)
+15 (tin-)	15 (tinio)	16 (tinin)	17 (tinoh)	18 (tinee)	19 (tinur)
+20 (vent-)	20 (ventio)	21 (ventin)	22 (ventoh)	23 (venteh)	24 (ventor)

This table is the phonetic chart to the twenty-five words for the dwarf numerals. Every digit has the same word for the numeral, not matter where it is in the number, with only a slight modifier for each base ordinate.

The phonetic chart above better describes how such a bold system can operate. The top row defines the right hand, the five fingers represent the singular units of the number from 1 to 5. The left-most column defines the left hand, the five fingers represent the basic units in this exotic counting. Each finger on the left hand counts as five rather than one, therefore the fingers are 5, 10, 15, 20, and 25. These two tallies combine to form one number, theoretically between 0 and 30 (25 + 5), and in fact, in cases dwarves do occasionally count up to 30 with this method.

When constructing numbers greater than 25, the phonetic chart is still used to create the numerals however, one final additive is placed in order to assign base ordinance. For example, the number 125 is written as *fiyost-io*, the -st at the end of the fiyo- numeral denotes it as the ordinate 25^1, in the same way that in the common counting system the 7 in the number 75 is in the ordinate 10^1.

This counting system gives the dwarves an adept knowledge in both standard quinary and quinquinary counting, as the latter is a more complex variation of the former. As novel as dwarves are in identifying such numbers, there has not yet been any application of quinary in complex mathematics. Instead, guildmasters adorn their buildings with mathematical architecture. Two examples of this kind of design are the Guild of Engineering, and the Great Vault of Hvelv. The Guild of Engineering is the official establishment of the engineers, architects, stonemasons, and carpenters, and the managers and planners of each city within the mountains. The architecture of the Guild of Engineering is a stepped steeple of ascending stone pillars that frame the imposing structure. The pillars are arranged in such a way as the façade appears as a curved peak. The middle column stretches up to the height of the mountain in which the guild resides, each pillar after it is reduced in height by a fraction of the middle. The centre pillar of the building is one of the foundation pieces that keeps the peak of the mountain over the head of the city. Each proceeding stone column of the building is a fraction of 3/5 the size of the previous column, creating the sloped surface of the structure. At the base of each pillar are known mathematical proofs by dwarves that have been recorded personally by the guildmasters.

By contrast, the Great Vault of Hvelv is a marvel in both architecture and history. The original Great Vault was besieged and destroyed by the orcs during the Age of Destruction, it has since been restored and has had installed a work of chiseled art and stonework. The outer wall of the vault rises to the height of the mountain itself, with the façade completely decorated in exotic patterns, sculptures and cravings into the rock. The scene is an artist's depiction of the Siege of Hvelv, in which the bodies of each dwarf and orc have accurate proportions yet based on abnormal mathematical ratios. The dwarf depictions were constructed from a standard height of exactly 11/25 the height of the orc depictions. The ratio of 0.44 is a highly apparent number in the biology of smaller creatures, mostly within the general body shape of sprites, fairies, halflings, dwarves, goblins, and magical creatures with a similar size to these. The carvings across the Great Vault are blocky and abstract in their visual representation, yet the detail in the image has a striking quality. The orc images also have a regular bodily proportion of exactly 16/25, the ratio of 0.64 is remarkably close to the actual proportion of 0.627 in which orc bodies are in relation to their chest, and their chest compared to their legs.

The mathematics of Mundus is rich and ever present in many facets of culture, architecture, religion, science, and of course the mathematics itself. Whether through the use of Ξ or δ in one's equations, or Finger-Counting to determine the next Eldar Prime, the evolution of arithmetic is an essential part of perception – how we see the world, and how we interpret things that are not obvious.

Appendix D

Albiology – the Study of Summoned Creatures, a Beginner's Guide

"Magic is the application and manipulation of various Manae in order to conjure a hex, bestow an enchantment, or summon a creature. This is true for all forms of magical sciences; Alchemistry relates to the molecular and physical properties of Manae, from Mana crystals, to aqueous Mana in the form of Magic Water, and molten Mana found in Fire and Earth Nodes. Alphysics describes how enchantments defend against either physical or magical attacks made to the person, or how wind walking is possible by the use of magic upon subjects, as examples. Albiology however, is a more

subtle and counterintuitive science. Summoning anything from a 'magical realm' makes no more sense than stopping time, or reversing the effect of gravity, or teleporting one's self at will. None of these things are capable in our world, yet we fall back on an old tale about creatures existing in other planes of reality. I'm not sure why this myth persists even today."

- Dimiourgós Plásmatos,
Albiogenisis: The Origin of
Summoned Creatures

The magic system in this world is a product of the most influential fantasy I was given at a young age, mostly from computer games. It is a uniquely complex system of disciplines, effects and weaknesses, and is used in different applications around Mundus. This will be one of a series of appendices over a few books that describe how it works and how to cast magic. This appendix will describe how fantastic creatures are summoned or cast into the world, the various orders and classifications of creatures, and a short list of the well understood creatures one can summon.

The Two Forms of Summoning

Before we understand the practice of summoning a creature, we must first appreciate the magic itself, and the process of a creature forming from it. Magic is a physical process, it requires the raw materials in the form of Mana of some kind, and a vessel to direct the energy from the Mana towards a source. Mana can exist in multiple forms; the most well known and documented sources of Mana are the variety of crystals scattered about Mundus. There are a total of nine basic types of Mana that have the crystalline structure we know today – Pure Mana, made of a type of tempered Adamantium, Quork Mana, a naturally occurring Silver-Adamantium alloy, Crysx Mana, a highly powerful Mana made of a Gold-Adamantium alloy, and the Elemental Manae. Air Mana is a crystal found in Nodes that are high up in the mountains, the Adamantium Oxide catalyses into a crystalline structure at very low temperatures. Earth Mana and Fire Mana are the only two forms of Mana that naturally occur as molten magic found in volcanic Nodes. Earth Mana is identifiable by its distinctive green glow. Earth Mana is a molten Iron-Adamantium alloy, Fire Mana is a molten Copper-Adamantium alloy. Similarly, Water Mana is the only known Mana that is naturally aqueous, the solution is often found in Nodes that are geysers spurting the Mana from the ground. Depending on the location of these geysers, the Node is either a lake full of Water Mana, or in the ocean diluting the liquid into it. Water Mana forms when Adamantium breaks apart the Dihydrogen Monoxide molecule – commonly known as water – and reforms it into the new molecule Hydro-Adamantium Hydroxide. Life Mana and Death Mana are the final types of Mana, neither of which are of note. Death Mana is formed in the presence of a hot, dense ash smoke. The result is an Adamantium Carbonate crystal. Life Mana is a crystal of Adamantium Sulphurous. All forms of Mana can be created from a process known as Mana Forging invented by the dwarves. By combining elements together Mana is producible en mass, except for Quork and Crysx.

The process of using Mana in order to summon a creature is an action of some sort to transfer the raw energy within the Mana into a living being. All magic follows the same principal of redirecting the energy of Mana towards an end, be it an enchantment on a person, or a hex to use against an enemy. It is important to stress that a summoned creature is in general regarded as an automaton and not at all sentient, until and unless such a time that the master deems it reasonable to discharge the animal to live its own life freely. In the magical sciences summoned beings are regarded as Adamantine Lifeforms, creatures that are mostly composed of Adamantium, and do not operate the same as the rest of the races on Mundus. By contrast, biologists today tend to see the races as Carbonic Lifeforms. This distinction is because of the fundamental nature of the summoned creature as created by the very Mana itself to produce it. Studies on such creatures who met terrible fates have revealed that their chemical makeup is almost exclusively Adamantine. Because they are not like natural forms of life, they experience life differently to the average person, a point we will discuss further in this appendix.

The first and most common form of summoning is called cast summoning, or simply 'casting'. Casting takes place in two ways, depending on the creature one intends to summon; small creatures can be cast by the hands of a mage, or a wand in their possession. Magicians can transmute a shard of Mana they physically hold into anything at will by focusing their technique into their hands and their speech. This is due to the fundamental nature of the practice of magic. Spell casting has been defined by Mathítria Orthgrafías, the father of Alphysics and one of the first recorded magical scientists, as:

> "...*the manipulation of sound, that travels across solid structures, to react with the crystal, and compels it to conform to the will of the caster. The casting of magic is a purely physical process that, through a truly intelligent use of oration, disrupts the Mana either into a new force that acts upon the world, that is not natural in any other sense, or into a new physical being that acts out the will of its master.*"

Small summoned creatures range from the various species of sprites found in Life Magic, to the baby kraken in Water Magic, to Hell Hounds within Fire Magic. The size of these creatures ranges from less than ten centimetres to up to fifty centimetres. High elves fancy the method of physically holding Mana in order to create life. It conforms to their belief in life. However, it is a practice that is used less and less across Mundus. Most spell casters use artefacts and objects that channel magical power to a specific direction, the use of wands and quarterstaffs are of note and popularity.

Wands and all types of staffs amplify a spell caster's power. They each possess a piece of Mana – elemental Manae compounds the multiplication of power – and acts as a conduit of arcane power. This feature of magical objects grants the caster a wider range of creatures to summon; wands can summon small to moderately sized beings, while even a quarterstaff can produce a few large beasts such as the Zephyr bird, an enlarged eagle-like creature with a wing span of between two and three quarters, and three meters. Full length staffs can produce the gamut of summoned beings below the two extreme species; large creatures include werewolves, the minotaur, the Efreet, ice giants, the lava beast, giant spiders, and the Hydra, each of which occur across various magical disciplines.

However, there is one drawback in casting creatures as opposed to summoning them, they are unstable on a molecular level. The bonds that form the creature are in a state of constant flux, due once again to the nature of spell casting. Cast creatures are mostly stable and function as any other summoned creature for a period of time, yet as they continue to exist the sounds and vibrations from other sources affect them, just as the incantation to produce the creature also affected the Mana to form them. Smaller creatures are significantly more stable than even moderately sized beings however, they too are not immune to this transient nature. Additionally, the effect of a wand or staff does also extend the lifespan of a cast creature, but not significantly. Presently, the Standard Lifespan of a cast being is between ten and thirty minutes, depending on factors such as the size of the creature and the method by which it came into being. The only exception to this standard is the Magic Vortex in the specialist form of Storm Magic. The Magic Vortex is the only 'creature' that is defined as such yet is not a living being but rather a phenomenon that is affected by weather. No matter by which means it formed, a Magic Vortex that was cast lasts exactly sixteen minutes and forty seconds. No one knows why the lifespan of a cast Magic Vortex is this stable.

The second method of summoning creatures is a ritual summon however, as cast summoning is shortened to 'casting', ritual summoning is also reduced to the term 'summoning'. One must understand the difference between the technical and colloquial terms. Ritual summoning requires much more Mana and materials, and an open space to imbue a creature into existence. One begins by using a shard of Pure Mana to draw a pentagram inscribed in a circle along the surface of flat ground. This shape is known as a *summoning circle*. Again, depending on the size of the creature, the summoning circle must be a set diameter in order to summon a being into the world. At the points of the pentagram that met the circle, place equal piles of Mana of any sort. Perfection is not necessary however, the more one sided the distribution is, the more likely the creature will be misaligned and the summon may fail. Lastly, one must proclaim the correct summoning chant clearly at the circle with great affect. A magician knows the summon has began when the energy from the piles of Mana ejects into the summoning circle.

A complete understanding of the process of a summoned creature being created is not available presently, some sources and research conflict with each other. A successful summon portrays a large circle glowing in energy with haggard shafts of light from it. It is here where accounts differ, as the light from the summoning circle is simply too bright to make clear observations. After a few moments of turbulent shine, the beast forms in the bath of light. The creature emerges from the circle, and lands on the ground. Shortly thereafter, the light disappears, and the creature has been brought into existence. Most albiologists agree that this is the sequence of events in producing a creature from a ritual summoning however, some argue that the summoning circle is in fact a portal that things travel between. This is currently being tested.

The distinct advantage of ritual summoning is that unlike cast summoning, fantastic creatures are totally stable and can exist indefinitely. This is due to the wide area in which the summoning circle covers, and the amount of Mana used to form the creature. The incantation takes time for the materials to coalesce into the beast of choice. The area and materials produce stable chemical bonds that interact into cells and known biological systems, at which time the systems conform into a specific shape. The resulting mass acquires cognitive function from the residual electromagnetic energy that activates the creature's brain and heart. The beast becomes in all respects a living, breathing being that forms from the chemical composition of the Mana, and materials involved to summon it.

Two reasons prevent ritual summoning in the modern era; the primary reason is the demilitarisation of fantastic beasts in all forms. The Age of Peace is a new era among Mundus, the heads of state have mandated the use of magic for the purpose of ending life, including the summoning of creatures, as illegal. Extraordinarily large beasts such as the Phoenix, storm giants, and the Earth Elemental have since been absent in recent history as they no longer serve a purpose and are very dangerous to remain rampant on the earth, unbound to anyone. The second reason is the expense of summoning such things. Often, cast summoning a fairy into the world requires little more than a single small piece of Mana and the concentration to affect the material into the creature. Summoning a fairy by ritual, while still is of little expense to the caster, requires significantly more Mana present, and typically takes a few seconds longer to form for the bonding to take place. With the interest of maintaining peace in the world, and the inflated cost of resources, especially with larger beasts, policies and mandates have diverted from pooling a Mana reserve towards research into the sciences. While all apprentices learn these practices as a matter of academia, they rarely conduct a ritual summon unless it is necessary.

Elementals, Dragons, and the Orders
of Size of Fantastic Creatures

There are five orders of size, where every single known summoned creature is classified: small, moderate, large, elemental, and dragon. Each order of size provides wizards and students alike with a concise description of the amount of Mana they require in a ritual summoning. Small creatures require little investment of Mana and a short, contained summoning circle. Moderately large beasts are the most varied category of size as all eighteen magical disciplines hold at least one or two of these in their repertoires. Large lifeforms require up to ten times the casting cost via a staff, and they alone are already quite exorbitant in cost. As a general, unwritten rule, most mages restrict themselves to creatures no greater than themselves in stature. Between the first three and the last two sizes there is a gap in height. Large creatures are typically between two to three meters in height, the two extreme classifications are no shorter than seven meters in length. Below is a list and brief description of the most well-known summoned creatures.

Zephyr Bird

Large, avian creature. Approximately 2 metres tall, a wingspan of between 3 and 4.5 metres wide. Eagle-like, except significantly larger in size. Oak-brown colour, grey beak and talons. Neutral attitude to strangers, protective of its young. Will pursue if it thinks you are a threat to its nest, will attack if you have physically injured it.

Originally mastered by the halflings in bygone ages, Zephyrs are no longer summoned by them or any other race. The history of their use on Mundus is limited to aerial assaults. Some believe they can be tamed and ridden upon like dragons. There are three known roosts scattered deep within the Great Wall Mountains past the dwarf cities. According to legend, the dwarves were initially frightened by the monstrous birds and did attack nests. Once the noblemen understood the behaviour of the Zephyrs, they ceased attacking and allowed them to settle.

Kharluu – Black Dragon

Dragon, born from Darkness Magic. Between 8 and 10 metres long. Named from the dark elven term *khar luu*, meaning 'death demon'. Scaled skin, sharp leading edges of their wings, luminescent sulphur yellow eyes. Pitch black in colour. It breathes an acrid, toxic breath that can wither and kill. Aggressive attitude towards strangers, looms over prey before it strikes. Will pursue to kill at first sight.

In known history only four Black Dragons have known to exist, none are alive today. Upon settling in the wasteland at the bottom of Mundus the dark elves took possession of Death Magic and wrought havoc against the elf clans during the Second Age. During the height of the Black Wars, two Black Dragons decimated elves on both sides, at the cession of hostilities the Khan released his pets to roam the world. Records of the dragons afterward are scarce until they reappeared in separate instances in the desert and the mountains. In each case a party of Heroes and Templar Knights slayed the beasts, the names of these fighters are lost to history. As the Age of Destruction loomed and the threat of the orcs appeared, the Khan once again summoned Black Dragons to defend against them. The third dragon was felled by an onslaught of orcs. The fourth dragon survived the entire period of war. When the Council's Mandate was enacted the Khan dissolved the creature back into power that flowed back into the earth.

Dark Angel

Deathly elemental creature. Approximately 2 metres tall, a wingspan of between 6.9 and 7.5 metres wide. Humanoid with giant feathered wings. Pale skin, black attire and feathers, large steel sword. Aggressive attitude to strangers, especially towards holy men and creatures aligned to goodness. Will pursue at first sighting, will attack either when it perceives a threat or when it identifies its prey as misaligned.

Until the Age of Peace, Dark Angels were the personal guard of the Khan. Like the Kharluu, Dark Angels were employed in both the Black Wars of the Second Age, and the Age of Destruction against the orcs. However, unlike the dragons, the Dark Angels remained in the Khan's court as guards during combat, and as enforcers of the law domestically. During the orc campaign the Dark Angels led regiments of troops to victory. Upon the end of the Great War the Khan retained the right to keep his Dark Angels as a personal guard and as enforces of law. One Dark Angel roams in each of the seven cities of Kharankhui ger Ongontsny.

Basilisk

Dragon beast, born from Earth Magic. Between 7 and 7.5 metres long. Physical descriptions are vague and prone to conflict. Scaly skin, frilled neck, said to have stone eyes. Green in colour however, shades vary. In general, earthy hues. Some accounts claim that the beast possesses metal claws, others suggest fleshy feet like humanoids. Aggression ranges between moderate and very high.

Basilisks are one of the least known creatures. Their ability to petrify prey on sight is a large deterrent for detailed observations. Known accounts of their use is similarly scarce. None of the races admit the use of such beasts however, given their alignment to nature and the earth, speculation puts the goblins as the culprits. No surviving records place Basilisks anywhere in history. The little information that is known on them is that several of them exist within the Great Wall Mountains guarding Earth Nodes.

Arcanier

Moderate, humanoid creature. Between 1.5 and 1.8 metres tall. Human in appearance with subtle differences. Malformed ears, similar to certain elves, bright purple skin with strobing light under it. Eclectic and varied hair and attire, bold and imposing. Neutral attitude to strangers. Will pursue within a set distance, will attack if you have physically injured it.

Arcaniers are often misrepresented as elf bands of magicians who melded Mana crystal within themselves. Their appearance is so striking they do not conform to any subdivision of any race on Mundus however, the shape of their ears is like the elves and are often the identifying characteristic. In truth, Arcaniers are a purely alchemical lifeform, the clue is their skin. Their exterior is Adamantium, which makes them immune to all magical attacks and gives their distinctive purple hue. They are so completely charged with the energy of the Mana they formed from that their blood vessels glow. Arcaniers were at one point one of the most widely used summoned creatures. Their superior skills in projecting magical attack in battle gave the peaceful races dominance in magic, as a result the elves, men and dwarves all invested in regiments of Arcaniers. The surviving creatures were all dissolved at the end of the Great War.

Fire Elemental

Fiery elemental creature. Between 7.5 and 9 metres tall. Giant ball of fire, floating in midair. Aggressive attitude to strangers. Will not pursue, will attack if your magically attack it.

Arguably the most abnormal beast ever conceived, the Fire Elemental is the most basic of these. It is a large, contained ball of fire that is capable of movement and defending itself. It has no physical presence, no body, no weapon, no distinct features whatsoever. Each Fire Elemental is the same floating ball of orange flickering light as the next. However, what gives the fire its unique quality is its ability to float above the ground, and that in battle it moves about the field and attempt to burn threats on command. The Fire Elemental epitomises the nature of summoned creatures, it is nothing more than an object that obeys the direct orders of its master. Today the few Fire Nodes in the mountains are guarded by the command of the dwarf Doge Smeltet V by a Fire Elemental.

Báilóng – White Dragon

Dragon, born from Healing Magic. Between 7 and 7.5 metres long. Named from the high elven term *bái lóng*, meaning 'pure sage'. Smooth, fleshy skin, no claws or talons, curved features. White in colour. Its breath is of note; the chemicals from the breath of the Báilóng can heal the wounds of the injuries it comes across. Friendly attitude to strangers. Will pursue on sight, cannot attack.

Docile dragons are much more favoured in the modern age than in any other period. The White Dragon is the most favourable of them all, a beast that heals instead of attacks. The Báilóng is a treasured dragon to the high elves, several freely roam the northern lands and the feet of the Great Wall Mountains. The high elf banner is a White Dragon in flight under a white sun, surrounded by sky blue. The Báilóng that dwell near cities are considered patrons and are named by the population; the pet of the Elfinqueen is known as Xīhé Jīngshén. Others include Shānlóng, Jiùshēngquān, and Jiāngōng, all of which live near the thresholds of cities. The Archonian men also express reverence to White Dragons. Two White Dragons roam the golden coast, and just like the high elves, they are named Aceso and Iaso, the daughters of Apollo who protect the world.

Ice Giant

Large, humanoid creature. Between 2.5 and 3 metres tall. Pale skin, broad stature, often clothed in a tunic or loin cloth. Armed with a club of an unknown material. Neutral attitude to strangers. Will pursue on sight, will attack if you have physically injured it.

Ice Giants were a field of interest in early Albiological study, their ability to affect the weather and temperature about them made them an intriguing beast. Their resistance to the cold is a direct effect of their endothermalism, their natural ability to draw away heat and persist coldness. The body temperature of an Ice Giant appears to fluctuate between +2 and -16°Θ. By comparison water boils at +100°Θ and freezes at 0°Θ. This ability to always maintain an area of cold about them makes an unusual yet effective natural defence. Lengthy physical exposure of their skin has been known to lead to numbing of the exposed skin. Persistence may cause frostbite to occur, and bone chill may petrify. There is no recent report presently, yet Ice Giants are said to dwell near Air Nodes at the tops of the mountains in the extreme northeast, far beyond any city or national influence.

Lava Beast

Large, amorphous creature. Between 3 and 4.5 metres tall. Composed entirely of lava. Aggressive attitude to strangers. Will pursue on sight, will attack if you have magically attacked it.

Like the Fire Elemental, the Lava Beast is one of a group of beasts made from molten lava that can act the will of its master. Lava Beasts have no distinctive features amongst each other, they all appear to be large, thick humanoid creatures dripping in superheated metal. They are difficult to destroy, the heat is extremely high, making them very tough to deal with without magicial intervention. Even a glancing blow is enough to damage the skin. Very few mages have used Lava Beasts, mostly the Runemasters, a specific class of dwarf magicians. The Runemasters summon Lava Beasts and other lava creatures as a quick defence against enemies.

Shénlóng – Divine Dragon

Dragon, born from Life Magic. Between 7.7 and 8 metres long. Named from the high elven term *shén lóng*, meaning 'enlightened sage'. Shining scales, hardened claws similar to fingernails, curved shape. Golden shine in colour. The breath is sulphurous which burns the skin, and particularly damages unholy deviants.

Neutral attitude to strangers. Will pursue on sight, will attack if you physically injure it.

Divine Dragons, sometimes called Golden Dragons for its colour, are extremely rare and highly prized by nearly every race on Mundus. There is no exact number of the remaining Divine Dragons in existence however, legends claim that three still live. The reason for the ambiguity is that Divine Dragons were prevalent in the period before the Age of Discovery. Elf tradition claims that during the Black Wars against the dark elves, the other two clans summoned many Divine Dragons to exterminate the race however, there has since been no physical evidence of any remains of these beasts. Priests of Xihe have the incantation to summon Divine Dragons and have demonstrated their ability to do so in the Age of Destruction for the purpose of war against the orcs. After the war the new dragons were dissolved back into the earth, yet the high elves claim that deep within the Great Wall Mountains three of the ancient creatures roost. No expedition has yet uncovered any Divine Dragon den.

Sprites

Small, humanoid creature. Approximately 10 centimetres tall, a wingspan of between 10 and 15 centimetres wide. Humanoid in appearance, resembling various races. Insectoid wings, similar in appearance to a hybrid of a dragonfly and a butterfly. Exclusively female in gender. Very friendly attitude to strangers.

Will pursue on sight, will attack if you physically injure it.

By far the most commonly summoned creature is a wisp of sprites. Sprites are a surprisingly unique creature as they are subdivided into a few species based on the discipline of magic used to summon them. Sprites summoned from the elemental Life Magic seem to have the appearance of elves, specifically the high elves in terms of complexion and physical attributes. Sprites summoned from specialist magics differ slightly; Terrain Sprites have a brown skin colour and as a result appear wood elven. Light Sprites have ears without points, taking the appearance of a human with exceptionally bright hair. Finally, Sun Sprites have a tanned complexion as well as ear without points. They do not resemble a human clan, rather they mimic the appearance of islanders found along the Discovery Archipelago towards Midgard. Each variety of Sprite can launch different magic when provoked; traditional Life Sprites cast Life Magic in order to upset unholy demons, Light Sprites fire intense beams of light that can set alight flammable materials, Sun Sprites launch miniature fire balls that explode upon impact, and Terrain Sprites sling mud balls, their viscous material sticks to most surfaces and slows down potential threats. Thousands of Sprites live in communes around Magic Nodes scattered across the world. These are known as Bivouacs and are often divided amongst the species of Sprites.

Aerí – Sky Drake

Dragon, born from Lighting Magic. Between 7.5 and 7.9 metres long. Named from the halfling term *aer rí*, meaning 'master of the sky'. Iridescent scales, hardened claws similar to fingernails, sharp leading edges of its wings. Sky blue in colour, yet its scales reflect natural light as certain colours, depending on the dragon itself. Bright magenta eyes. The dragon always holds an electric charge, making the belly of the beast glow and spark. This property allows the dragon to fire lightning bolts from its mouth instead of fire or other projectiles. Aggressive attitude to strangers. Will pursue on sight, will attack if it perceives you as a threat.

The Aerí is a legendary creature considered to be the single strongest animal in existence. Its hide is the strongest material known, capable of resisting most attacks, magical or physical. The Sky Drake is neither the fastest dragon, nor the dragon capable of reaching the greatest height however, it has the most endurance of all the breeds, making it the most amenable to transport one's self across Mundus. However, their greatest advantage is their attack. Most dragons, including the White Dragon, expel a fire or a gas of some kind. The inner workings of the dragon's organs provide the beast with its own natural furnace and supply of flammable material, giving dragons their breathing abilities. The Aerí has a similar property insofar as the creature does expel a harmful material however, it is not at all the same. As it flies through the clouds it gathers the electrical energy built up in them and holds the negative charge inside itself. When the Sky Drake intends to, it opens its mouth and cause a discharge to fire from itself out towards an enemy it has encountered. This made the Sky Drake the most sort after dragon to possess for those with an intent to rule, they were the very first summoned creatures to dissolve away for the safety of Mundus however, there are unconfirmed rumours of some that still exist today.

Mud Men

Moderate, amorphous creature. Between 1.5 and 1.8 metres tall. Composed entirely of mud. Aggressive attitude to strangers. Will pursue on sight, will attack if you have magically attacked it.

Mud creatures are the opposites to Lava creatures. While creatures such as Lava Men and Lava Beasts attack enemies by strength and heat, Mud Men and other Mud creatures do not enjoy the same luxury of posing immediate threats. Mud Men are by far the weakest summoned creature as it cannot attack with real effect, block magical power, or assist the members of its party. Their effects are limited to their non-corporal state, physical weapons are useless against them. As a result of this Mud Men were never used extensively by any of the races. Mud creatures remain as one of the only acceptable summoning spells that can be used today as they cannot harm. Their use was almost exclusively limited to distraction, a looming threat of men impervious to blade and arrow. However, once they reached their targets, they did little to pose any serious threat. They slowed down armies but never affected them at all.

Giant Spider

Large, arachnid creature. Between 2 and 3 metres long from front leg to back leg. Enlarged spiders, black in colour. Thick, hairy legs. Red eyes, venomous pincers. Very aggressive attitude to strangers. Will pursue to kill on sight.

Spiders were an important part of the goblin army during their engagement with the orcs. Prior to their first meeting outsiders well into the Second Age, goblins frequently relied on Giant Spiders and Stag Beetles to manoeuvre about the caverns of the Bhoot. The arachnid's abilities to see well in the dark were and still are a valuable trait. Once intrepid goblins emerged from the underground and explored the land above, spider- and beetle-riding became known as iconic skills that identified the goblins from all other races. Contrary to popular belief, the goblins never knew about the Giant Spiders ability to create a large web. There was never a need to construct such a thing underground. Therefore, the goblins never knew about this latent skill until after albiologists studied the beasts.

Magic Vortex

Large non-creature. Between 4 and 5 metres tall. A large, randomly moving tornado. Very aggressive in general, will not pursue in a straight line.

Of all the summonable creatures the Magic Vortex is the least like a creature. It is defined as a *non-creature*, a summonable force that is not capable of sentience nor acting out the will of the caster, yet is producible in the same way as any other summonable creature. Because of this property Magic Vortexes are never summoned today and are strictly forbidden due to their danger. Prior to the Great War the human clans were the most prevalent casters of Magic Vortexes, as well as the halflings and the dwarves. The storm is quite literally a large spinning tornado that moves in a random path and builds up an electric charge that causes it to fire lightning as it goes about. Vortexes were used with great effect to cause disarray against enemy parties, the added danger of the storm was both a distraction and unexpected threat that may or may not attack multiple times. By the middle of the Age of Discovery the Magic Vortex was deemed too unstable a 'being' to rely upon for any real effect, as a result it was largely left alone. At the end of the Great War this was further codified by laws that restrict the use of Mana and magic to non-life-threatening practices.

Vasiliás Drákos – Great Drake

Dragon, born from Sun Magic. Between 8 and 8.5 metres long. Named from the Archonian term *vasiliás drákos*, meaning 'king of the dragons'. Scaled skin, sharp leading edges on its wings, fire lit on the very edge of its tail. Bright red orange in colour, golden eyes.

Neutral attitude to strangers. Will pursue if it perceives a threat, will attack if you physically attack it.

The Great Drake is the largest dragon summonable. The dragon is not remarkable in any way beyond its colour, a bright orange like a hot fire. The Great Drake is also referred to as the Vasiliás Drákos by the Archons due to its size. The high men and the dwarves were the only races that possessed and, in the case of the high men, ridden Great Drakes. One noteworthy rider of a Great Drake, and dragons in general, was the Archon Templar Íroas who fought during the Race Against Peace in the Fourth Age. The Templar fought entire troops of orcs singlehandedly with the Great Drake, providing additional fire. Íroas is noted as the most well-known Templar in history and representing the values of the Templar Knights. After the Great War, the Great Drakes were all dissolved except one, Íroas' dragon, which lives within the compound of the Templar Insular as a symbol of loyalty and purity, two of the fundamental traits of the Templar Knights.

Fairy

Small, humanoid creature. Approximately 15 centimetres tall, a wingspan of between 20 and 27 centimetres long. Humanoid in appearance, resembling elves. Enlarged butterfly wings, often with bright and vivid patterns, flowing silken clothing. Very friendly attitude to strangers. Will pursue on sight, will attack if you physically injure it.

Fairies are the largest of the small summoned creatures and they tend to vary to a lesser extent than their Sprite counterparts. Fairies also have similar facial features to the elf clans. Unlike the Sprites, Fairies differ in skill and not in appearance. Fairies cast from Life Magic are the only ones capable of attacking as they fire bolts of Life Magic against threats, whereas Fairies cast from Healing Magic can only heal passing travellers of their wounds, and Fairies from the domain of Terrain Magic serve to revitalise and maintain the natural environment of their surroundings. Fairies also create societies for themselves like Sprites however, they are more complex. Tens of Fairies settle within dense forestland and adopt shelter from its canopy, not unlike the wood elves. Each one is ruled by a Fairy Queen that speaks for the shelter and brings harmony to all the other Fairies that live amongst her. Her subjects fill rolls that maintain the shelter, such as protecting it from malcontents, drawing out magic from the Queen, and enchanting the forest, to name a few. Fairies are very rarely mentioned in any war journals and are often fodder or distractions. So many have abandoned their masters to establish their own society of melody and peace. Fairies are friendly to kind strangers, but Fairy Queens maintain a distrust of the races of Mundus.

Water Dancer

Moderate, amphibious creature. Between 1.5 and 1.7 metres tall. Slimy skin, long thin limbs, can stand, walk and run over water. Green blue in colour, webbed fingers and toes, yellow frog eyes. Neutral attitude to strangers. Will pursue to kill if you physically injure it.

This creature has the unique property of being able to walk on the surface of bodies of water. The Water Dancer is a frog-like creature with elongated arms and legs. The beast was often used to scout nearby islands from coastal cities, or to defend Water Nodes. The Midgardian men enjoyed the use of Water Dancers not long after discovering magic and learned the use of Mana. Many scouting expeditions were passed over from fleets of ships captained by the great admirals to regiments of the creatures. The upkeep of the Water Dancer was much cheaper than the that of a ship and its crew. Other races did not take much of an interest in them. The Archons held no Water Nodes to protect, and the halflings were too disgusted by the creature's appearance to even consider it. As time went on, and more of the sea was discovered, the Water Dancers were slowly discharged from their service and roamed freely about the Western Sea. Today there is a recent report which catalogues each island along the Discovery Archipelago where Water Dancers live.

This is a significant fraction of the summoned creatures that lives or has lived on Mundus. There are more beasts and dragons that are yet to be covered in the story and this appendix.

Appendix E

Inspirations and Connections to Earth's Culture

Ever since I was exposed to high fantasy in various forms, I had always found and attributed similarities between them and cultures I learned about on Earth. One of the oldest cultural traits I encountered was the similarity to the use of wooden architecture in depictions of elves, and traditional Japanese architecture, the style of feudal Japan struck me as very elvish at the time. My interest in other cultures expanded as I came to appreciate global history more and more. In this appendix I like to take the opportunity to discuss and illuminate the influences in the narrative and how there are drawn from real world practices, artefacts, history, and culture in general.

This appendix will feature the direct root of Halfling culture, Ireland, by describing references to Irish cultural fixtures and symbology, a real life case of the Doge and the government they operated in during the Italian Renaissance, how a book about mathematics became a less than subtle reference in the story, and Alchemy as a real science in the ancient and medieval periods, and how it shaped modern chemistry.

Symbiosis of Halfling and Irish Cultures

It may not be a total surprise that when constructing the culture and behaviour I drew generally from Irish culture, and admittedly stereotypes of Irish people. I will explain the use of stereotypes in a moment, but first a brief overview of the elements of Irish culture beyond simple names. Much of the landscape of Leath Langa is drawn from the geography of Ireland. The Irish landmass is mostly lowlands and vague hills, surrounded by coastal cliffs. Instead of a sea surrounding the nation, a large river is used to denote the maritime trait of the halflings. The lyrical nature of the halflings is directly rooted in Ireland's artistic bent. While the Irish are far more well known as a people of great literature and poetry, music is as much a significant part of Irish culture. Since the 1960s Irish folk music has seen popularity, notable musicians include Van Morrison, Enya and the Corrs. Riverdance was a group of performers who defined the essence of Irish culture in the 1990s and early 2000s. They conveyed story and strong emotion though the unique combination of music and traditional dance. Fishing is a popular pastime in Ireland, the many lakes provide excellent spots for angling, and the island is a known tourist destination for fishing. Salmon and trout are commonly caught in Ireland, which is the reason

I mentioned these species at the beginning. Lastly, a common fixture in modern cities today are Irish pubs. Themed saloons with a friendly atmosphere, and images of Ireland and the sound of its music are commonplace is many large cities. Other aspects of halfling culture are taken from representations in other fictions.

Stereotyping has become a primary point in this story, it is an aspect of society that exists both consciously and unconsciously. The use of a character that is incapable of dishonesty, yet judgemental and infers the stereotypes of their era, is deliberate and designed to expose the harmful and often misunderstood consequences of such judgementalism. In general, a stereotype is a statement that overgeneralises a group of people, this can be people from a country, a belief, a gender; any grouping is capable of being stereotyped. The Irish are certainly not immune to stereotypes. Casual comments of their drunken behaviour, short tempers, or religious piety are attached to the Irish. Therefore, the creation of a character that have these traits, and a narrative that points these out at given opportunities, is designed specifically to demonstrate how this thought pattern is absurd.

The character of Ceannte is inspired by a particular person, one of my favourite comedians, Dylan Moran. Moran is known for his stand-up performances; his highly intellectual observations and jokes counterbalance the character he creates as mildly drunk and vulgar. Moran has appeared in a few movies, most notably Notting Hill, Shawn of the Dead and Run Fat

Boy Run. However, his most well-known appearance in entertainment was the permanently drunk and ill spoken character Bernard Black from the television show Black Books. The character is an excellent representation of the sort of stereotyping attributed to the Irish and is the reason why I draw from the character and imbue that into Ceannte.

The Role of the Doge and the Maritime Republic

The term "Doge" is not very well known today. The word itself is in use, but as a meme. This was popularised in 2013 with a simple picture of a dog and the sort of internal monologue that is typical of internet culture. The concept of a Doge in the context of the story – as a merchant ruler – is rather a bit removed from the reality of what a Doge truly was in history, this part of the appendix will briefly explain the Doge, his domain, and what a maritime republic actually means. The Doge was a title given to monarchs during the Italian Renaissance, they were often lords of the then city-states. The greatest of these cities were Venice and Genoa, they were rivals who grew into maritime and commercial empires. Started by the Venetians, an election of a Doge was conducted by a council of forty elected officials, these members were chosen by electors, who they themselves were chosen by the public. The Genoese originally chose their Doge by direct election, they later adopted a similar process in 1528. Like any other king or warlord, a Doge remained in office for their natural life, and while they did hold great power a Doge was under constant surveillance. The Doge was held to account by the elected members who put him into his position, even after death an inquiry into his actions would be launched, and if the departed was found to have made indiscretions the family estate would have to pay fines.

One notable Doge of the Renaissance was Enrico Dandolo of Venice, a man that led his city to its peak. Born in 1107, Enrico Dandolo emerged as the most influential, and controversial Doge in the history of the Republic of Venice. In truth, little is known and Enrico's youth or even middle life. He worked in administration positions until 1171, when at the age of 64 he entered the diplomatic service for the then Doge Michiel. He accompanied the Doge to the Byzantine Empire on an ill-fated military campaign. The Emperor Manuel Comnenus displaced Venetians in Constantinople, many fell into prison. Public pressure compelled the Doge to gather a response and send it to Comnenus. However, it was never meant to be, en route to Byzantium the army suffered the plague. They returned to a furious Venice, so irate were the public that an angry mob killed Doge Michiel in 1172. Dandolo continued to serve as negotiator and legislator for the next twenty years, talking with Sicilian King William II and the Byzantine Emperor of the time.

After the abdication of Doge Orio Mastropieto in 1192, Enrico Dandolo became the 41st Doge of Venice. His first years were iron fisted. His first decree was to evict foreigners from Venice, and to disallow Venetians to lend money to outsiders. Oddly, he took exception to citizens from Umana and Ragusa. The following year he ordered the harassment of the city of Zara, a meddlesome vassal to Venice who recently rebelled. He reformed the currency in order to float the silver penny and, perhaps unintentionally, expand the use of the new coin – the silver *grosso*. Dandolo participated in the Fourth Crusade by transporting knights, mercenaries and soldiers to the Holy Land for a fee. However, the knights failed to pay for the transport without borrowing from elsewhere. The knights owed 85,000 marks and despite pooling all their available funds they were 34,000 marks short. Dandolo arranged for the spoils of war to pay the remaining debt. He further used the knights in his own personal war with Zara. This angered Pope Innocent and threatened them with excommunication if they attacked. They attacked, but Dandolo hid this information for the crusaders in order to carry on with the Crusade. Lastly, he orchestrated a campaign to help the Byzantine prince Alexius Angelus reach Constantinople and sack the city to install himself the new Emperor. Enrico Dandolo died in 1205, his brief thirteen-year legacy of commercial and militaristic expansion shaped the future of the Venetian Renaissance.

Venice is just one example of a form of a maritime republic, a type of government that, while it has a general definition, is uniquely associated with the Italian Renaissance. As a basic, general definition, a maritime republic is a state largely governed by its naval domains; naval trade routes, a powerful navy that engage in naval warfare, blockades against hostile cities, ect. In the Renaissance, Italy in general relied on naval power in the Mediterranean. Cities that flourished during this period include Pisa, Genoa, Amalfi, Ragusa and Venice. Because Italy was en route to the Holy Land, these cities capitalised on transporting kings during the Crusades. The rise of maritime republics came about due to the dangers of land trade over mainland Europe. This was coupled with the emergence of powerful independent coastal cities. The threat of piracy at the time compelled them to bolster their naval defences and levy large navies. The events leading up to the Crusades also played a minor role in this development.

Matt Parker, Humble $\tau/2$, and the Use of Mathematics in Narrative

As I have mentioned before I am a recreational mathematician. Maths was one of my best subjects in school. I am personally proud of the fact that I was the only student in my grade to get 100% in statistics. While working does taking my mind off hard maths, I still play around with factorials and irrational numbers and what not whenever the mood takes me. Work occupies my mind, but it does not deter mathematics entirely for me. Even at a fundamental level for my job, three-dimensional geometry has managed to become a useful tool. But when it comes to writing, especially fiction writing, it is hard to find any real use for such a concept as precise and abstract as maths. Is it appropriate to use Euler's Identity as a metaphor for divine beauty? Will people even understand the reference? Can you build an entire story from the madness of complex numbers? Or the concept of two-dimensional space? People have certainly tried, but are they effective and memorable for the reader? Can the creative abstraction of mathematics reconcile into creative narrative?

Honestly yes, the metaphor works as an image of beauty.

Probably not unless the reader can already imagine Euler's Identity in the story as some sort of physical manifestation.

Well, that is the conspiracy theory about Alice in Wonderland. It is unconfirmed, but that would be one hell of a great idea.

Yes. Flatland is a remarkable, and very real narrative set in 2D space. Class structures are represented as regular polygons, and the concept of beauty and popularity defined as perfect circles. I should not say more if you have not read it. Please do, it is remarkably well structured for a creative idea based purely around a mathematical concept.

The honest answer to the last question is I really do not know, but it is that challenge that makes me want to try. In this part of the appendix I will talk specifically about why I decided to spice my narrative with mathematics, and why the book *Humble Pi: A Comedy of Maths Errors* became such a prominent fixture in it.

It surprises people when I tell them that I have not read many books. The way I talk and how I conduct myself hides this fact rather well. The fact of the matter is years ago in school I was simply not motivated to read. Apart from the occasional book review or assignment, reading was not at all a recreation I picked up. This was also during the time when I was creative as a writer. Ideas simply entered my head naturally from the environment around me, not by the things I read. My imagination was fuelled by visual media such as television and movies, artworks, and video and computer games. I read Tintin more than I read the Lord of the Rings, and I only ever read the Tintin comics once. As a child I had no patience for reading, the words did not conjure images in my mind. This stubborn attitude lingered well beyond my adolescence, until I heard about a book. It was a book from a comedian I enjoyed as a child, and I found it personally interesting that it was a maths book of all things. The book was *World of Numbers* by Adam Spencer. It is an excellent book, if you personally have a child with an interest in mathematics, I genuinely recommend getting this book for them. But for me it was a revelatory concept. Mathematics had been espoused by the people around me for all my life up to this point. Maths was hard, uncool, and nerdy. It had no place in the world. The idea of a popular book about maths was something that made no sense to me. I visited a bookstore for the first time as an adult, bought *World of Numbers*, and read it, and I enjoyed it greatly. It is not a narrative about grand adventures or remarkable science fiction, it is literally a book about mathematical trivia. From then on, I committed time in the day to read a book.

While I am here bigging up Adam Spencer, *Time Machine* is another book I highly recommend. It is a straight up timeline of the world mathematically and scientifically.

This is not the first narrative I made which involves some mathematics however, it is the first proper story I would work on that does. In my youth, I produced a mathematical proof that was a love letter of sorts. It is a simple idea I want to polish into a better short story in the future.

Mathematics is a difficult subject to simply insert into a narrative. Unless your story is specifically set in an environment that needs a knowledge of maths to operate in, one cannot just casually write in $e^{i\pi} + 1 = 0$ and expect everyone to a) not notice the statement, and b) not begin to question why it was there in the first place. I had given it a lot of thought for the time I spent writing and until recently it was irreconcilable. It was at this time that I learned about YouTube's educational content. I was a teenager during the infancy of the site, when funny cat videos were the rage, and the concept of the modern meme began its evolution into the zeitgeist. Returning to it in 2017 I found, to my amazement and sheer delight, that while the baser entertainment did indeed carry on unabated on YouTube, education had found a niche to thrive as well. My absolute favourite channels on YouTube are *Kurzgesagt – In a Nutshell, Numberphile, PBS Spacetime, CGP Grey,* and *Overly Sarcastic Productions.* And the plucky channel of an ex-patriot math nerd living in London, Matt Parker's *Stand*

Up Maths. Watching Matt's exploits in numbers made me personally excited about mathematics again, after having it slowly drain out of me after high school. Matt reinvigorated my love of maths, and that is something I am grateful for.

During the development of this book, I got myself a copy of Matt Parker's *Humble Pi* for myself. I've mentioned it before already, but seriously, if you love a good yarn about people getting things wrong, sometimes very simple things that seem unbelievable to think could be a thing to do, *Humble Pi* is not at all a book about straight up maths, but all about stories of humans turning out to be human. Seriously consider getting this book.

At about this time the first draft of the story was done, and I passed the manuscript to my editor. He informed me that my story was lacking foreshadowing and it would be improved upon by adding more. I gave it a lot of though about adding something to use as a foreshadowing device throughout the saga. Then one day, while finding a Christmas present for my father, it occurred to me. A tome. A book within a book. A travelling homage to my love of numbers and its application to most things constructed by humans, and yes, a not at all concealed reference to my favourite mathematician, or his recent book. The idea to imbue the narratives of *Humble Pi* into *Tales of Mundus* is exactly that, a homage to the humour and the lessons within the book, and how the stories of *Humble Pi* are just as applicable in a fictional world such as Mundus, even in a fictional world with abstract concepts such as magic. That is ultimately the point of the fictional book *Humble Phi?* It tells short stories about themes within the story, in this case the behaviour that money causes and motivates, that reframe these themes into humorous viewpoints, as well as foreshadow the plot of the story.

I was so pleased, and to be honest surprised to be given the chance to reframe *Humble Pi* in this context with Matt's permission. His zest for mathematics has left its mark on me in a way I never really expected. I do want to find an excuse to inject a little cheeky maths in my works, and I feel that valorising my favourite maths book is a good place to start.

Maths is fvn! Keep doing maths.

The Development of Alchemy and its Role in Science

It should come as no surprise that many, if not all ancient cultures had created their own form of magic and mysticism. Archaeological evidence of it exists literally everywhere where humans have lived. However, it may surprise you to know that what historians call 'alchemy' today actually has three main cultural roots; Greco-Roman alchemy, which influenced Western knowledge, East Asian and Indian alchemy, and Muslim alchemy after the fall of Rome. For me personally, the idea of marrying the precision of science with the arcane nature of magic was a concept I held since high school over a decade ago and is a world I find truly fascinating. The more esoteric principles of the chemical composition of Mana crystals and the magical sciences for example are directly inspired by genuine, real world alchemical practices. The concepts of what was alchemy in the ancient and medieval worlds will be covered in this appendix; the skills and quests alchemists attempted to fulfil, the meaning of riddles, what was magic and what was science, and how alchemy evolved into chemistry.

Before we start, the first thing to understand about alchemy is that it is not all about magic or illusion, alchemy was very much spiritual. It required a great deal of thought and philosophy from practitioners. Substances and material processes were used as metaphors rather than to be taken in a literal sense. Often the quest to transmute metals into gold, or to create the elixir of life, were just beliefs hidden within the text. In fact, the fabled philosopher's stone was itself a metaphor for what alchemists ultimately tried to achieve, evolving humanity from corruption and imperfection to a world of purity and eternal health, not unlike what scientists, doctors, biologists, and many other intelligent people seek to achieve today.

Initially research into the history of alchemy had divided the exoteric, practical methods such as early laboratory practices, and the first scientific method prior to the Scientific Revolution, from the esoteric, spiritual philosophy that existed for years before, such as the antiquated belief in the 'four elements'; air, earth, fire and water. Modern research has instead adopted a practice of dual understanding as the connection between the experiment and the thesis becomes more obvious. Lawrence M. Principe said it best on the matter;

> *"Most readers probably are aware of several common claims about alchemy – for example…that it is akin to magic, or that its practices then or now is essentially deceptive. These ideas about alchemy emerged during the eighteenth century or after. While each of them might have limited validity within a narrow context, none of them is an accurate depiction of alchemy in general."*
>
> *- Lawrence M. Principe,*
> *'The Secrets of Alchemy'*

Understanding that alchemy is a practice of mind as well as spirit is essential, that the pursuit of oneness with nature was as important as finding exquisitely rare artefacts of great power. I will take the time to outline the quests alchemy attempted to complete, such as the search for the philosopher's stone, the elixir of eternal life, and developing panaceas, great universal curses of all illness.

Western alchemy began in Ptolemaic Egypt, the Greek rule of the Nile after Alexander of Macedon liberated the land from Darius II of Persia. Alexandria was the centre of knowledge and alchemy in most of the Mediterranean. Now a ruin consigned to history, The Great Library of Alexandria was at its time one of the largest repository of scrolls and tablets of knowledge. Contrary to popular belief, the Romans did not cause the library to burn to the ground, although they were complicit in one minor accident involving fire and the building. In fact, the fall of the library took place over a period of centuries with attacks against intellectuals; Ptolemy VIII Physcon conducted a purge in 145 BCE where most of the staff fled Egypt. Julius Caesar is generally attributed to the raising of the library, while he did cause a fire, the building remained. The destruction was minimal and some time after the affected areas were reconstructed. Roman support for the structure dwindled until around 260 when it stopped completely. A decade later a rebellion struck Alexandria with imperial forces quelling the malcontents, these attacks likely destroyed what was left of the building however, there is doubt on whether the Great Library still existed then.

It was there, in that period of history, where the first records of alchemy stirred in the West. Collections of scrolls emerged that combined Greek concepts of technology and mysticism. However, it would be after this when the first noted alchemist would emerge – Mary the Jewess. Mary was an Egyptian living in Alexandria in the first century, she is referenced a great deal by alchemist and countryman Zosimos of Panopolis, who is credited with the oldest known books on the subject. Mary herself wrote pieces describing the cryptic nature of alchemy that would later be analysed by psychiatrist Carl Jung, and is said to have been the first person to create hydrochloric acid, although as of right now the scientific community does not agree with this assertion.

Mary also developed scientific instruments such as the *tribikos*, a vessel used for distilling, the *kerotakis*, a device made to boil substances in order to capture its vapour, and the *bain-maria*, an ancient form of what is now more commonly known as a double boiler.

As the major proponent of alchemy of the region, Zosimos of Panopolis imbued classical mythologies of Greece, Egypt and Rome into his works, referring to gods and heroes. Technology also played a large role in alchemy, as already mentioned earlier. Metallurgy was developed as far back as 3500 BCE. The Roman emperor Diocletian ordered the destruction of alchemical books in 292. Additionally, Alexandria at the time was a melting pot of the collected though of ancient philosophies from thinkers such as Pythagoras and Plato, and the emergence of Gnosticism, the belief of the divine spark of knowledge descended from a lesser god that can be liberated. Most alchemists after Zosimos of Panopolis referred to themselves by pseudonyms such as Moses, Isis, Cleopatra, etc., and they all built upon the works of their predecessors. By the 7th century alchemy was almost lost entirely to myth and legend however, by the 8th century Khalid ibn Yazid of the Umayyad Caliphate learned of the works and moved from Alexandria to Damascus with them, starting Islamic interest in the science.

The ancient Vedic culture from India began its own alchemy during the 2nd millennium BCE with the surviving religious text *Vedas*. It described the connection between gold and eternal life. Several centuries later the document *Arthashastra* accounts the first use of mercury in alchemy. Texts in Buddhism had emerged between the 2nd and 5th centuries describing the transmutation of lesser metals into gold however, this may be influenced by Greek sources as by 325 BCE Alexander of Macedon encountered and disrupted the ancient Maurya Empire of northern India. As alchemy expanded in India it intertwined with a vast array of religions. Early writings seem to be rooted in traditional Hinduism such as Shaviaism, by Matsyendranath, a yogi and saint of Buddhism and Hinduism. Early authors of alchemy include the Buddhist monk Nāgārjuna whose laboratory was in Nagalwadi in southern India, and Nityanātha whose work *Rasaratnākara* was held in exceedingly high regard. Nāgārjuna is credited with recording a method of converting mercury into gold.

By contrast, Eastern alchemy is less interested in forming noble metals and leans towards medicine. The grand elixir of immortality was the great alchemical quest of China. It possessed similar qualities to the philosopher's stone, yet they were both sought after objects rather than one representing the other. Black powder was invented by Chinese alchemists originally as a solvent that gives eternal life. The substance evolved into the creation of fireworks in the 10th century and eventually used in the development of cannons in 1290. Gunpowder spread from China to the rest of the world by way of Mongolia's expansion across the Eurasian supercontinent, reaching Europe by the 14th century. Acupuncture also arose from Chinese alchemy. One of the more dangerous practices in alchemy occurred within Taoism, the polytheism of dynastic China.

The elite of the Song dynasty ingested a rather toxic compound; mercury sulphide, also known as cinnabar. At low levels the human body can tolerate cinnabar in the system, but like everything, too much of it will cause death. This led to the freedom to access the heavens and interact with the gods, many Taoists not only engaged in the practice at the time but encouraged it throughly.

Much of the ancient philosophy was lost to the world, and it is entirely possible that without intervention Europe may never have continued the traditions of earlier times. However, the Islamic world would resurge the science and refine it into a more familiar profession. First and foremost, we know more about Muslim alchemy because they were much more vigorous recording their work. Khalid ibn Yazid translated the works he acquired in Alexandria into Arabic, providing the foundation for the expansion of the science in Islam. The works of Plato and Aristotle became common knowledge in the Middle East and moulded them into their own works. Even the term 'alchemy' arose, the word is Arabic in origin and comes from *al-kīmiyā*, a hybrid term incorporating Greek meaning 'the fusion of metal' amongst other interpretations. The most noteworthy Muslim alchemist is Jābir ibn Hayyān. He revolutionised the process by establishing a method of controlled experimentation rather than the allegory and riddles of the ancient past. Jābir created the first scientific method, a ruleset that all scientists in every single field of practical study uses today to conduct experiments, observe, and draw conclusions;

> *"The first essential in chemistry is that thou shouldest perform practical work and conduct experiments, for he who performs not practical work nor makes experiments will never attain to the least degree of mastery."*

> *- Jābir ibn Hayyān*

Jābir's scientific method paved the way for the golden era of advancement in Islam. He and his contemporaries like Al-Kindi and Muhammad ibn Zakarīya Rāzi progressed chemistry with the discovery of hydrochloric, sulphuric and nitric acids. Jābir theorised the concept of creating artificial life within the laboratory, including human life. He established a numerology, and drew from Aristotle's observations on property, both to devise methods of transmuting metals. Jābir took licence from another ancient belief, the five elements from Ancient Greece; air, earth, fire, water, and *aether*, an element that is tied to the gods. He initially added sulphur and mercury to his seven elements, sulphur for its combustibility and mercury for its liquid state at room temperature, and he later added salt as the eighth element for its hardness.

During this period, the Middle East expanded all intellectual fields. Algebra, optics, trigonometry, cartography, geometry, medicine; these fields of mathematics and science and more were enriched by Muslim thought. Their influence shaped Europe as it entered the medieval age.

The exact day the West was reintroduced to alchemy may have been Friday the 11th of February 1144, we know the date for certain because that was the day Robert of Chester published a translation of the Arabic work, the 'Book of the Composition of Alchemy'. Robert notes the lack of knowledge on the subject in his time. Spain in particular translated many Arabic books in the 12th century, due in no small part to Iberia being occupied by the Almohad Caliphate before the Reconquista a century before. The translations led to the extension of the English vocabulary via Arabic. The terms *alcohol* and *elixir* are just a couple of examples. Theologians began to integrate these new texts into their religion. Anselm of Canterbury argued the compatibility of rationalism with God and encouraged it within the context of Christianity. After his death he was sainted as the Doctor of the Church. Pierre Abélard followed suit by establishing an acceptance of Aristotle's thought before any copy of his work itself ever reached Europe, let alone France. By the 13th century Robert Grosseteste used Aristotle and Abélard's outreach to build upon their work and base his investigations on observation and experimentation.

For the first two centuries Western alchemy was not properly scientific yet, Europeans were still translating texts. Two friars translated and commented on works of alchemy: Albertus Magnus and Roger Bacon. Magnus compiled several previous works and made observations from them, he focused especially on transmuting metals. After his death almost thirty claims in alchemy were misattributed to him until the 15th century. Bacon did not view alchemy as more or less important than other science, but he wrote to Pope Clement IV to reconsider the curriculum at universities to incorporate alchemy amongst other subjects. After them came the first influential alchemist, Pseudo-Geber. There is currently no consensus on the identity of Pseudo-Geber, only that a few alchemical works arose before 1310 which have the name Geber as the author. These books, 'the Height of the Perfection of Mastery', the 'Book of Furnaces', 'On the Investigation of Perfection', and 'On the Discovery of Truth', cemented the beliefs and structure that alchemists after them practiced.

By the 14th century alchemy left the confines of scholars and the clergy and entered a more public realm. Unfortunately, that led to some distasteful attitudes. Writers such as Dante and Chaucer wrote of the alchemists as charlatans, and the practice as thievery. Pope John XXII decreed the illegitimacy of the claim of transmuting metals from pseudo-alchemists. Despite the alchemists, the world appeared to turn away from the pursuit of perfection to a fear of hollow promises. It is this time when the most famous alchemist emerged; Nicolas Flamel. His name is attached to many legends however, he was born into the world during the 14th century, and the things he is often attributed to began to surface in the 17th century. Flamel was a French scribe with an interest in the philosopher's stone, he described many reactions but never the formulae to produce them, and like his contemporaries he wrote about work before him. One legend suggests that Flamel discovered the philosopher's stone and as a result is now immortal.

Today Nicolas Flamel is a popular character in fantasy literature and media, the person and his work has appeared in well known fiction such as 'Harry Potter and the Philosopher's Stone', mentions of it in 'the Da Vinci Code', the anime 'Fullmetal Alchemist', and most prominently in the Michael Scott series 'the Secrets of the Immortal Nicolas Flamel'.

The Renaissance saw sporadic changes in alchemy as the utility of the science became open to the interpretation of the alchemist and the public. Florentine scholar Marsilo Ficino translated Plato directly into Latin rather than from later works, and for the very first time exposed the Ancient Greek philosophies to Europe. Humanism and Neoplatonism emerged consequently, and redirected minds away from physics. German polymath and theologian Heinrich Cornelius Agrippa attempted to merge alchemy with the Jewish tradition of Kabbalah, a set of values explaining God's connection with man.

His countryman Paracelsus took a more extreme interpretation of alchemy, rejecting the original purpose of transmuting metals into gold and focused on medicinal applications. His type of healing alchemy differed from the norm, instead of purifying the soul he considered the idea that the body lacked balance and certain minerals can restore that balance and cure illness. John Dee carried on from Paracelsus' work and expanded into divination and *angel summoning*. Dee's 'Monas Hieroglyphica' described a new alchemy again, a spiritual connection to the stars, defining his interest in astrology. By the 17th century alchemy changed once again into a supernatural context, scholars suggested the philosopher's stone was capable of conferring and even summoning forth angels.

Suddenly, alchemy gained the interest of kings, dukes and princes for their private, selfish purposes. Nobles and royalty contracted resident alchemists for various reasons, healing and medicine, the production of chemicals and jewels, and the improvement of mining. Known clients include King James IV of Scotland, Henry V, Duke of Brunswick-Lüneberg, and Maurice, Landgrave of Hesse-Kassel. However, the most noteworthy of these leaders was Rudolf II, the Holy Roman Emperor, who hired a suite of alchemists to his court in Prague, including John Dee himself.

Pseudo-alchemy persisted in this time, as did the disdain from the public. Confidence artists used sleight of hand or claimed to have insider information as methods to profit from alchemy. Legitimate scholars would write about these fraudsters to distinguish themselves as the real deal. However, the wheels of fate were turning during the 17th century. The terms 'alchemia' and 'chemia' were interchangeable in their meanings. There was no clear definition that split alchemy from chemistry. In fact, many alchemists of the era indulged in many of the sciences. Tycho Brahe was both an alchemist who made use of astrology, and a chemist with a deeper interest in astronomy in general. Michał Sędziwoj, or Michael Sendivogious, was both a Polish alchemist who wrote his own works of transmutation, and a medical doctor whose pioneering work in chemistry includes the first person to distill oxygen in a laboratory.

And then there is the most famous, yet least appreciated alchemist in history, Sir Issac Newton. Everyone is at least somewhat familiar with Newton, he was the Englishman who understood the force of gravity, albeit at a basic level, and applied his knowledge in mathematics to codify laws of thermodynamics and motion. However, he devoted just as much time into alchemy and the occult. From his interest of natural science, Newton wrote of his goal to discover the philosopher's stone and the elixir of life. During this time however, England treated alchemy as a punishable crime. He was fearful of revealing his works with his colleagues, which prevented him from publicly publishing the work.

Indeed, the late period of history saw the beginning of the end of alchemy as the science tended towards clearer definition of chemistry and an abandonment of philosophy. Robert Boyle was the proponent of this, his experimentation was meticulous, and he took note of every single detail no matter how trivial it was in case it all proved to be relevant either now, or in the future. This detailed method was the start of modern chemistry, it was followed by discoveries that revolutionised the science by Antion-Laurent de Lavoisier and John Dalton. Chemistry became more and more distinct from alchemy. By the 1740s alchemy was confined to transmuting metals, where the perception of thievery and contempt still fostered. The practical methods of experimenting with chemicals and reactions became the realm of chemistry, and the application of physical methods to heal the body and restore its balance evolved into the science of medicine. To further disassociate from alchemy, scientists and chemists during the Enlightenment and subsequent Scientific Revolution described it as 'old science', whereas the science of the day was labeled the 'new chemistry'.

The move worked and alchemy was delegitimised over time. Brief revivals did occur, but they were never major nor highly influential. We will finish with the major defining features of the science; transmutation, the elixir of life, the fundamental elements, panaceas, and the philosopher's stone, as well as other discoveries connected to alchemy.

Elements in alchemy varied depending on the region. As mentioned before Ancient Greek thought held that there were four physical elements in nature; air, earth, fire and water, and a fifth element, aether, that occurred only in the presence or application of divinity. The physical elements were divided into subgroups of vague but useable characteristics of temperature and, for lack of a better word, moisture. For example, the water element is classified as being cold and wet. Each of these elements took one unique description within this simple structure of hot (air) or cold (earth), and dry (fire) or wet (water). India has the same five elements in its table, yet they are arranged differently. The Indian elements are ordered based of the five senses: hearing, touch, sight, taste, and smell. Earth is the lowest element because it engages all five senses, the structure is determined by the increasing lack of sense to detect and be aware of them. Let me demonstrate this; from earth, water is the next highest element because it can be heard, felt, seen, and tasted insofar as it can be ingested, but it cannot be smelt. Fire is the next element up as it can be heard, seen, and felt but it cannot be tasted. Air is the second highest element since it can only be heard and felt. Aether sat at the top of the hierarchy of Indian elements as it can only be heard.

Chinese elements are distinctly different because unlike the Greek interpretation of differing materials, these elements are based on states of matter that change constantly. In an unusual coincidence, these elements can be loosely thought of as an ancient context for the states of matter chemists and physicists define materials today; metal (supersolid), earth (solid), water (liquid), wood which is closely related to the air (gas), and fire (plasma). The elements govern a great deal of Chinese mysticism; each of the five planets that can be seen solely by humans – Mercury, Venus, Mars, Jupiter, and Saturn - were the residences of the gods associated with each element. Seasonal cycles emerged from the elements that alternated between them, and between cycles of creation and destruction.

As mentioned earlier, Muslim elements incorporate specific metals with the four traditional elements as they each represent a certain characteristic: sulphur for its flammability and combustion, mercury for its volatility, and salt for its solidity. These extra elements form the *tria prima* and serve as fundamental properties of all things. An example of this principle is the process of burning wood; the smoke it caused represented mercurial volatility, the heat the fire gives off is produced by sulphuric flammability, and the resulting ash mimics solidified salt.

Other cultures adopted their own elemental structures. The Bön culture of Ancient Tibet for example holds a similar framework to the ancient Indians except for aether being replaced with the element of the void, sometimes referred to as 'space'. Japan especially is a creative mix of Buddhist elementalism blended with Taoist culture. They share a similar set of elements from the Bön but also recognise and accept aspects of Chinese mysticism such as the veneration of wood and metal.

In alchemy the term *chrysopoeia* literally means 'to transmute into gold'. The term is Greek in origin and it was defined by Cleopatra the Alchemist who was a contemporary of Zosimos of Panopolis. For the most part transmutation and the philosopher's stone was a metaphor of spirituality, it represented the notion of transforming one's self into perfection and enlightenment. However, as with all things, some alchemists took the concept literally and actively searched for such a process. Chemists, scientists and other alchemists debated over the existence of chrysopoeia and the philosopher's stone since the medieval era. The concept of a physical object that transmutes, never mind transmutes things into gold, was a common point of ridicule against alchemy, and was ultimately portrayed as the sole feature of the science.

The search for the philosopher's stone yielded a number of scientific, and specifically chemical advances. The first acids were produced by alchemists as possible solvents that achieve chrysopoeia. Today we know acids and bases as corrosive solutions that easily react. Acids are defined by the abundance of hydrogen ions that chemically bond with materials. Bases are defined by the corresponding hydroxide ions that bond with reactive material, hydroxide is a molecule made of a single hydrogen and oxygen atom. This is one physical reason why pure water has a purely neutral acidity, it has neither hydrogen nor hydroxide ions to react with, rather it is an equal measure of each component: $H + OH \rightarrow H_2O$.

The philosopher's stone is also said to be a component to the elixir of life, a liquid that can cure all disease and grants longevity and an immunity to natural death. Mentioned earlier, China propagated the concept of ingestible mercury as a form of eternal life, even though it is a poisonous substance. Apart from mercury, Chinese alchemical recipes included sulphur, arsenic, and many salts from mercury and arsenic, all of which were entirely acceptable drinks to consume. India had similar creations within its own legends, but immortality was nowhere near as important compared to China. In Europe, the quest for the elixir of life was the quest for the philosopher's stone, the mythical substance was a critical ingredient in order to make the solution.

The stone and elixir were a panacea, a substance that could cure all illness. Alchemists that branched away from chrysopoeia instead took the search for the elixir of life very seriously. Despite not being able to truly form either the philosopher's stone or the elixir of life, two substances in all recorded history were used as genuine panaceas. The Cahuilla tribe of native North America use the sap of the Elephant Tree, found almost exclusively in the Baja Peninsula in the Southwest, as a panacea. A more widely known panacea is ginseng, an ingredient commonly found in ancient Chinese remedies, and is still treated as a generally beneficial food to eat. In biology, the food is given the genus name *Panax*, literally meaning 'panacea'. A common misconception is that the element phosphorous was originally named as the philosopher's stone; it was discovered by German alchemist Hennig Brand who was in fact attempting to create the philosopher's stone. He distilled certain salts from a vile of urine and created a white material capable of glowing in the dark and burning brightly. Brand named the substance the 'miraculous bearer of light', *phosphorus mirabilis*.

Alchemy's effect on history is immeasurable. Without the curiosity and the research from the earliest scientists of the world, the very nature of how we discover and learn becomes greatly reduced. The reason we know how to desalinate sea water, study how chemical compounds affect the body, and observe the particles of the universe is at least an indirect result of the fact that at the very beginning of science intelligent people believed in immortality, purity, and eternal health, and strove to understand how to achieve these things.

For the Interested Reader

I mentioned earlier that I am a prolific watcher of educational YouTube. Below is a list of videos that you may or may not already know of that either have influenced the making of this story or the lore the story contains, or provides additional context to the ideas in the story or in the final appendix in which I talk about the real world influences into the story. Look up each of these videos and enjoy at your leisure.

History Summerized: Ireland, by Overly Sarcastic Productions

58 and Other Confusing Numbers, by Numberphile

History of Venice & Genoa | Italy Part 3, by Suibhne

Alchemy: History of Science #10, by Crash Course

Trope Talk: Dragons, by Overly Sarcastic Productions

How to Be a Pirate: Captain Edition, by CGP Grey

The theme surrounding *Tales of Mundus: Puppets* is inspired by ideas from *Time: The History & Future of Everything – Remastered,* by Kurzgesagt – In a Nutshell.

Lastly, the writing of the story was also inspired by a playlist of songs and music. The music helped me illustrate the scenes and moods I wanted to convey into the story. The playlist is unlisted on YouTube, it can only be accessed from manually typing in the address of the link, or via the link in the digital copy of *Tales of Mundus: Puppets.*

https://www.youtube.com/playlist?list=PL7baCBInMSJ49s84Fta2yhfsfh5oa-0HJ

Kakariko Village, *from the Legend of Zelda 25th Anniversary Orchestra, composed by Koji Kondo*

Trust, *from the Kurzgesagt Soundtrack Volume 6, by Epic Mountain Music*

El Dorado, *from the Symphonic Jean Michel Jarre Volume 2, composed by Nic Raine*

The Serenians, *from the Myst VI: Revelation Soundtrack, composed by Jack Wall*

Nuke a City, *from the Kurzgesagt Soundtrack Volume 6, by Epic Mountain Music*

Computer Weekend, *from the Symphonic Jean Michel Jarre Volume 2, composed by Nic Raine*

Libra's Lever, *from the Myst III: Exile Soundtrack, composed by Jack Wall*

Magnetic Fields Pt. 1, *from the Symphonic Jean Michel Jarre Volume 2, composed by Nic Raine*

This Machine, *from This Machine, by Fourplay Electronic String Quartet*

Have Your Cake, *from This Machine, by Fourplay Electronic String Quartet*

Time Remastered, *from the Kurzgesagt Soundtrack Volume 5, by Epic Mountain Music*

Maps

The following pages contain two maps. The first is a map of Mundus in the present day; the one hundredth year of the Fifth Age. The second is a map of the Dogedom of Leath Langa, showing Ceannte's journey across the river.

Full sized, colour maps of the continent of Mundus, and the nations it contains can be found on my website; www.chrissifniotis.com/maps

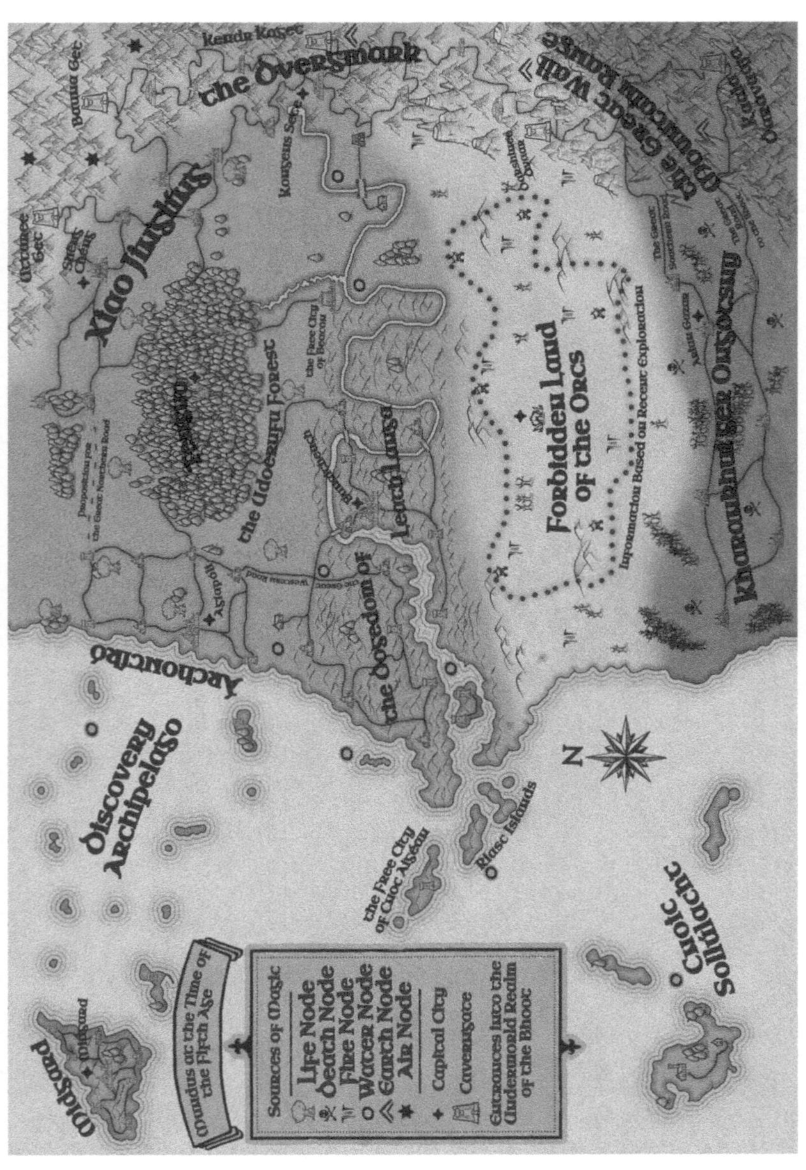
the Overstork
Xiao Jiushing
Kenir Kaget
the Great Dominion Range
the Great Dominion Wall
Kharaunhut Ser Orgorsuy
Forbidden Land of the Orcs
Information Based on Recent Exploration
the Udocxuru Forest
the Free City of Beotou
the Osedom of Letroh Imya
Archoucho
Discovery Archipelago
Riasc Islands
the Free City of Cuoc Ahséou
Cuotc Solildacht
Oldsoad
N
Sources of Magic
Life Node
Death Node
Fire Node
Water Node
Earth Node
Air Node
Capital City
Cavemagate
Entrances into the Underworld Realm of the Bhoot
Mundus at the Time of the Fifth Age

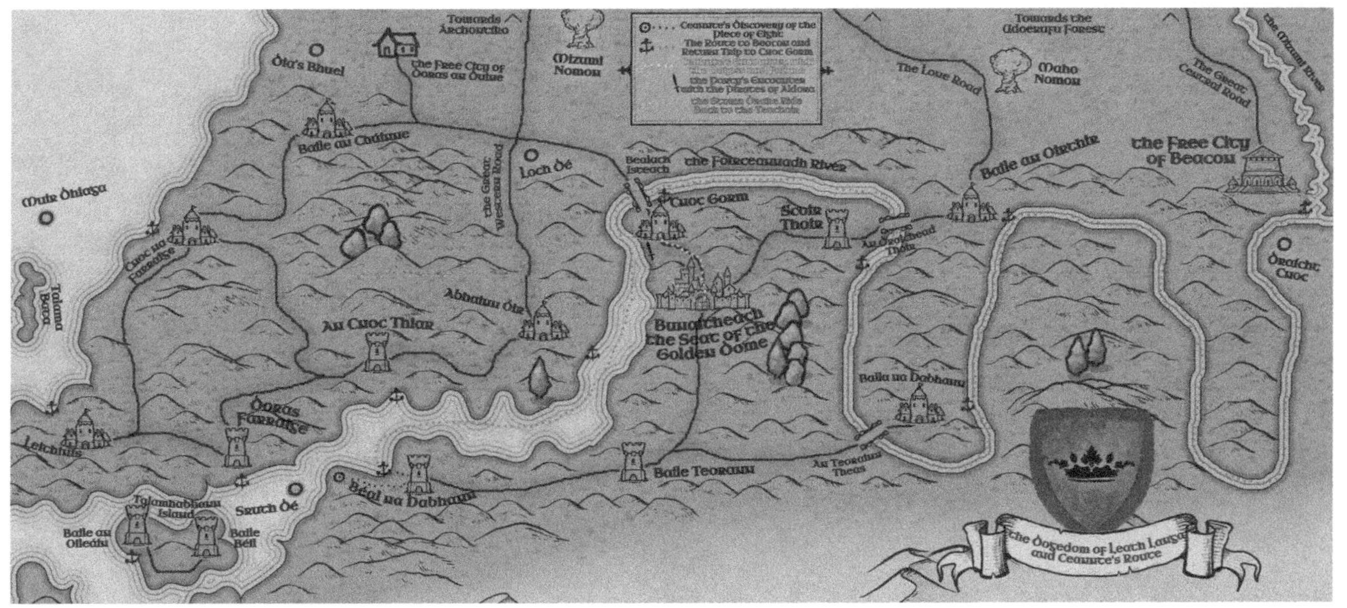

Towards Aschorutho
the Free City of Ooras au Ouine
Mizuni Nomon
Towards the Adoerufu Forest
The Long Road
Maho Nomon
The Great Cascad Road
the Mizuni River
Ceannate's Discovery of the Piece of Eight
The Route to Beacon and Recent Trip to Cnoc Goem
the Doxcy's Encounters with the Pirates of Aldona
the Broken Oynte Ride Back to the Teochnis
Olar's Bhuel
Baile au Cnuime
the Great Western Road
Loch Dé
Bealach Isteach
the Foirceannadh River
Cnoc Goem
Scoir Thoir
Baile au Oirchir
the Free City of Beacon
Deaiche Cnoc
Muir Dhiaga
Cnoc na Forraise
An Croichead Thoir
Abhainn Óir
Bunaicheach the Seat of the Golden Dome
An Cuoc Thiar
Balla na Dabhann
Talama Bata
Ooras Forraise
Leteninis
Baile Teorann
An Teorann Theas
Tgloamhabhann Island
Baile au Oileain
Baile Béil
Sruth Dé
Béal na Dabhann
the Kingdom of Leach Lausa and Ceannce's Rouce